DRAWN IN

by

Barbara Elsborg

COPYRIGHT

Drawn In is a work of fiction. Names, characters, businesses, places and incidents are the product of the author's imagination or are used in a fictitious manner. Any resemblance to actual events, locales or persons, living or dead is entirely coincidental.

DRAWN IN

Undercover police officer Kell has crossed the line. He's become trapped in an abusive relationship with his violent thug of a boss and sees no way back without wrecking months of work. His hope of ever being involved with someone who respects him seems a distant dream.

Private investigator Gethin doesn't like his job following unfaithful partners. Hard not to question the ethics of what he's doing, but he knows *just* what it's like to be cheated on. His relationship with an ex named Jonnie is complicated and Gethin can see no way of breaking free of a guy who still needs him.

A chance encounter brings Kell and Gethin together in explosive sexual need, entwining their lives with secrets and danger. Both have their reasons to stay away from a real relationship, but casual sex is fine. More than fine.

But there are consequences to zipless fucks. Now, they not only do they have to survive people trying to kill them, they need to trust each other, keep their wits about them, and ensure their hearts stay intact.

WARNING

Due to the adult nature of the contents, reader discretion is advised. Scenes of violence and sexual assault.

ACKNOWLEDGMENTS

Thanks to all my readers with a special thanks to Rita for all her advice and thoughts.

Chapter One

Kell's head snapped to one side with a force that made him gasp. The blow from Marek had taken him by surprise. Knowing the bastard rarely stopped at one strike, Kell tensed and made sure his teeth were nowhere near his tongue. The second punch caught him in the stomach and Kell let out a long moan.

"I said strip." Marek glared at him.

It wasn't as if Kell had hesitated. The fucker just liked to hit him. Kell toed off his shoes and folded his clothes as he removed them. Not because he was a neat-freak, as Marek thought, but because it gave him time to get his shit together for what would follow. Though delaying had the disadvantage of allowing Kell a chance to wonder if on this occasion the fuckwit would go too far.

By the time Kell had everything in a pile, Marek was naked. Kell was tall, but Marek was a couple of inches taller at six four, and several years older. He was far stronger than Kell, bigger, broader, though not as quick. Usually. Kell barely saw the guy move before he found himself pulled back against Marek's chest with the guy's shirt wrapped tight around Kell's neck, his erect cock poking Kell's arse.

"You're not hard," Marek said.

Guess what, dickhead? Punching then strangling me tends to have that effect. Kell wasn't into autoerotic asphyxia, well not when performed by a psychopath who didn't know when to stop. Actually, he probably *did* know when to stop. If Marek wanted him dead, Kell would die. He didn't speak because he couldn't. He didn't struggle because he thought even if Marek actually intended to end his life, he'd fuck him first which would give Kell a chance of survival. Was the bastard playing his usual games or had he found out the truth about his latest fuck toy?

Marek slackened his hold and pressed his mouth against Kell's neck. "You have no sense of self-preservation."

"Yeah, well maybe I don't want to be a mummy…sir," he choked out.

Marek laughed. Kell knew a fight was best saved for a day when the odds were in his favour. He hoped it came soon. Marek released him from the shirt and shoved him hard so he fell onto his knees. *Christ, I'll have bruises there too.*

"While you down there, suck me."

Kell lifted his head and shifted round so he could lick the crest of Marek's cock. A swipe with his tongue, a sweep around the tip, a long suckle at the top couple of inches should do the trick, and when he glanced up, sure enough the belligerence had faded from Marek's face along with any remnant of intelligence. Though that was only temporary. The time it took to give Marek a blow job was one of the few occasions Kell felt safe with the guy. Relatively speaking.

"Shhhiiit. Your fucking mouth!" Marek gasped. "Deeper."

Kell took him straight down without gagging, his mind straying onto the idea of swallowing *all* of the guy, like a gigantic anaconda consuming its prey. Marek *was* Kell's prey, the guy just didn't know it.

"Yeah, like that." Marek groaned.

The fuckwit sometimes stood in the club with his hand on Kell's neck, stroking him like a puppy that had been taught to sit up and beg, bragging to strangers about Kell's lack of a gag reflex. Marek was amused when he had offers to pay for Kell's services. Kell wasn't sure what he'd do if Marek actually took anyone up on that. Bad enough that he had to do this with a guy he loathed. He sucked harder, hard enough to hurt.

"Fuck, that's good." Marek threaded his fingers in Kell's hair and gripped tight as he pulled Kell against him, arching his hips to thrust deeper.

Kell snatched breaths where he could. As he worked dark magic with his mouth, lips and tongue, Marek stopped speaking English and switched to Albanian, of which Kell knew only a few words. Then his comments stopped making sense at all as they

2

turned into guttural groans and breathy gasps. With another man Kell would have felt a degree of pleasure in bringing a guy to incoherency. As it was his satisfaction came from thinking about what he'd like to do to this bastard, what he eventually *would* do to him. It almost made sucking his dick enjoyable.

For the time being, Kell was obliged to cooperate and do everything Marek liked, at work and at play. But the guy was poison, it ran in his veins, oozed from his pores and seeped into Kell every time they were together. He mouthed Marek's balls, fingered his hole, teased his slit with the tip of his tongue and jerked himself to full hardness at the same time because if Marek thought Kell wasn't at least in part enjoying this, he'd be lucky to leave the room without limping. Marek didn't usually hit his face. He left bruises elsewhere, but Kell's cheek still stung.

As Kell felt Marek's balls draw up against his chin, the guy pulled out, grabbed his own cock and within a couple of strokes had spurted all over Kell's face, hitting his lips, cheeks and chin.

"Swallow rest." Marek put his dick against Kell's tongue.

Kell didn't mind swallowing come which was just as well. Any sign of distaste would get him into trouble.

When Marek had finished, he pulled Kell to his feet and licked his cheek, one long drag of his wet tongue. Kell shuddered.

"You like that?" Marek asked.

I'm shuddering with disgust not desire, you twat. "Yes, sir."

Marek licked Kell's face clean — his version of clean — and Kell had to fight the impulse to race to the bathroom and stick his head under the hot tap.

"Now I can fuck you for long time before I come again," Marek said.

Oh joy.

Marek pushed Kell face down on the bed. "You have pretty arse. Looks even better with my cock in it. Want to see? I take picture."

"Please don't, sir." Kell wanted that back the moment he said it. Marek would do what he liked anyway.

3

"Where's your phone?"

Marek rummaged in both piles of clothes before brandishing their phones. He returned to the bed, dropped the mobiles next to Kell and picked up the lube. Kell did everything he could to relax. The looser and more compliant he was, the less painful this would be and the easier he'd find it to imagine himself somewhere else. Marek squirted lube on his fingers and then pressed two of them into Kell's hole. Kell tensed and bit down on his arm to stop himself crying out.

Then it was three fingers and Kell worried. The stretch was too much, too fast.

"You really want this," Marek crooned in his ear as Kell wriggled beneath him.

Kell couldn't bring himself to say yes.

"Ever been fisted?" Marek asked.

Kell tensed. "No and I don't wanna be." He grunted. "Sir."

Marek sniggered as he pushed his fingers in and out of Kell's butt. When he rotated them, Kell found himself twisting against the guy's hand, but not through enjoyment. Without Marek's arm pressing in the middle of his back, he'd have been out the door. He was *not* going to let Marek fist him. That was too much, going too far. He wasn't fucking paid enough for that. He wasn't fucking paid enough for this. Though officially, he shouldn't be doing this. Officially, he'd never done this.

"A pretty face and a nice tight arse."

The rough finger fucking had Kell struggling to breathe. *Christ, it hurts.*

"Tell me how much you want me," Marek said.

"I need you inside me, sir. Your thick cock, not your fingers. I want to feel your dick pushing deep into me." *I wish your fucking cock would shrivel up and fall off. You think I like doing this with you, you stupid prick?*

Marek pulled his fingers out and Kell heard the rip of foil. *Thank fuck for small mercies.* No way would he ever —

"One day I take you without," Marek said.

4

And on the day you try that, you will fucking die.

Marek gripped Kell's hips and spread his butt cheeks apart. "Look at that tight hole."

Not something Kell had ever done, looked at his own arse hole and if Marek forced his fist in him, it wouldn't stay tight.

"You like that? Just me. No rubber?" Marek spat on his butt.

"My mother would kill me."

Marek laughed, then he was in him and Kell cried out. The fucker was big. For a moment Kell lay there like a man impaled on a steel pole, barely able to move, fighting to breathe, his body struggling to eject before reluctantly accepting what had been forced into him. He saw Marek reach for the phones and he cringed.

"Shall I sent to all your contacts?" Marek asked.

"I'd rather the local pizza place and my dentist...didn't get shots of my backside...or your cock, sir."

"Keep this on your screen. If I look and you've taken it off, I'll put it on website. Maybe people pay to have you perform live for them. Fuck yourself with big black dildo in back room. Maybe I pay." He laughed.

That was the way Kell would kill him, with a big black dildo. But he'd stuff it down his throat. *List the ways I'd like to kill him. Suffocation. Decapitation. Exsanguination.* Marek began to drive into him and knowing what would happen if he didn't show willing, Kell began to buck against him, lifting his hips into Marek's thrust. How the hell could the guy stay so hard after he'd just come? Maybe he'd taken something. There was plenty of stuff floating around the club for those who wanted to get and maintain erections. Could you die from an overdose of Viagra? *Please let that happen.*

Kell put more effort into lifting his hips because the quicker Marek came, the sooner Kell could leave. His actions had the added benefit of him rubbing his own cock against Marek's bed, hard and fast enough — given time — to bring himself off, provided he could think himself somewhere else or blank his mind. Except he found himself rolled over with his legs pushed back against his chest, and now he had to cope with Marek's face. The guy wasn't bad looking, close cropped hair, dark eyes, thick lips, but the Albanian was fucking crazy, veering toward gentle one moment, then vicious the next and Kell hadn't yet worked out how to predict which Marek he was going to get.

I need to make myself come. He didn't want to. Well, making himself come wasn't that difficult, but mentally he was struggling with this, and it was getting harder to keep himself together, not easier. He'd tried to condition himself to ignore the physical pain, but had increasingly uncomfortable issues with the way he felt, his guilt and self-disgust. His motives might be backed by a belief in a greater good, but it was getting harder to see that. He'd gone too deep and was steadily drowning.

But — Kell had a point to prove with his boss. A point to prove to himself after the last disaster. He *could* get results. After all, this was something he was good at, pretending to be someone he wasn't. It had worked at school when he'd hidden he was gay until he was fifteen, and had worked at home when he'd hidden the bulk of his unhappiness from his parents.

He wrapped his hand around his cock and jerked himself off as Marek powered into him. Kell didn't dare take his gaze off Marek's face, but his head was elsewhere, thinking of fucking around with someone he actually liked, someone he'd look forward to coming home to at the end of the day, someone he could trust. Kell hadn't found him yet, but he knew he was out there. Not that he was looking. It would be a fucking disaster to meet him now. But when this job was done…

He felt Marek's shudder of pleasure and as the guy came, Kell yanked harder at his cock, dragging himself over the edge. His come spurted over his belly and chest in long, sticky, white ropes. There was *some* relief in that, but he could never relax, never let his guard down long enough to enjoy sex with a guy he knew could kill him in a blink. Marek ran his fingers through the streaks and fed the mess to Kell, watching him intently. Kell licked his come off every one of Marek's fingers as though there was nothing he'd rather be doing.

"The bathroom's through there," Marek said. "Get cloth and wipe me down."

"Yes, sir." Kell pushed to his feet and took the used condom Marek held out. *Lovely.* This was the first time he'd been in Marek's flat, but he doubted he'd find anything of interest in the bathroom. He had no excuse to open the cupboard under the wash basin so he didn't. Marek might be watching from the bed. He got rid of the condom, wet a facecloth and came back to the bedroom. Marek looked as though he was sleeping, but when Kell dabbed at his crotch, the guy opened his eyes.

"Want to make some extra money?" Marek asked.

"I'm not going to let you fist me."

Marek snorted. "When I do that, I won't pay. You beg for it."

In your dreams, you wanker.

"I have little job to do before work tomorrow. You can help."

Shit. Kell's disappointment was genuine. "I can't. I swapped my day off. I fixed it with the boss. I promised a friend I'd go to his party."

"A party? Make excuse. This is good money."

Kell shook his head. His other boss would kill him for turning this down. Kell tried to rationalize refusing. It might be the break he'd been waiting for, but maybe saying no would make Marek more likely to trust him. *Christ.* Like his boss was going to accept *that.*

"You sure?" Marek asked.

"Yeah. I promised. I don't break my word."

Oh yes he did, but Marek actually looked vaguely impressed. Kell hadn't been working for Marek, and Warner, their boss, for long. Five months, though it felt a lot more. Kell's background was solid, his life depended on it, but so far he'd not uncovered much, not enough to end the operation. Becoming Marek's fuck toy had been a calculated risk. One he'd not told his real boss about, not in so many words, though he had to have guessed.

7

Kell had been chosen for this operation because he was gay and the club he was working in was a gay club. The chances of Kell *not* having sex were small, but there would never be anything acknowledged. Kell felt guilty not jumping at an opportunity to get further intel by doing something extra for Marek, but he *had* promised his childhood friend Quin he'd go to his party, plus he needed the break, needed his head back in the real world just for a short time. It would be like coming to the surface for air after a long free dive. Kell could almost taste the relief. Working undercover was a minefield of a mind fuck and he was always one breath away from disaster.

"Maybe next time," Marek said, which was exactly what Kell needed to hear. "Make sure you close door when you leave."

Marek's eyes shut and Kell pulled the covers over him. The guy's hand shot out and he grabbed Kell by the throat. Kell gurgled.

"Don't be kind. You won't last." Marek closed his eyes again.

Kell wasn't being kind. He'd hoped to cover Marek's face, encourage him into sleep so he had a chance to snoop, but the guy was too alert. Kell didn't want to shower and risk another fucking so he pulled on his clothes. When he emerged from the bedroom he hesitated. He didn't feel confident enough to search the living space, but he could at least look in kitchen drawers and cupboards while he made a drink.

He over-filled the kettle so it took longer to boil, and hoped he didn't find the mugs and coffee too soon. The first cupboard held the mugs. He sighed and put two of them on the work surface. The coffee wasn't so easily found, but there was nothing interesting in the cupboards. He pulled open a drawer and spotted two burgundy passports, one Albanian, the other British.

"What you looking for?" Marek asked behind him.

"Spoon." Kell closed the drawer and opened another. A gun in with the cutlery. *Shit.* He picked up a spoon.

The kettle started to boil. Kell put a half-smile on his face and turned to him. "I was desperate for a coffee. You don't mind? I was going to make you one too."

"Go buy from Starbucks," Marek said.

Kell let his shoulders fall. "Sorry."

He dropped the spoon back in the drawer, but before he could shut it, Marek picked up the gun and held it against Kell's head. Kell stopped breathing. He stared at Marek and waited. He didn't want to die. He particularly didn't want to die at the hands of this bastard, but the one thing he wouldn't show was fear.

"Nothing to say?" Marek asked.

"I left a million quid in the...arggh."

Marek shook his head. "Funny guy." He put the gun back in the drawer.

Kell grabbed his jacket and headed for the door of the apartment.

"See you Sunday night," Marek called.

Kell made his way to the lift trying to keep his shakes under control. He'd been pretty sure Marek hadn't intended to use the gun. Too noisy, too messy. Marek had said he'd see him on Sunday with a confidence that suggested he knew that was when Kell was due back at work. Had that offer of a job on the side been a test? If Kell had agreed to change his plans would that have made them suspicious?

Undercover work had to be carried out at a slow and steady pace. Kell needed to be suspicious of everything and everyone. This was the most dangerous thing he'd ever done. Fucking up could get him killed. He couldn't deny the danger of it gave him a buzz, but he wished Marek didn't exist. When the guy had cornered him the first time, Kell had fought him off. The second time Marek raped him.

No sugar-coating it. That's what had happened and Kell had to live with that, live with the excuses he'd made to convince himself it didn't matter, that he might as well let the guy fuck him anyway, because then there was no chance he'd be taken for a cop. But his heart still ached when he thought about it.

When he was well clear of Marek's place, and sure he wasn't being followed, he took out his phone. He winced when he saw the photo. Marek had made sure Kell's face was in the shot, his eyes screwed shut, his features twisted in a grimace, but unmistakably him.

Kell called his boss. "Hi, Uncle Bob. Can I ask a favour?" Code for *I'm okay*.

His boss, Detective Superintendent Nigel Lane, sighed. "Where the fuck have you been? You were supposed to check in this morning and let us know you were still alive."

"I *am* checking in. I've been in Marek's apartment."

"Great. Anything useful?"

"Albanian and British passports in a kitchen drawer. I didn't have chance to look inside them. And a handgun."

"Right. A computer?"

"Not that I saw." Kell heard his boss's disappointment and braced himself. "He asked me to do a job before work tomorrow. Extra cash."

"Brilliant."

"I said no."

"You fucking what? What the — ?"

"I'd already asked Warner for time off. I told you. I'm going away until Sunday afternoon. It would have looked suspicious if I'd changed my plans."

His boss didn't say anything.

"I need this break," Kell said quietly.

"We spent a lot of time and money on your cover."

"There won't be a problem. Something Marek said made me think he was testing me, to see if I'd change my plans. This time saying no was the right thing to do."

Lane sighed. "Okay. You have to go with your instincts. Anything else?"

"Nothing significant."

His boss disconnected.

"Fuck you." Kell stuffed his phone back in his pocket.

Chapter Two

Gethin sucked in a breath as the gun barrel drilled into his forehead forcing him against the wall.

"What the—?" he gasped.

"If you've touched her, I'll kill you. If you've so much as breathed on her, I'll kill you." The guy twisted the gun and Gethin gritted his teeth. This had to be Brian Charlton, Izabela's husband.

"He has done nothing." On the other side of the room Izabela struggled into a cardigan, then sat sobbing.

"You're making a mistake." Gethin's heart was hammering. The last thing he'd expected when he'd sat down to talk to Izabela was that a guy would burst into the lounge brandishing a gun.

"You're the one who's made a mistake." Charlton's face was turning red from the neck up.

Gethin widened his eyes. "What have I done?" He hoped to hell the guy didn't know.

Izabela had told him her husband flew into rages, but Gethin hadn't thought he'd be the subject of one of them. He never imagined he'd ever come face to face with the guy. Charlton was at least twice Izabela's age; a jowly, balding accountant whose stomach bulged over his belt. He was supposed to be at work, but had come home and found Gethin with his young, attractive and now Gethin came to think of it, rather scantily clad wife. Izabela wore a short, tight red dress with a low neckline. The sort of dress she'd go clubbing in, not a dress most women would wear to hang around the house. She'd been quick to pull on that cardigan.

Shit. What's going on here? Thoughts whirled in Gethin's head.

"What's his name?" Charlton didn't take his eyes off Gethin.

"Rhys Jones," Gethin spoke before Izabela could contradict him.

"Was I talking to you, you piece of shit?" Charlton spat out the words, the spray hitting Gethin's cheek.

"Look, there's been a misunderstanding." Gethin was desperate to wipe his face.

"Shut up," Charlton shouted.

He could plant his fist in this guy's mouth, but there was that gun, a surfeit of nervous energy and an itchy finger on the trigger. Better to talk his way out. Maintaining his cover would keep him and Izabela safe as long as she stayed calm. She sat rocking on the couch, her arms wrapped around herself, her eyes wide.

"How long have you been fucking her?" Charlton asked through clenched teeth.

"I'm not."

"He's not," Izabela said at the same time.

"Shut the fuck up, Izabela," Charlton shouted. "All those questions about when I was leaving for work, whether I'd be out the whole day, what time I'd be back. You think I'm fucking stupid?"

"There's nothing going on between us," Gethin said. "Not like that. When you came in we weren't even sitting together. Apart from shaking her hand when I arrived, I haven't touched her."

Not quite true, she'd burst into tears the moment she had Gethin in the house and wrapped her arms around him. He wasn't going to be telling Charlton that. He could have told the guy he was gay but decided to keep with the plan he'd had in place but never had to use.

"You probably moved apart when you heard my car pull up outside."

For Christ's sake. Though if Charlton had arrived five minutes earlier… A bead of sweat trickled down his back. "I know I promised confidentiality, Izabela, but that was before your husband decided to hold a gun to my head."

"Husband?" Charlton's brow furrowed.

Oh hell. One word that shoved Gethin onto shifting sand. She'd lied.

"We're not married," Charlton said. "But that doesn't mean she's not mine."

It had to be Gethin's imagination, but it felt as though the barrel was embedding itself in his skull. At this rate there'd be no need to shoot him. It would be a new one for the coroner — victim impaled on a gun barrel.

"You only go for married women?" Charlton asked. "Do you get a kick from fucking another man's wife?"

Gethin decided to go for broke. "You've got this all wrong. I'm a party planner. And I'm gay."

Charlton snorted.

"It's true," Izabela said.

Gethin had told Izabela to say that's what he did if she was ever challenged, but if she didn't help him out with this, he'd be in trouble because if it wasn't Charlton's birthday or the celebration of some major deal or a salute to the day he'd discovered Viagra, this guy wasn't going to believe him.

"A party planner?" Charlton narrowed his eyes.

Is that blood trickling down my face or sweat? He didn't seriously think Charlton could push the barrel through bone, but he was a big guy. Bigger than Gethin.

And I'm fucking gay, you moron. "I work for a company that plans parties. We arrange venue, food, entertainment. Sorry, Izabela, for spoiling things, but I'm not going to get killed because you asked me to arrange a surprise party."

Back me up and don't tell him the truth — whatever the fuck that is — if you want to keep your carefully feng shuied room free of blood. Gethin was *almost* certain the last thing Izabela would want to do was inform Charlton she suspected him of cheating, that she'd hired Gethin to find out if he was and also to ascertain how much he was worth in case she wanted to divorce him. Except she wasn't married to him so this had nothing to do with a divorce settlement. Almost as if she sensed Gethin's annoyance, she cried harder, snuffling into a tissue.

14

Why was the gun still pressed against his head? Gethin wondered what the hell he'd stumbled into.

"No car on the drive?" Charlton asked.

He never parked on a client's drive. The whole point was discretion and a desire to avoid difficult questions from neighbours, friends, and jealous, gun-wielding boyfriends.

"I grabbed a spot around the corner. I hadn't thought to ask if there'd be a place to put my vehicle." Gethin took a deep breath. "The party's supposed to be a surprise. Izabela said you didn't have many surprises and she wanted this to be…special."

How much more waffley could he be? But specifics could kill him.

"Why did you think she was my wife?"

"I assumed." Protecting someone who'd lied to him was irritating, but until Gethin understood what this was about, he had to be careful.

"Put gun down, Brian," Izabela said. "Please."

Gethin took a couple of shaky breaths, clenching and unclenching his fists. The gun was an attempt to scare him and it had worked, but Charlton didn't want to kill him or he'd already be dead. Though for once in his life, Gethin wished he actually looked gay.

Charlton glared. "What sort of party?"

Izabela! Stop leaking into your tissue and say something. If Gethin said birthday and Charlton had only just had one, the guy wasn't going to believe him, but too long a gap before answering and Gethin might end up with a neat hole at the front of his head and an untidy one at the back. Hard to convince himself Charlton wouldn't shoot when the guy's finger still rested on the trigger.

"To celebrate day we met," Izabela choked out. "Six months on seventh of November. I want to do something special for man I love."

Six months? Oh Christ.

"Using my money?"

"No, I pay." The hurt in her voice sounded genuine, but Gethin wasn't going to believe another word that came from her mouth.

For the first time since he'd pressed the gun to Gethin's head, Charlton stopped staring at him and turned his attention to his girlfriend. It was an opportunity for Gethin to get the upper hand, but he didn't take it. While there was still a chance to emerge from this with Charlton ignorant of the truth — whatever that was, Gethin might as well take it.

"Where's this party going to be?" Charlton asked.

Izabela gave Gethin a frantic look.

"No decision's been made," Gethin said. "We were about to discuss venues."

Apart from hacking into the guy's computer, he'd also expected to be given a schedule of where Charlton would be over the next couple of weeks so Gethin could follow him. But moments after he arrived, Izabela dried her tears and pushed him into Charlton's office. Gethin could smell all manner of rats and Charlton's obsessive suspicion was adding to the aroma.

"Did you bring brochures?" Charlton asked.

Note to self. Put some in the car. "Not at this stage. This is a preliminary discussion. I need a budget before I get a client too keen on a particular location. But the choice would be between a hotel in London, a country house or castle — there are some lovely places in Surrey, or perhaps using katas. They're becoming increasingly popular."

Charlton frowned. "What the hell are katas?"

"Tipi style tents based on those used by reindeer herders in Lapland. Much more interesting than ordinary marquees. We've done Viking feasts in them with reindeer skins draped over the benches. Christmas parties with Santa Claus. Weddings. At this time of year we provide fan heaters, but there's a fire pit to sit around too."

Thank God he'd listened to Angel rattle on about them. Gethin was not a blatherer, but he thought that might have just convinced Charlton.

"Tents?" Charlton looked aghast.

Gethin turned indignation on full blast. "A lot more than a tent. But I'm not sure yet how many guests Izabela wants to invite. A few select friends or everyone you know."

"I didn't know if you want to invite neighbours," Izabela said.

Charlton scoffed. "I thought you didn't like the neighbours. You said they look down their nose at you."

"It would be a chance to get to know them."

Gethin was relieved Izabela was running with the cover, but still wondered what she was up to.

"I don't know which relations you still speak to and if you want employees or clients to come," she said.

The gun seemed not be pressing so hard on his head, but Gethin stayed tense.

"If I invite just one person you don't like, I spoil everything." She stifled a sob. "I want party to be perfect. I want you to walk in, gasp, then smile. I want to make up for all times you don't get parties."

All this fuss to celebrate you'd been with someone six months? Though looking at the pair of them, Gethin was surprised it had lasted so long. Would this guy fall for it? Didn't he already wonder why a young, attractive woman was with a bad-tempered, overweight guy like him? Couldn't he see it had to be about the money?

"What's the name of your company?" Charlton's focus returned to Gethin.

"Party Solutions."

"Give me the phone number."

Charlton took out his phone, and Gethin reeled off the number.

A moment later Tilda's chirpy voice rang out. "Party Solutions large and small for all your entertainment needs. Matilda speaking. How may I help you?"

Gethin's anxiety retreated as it sank in that Tilda had remembered what he'd asked her to do, not only what to say, but the way she said it.

"Do you have someone working for you called Rhys Jones?" Charlton asked.

"Yes, we do. I'm afraid Rhys isn't in the office right now. Is there anything I can help you with?"

"What does he look like?"

"Look like?" Her voice faltered.

"It's not a difficult question."

"Tall, skinny, floppy dark hair. Green eyes. Early thirties. Doesn't smile much."

"Where is he?" Charlton asked.

There was a pause before Tilda spoke. "What is this? Do you have a problem? Is Rhys all right? Has he been in an accident?"

"I want to know where he is."

"May I take your number and ask him to call you?" Her tone had flattened and her voice veered away from the posh accent she'd assumed and moved closer toward her Essex one.

"You don't know where he is?" Charlton glowered as he glared at Gethin.

"Yes, I know where he is. Well, I know where he told me he was going this morning—to see a client—but I have to maintain confidentiality. We specialize in *surprise* parties. I have no idea who you are. I'm not—"

"Contact him now," Charlton barked. "Tell him to call Izabela."

"Will he know the—?"

Charlton cut off the call and waited. A moment later, the phone rang in Gethin's pocket.

"Answer it," Charlton said. "I want to listen to what she says."

Gethin pulled it out, swiped his thumb across the screen and put it on speaker. "Hi, Matilda."

"An extremely rude man has just phoned and told me to tell you to call Izabela. No second name. Are you okay?"

"Yes, thanks." Gethin ended the call and stuffed the phone in his pocket before she turned a brilliant con job into a disaster.

When he'd discussed with her and Angel the remote chance of needing to do this, they'd said it sounded exciting, and Gethin had thought the occasion would never arise. They were all wrong.

The gun shook against Gethin's head and he worried Charlton would shoot him accidentally.

"See?" Gethin said. "This isn't what you thought."

He took a risk, raised his hand, wrapped it around the barrel and moved it aside. His heart lurched, then settled.

"Let me put the gun down," Gethin said. "You don't want to shoot me. Izabela's already warned me twice not to get the carpet dirty."

Gethin was surprised when he found himself left holding the gun as Charlton crossed the room to his girlfriend.

"It's not loaded," Charlton said as he pulled her into his arms.

Gethin put the gun on the floor behind the couch and kicked it underneath. Now was the time for him to leap on Charlton and knock the fucker from one side of the room to the other before calling the police. Except Gethin was the most likely to get beaten up. Even if he phoned the police, he could imagine what would follow. Charlton's lawyer talking him out of custody — *my client was faced with a home invader, his girlfriend was threatened. A gun? No it was a replica, a cigarette lighter, a kid's toy* — then the guy would be back in this house, demanding to know who Gethin really was and giving Izabela more bruises. Gethin hadn't missed the fingerprint marks on her arm.

He leaned against the wall, and imagined Charlton bleeding profusely over his pristine cream carpet as he pleaded for mercy. A quick swipe of his forehead told Gethin he wasn't bleeding, but he was bruised. *The wanker.*

As the pair kissed, Gethin allowed himself a silent sigh of relief. He'd been reluctant to come here for a first meeting, but Izabela had insisted. She'd said although her *husband* would be at work all day, Charlton frequently checked up on her by calling on the landline so she couldn't go out. Classic controlling behaviour, but it had given Gethin a chance to look at Charlton's computer.

It had been more heavily protected than he'd expected. His usual password cracking method didn't work, but eventually he gained access and embedded software that opened up the hard drive. Luckily, he'd downloaded everything onto a memory stick before Charlton arrived, though that sliver of metal and plastic was burning a hole in his pocket. Gethin had done what he could to reduce the risk of Charlton discovering his files had been accessed, but a lot depended on how computer savvy the guy was. Hopefully not as savvy as Gethin.

Now Gethin was torn. Izabela had lied to him. Charlton had massively overreacted and threatened him. *With a fucking gun.* Gethin had been shocked into immobility when the guy produced the weapon. This was the UK not the US. It was illegal for people to have handguns in their houses. Why have a gun and not load it? Assuming it *was* unloaded. Why did he need a gun? Why was he so suspicious? Why had Izabela lied about being his wife? Gethin thought he'd already figured out part of that. Because she wanted to know what was on Charlton's computer and had come up with a story to con Gethin into doing something illegal.

When Charlton walked across the room, Izabela hanging onto his arm, Gethin tensed, but the guy held out his hand.

"Sorry," Charlton said. "But you can see how it looked. She asked me too many times if I was going to be out, then I come home to find her with a good-looking guy."

Who's gay. Weren't you listening?

"As if I want anyone but you, my big poppa bear." She nuzzled his arm. "But you spoil my surprise."

Gethin reluctantly shook Charlton's hand. "You don't want the party, then?"

Charlton gave a short laugh. "Not much of a surprise now." Gethin wasn't done with this wanker, but it was time to leave. On the way back to his car, he did subtle checks in case Charlton had told someone to follow him, but there was no one around. Yet someone had to have been watching the house for Charlton to have known he was there. Or was there a camera Izabela didn't know about that Gethin hadn't spotted? A nosy neighbour? *I should never have come to the house.* If Gethin hadn't thought Charlton finally believed him about the party planning, he wouldn't have left Izabela alone with him. But he still worried.

He wasn't sure of the next play in the game. Izabela wasn't going to tell Charlton the truth, but a guy that paranoid might discover Gethin had been on his computer. Debatable whether Gethin should keep his mouth shut about this. Christ, the guy was crazy. You can't just pull out a gun and threaten to shoot someone.

He allowed himself an audible sigh of relief once he was in his car with the doors locked. He glanced in the rear view mirror as he drove away, but no one followed. What he *did* see, right in the middle of his forehead, was a circular red bruise that looked like one of those marks Hindus put on their head.

Gethin thought again about calling the police, but it would be his word against Charlton's and he *was* concerned about Izabela, even though the bitch had tricked him. There were plenty of ways to explain the bruise, and plenty of opportunity for Charlton to get rid of the weapon before the police arrived. It was more than likely Izabela would back up Charlton's version of events. Gethin was well aware how abused women reacted when pressurized. Maybe she'd wanted to get her own back on Charlton for hitting her, planned to steal his money and run. Gethin would help her run, but not steal her boyfriend's money.

Once he'd checked out the memory stick, he'd decide what to do. *Christ, I hate my job.*

Chapter Three

When Kell reached his crappy bedsit, he took a long, hot shower and scrubbed Marek off his skin, though his arse still ached and so did his face. His left cheek was grazed.

The Metropolitan Police weren't supposed to encourage their undercover officers to sleep with suspects. The force was still reeling from the damage done by cops who'd fathered kids on activists they were supposed to be spying on. The press got hold of the story and all hell broke loose. The women had sued.

But this was different, his boss had said, while still telling Kell not to go too far. Kell wondered how different. Apart from the fact that Kell wasn't going to get anyone pregnant, or *get* pregnant, the people who worked for Warner were far more dangerous than tree huggers. In any case, Warner was the one Kell was investigating, not Marek. Warner was into much younger guys.

Silas Warner ran an upmarket gay club in London called No Escape. He had clubs in other cities, plus he owned sex websites, online adult stores, physical stores, and made porn films. Shady stuff, though legitimate. But Warner was suspected of involvement in organized crime: people trafficking, drugs smuggling and money laundering. Kell didn't have much to show for his efforts although drugs were being sold in backrooms of the club. Not difficult for Warner to claim ignorance. Kell wasn't even being paid in cash. He had proper wage slips with tax and national insurance deducted. There was a computer in Warner's office, but the door was always locked.

The lack of useful information after five months of anxiety accounted for much of Kell's depression. A few faces snapped on his phone, a few names to give his boss, but nothing concrete, nothing useful. Kell packed his bag for the weekend and tried to think himself into a better mood.

Quin's thirtieth birthday party wasn't just a booze up in the pub. His parents were mega-wealthy and had organized a whole weekend of events. Quin had been Kell's friend since they were young boys. It was Quin who'd stood by Kell when he'd come out age fifteen. Quin who'd stopped him getting bullied at school. Quin who'd been there when Kell's family imploded. He was like the brother Kell wanted rather than the one he'd got.

Kell froze at that thought and let out a mouthful of curses. He'd forgotten his twin nephews' birthday. Despite his brother's deep dislike for him, Kell had been determined to be a good uncle to the boys. Just because his brother was a dickhead, didn't mean his kids would turn out the same. He tapped Oliver's home number into his phone. Oliver would be at work, but he hoped Lyndsay was in, though she wouldn't recognize this number.

"Hello?" she said.

"Hi Lyndsay, it's me. I wondered if I could come by with the boys' birthday presents."

"It was two weeks ago, Kell."

"I've been up to my neck. Sorry. When do they get out of school?"

"We're busy then. Come at one." She disconnected the call.

Bitch. She wasn't as bad as his brother, but the pair of them were well suited. *Pompous twats.*

Kell picked up his bag and headed out. He didn't see much of the five year olds because he was never invited to his brother's house. He always had to call to make a fucking appointment though Kell didn't mind much because any time spent with his brother was torture. Kell had always taken birthday and Christmas presents to his nephews and never turned down the chance to see them when they were at his father's place. Oliver rarely tried anything there. Kell shouldn't really be going anywhere near his family while he was undercover, but buying presents for the boys was his rather pathetic attempt to show Oliver he wasn't hurt by the way his brother treated him.

Except he was.

Once Kell stepped into the toy shop he was overwhelmed by choice, undecided as to whether to buy the boys the same thing or not. He didn't know them well enough to be sure of what they'd like. Lego seemed a good option and he picked out two different Star Wars sets, big boxes, then added another to give Quin as a joke. What could he get for a guy who had everything? The twins weren't really old enough for the Lego which he hoped meant they wouldn't already have it with the additional bonus of Oliver having to help them built it which would annoy him, though he did love his kids. Kell paid extra to have everything gift wrapped and wrote out three birthday cards.

His phone rang as he left the shop and when he saw who was calling, he sighed. "Hi, Lyndsay."

"Make it two instead of one, would you?"

"Yeah. Lyndsay, would you do me a favour? Wipe this number off your phone. I'm not supposed to have personal calls on it."

"Fine." She cut him off again.

If he'd asked Oliver to do that Kell would have been besieged with texts and messages, but then he wouldn't have called Oliver. If he got the chance, he'd make sure Lyndsay had done what he asked. The last thing he needed was Marek checking his call history. Kell headed toward a café on the other side of the road. He might as well get something to eat while he waited.

When Kell saw his brother's car parked outside the smart Georgian townhouse, their London home, he swore under his breath. Didn't mean Oliver was there. He really hoped he wasn't, but when Kell rang the bell it was Oliver who answered.

"Look what the cat's dragged in," his brother said.

"You'd be the cat, would you?" Kell pushed past him into the house.

He'd been tempted to thrust the parcels at Oliver and leave, but he refused to give his brother the satisfaction of acknowledging he wasn't welcome.

Oliver followed him to the kitchen. Lyndsay gave Kell a tight smile.

"Hi, Lyndsay. How are you?" Kell could be polite.

"Fine."

But she couldn't. Kell put his overnight bag down and lifted two of the Lego sets and cards out of the large plastic carrier. "Sorry I'm late with the presents."

"They thought you'd forgotten," Oliver said at his shoulder. "What crap have you bought them?"

"Something that should keep them busy." Kell had spent more than he could afford on his current wages. He had no access to his police salary until this work was done.

"Who's the other gift for?" Oliver asked.

"A friend." The less Oliver knew the better. If Kell had told him he was going to Quin's party, his bastard of a brother would have found a way to spoil it.

"Maybe I could come with you to collect the boys from school," Kell said to Lyndsay. "Just say hello to them."

"We're going out to eat."

Her phone was lying close to the coffee maker and Kell tried to work out a way to get to it.

"Father tried to call you," Oliver said, "but your number was disconnected."

Someone at headquarters was supposed to monitor calls to Kell's phone, the one he couldn't use while he was undercover. He should have been told his father had called. Then again, maybe he hadn't called.

"Not pay your bill?" Oliver smirked.

"Could I have a coffee?" Kell asked.

Not that he wanted one, but he definitely needed to get hold of Lyndsay's phone. He regretted calling her. He should have found some other way to get the gifts to the boys.

She huffed but set up the complicated looking black and silver coffee maker that sat on the sparkling marble worktop.

Kell thrust the gifts at his brother. "Want to put them in the playroom?"

Oliver sucked in his cheeks, but walked out with the boxes. Kell went straight to the coffee maker, distracted Lyndsay with a comment about a mark on the floor, and slipped her phone into his pocket.

"I'll just nip to the bathroom."

Kell shut himself inside as he spotted his brother coming back down the hall. He locked the door and sighed with relief when he realised there was no password, otherwise he'd have had to drop it in the toilet. By the time he emerged, his number was no longer there.

Back in the kitchen, he expected Lyndsay to confront him, but she said nothing. Hopefully she hadn't noticed. One cup of black coffee sat next to the coffee machine.

"Thanks." Kell put a broad smile on his face and returned the phone to where he'd found it before swivelling round and keeping his back to the machine.

Oliver had fucking eagle vision and he'd likely notice the sudden appearance of his wife's mobile.

"How's Westminster?" Kell asked.

His brother was a Member of Parliament and Kell still couldn't figure out how he'd convinced people to vote for him. But then again, it was only Kell that Oliver treated like shit.

"Drink your coffee and leave."

"Put it down on your expenses. Entertaining a potential constituent."

"You're moving to where we live?" Lyndsay looked horrified.

"Thinking about it," Kell said, just to be bloody-minded.

"What do you really want?" Oliver narrowed his eyes.

A pang of disappointment seized Kell's heart. He never expected anything different from his brother, but it still hurt.

"To give the kids their presents. That's all." He took a sip of the coffee and set it down.

Oliver gave him a triumphant smirk and Kell wondered what he'd put in the drink, if he'd spat in it. *Shit. Thank fuck I only had a sip.*

"Tell the boys I'm sorry I didn't get their gifts here sooner," he said and picked up his bags.

Oliver followed him to the door. "You think we'd actually give them to them?" He sounded astonished. "What did you get them? Barbies? That's what you liked to play with."

"You know I didn't."

"They'll go in the trash."

"I've already told dad what I bought them so I wouldn't do that if I were you."

Oliver slammed the door as Kell walked away. He stopped at the first public phone box he found. His father wasn't in so he left a message.

"Hi, Dad. I've just taken the twins their birthday gifts. Star Wars Lego. Maybe you could give them a hand with it. I don't think Oliver has the patience. I'll be in touch."

Gethin's phone rang as he headed for his car with a box of cakes. He'd wondered how long it would take Izabela to call him.

"Party Solutions," he said, aware Charlton might be listening in.

"I'm so sorry. Oh my God. I had no idea he had gun."

Was that true? "Are you okay?"

"Yes. He gone to work. He promise to take me out tonight to make up for spoiling surprise. Can you come back with information you took off computer?"

"You told me you were married."

"Sorry." She sighed. "I thought you not want to help me if you knew I was only girlfriend."

"You've no entitlement to his money."

"I just like to know whether he lie about how much he have."

27

What a bitch. If Charlton hadn't been such a bastard, Gethin might have felt sorry for him.

"Can you bring memory stick?" she asked.

"Not right now. I've somewhere I need to be. I'll be in touch." Gethin ended the call.

An ache had started up in his head to match the heavy weight in his stomach. He'd been too eager to take this case. Too desperate for work to refuse to hack into the computer. He'd put an ad in the Metro newspaper and been so pleased to get work from it he hadn't thought hard enough about why she'd picked him. Had she known his background? He couldn't see how, but now it was a niggling concern. What had seemed relatively straightforward had turned out to be anything but.

Gethin drove back to the office, parked his car underneath the building and climbed the stairs to the second floor. He pushed open the door to Celebrations—the real party planning business— and put the box of cakes on Tilda's desk.

She finished the call she was on and smiled at him. "Yum. So I did good with the bat phone?"

"You did good, thank you. That man might phone again. If he does, use the voice you used before, ask for his number and tell him you'll get me to contact him. Under no circumstances tell him where the office is. Any concerns whatsoever you cut off the call, switch off the phone and contact me from a different one."

"You're scaring me now."

"I'm being cautious." Gethin forced a smile to his face.

"So what happened?"

"My spidey senses let me down. Client's partner came home, decided I was messing around with his girlfriend and overreacted."

There was a lump in Gethin's throat. He swallowed, but it didn't shift. Maybe it was belatedly hitting him that he'd had a narrow escape.

Angel, the owner of the party planning business, poked his white-haired head out of his office. His eyes lit up when he saw the cakes.

"All mine." Tilda grabbed the box.

"*What, wouldst thou have me go and beg my food?* Make us coffee, darling." Angel stared pointedly at the box, then beckoned Gethin.

"Macbeth?" Gethin asked.

Angel tsked. "As You Like It."

No way would Gethin ever get any of Angel's Shakespearian quotes, so he always said Macbeth. Gethin dropped into the leather chair opposite Angel's huge desk.

Angel was forty, looked thirty, and had the energy of a twenty-year-old. Today he was wearing a gray Nehru jacket threaded with sparkling silver strands and pink chinos. Gethin wasn't sure he'd ever seen him wear the same thing twice.

His office was just as flamboyant, an Aladdin's cave of eclectic styles and colours. A smoky black and white print of a debutantes' ball, supposedly featuring Angel's grandmother, was positioned above a Louis XV style cream chair. On his clear acrylic desk sat a turquoise retro telephone, a stone gargoyle, a fake chocolate wedding cake and a lamp that could have been an authentic Victorian piece. Plus there were containers of fresh flowers everywhere so the room smelled and looked like a confused summer garden. Yet Angel orchestrated tasteful, highly successful themed parties that people booked over a year in advance. It was a mystery Gethin couldn't solve.

"*Full of sad thoughts and troubles?*" Angel settled in his chair.

"Macbeth?"

Angel groaned. "Henry VIII, you ignoramus. What happened to your forehead?"

"Nothing." Gethin pulled at his fringe.

"Come to blows with Jonnie?"

Gethin glared. Jonnie was out of bounds and Angel knew it.

"Let's try an easier question," Angel said, his face full of excitement. "Why did you require Tilda's dubious acting skills?"

"A woman's boyfriend came home and got the wrong idea when he found me with her. He rang to check I worked where I said I did. Tilda did a good job."

"He didn't guess you were gay? The idiot."

Gethin laughed. Very few people looked at him and thought he was gay. "I told him I was, but he didn't seem to believe me."

Tilda came in with coffee and two chocolate digestive biscuits. Angel stared at the biscuits and whined.

"I'm saving you from yourself," Tilda said.

Angel whined harder and Tilda huffed, left the room and returned with two macaroons.

"Sweet cheeks, you shouldn't have." Angel pinched one as she tried to whisk the plate away.

When Gethin had moved into the building just over a year ago, as a fledgling private investigator, Angel's party planning company had been in operation for almost a decade. Without Angel's help, Gethin couldn't have set his business up, couldn't have afforded the office he currently used — in truth he still couldn't afford it. Angel subsidized him. PI work largely came from word of mouth, but Gethin hadn't done enough jobs to rely on that. He'd paid a fortune for the ad in the Metro and it had nearly got him killed. *Fuck.*

"Are you okay?" Angel asked. "You look pale."

"I'm fine."

"Eat that to stop me scoffing it."

Gethin took the macaroon.

To make him feel better about his deal with Angel, they'd come to an arrangement. Gethin collected debts from clients who were reluctant to pay and if any calls for Rhys Jones came in on the phone Gethin had supplied, Tilda or Angel would confirm he worked for a party planning company called Party Solutions. Angel had wanted to say Gethin worked for Celebrations, but Gethin knew it was safer not to be linked to Angel's company.

He'd told Angel and his staff to deny they knew him if anyone came asking, admit to passing him in the corridor, but that was all. Angel thought he was paranoid. Gethin hoped he was.

"I need a favour," Angel said. *"With the help of your good hands.* That's a quote from The Tempest because you won't guess. I'm running a thirtieth birthday party in a castle in Sussex this weekend and I'm so short staffed I'm having heart palpitations." He patted his chest.

"Wrong side."

Angel glared. "No it's not. Can you help me out? Setting up, waiting tables then dismantling everything the next day? I've arranged accommodation at a local hotel, and transportation. I'll let you off two weeks rent."

The money was tempting. Gethin wouldn't get paid for this morning's fiasco, but he was busy on Saturday night. He was busy *every* Saturday night and Angel knew it.

"I can't."

"Please," Angel begged. "I've had three guys cancel on me."

Gethin thought about what he was supposed to be doing, how much he dreaded it, and knew Angel had just offered him a legitimate excuse. Work. Jonnie would understand.

Crap, no he won't.

"Sorry. No."

"Bring your boyfriend," Angel said. "He can help."

"I can't." Gethin regretted telling Angel about Jonnie. Not that he *had* told him. Angel had eavesdropped on a call, then assumed he knew everything when he knew virtually nothing.

Angel stared at him. "Tilda helped you out today. Now I need you to help me out or maybe that phone won't be answered next time."

"Shit, Angel. Blackmail?"

"I'm desperate. It's not that big a deal is it? I'm asking nicely and of course Miss Moneypenny and I will keep up the subterfuge even if you say no. But please. I don't want to ask an agency and get some pimply youth. You look right. *Three* weeks rent."

31

Gethin sighed. "Okay."

Angel clapped his hands together and smiled, his look of distress gone in an instant. "Great. I'll get Tilda to email the details."

Gethin pushed to his feet.

"I meant it about Jonnie," Angel said. "It's about time I met him, decided on his suitability for my favourite PI. Bring him. I'll pay him."

"No." Angel could interpret that any way he liked.

Chapter Four

Gethin headed for his bolthole at the far end of the corridor, tapped the code into the keypad and pushed the door open. The only uncluttered thing in his small office was the filing cabinet. Inside *that* his paperwork was in perfect order, receipts in dated folders, and handwritten notes in others — keep everything, he'd been told by the guy on the PI training course. But the surface of his desk could hardly be seen. His laptop was surrounded by what looked like crap but actually wasn't. Sheets with scribbled sentences, maps, clippings from newspapers and magazines, all relating to missing persons cases he was no longer being paid to work on, but that he'd not let go. He had difficulty letting go of anything unfinished.

On the left hand side of the desk were piles of manuals on burglar alarms together with leaflets on locks, safes and surveillance equipment, a Jenga-style interlocking pile of chewed pencils created when he was thinking, and two identical pairs of eye glasses he needed for close work. On the floor, boxes held computer parts, wires, circuit boards and various components he knew needed sorting out, and on the other side of the room was another desk holding two more computers, a printer and random stuff he ought to put into some sort of order and probably wouldn't. His inclination to tidy anything that wasn't important disappeared almost as soon as it had appeared.

Gethin sat at his desk, switched on his laptop and put on a pair of black rimmed glasses. He'd fucked up with this case, made mistakes that could have gotten him or Izabela killed, and might lead to trouble for Angel. Izabela told him she'd gotten his name from the ad, and looked him up on the Internet, but he'd not asked why she'd chosen him in particular. It wasn't as if he was anywhere near the first page on Google. He should have checked himself that Charlton was occupied elsewhere, made the decision about whether to go to the house based on his own intel and not

Izabela's. He should have looked the guy up, done some preparatory work.

Very rarely did a client come to Gethin's office, more for their safety than his, though his untidy rabbit hutch, minus the cuddly carrot-chewing animal, wasn't likely to impress. Gethin figured the fewer people who knew where he worked the better because he didn't need visits from pissed off partners, particularly those violent toward their other half, or now — as it appeared — those with access to guns. He was still having difficulty getting his head around what had happened that morning.

It was more sensible to meet clients in a public place, somewhere away from their normal environment; Kew Gardens, the Tate Modern, a café at the end of a tube line, Kings Cross station. Once he'd even had a meeting on the London Eye. The only reason he'd given in to Izabela's request was because she'd offered five hundred in cash up front which he'd now never see. She'd wanted him to get information from the computer and had presented him with what she said was the perfect opportunity. Gethin had assumed abuse when he'd seen the bruises and yet... Izabela hadn't known the computer password. What he'd done was illegal.

He took the memory stick from his pocket and laid it on the desk in front of him. What was on it that was important enough for her to come up with this ruse? She'd sounded sincere when she'd told him she suspected the man she said was her husband was cheating. The bruises looked real. But now Gethin wondered. Izabela had been perfectly made-up. She'd worn a dress most men would have found sexy though it exposed those marks. Had she faked them, made sure he'd seen them? Then pulled on that cardigan to stop Charlton seeing them?

He was no longer convinced by anything Izabela had told him. Gethin hadn't liked her boyfriend and now he didn't like her either. She'd engaged his services purely to get information off that computer. Maybe he wasn't the first PI she'd contacted, just the first to not use his brain.

His phone rang and he pulled it from his pocket assuming it would be her asking for the stick again. But it was an unknown number.

"Hello?" he said.

"Is that GRJ Investigations?"

Gethin didn't recognize the woman's voice, but that didn't mean she wasn't a friend of Izabela's, or an enemy of hers.

"How can I help you?"

"My name's Zena Hoehn. My son Dieter is missing." The woman let out a strangled sob.

Gethin felt guilty for his sigh of relief that he wasn't listening to someone threatening him about the memory stick. He pushed it into his laptop and started a virus check.

"How did you get my number?"

"I saw your ad in the Metro."

"And why did you choose me?" Gethin had just learned a lesson in being extra cautious.

"It says on your site how much you charge. Not many do that. Forty pounds an hour, right?"

"Minimum of four hours, plus travel costs and out of pocket expenses."

"That's fine. I can afford you for four hours. Maybe more if you need it."

Gethin swallowed his groan. Was this going to be another case he ended up not charging for? "How old is your son?"

"Seventeen."

"The police—"

"Are useless. They won't do anything. Please. I need help. I need someone to be looking for him." She burst into tears and Gethin winced.

"How long has he been missing?"

"Twenty-eight days."

"What's your address?"

He wrote it down. *Oh shit. Edgware.* He should just tell her he'd need two hours of her four getting there and back. More probably. But this was a mother concerned for a missing son and Gethin kept quiet.

"Can you come now?" she asked.

"Give me a couple of hours."

"Thank you."

Gethin put down his mobile and stared at the screen of his laptop. No viruses. He had top of the range programs to keep his computer safe, but he was still relieved to see no problems. He copied the contents of the stick onto the machine and onto another storage device just in case, his mind already drifting to thoughts of the missing boy.

The chances of finding a seventeen year old who'd run away from home were not good. Desperate partners, parents, siblings or friends of the missing only approached private investigators after the police had failed and the trail was cold. Unless it was a case of abduction, and that didn't happen often to kids that age, people generally disappeared because they chose to. Those left behind often found it impossible to accept their loved ones had gone of their own volition. He found brief details of Dieter's disappearance online, a photo of the teenager in the local paper. At least he knew his mother was telling the truth, unless she'd killed him.

While he was looking at photos, he searched for one of Izabela, inputting Brian Charlton's details. He found one picture of the pair of them at a charity event. Gethin took a shot of it with his phone. He couldn't find anything about Izabela. Without her surname there was little more he could do.

Gethin clicked to open the file he'd created from Charlton's computer data. He'd copied everything: documents, pictures, videos, excel spreadsheets, emails and the contents of the recycle bin. He should have covered his tracks well enough that the guy never found out, but Gethin knew he might. No matter how good a hacker you were, there was always someone better. He opened up the spreadsheets and worked on decrypting the one Charlton had most recently closed. When he saw lists of bank accounts and amounts of cash being moved about, he groaned. That didn't look legit, though the guy *was* an accountant.

He scanned through the other stuff. More decryption was needed. The pictures and videos were a mix of decent and indecent, though nothing perverted. Izabela looked happy to be posing like a porn star. Maybe she *was* a porn star.

Normal decryption techniques didn't work with all the documents, but he uncovered one embedded folder within a folder within another folder holding photos of young women whose pictures were arranged like a series of mug shots. The first of a woman's face, the next of her standing naked. Not posing. Just standing and not looking happy. Amounts in Euros beneath made Gethin wonder if the women were for sale or had been sold. Or was he jumping to conclusions because he wanted to find Charlton guilty of something?

Regardless of what else was on the stick, this felt like information the police ought to have along with the detail that Charlton had an illegal weapon. Gethin could do it anonymously, though there was no way of knowing if the police would take it seriously. Plus if the police seized the computer, maybe Izabela would give them Gethin's name and Charlton would discover what she and Gethin had done. If hadn't been for that gun, he might not have been so worried, but if the guy wasn't kept in custody, and it was unlikely he would be, then Gethin and Izabela were in danger.

In addition, the way Gethin had accessed the computer, let alone the fact that he'd illegally copied the data, was an offence under the Computer Misuse Act. It wasn't Izabela's machine so Gethin couldn't claim her involvement to justify what he'd done. In the long term, it would eventually be up to a trial judge to decide whether what he'd discovered could be excluded because it had been unfairly obtained. The whole case, assuming there was one, could fall apart.

Gethin ground his teeth. He'd been warned about this on the training course, that more and more PIs were getting information off computers, mostly illegally. It was one thing Gethin was good at. He'd thought hacking to help people out would be a good thing. Now he wished he'd not done it. For the moment, he was reasonably certain Charlton didn't suspect anything and that gave him time to think how to handle this.

He called Izabela.

"Hi," she said.

"Can you talk?"

"He's at work. I was just going to call you."

"How did you come to choose me?"

"I saw your name in paper. You could do work fast, come to house straight away."

"Why not a big firm?"

"Why all these questions?" she snapped. "If Brian finds out what we did, I'm frightened he do something stupid. Just bring memory stick and I pay you."

Of what value is the stick to you?

"Can you come today? Brian won't be in until late. Or I could meet you."

I thought you couldn't leave the house?

"Was I the first PI you spoke to?"

"Why you make big deal about this?" she screeched. "Two hundred pound more if you bring it back right now."

"Just tell me—"

Izabela gasped, then cut him off and when Gethin rang back, he couldn't even get a dial tone. *Fuck.* What had she done to the phone? He took off his glasses and rubbed his forehead, belatedly remembering the bruise and wincing. *I've been used.* Had he really been picked at random? Or because he was a sole operator and not very experienced? Or because she knew he could hack into computers? But how could she know that? Questions niggled away at him.

Gethin picked up the spare memory stick. Now he had three copies, including the one on his laptop. He closed down his computer, and pushed to his feet. One stick went into his pocket, the other he hid behind the loose skirting board at the back of his chair. He glanced around. As far as he was aware, neither Izabela nor Charlton knew the location of his office. All the information on his computer was backed up remotely. If anyone came here, they wouldn't find every copy of what they were looking for.

Life had seemed so simple this morning and now Gethin worried he'd stumbled into something bigger than he could handle.

Before he left the office, he entered Zena Hoehn's address into his phone. After he'd spoken to her about her missing teen, he'd call in at a supermarket to buy the things Jonnie needed then go and explain why he wouldn't be there as usual on Saturday. It was pointless phoning. Gethin had a better chance of getting him to understand if he talked to him face to face.

He changed into his leathers, left his car under the building and took his bike, his headset plumbed into his phone. He never seemed to get time to himself, a few hours to unwind. Even when he wasn't working, his mind raced. There was always something he was trying to figure out, some current case bothering him or past cases where he'd not been able to help, or cases where his help had caused such anguish he'd wished he did any other job. Now he had a missing seventeen year old to find, who even if Gethin *did* locate him would most likely refuse to go home, plus the curious case of a guy with strange photos on his computer, along with details of complicated money transfers, and Gethin had only managed to look at part of it.

Then there was Jonnie. Gethin's emotions went into overload as soon as he thought about him. Regret, guilt, affection, sympathy, resentment, hatred. It was impossible to define how he felt because he felt all that and more. In trying to be kind, to be a good man, Gethin had trapped himself, fucked up his world and he could tell no one, not without looking weak, stupid and selfish. Yet however bad Gethin's life was — Jonnie's was worse.

By the time he pulled up outside Zena Hoehn's semi-detached house, he'd made a decision about the memory stick.

After he'd decrypted everything that was on it, even if the photos of those women and the bank transfers were the only odd things, he'd still go to the police.

Zena Hoehn pulled open the door before he reached it. She was a petite blonde in her late thirties. The dark rings under her eyes and her agitated fingers betrayed her anxiety.

"Thank you for coming so quickly."

"You caught me between jobs."

She ushered Gethin into a tidy lounge, and gave him a photo of Dieter. It was better than the one Gethin had downloaded, so he took a picture with his phone and handed it back.

"Good looking boy."

She took a shaky gulp. "He is. Takes after his father, but not in temperament."

"Start at the beginning."

"Six weeks ago, Dieter set off for school but never arrived. It was only when he didn't come home that I discovered he'd taken a bag of clothes and his toiletries, but left his phone and keys. I called the police. They checked local hospitals and contacted neighbouring forces, but couldn't find him."

With no evidence of foul play, Gethin knew they'd only make perfunctory further enquiries, no matter how much his mother insisted Dieter wouldn't have just upped and left.

"I spoke to all his friends, and contacted my ex-husband who lives in Manchester, but Mike hadn't seen him. I went to every place I thought Dieter might be. I assumed the police would keep looking, but they didn't." She gritted her teeth. "They made me feel as if it was *my* fault he'd gone, that he'd run away from *me*. But he had no reason to. We got on fine. Once I understood the police weren't doing anything more to find him, I looked for a private investigator."

Everything poured out: every memory, fact, and theory. Gethin sifted through the torrent of information and made notes. Details about scars, nicknames, hobbies, Dieter's medals for gymnastics, medical history, places he liked to visit, pop stars he followed, movies he'd watched, books he read, contact numbers for family, his school, and school friends.

When she began to repeat herself, he asked to see Dieter's room. She led him upstairs.

"The police are the only ones who've been in here apart from me. I haven't disturbed anything. When he comes back, I want it to be as if he'd never left."

Gethin stood on the threshold and ran his gaze over everything, getting an impression of the boy before he stepped inside. His mother stood watching. He asked questions as he went through drawers, checked underneath them and looked in the wardrobe, noting what Dieter hadn't taken. He examined places where he might have hidden stuff if this had been his room, but found nothing.

He switched on the computer. "Could you get me a cup of black coffee, please?"

She looked mortified she'd not thought to ask, but he only wanted her out of the way while he checked the computer, and had a quick glance in the other bedrooms. By the time she came back with the drink, Gethin had seen as much as he needed to.

What he'd gathered on this visit looked like a mass of random information, but it enabled him to create a profile in his head to tie to the photo of the good looking, slender kid, who seemed much younger than his age. Dieter had curly brown hair and a cheeky smile, a slight gap between big front teeth he'd not yet grown into. He was regularly on Facebook, Twitter and Instagram, but hadn't logged on since the day he disappeared. That, plus leaving his phone and keys, confirmed to Gethin, as it would have to the police, that Dieter had thought this through and didn't want to be traced.

His mother insisted she had no idea why he'd run and Gethin was inclined to believe her. He couldn't help wishing he'd had someone who'd loved him as much when he was seventeen. He asked her to phone Dieter's best friend Sam and push Sam into meeting him at McDonalds after school. Gethin filled in the time until then by talking to neighbours and local shopkeepers, showing them Dieter's photo and asking questions he suspected they'd answered before.

Gethin already knew what Sam looked like from a photo Zena had shown him. A shorter, plumper version of Dieter. He waved to the boy when he walked in. Gethin had picked McDonalds because it was non-threatening, but Sam looked petrified. Buying him a burger and chips didn't take the fear off his face.

"Dieter's mum is frantic," Gethin said.

"I don't know where he is. I told her."

"You know why he ran?"

Sam shook his head and didn't meet Gethin's gaze. Gethin didn't believe him.

"Did he ask you to go with him?"

"No. I wouldn't have gone. He knew that."

"So you're happy at home?" Gethin asked.

"Yeah."

"Why wasn't Dieter?"

The boy gave him a frantic look. "Dieter loves his mum."

"Then why did he run?"

"I don't know." The expression on Sam's face had changed to one of defiance.

"Do you have any idea where he might go?"

"No."

Gethin leaned back in his seat and took a bite of his burger. "Tell me what you do together, what sort of friend he is, what school's like. Is he cleverer than you?"

"No. Well, yeah in some subjects. He's good at maths. I'm better at English. He's brilliant at gymnastics and dancing. I'm not."

"Are you gay too?"

Sam went so red Gethin worried for a few seconds that he wasn't going to start breathing again. It had only been a guess about both boys, but an intuitive one.

"No," Sam whispered.

"Sam." Gethin leaned forward. "Tell me the truth. I promise I won't tell anyone."

"We haven't done anything."

"It's nothing to do with me if you have." Gethin stared at him. "So you're both gay."

Sam nodded once, the smallest possible movement of his head as if he couldn't even admit his sexuality to himself.

"Did Dieter have a boyfriend? An older guy?"

"No."

"Did he meet someone online? Chat to them?"

"No. He hasn't been groomed. We know what to look out for. We've talked about it. But I can't tell you why he ran. I promised and I won't tell. I don't know where he is. He said if he told me someone might make me tell them. He also said he'd call me, but he hasn't."

Gethin needed more information from Sam before the kid clammed up.

"Dieter's mother is worried sick. She's thinking the worst, that Dieter's lying dead in a ditch or he's being held against his will and bad things are being done to him."

Sam gulped.

"I know he must have had his reasons for running and I'd never try to persuade him to come back home if he didn't want to, but I need to be able to tell her he's safe."

"I really don't know where he is."

Gethin thought he was telling the truth about that. "Tell me about him, what he likes, what the pair of you did together."

Gradually, Sam unwound and started to talk. By the time Gethin waved him off, he'd added to his mass of information, but Sam refused to budge on why Dieter had run. The kid promised to call him if he thought of anything or if Dieter got in touch. Gethin sent Dieter's photograph to a few of his contacts but he wasn't optimistic. London was a big city to disappear in and there was no guarantee the kid was even in the capital.

After he'd called in at the supermarket next to McDonalds and bought the stuff Jonnie needed, he went back to Dieter's mother's house.

For a split second when she opened it, he saw light in her eyes before it faded. He guessed every time someone knocked on the door, she hoped.

"One question," Gethin said. One he needed to ask her face to face. "Is your son gay?"

"Yes. Is that a problem?"

"No. Not at all. I just wondered if it was for you."

"That wasn't the reason he ran. We talked about it a couple of years ago. He knows I'm okay with it. I know Sam's gay too, but he's not told his parents. I don't think he and Dieter were into each other. They were just good friends."

"Are you seeing anyone?" Gethin asked.

She gave a short laugh. "I was. I'm not now."

"I'll work on a few ideas and be in touch."

Gethin returned to his bike, and reset the destination in his sat nav.

Chapter Five

By the time Gethin had parked, retrieved the shopping from the box at the back of his bike and put his helmet in there instead, his mood had plunged to its usual low whenever he was in the vicinity of this place. He climbed the steps of Wellbrook Manor — was there ever a worse name for a nursing home? — and the glass doors swished open at his approach.

Candy, the Jamaican receptionist, smiled when she saw him. "Leather man! When you going to take me on dat bike?" She let out a raucous laugh.

He managed a smile. Candy was so large, there'd be no room for him on the bike as well or he might have surprised her and offered her a ride. It seemed incongruous to have someone who was always happy and smiling working at a place where people were struggling to survive, but maybe she was a reminder to visitors that life goes on.

Jonnie didn't want to be here. At first he'd kept asking if he could live with Gethin, but that was impossible. All Gethin could afford was a small bedsit on the fourth floor of a dilapidated block in Deptford with no lift. Jonnie needed his own room, space for his carers, electric wheelchair, hoist, special shower and a shit load of other stuff. Gethin felt guilty to be relieved it couldn't be done.

The smile on his face was firmly in place before he knocked on the door of Jonnie's room. He checked no one else was in there before he walked all the way inside. Jonnie was sitting in his wheelchair, facing the TV, his head cushioned by neck supports. He swivelled away from the screen to face Gethin and scowled. Jonnie's hair was just as blond as the day Gethin had met him, though much thinner, not that Gethin would ever tell him or about the bald spot at the back. Jonnie was still vain about his appearance and it broke Gethin's heart.

"Late," Jonnie said.

"I'm not late." He hadn't even been due to come, but there was no point telling Jonnie that.

"Sorry. Miss you."

Not everyone could understand him. Gethin mostly could, though sometimes Jonnie's speech was so slurred it was a struggle to decipher. His lungs and voice box were under pressure from his slumped posture.

Jonnie used the small amount of movement he had in his fingers to work the controls to bring the chair across the room. Gethin bent to kiss him. He pulled away the instant he felt the tip of Jonnie's tongue touch his. *Oh Christ. Don't.*

"Get me everything?" Jonnie asked.

"Yes, your highness." Gethin put the bag on the bed. "They were out of Beluga caviar and I had to settle for Sevruga. Hope that's okay."

That raised a quiet laugh. Gethin put away everything that he'd bought, either into the cupboard or the little fridge Gethin had paid for. He'd been joking about the caviar, but Jonnie's tastes had always been expensive and the nursing home was happy to let friends and relatives bring in things patients liked to eat. Jonnie's carers would get the food out when he wanted it. Gethin laid the magazines on the tray table across the bed and put a box of mint chocolates on top.

"Get alcohol?" Jonnie asked.

"You know you're not supposed to have it."

Jonnie glared.

"But yes I did, slave driver. You have to drink it now so I can sneak the can out."

Gethin pulled the tab on the beer and stuck a straw in it. He put the straw between Jonnie's lips and he sucked hard.

"Nice." Jonnie smiled at him.

Oh God, I hate this. But not as much as Jonnie did.

"What are you watching?" Gethin glanced at the TV.

"Crap. Waiting for you."

"I wasn't due to come today." *Why did I say that?*

Jonnie's face fell. "Not been for ages."

Yes, I fucking have.

"Toes moved today."

Gethin tried to look excited. "Your toes moved?"

"Yeah." He grinned.

"That's great."

Jonnie's smile faded. "You don't believe me."

"Of course I do." *No, I don't.*

"Getting better."

According to an endless line of doctors called for a second opinion by Jonnie, the chances of him getting better were nil. Well, not better in the sense of back to how he used to be. Some improvement might be on the cards, but it would never be as much as Jonnie wanted.

A complete quadriplegic with a C4 injury, Jonnie had lost the ability to control his limbs. He could move his head to a small extent and breathe unaided, though he'd spent a long time on a ventilator. He had a limited amount of movement in the fingers of one hand, enough to manoeuvre his powered wheelchair, and using a variety of devices, exercise some control over a computer, the position of his bed, and whether the light or TV was on or off. He could read a book or a magazine using a machine that turned pages operated by his finger. Gethin had bought him an electronic reader, but knew Jonnie had not finished any book he'd started. He lost interest and patience. Magazines were better, particularly because Gethin could sit beside him and read them to him, show him the pictures.

"Has the doctor been to see you about your toes?" Gethin asked.

"No. No one comes."

That wasn't true. There was a team of therapists who helped: physical, speech, recreational, occupational. A program had been drawn up to meet Jonnie's needs and abilities. Realistic goals had been set, but Jonnie refused to accept that was his future. Gethin knew he'd feel the same. How could anyone accept this after they'd been flying so high? Stardom had beckoned and been taken away by one moment of stupidity. Not just Jonnie's.

"No one ever visits," Jonnie said.

"I come."

"Only one."

Which was Gethin's problem. At first Jonnie's friends had come to see him. Members of the band had been regular visitors, but now they rarely stopped by. Gethin knew they were angry Jonnie had wrecked things for them too.

He put off telling Jonnie he couldn't visit him the next day until he'd spent an hour reading magazines, discussing the news and chatting. Jonnie laughed when Gethin told him about the gun, and the mark on his forehead, though Gethin had narrated the story in an amusing way.

"You wouldn't have thought it was funny if I'd been killed. Who'd visit you then?"

"No need for people to visit if I was dead," Jonnie said.

Gethin's stomach twisted. He knew exactly what Jonnie meant and had to stop himself saying—and how the fuck are you going to kill yourself? He could feel the conversation looming that he didn't want to have.

"I have to go now." Gethin pushed to his feet.

"Stay longer."

"I can't. I have to work tomorrow, mate. I'll come Sunday instead."

"No." Jonnie gave him a stricken look. "You always spend Saturday with me. Date?"

"No, I don't have a date. It's work."

"Come after."

"It will be too late."

"Don't care. Come after."

"I'll be in some castle in Sussex. This place is miles away."

"I see no one." Jonnie's voice began to rise. "Might as well be dead. Wish I was dead. No trouble to you then."

"Don't say that. There are medical advances happening all the time. You just have to be patient. You moved your toes, didn't you? See, that's progress." *Oh Christ, what the fuck do I say to him?*

"Want to die," he whispered.

Gethin sagged.

"Love you." The desperation in Jonnie's voice and the look on his face hurt as much as if the guy had reached into Gethin's chest and squeezed his heart. "Love you forever."

"I love you too," Gethin said and part of him did. Just not the part Jonnie wanted.

If it hadn't been bad enough Jonnie had been left paralysed in the accident, he'd hit his head as well and suffered from retrograde amnesia. Gethin and Jonnie hadn't been an item for six months before that fucking terrible day, but Jonnie didn't remember that. He thought Gethin was still his boyfriend.

"Stay. Lock door," Jonnie said and Gethin swallowed.

"No."

"Want you to jerk off for me."

"No."

"Please."

Gethin shook his head.

"Put your cock in my mouth. Let me suck you off. Can do that."

"I can't." Gethin headed for the door.

"Come tomorrow."

Gethin sighed, already capitulating. "It'll be very late."

"Still come."

"I'll try." *Fuck.*

By the time Gethin reached his bedsit, he was wired tight enough to snap. He looked at the dump he called home and couldn't stand the idea of spending the night lying in his uncomfortable bed, trying to get to sleep when he knew it wouldn't happen. He grabbed his backpack and few things from his closet, put his toiletries in a plastic bag and returned to his bike. The place where he was working tomorrow for Angel was close to Brighton. If he left now, he had a chance to go to a club, find someone to fuck and stay with them overnight.

Gethin abandoned most of that plan on the way down. He wasn't in the mood to go to a club, not in the mood to fuck anyone or to spend the night with a guy he'd never be able to see again. He hadn't been with anyone for over a year. He couldn't muster enthusiasm for sex. If it hadn't been for all the crap going on in his life, he might have been worried.

He weaved his way through the streets, slowed by congestion until he reached the outskirts of the city. Maybe he'd made a mistake becoming a PI but he hadn't wanted to be office bound and it had seemed like a good idea at the time. Except most of Gethin's work was matrimonial and involved him creeping around taking pictures that would end up wrecking lives: photos of middle-aged men with their tongues or dicks down the throats of their secretaries, women on their knees sucking off the repair guy, gardener, next door neighbour. 'Straight' men fucking other men, men picking up prostitutes of all genders, men flirting with teenagers who looked barely legal, and in one case wasn't. He'd gone straight to the police with that.

Every time he thought he'd seen it all, he found he hadn't and took pictures to prove it, though he didn't always reveal everything he knew to his client. Some people could take the whole truth, others couldn't. He appreciated the lives of those involved had already been wrecked by suspicion if not by deceit before they approached a PI, but it didn't make him feel any easier with himself. Telling someone they'd been right, their spouse was unfaithful, always made him feel sick.

Sometimes he wondered if there was any part of his job he liked. Finding missing people? Yes but it didn't happen often because those who went missing usually had a reason for disappearing and had no intention of returning home. The best Gethin could do was prove they were still alive. He'd done that once and failed to find any trace on three occasions. He didn't hold out a lot of hope of finding Dieter.

He pulled onto the motorway and was finally able to speed up. As if his working life wasn't bad enough, his personal life was non-existent outside of visits to see Jonnie. Gethin went to the nursing home three times a week. *Three times too many.* He'd tried to go less often but he knew how much Jonnie looked forward to seeing him. He'd been drawn into the emotional trap of feeling obliged to keep going, allowing Jonnie to suck the life out of him like a bloody vampire. When no one else visited, not even his parents, who'd buggered off to Portugal — the complete bastards — how could Gethin abandon him too?

Jonnie swung between thinking he was going to get better, that he and Gethin would live happily ever after, and accepting this was all the life he could ever have and wishing he was dead. He was always complaining Gethin hadn't been to see him, simply because he forgot Gethin had come. Gethin wished Jonnie could forget him, wished he was free of him, but they were tied by Gethin's conscience and Jonnie's faulty memory.

The guy wasn't just an emotional drain but a financial one too. The local authority funded Jonnie's care to a point, but required a top up contribution for his upscale nursing home. Jonnie thought he was still paying, but his money had long run out. When the nursing home manager had talked to him about going somewhere else, Jonnie had asked Gethin to go and look at where they wanted to send him and take photos. Gethin had left the other places knowing Jonnie would hate them even more than Wellbrook, so Gethin made up the shortfall. Was *still* making up the shortfall. *And* buying food Jonnie wanted, plus a fridge, a TV, designer clothes and a whole lot of other crap. His savings had gone.

Gethin knew he was an idiot. He wasn't even a good man because he didn't act out of altruism. This was no selfless desire to help someone worse off than him, but a duty borne out of obligation and guilt. When Jonnie had lain in hospital, wired up and on a ventilator, Gethin had hoped his friend died before he understood the extent of his injury. But he hadn't. Jonnie might live as long as Gethin. Whenever Gethin wished Jonnie would pass away in his sleep, he was crippled by remorse. Just because he didn't think life in a wheelchair, paralysed from the neck down, was a life worth living, didn't meant he had the right to choose for Jonnie.

But Jonnie had started to ask him to kill him. At least he'd not done that tonight. Just wished he was dead. Gethin couldn't kill him, and yet he was hypocritical enough to hope someone would do it for *him* if he were ever in Jonnie's situation. *Christ, what a fucking mess.*

He caught sight of blue flashing lights in his mirror, checked his speed and groaned. He hadn't been going much over the limit. But the police car flashed past him and Gethin sighed with relief. Was his luck changing?

When he reached Brighton, he pulled up outside the first bed and breakfast with a vacancy sign. After he'd dumped his bag in his room, he walked to the seafront, bought a bag of chips and sat looking out at the starlings swirling in the sky. When he had ever felt so free, so joyful? Assuming the birds were capable of that.

Kell sat on the seafront feeling happy, eating a bag of chips he'd overloaded with salt and vinegar. It took being miles away from London to make him realise how much his job weighed him down. He was living a life where he hardly dare take a crap without checking he was safe, but just sitting here in the failing light, looking out to sea, eating freshly cooked chips, made him feel so much lighter, though not warmer. He had his jacket on, a scarf wrapped twice around his neck, a beanie hat pulled down over his ears and he was still cold. But he'd take cold and safe over warm and not safe any day.

He'd caught the train from London, checked into a bed and breakfast he'd chosen at random, dropped onto the bed and fallen into a deep, dreamless sleep until he'd woken with a jolt an hour ago. After a shower he'd felt almost human though his arse still ached from Marek's rough fucking and his cheek was bruised.

Technically, Kell didn't need to have come down today, tomorrow morning would have been fine which meant he could have worked tonight, but he was so tired, mentally exhausted from being a guy he wasn't. It was a short cab ride to Quin's parents' place from Brighton and now Kell had this evening to unwind giving him time to find another face — still not quite his own — to put on tomorrow.

He finished the chips, screwed up the paper and tossed the ball into the bin at the side of the seat. He spotted another guy sitting on a bench further up the promenade doing the same as him, eating chips, watching the birds. Kell looked into the sky. It was already streaked with starlings, not yet a full show but getting there. The birds had spent the day scavenging Sussex fields for food before flocking to a communal rooting site under Brighton pier. Prior to settling down for the night they'd perform an exotic aerial dance, one Kell hadn't seen for a number of years.

Gradually the number of birds in the sky increased, and coalesced into the huge swirling mass called a murmuration. Thousands of starlings swooped, glided and fluttered through the air, swirling black clouds of birds morphing into strange shapes, transforming into alien creatures in the twilight. Kell thought it was a miracle none collided. When he was a boy, he used to expect to see a few birds falling into the sea but they never did. Like shoals of fish, they appeared to instinctively adjust to the movement of those around them so it seemed as if they were one huge shape-shifting monster.

He'd looked up what murmuration meant — the uttering of low continuous sounds — and it fitted because you could hear the strange noise of all those wings rippling and flapping as the birds danced together. Yet the fancy word didn't say enough, didn't hint at the magic of what he was watching. Kell pulled out his phone to take a picture and winced when the screen lit up. He pressed a few keys to change it, mentally reminding himself not to forget to change it back. He took a few shots, and captured one where the mass appeared to look like a gigantic prehistoric bird.

Kell sat and watched until the sky was empty, the starlings safely roosting for the night. Then he went back to the bed and breakfast and fell into a deep sleep.

Chapter Six

Gethin woke with a start, registered he was in a warm comfortable bed with no peeling paint on the walls, no roar of traffic outside and sighed with pleasure. The moment of satisfaction was fleeting. He was an idiot for coming down last night. He'd forked out money for a bed and breakfast when he could have stayed in Deptford and come down this morning. Though he'd watched a dazzling display put on by thousands of birds and he'd slept well so maybe it was worth it. He checked the clock, then rolled out of bed and put on his exercise gear. He had time for a run before the landlady stopped serving breakfast.

It was barely light when he stepped through the door. He did a few stretches, warming his muscles, then headed for the seafront, looking forward to running somewhere different. He ran most mornings, usually the same route, crossing Deptford Creek, heading down to the river and along the Thames path in the direction of the Dome. When the route turned away from the water, he reversed the journey, sometimes stopping for a coffee in Greenwich.

Running was one of Gethin's few pleasures. He drew comfort from the rhythm of his feet pounding the pavement, the flow of the river by his side. Running cleared his head and fired an endorphin rush, though the high never lasted because he eventually found it impossible to ignore what he was running past. The detritus of people's lives, items left behind, lost, and abandoned, sometimes treasures, mostly rubbish. Fast food wrappers discarded by the lazy or thoughtless, a child's tatty toy — how long had that been mourned before it was forgotten, replaced? A shoe — who loses one shoe and doesn't go back for it?

Was Dieter lost for good? Would Gethin have to tell another grieving parent he'd failed?

He picked up his pace on the promenade. The wind whipped off the water, made his ears tingle and tears leak from his eyes.

Dawn broke as he ran, the sky infused with pink. *Concentrate on the beauty of that and not your crap life.* He ran faster. Too fast. Pumped his legs and sprinted as if he were trying to take off and launch himself into a parallel dimension where he'd made the right decisions and Jonnie wasn't paralysed.

Gethin felt as if he'd spent his life making one mistake after another and sooner or later, they'd catch up with him no matter how fast he ran. His errors would pull him down like a pack of raptors and he'd not have the strength to get up.

Eventually, he had to slow because he could hardly catch his breath. His jog turned to a full out stop. As he bent with his chest heaving, his hands on his hips, he saw a guy heading toward him in running gear and a red beanie hat, dark hair escaping at the sides. He flashed Gethin a dazzling smile as he passed. He was good looking, about the same age as Gethin and Gethin couldn't even manage to smile back. *Shit.*

Smiling was off the agenda for the next five hours. Gethin surprised Angel by arriving early, but the list of jobs was long and Gethin worked non-stop to get everything finished by the time the guests began to arrive. His mood wasn't helped by Jonnie pestering him. Eventually Gethin stopped answering his phone.

"Christ, you've not changed your clothes." Angel wailed when he found Gethin coming out of the kata, where he'd spent the last fifteen minutes rolling red and blue blankets, stacking them in identical piles for guests to use if they were cold. They would be.

"Your outfit's in the room next to the pantry," Angel said. "Get dressed and start serving. God, it's going to be close."

"Everything's done. Stop panicking."

"Don't tip champagne over anyone. Be polite and bloody smile."

Gethin found tailored black trousers, red waistcoat, red bow tie and a crisp white shirt waiting for him in a suit bag with his name on, and belatedly realised this was not a day to have gone commando. Fortunately, he managed to change before anyone came in and freaked out at the sight of his naked arse. He put his bow tie on after a fashion but with no mirror to check, he didn't know if it would pass muster with Angel.

When Gethin's phone vibrated yet again he felt like flinging the fucker on the floor and stamping on it. It didn't have to be Jonnie, but since the last five calls had all been from him, Gethin suspected this was too.

He was right.

He stuffed the phone in the back pocket of his trousers and picked up a tray of hors d'oeuvres, tiny Yorkshire puddings filled with cubes of rare beef and topped with smears of horseradish. He'd chosen to serve food rather than champagne so he could eat a couple of the canapés. They were delicious. The buzzing in his pocket stopped and he gave a quiet sigh of relief. Just as he'd almost emptied the tray, it started again. *Fuck.* He headed to the far side of the room where he'd seen a small nook he could stand in.

"Yes, Jonnie." Gethin made sure his voice was even. There was nothing to be gained by showing his irritation.

"What are you doing now?"

The thin hesitant voice piled guilt onto Gethin's annoyance. "I'm serving hors d'oeuvres at Denborough Castle."

"When will you get here?"

"I told you I'd be very late."

"How late?"

"I don't know."

"They won't let you in."

"I promised I'd come and I will. Please don't keep ringing me. I'm going to get into trouble for being on the phone."

"Sorry to be such a nuisance."

Jonnie cut him off. The guy had the ability to turn screws without even trying. Gethin stuffed his phone in his pocket. He wished he could switch it off, but he couldn't afford to miss a call about potential work. Izabela wouldn't be paying him and he had a feeling he'd end up refusing money from Dieter's mother when he failed to find her son. He wondered if he'd hear from Izabela again. He hoped not. The phone pinged with a message and Gethin scowled as he yanked it out.

Sorry. Miss you. xxx

Gethin hesitated, then texted, *C U soon.* He added an *x* then took it off, then added it again. He put his phone away, and as he headed toward his abandoned tray, he spotted Angel approaching.

"*There's daggers in men's smiles.* Take that look off your face," Angel said through clenched teeth when he reached him. "You're about as attractive as a vampire bat. Oh God, a vampire bat who can't manage a decent bowtie."

"Was that Macbeth?"

Angel groaned. "By the law of averages, you were going to be right one day. Yes, it was." He nudged Gethin to the side and redid his bowtie. "Please smile."

"You blackmailed me into helping out. I don't recall any requirement to look happy about it."

"Blackmail?" Angel glared at him. "It was no such thing. I did you a favour, I'm still doing it and now you're doing one for me."

Gethin pressed his lips together.

"Darling, I pride myself on my staff being as delicious as my food and when you smile, you're the most delicious of all, despite being on the scrawny side. Please try harder to look as though you live to serve extraordinarily yummy canapés to fabulously wealthy people who might or might not deign to say thank you."

Gethin sighed, grabbed the now empty tray and made his way toward the kitchen with Angel on his heels.

They were almost there, Angel still muttering at his back, when Maisie came running up. She was one of Angel's waitresses. "There's trouble in the front courtyard."

Angel flapped his hands. "What sort of trouble?"

"A fight," said the petite blonde.

"Oh my God." Angel turned to Gethin and did his puppy dog face.

"I'll deal with it." Gethin handed Maisie the tray and hurried to the main entrance.

A small group of men had gathered on the gravelled forecourt. They were watching two guys, jackets off and shirt sleeves rolled up, who were circling each other with fists clenched. The smaller one's face was bloody. Gethin didn't hesitate. He pushed his way through the jeering spectators and positioned himself between the two men, facing the biggest.

"Enough," Gethin said. "Not the time or the place."

"The fucking bastard was kissing my girlfriend." The bigger guy reached to grab the other and Gethin moved quickly, pinning the larger guy's arm behind his back, looping his foot around his ankle to unbalance him as he yanked him away without pulling him over.

"This is a party. You're going to spoil it," Gethin said quietly in his ear. "You need to calm down."

He carried on reasoning with him and when he felt the fight go out of the guy, he slightly relaxed his hold. Even while he was talking, Gethin was aware of what was happening at their side, the smaller man being cared for, no longer a threat, if he ever had been. Gethin walked the bigger guy down the drive away from the entrance to the castle and when he glanced back, he saw everyone but one guy had gone back inside.

"You can let me go now," the man said.

"Only if you promise not to throw any more punches. He was littler than you. No matter who was at fault, you're the one who'd look bad."

"And you treating me like a child hasn't done that?" the guy snapped. "Let me fucking go."

The man who'd been watching walked forward. "Need a hand?"

"We're fine," Gethin said, then widened his eyes when he recognized the guy he'd seen running that morning. *Fuck.* He looked hot in a tux. Dark hair, gorgeous eyes. Long and lean like him.

"Going to behave?" Gethin asked the man he was holding.

"Yes," he snapped.

Gethin released him.

"What you looking at, Kell?" the man asked, then glanced at Gethin. "Fucking the help?"

Kell laughed. "Only because your arse is too spotty."

The man chuckled and slung his arm over Kell's shoulder.

Once he was sure the fight wasn't going to restart, Gethin slipped past the pair and returned to the kitchen. He picked up another tray, this time of miniature fish and chips in paper cones. He tipped the contents of one into his mouth and tossed the paper aside.

"Serve them, don't eat them." Angel appeared out of nowhere. "You'll fuck up my calculations."

Gethin ate another just to annoy him and swallowed fast. "Thank you for letting me work all day without giving me something to eat. Thank you for sorting out that fracas before it turned into a blood bath."

"Thank you." Angel lifted the tray from his hand. "I'd like to say you're not just a pretty face, but you still look like the Angel of Death. Serve the champagne instead and remember this is a birthday party not a wake."

Gethin bared his teeth and Angel gave a mock shudder. "On second thoughts, don't smile. There must be someone here who's into the bad tempered bat look. In fact, I saw a guy —"

Angel was distracted by a handwringing chef fretting about a vegetarian who'd turned vegan, and Gethin made his escape with a tray of drinks. He headed down the cool flagstone corridor and walked through an open door. When he emerged onto the raised terrace at the rear of the castle, he shivered.

Before descending the steps to where guests were milling, Gethin took in the distant view of the English Channel, where whitecaps glistened in the sun. It was a cloudless October afternoon, and unseasonably warm in the lee of the breeze, but in unsheltered areas like the terrace the wind was vicious and doing its best to mess up hair and expose underwear.

As Gethin wandered around, handing out drinks, listening to posh accents, he caught snatches of conversation that reminded him of how far he was from this sort of life. Thirty year olds talking about mummy and daddy, polo games, trips to Mustique, Necker Island, boltholes in the country whose interiors had been designed by famous people, flats in Sloane Square costing millions, hedge funds, trust funds, film deals, modelling contracts, fast cars. Men and women around the same age as him but most with rich parents who'd provided a privileged upbringing, and intentionally or otherwise engendered an expectation of entitlement in their children. Most of these champagne-swilling, beautiful people hadn't had to work for what they had, it had been handed to them. And one of them was the guy he'd seen running, the one with cheeky blue eyes.

When he'd filled his tray with empty glasses, he made his way back for more champagne. Not just any champagne. This stuff was almost a hundred quid a bottle. No expense had been spared for this thirtieth birthday party. But then for a boy who'd grown up in a castle and was probably heir to the throne if ninety or so died ahead of him...well, Gethin supposed this was what you expected. Whereas *his* thirtieth passed unnoticed.

"Fucking smile," Angel hissed in his ear and Gethin made an effort not to scowl.

It was unlike him to let the way he was feeling show on his face. He'd learned as a child to school his features and had carried it through into adulthood. He was well aware his resentment was unreasonable as was his assessment of the guests. Not all these people were wankers. Just because they had money didn't mean they *hadn't* worked hard for it, or that they didn't get let down, were never cheated on, ripped off, or hurt. Maybe their parents didn't love them. Money was no replacement for affection. Gethin knew better than to judge by appearances. He finished filling the last glass and put the bottle down.

"There are plenty of good looking guys here," Angel said at his shoulder. "If Jonnie's not the one, and I have a feeling he isn't, you could take your pick."

When Gethin turned to face him, Angel posed and fluttered his eyelashes. Gethin laughed, flipped out of his funk.

"Finally, I get a smile and I'm insulted." Angel pouted. "Surely I'm the man of your dreams, darling."

Gethin knew Angel wasn't serious. Angel's partner Henry was the love of his life and couldn't have been more unlike Angel. Angel spoke like an old queen but behaved like a hyperactive teenager with OCD. He was a force of nature who'd turned doing favours for friends into a thriving company that had become a major player in the business of planning and arranging of upmarket parties.

While Henry worked at home as a web designer, content to spend his days in tatty jeans and holey sweaters, two dachshunds at his feet, Angel was a ruthless slave driver in designer clothes who demanded perfection. Tonight he wore an intricately embroidered grey jacket, collarless brilliant white shirt and tight black trousers. His short hair was currently dyed silvery white and his name, as Gethin had discovered, was not Angel or Angelo Murani as he claimed but Barry Ramsbottom. Gethin smiled at the thought. He was saving that nugget.

"You're gorgeous when you smile," Angel said. "If someone asks you out, for fuck's sake say yes. Though dump Jonnie first and don't waltz off into the sunset until you've finished here. I still need you."

Gethin stopped smiling. "I'm here to work not find a date."

"A fuck then. You surely wouldn't turn one down. If Henry wasn't so insanely jealous I'd offer my services."

"That's good of you."

"Tell me you can't resist."

"I'm too busy, sorry. My boss is a monster."

Angel moved closer. "If you can flirt with me, you can find a guy here, no problem."

"Not interested."

"Because of Jonnie?"

"No. I've told you that's complicated. I'm not going out with him."

"But whenever I ask you to come to anything, it's always him you're seeing."

"Yep."

"Look for someone else."

"No."

Angel put his hand on Gethin's forehead. "Hmm, I thought you must be sick but you feel fine."

"I *am* fine."

Angel stared at him. "I don't think you are."

Gethin mentally erected a series of barriers: doors, bars, padlocks, fire, and a heap of radioactive material.

"Can't you get it up anymore?" Angel whispered.

"Fuck off. Life's about more than sex."

"So you *can't* get it up. You poor thing."

Gethin knew Angel was teasing, knew he shouldn't react but that comment had hit too close to home. Not that he couldn't get an erection, he just hadn't had anyone to use one on if he didn't count his hand.

"That's such a pity because there's a guest who can't seem to take his eyes off you. Tall, dark, handsome. Cheekbones that could cut. Nearly as good looking as me. If he's staying the night in the castle, you could spend it with him. You'll have even more time to get to know him tomorrow. I can fix it for you to be helping with whatever activity he's signed up for. What do you say?"

"I thought you already had something lined up for me to do tomorrow?"

Angel blushed and Gethin's suspicions revved right up and off the page.

"If you make a date with someone, I'll let you off what I have planned."

Now Gethin was even more suspicious. "Stop meddling."

Gethin returned to the terrace with champagne. It was slightly alarming not to have noticed he was being watched, assuming Angel was telling the truth or not imagining it. But then Angel was continually trying to find him his own Henry, so lying in order to get Gethin to look around seemed likely. Or was it the guy from this morning with the interesting name? Kell.

What did it matter? There could be no Henry in Gethin's future, no moving in with a guy and living happily ever after because how could he ever explain Jonnie to anyone? Or expect Jonnie to accept he had a guy in his life when Jonnie thought *he* was that guy?

Gethin was fully aware there was always a solution to a problem, though it might not be a palatable one, but solving this was not something within his control. He couldn't kill Jonnie and he shouldn't wish he was dead, so Gethin was learning to live with the life he had while trying and failing to curb his growing resentment. He had little reason to feel such an intense level of guilt, but he did. Guilty because he was resentful and resentful because he felt guilty. And there was no escape from his emotions. Even his free time was blighted by his overdeveloped fucking conscience.

Serving drinks at a posh party and helping with the after party activities the following day was not the way he'd have chosen to spend the few hours of the weekend that belonged purely to him, and he didn't count shopping, cleaning or working as *his* time.

He walked back inside with another tray of empty glasses. He was annoyed he couldn't even get drunk. Not with a long ride to see Jonnie at the end of the night.

Chapter Seven

Whenever Kell saw Quin's mother heading in his direction, he slipped away before she spotted him. He found it alarmingly easy to lie about some parts of his life and disturbingly difficult to be quizzed about others which was why he usually tried to avoid going anywhere he might bump into someone he knew. Which begged the question as to why he'd come to Quin's thirtieth birthday party knowing Quin's mother would corner him sooner or later.

"Mother thinks you're avoiding her," Quin came up at his shoulder.

"I'd never do that."

"Then go and talk to her."

Kell winced. "I don't want to watch her face fall when she asks what I'm doing."

"It won't. Hey and thanks for my Lego. Good choice, mate." Quin squeezed his arm and headed for his girlfriend.

Nor did Kell want to answer awkward questions about his family. Quin's mother been good to him when he was a boy and he didn't like the thought of her thinking he'd let her down in some way by not reaching his potential. Even if he could tell her the truth, he suspected she'd be disappointed.

The canapés kept coming, the alcohol kept flowing. Kell almost relaxed. He told people he was working in a night club and added the word gay before they asked him to get them free entry. He was aware that the more people who saw him as a bit of a waster, a guy who'd slid off the rails and was neither of interest nor benefit to them, the better. It lessened the risk of the wrong thing being said at the wrong time. When you worked undercover, having someone recognize you was your worst nightmare.

He'd explained his bruised cheek on a collision with a flying rock cake, a church altar, a belligerent poet and a frisky horse. He made up something different every time. He wasn't quite being himself, but he was close to it. He liked Quin and his family, liked some of his friends, several of whom had been Kell's friends too, once upon a time.

He liked the look of the gently spoken, dark-haired waiter who defused that fight, though Kell couldn't work out if he was gay. He had a nice arse and in one quick full on glance at his face, when he'd offered Kell champagne and Kell had declined, Kell had seen startlingly green eyes lined with thick dark lashes, and lightly stubbled cheeks. No smile on those tightly pressed lips. Kell was six two and this guy was an inch or so shorter, and slimmer, sort of…rough looking even in his waiter's gear.

Exactly Kell's type. Kell watched him. He couldn't help it. Nor could he help noticing that for a waiter, the guy wasn't a natural. He looked as though he'd rather be anywhere else than here. Instead of being friendly and polite, he was awkward, slightly guarded and surly. Kell liked guarded and surly. He liked awkward guys who'd unbend for him, just for a while, guys he could *make* unbend. He wondered if Marek had guessed how much Kell liked to top. The bastard wouldn't care either way. Though maybe he did. Maybe part of his attraction to Kell was the same as Kell's attraction to the waiter.

Kell didn't want a relationship. He couldn't *have* a relationship. He had no time for dates, no interest in getting to know what films someone liked, where they'd been on holiday or whether they liked beans on toast or cheese sandwiches for lunch. Kell could only be interested in stringless sex, zipless fucks, hard fast encounters he could walk away from without feeling a further tug, any future need for that particular guy, or any urge for commitment because that couldn't happen.

But the longer he watched the waiter, the faster his heart beat. *My type.* Well, his type assuming the waiter was gay. Kell gave a quiet laugh. The guy didn't look or act gay, but Kell wasn't into fem guys, not to fuck. They often made better friends, were fun, made him laugh, but he liked sex with difficult guys who could be taken for straight, the sort of guy he had to control. *Like Marek controls me.* Kell tried to shove the fucker out of his head and concentrate on the waiter. Even if this guy *was* gay, it didn't mean he liked to be fucked hard or even fucked at all. And Kell wasn't going to waste his time trying to persuade a straight guy into bed no matter how physically appealing he might be.

Still… His gaze followed the waiter around the room. Was the guy straight? Bi? Would he bend?

Guests were called through for dinner by a master of ceremonies, and Kell's eyes widened in surprise when he followed the crowd into a spectacular tent. Three katas, Quin had pointed out, though that meant Kell kept saying tent just to annoy him. The katas were decorated with thousands of twinkling lights, and Quin's guests took seats on padded benches either side of rustic wooden tables incongruously laid with silver cutlery, sparkling glassware and linen napkins with folds sharp enough to cut a finger. Kell was relieved to see Quin's mother sitting with his father and their relatives close to the fire pit, nowhere near him. Kell was on Quin's table, opposite his friend.

Kell's birthday was coming up fast and he'd be lucky if he managed a takeaway and a can of beer while he watched TV on his own. Most likely he'd be working. He'd be *very* lucky if his brother didn't make an appearance. Oliver had no idea where Kell was living or working, but that didn't mean he couldn't find out.

Grownup party bags at each place setting held a selection of body products made by Quin's father's company, where Quin also worked. Kell pocketed one of the small tubes and hoped he got a chance to use it. His gaze strayed to the waiter he fancied who was working at the far end of the kata.

"Earth to Kell." Jenny, who sat next to him, tapped Kell's hand and Kell turned. "What activities have you put your name down for?"

"Bog snorkelling and snake wrestling."

She gave him a look of horror, then registered he was joking.

A whole range of things had been planned for the following day: shooting, quad bike riding, raft building — *in this weather?* —

paintballing and whatever the fuck else Quin had persuaded his parents to pay for, and Kell was actually looking forward to it. Well, not the raft building. But something so different from his usual daily grind would help him remember there was life after Marek.

When the cake was produced for Quin to cut, shaped like a red Aston Martin, apparently the real thing waited in the garage, an insanely expensive present from indulgent parents, Kell picked up his jacket and made for the other end of the tent. He persuaded Freddie, another school friend, to swap seats, then waited for the waiter to return to the table.

Kell deliberately stared at him as he approached with a bottle of champagne. *I really want to fuck this guy.* A one-off fuck and Kell would never see him again. When their gazes collided and Kell smiled, the tip of the waiter's tongue slid over his lips. The tiniest of gestures, but enough to make Kell's cock stir. There was a small bruise right in the middle of the guy's forehead and Kell wondered how he'd done that, wondered if the waiter was thinking the same thing about Kell's cheek. The guy circled the table away from Kell and when he finally reached him with the champagne, Kell moved Freddie's glass aside.

"I need a clean one," Kell said.

"I thought you weren't drinking."

Kell smiled. *You remember me refusing one before.* "I think I can handle one drink."

"You sure? I'd hate to be responsible for you lapsing. You need to call someone?"

Kell bristled. "I'm not a fucking alcoholic. Get me a glass."

"Yes, *sir.*"

That insolent emphasis filled Kell's cock and the smirk that accompanied it, made Kell think the guy was gay. Kell hadn't missed the irony that he was interested in someone for the reason Marek was interested in him. He called Marek sir but didn't want to, but he *did* want to hear the word on this guy's lips.

After the waiter left, Kell stayed long enough to not look obvious, then picked up his jacket and followed. His cock was already hard, his stomach churning in anticipation. He spotted the guy hurrying around the side of the castle, in the opposite direction to the kitchen, and Kell went after him. When he turned the corner, there was no one there. He barely had time to register he'd made a mistake and for disappointment to settle in his gut, before he found himself shoved behind a section of supporting wall, his back to the stone, his jacket falling from his fingers as an arm pressed across his throat. *Christ, where did you come from?*

"Are you lost?" The waiter's voice was quiet and calm, the hint of an accent Kell couldn't identify. "The bathroom's the other way."

Despite the arm at his throat, the lack of verbal threat and the ordinary tone of voice were reassuring. Instead of shoving him away, Kell cupped the back of the man's neck, threaded his fingers in silky hair and tugged him closer as he rubbed his nape with his thumb. *Decision time. You interested or not?* Seconds ticked by and nothing happened, then the pressure on Kell's throat lessened. When the arm fell away, Kell dropped his hold on the guy's hair. They stood face to face, inches apart. Kell let his hand brush over the front of the waiter's trousers, and touched an erection. He caught the sudden glare, and smiled.

"What's your name?" Kell asked.

"Why?"

"Isn't that how conversations usually start?"

"Are we having a conversation?"

Kell sucked his cheeks. "You're talking. I'm talking. I think that counts. Let's try again. What's your name?"

"Why would you care?"

Kell was annoyed he felt wrong footed. "I'd like to know."

"Tough."

Kell could feel the situation slipping away. But the guy was right. If all they were going to do was fuck, they didn't need each other's name, date of birth and blood group.

"I want to fuck you." Kell saw little point in not being open. He'd either get what he wanted or not.

"Before I get you a clean glass or after?"

Kell let out a snort of laughter.

When he reached to pull the guy closer, he found himself clutching air and blinked in shock. The waiter suddenly looked like a predator ready to eat its dinner and didn't *that* turn Kell on even more. After a brief tussle Kell reversed their positions and pinned the waiter.

The guy let out a quiet laugh. "I don't have time to play tag. I'm supposed to be working."

"I can be fast."

One dark eyebrow was raised. "You say that like it's a good thing."

"We keep seeing each other," Kell said. "This morning you were gasping for breath."

"I fucked up my timing. Got distracted by a guy in a red beanie. But I saw you before that."

Kell's stomach lurched. *Oh fuck. At the club?*

"Eating chips on the seafront," the waiter said.

Kell breathed out. "You were the guy on the other bench?"

"I'm offended you didn't notice me."

"I was watching the birds."

"I'm not into birds."

"Good." Kell swallowed. Why did the prospect of a quick fuck no longer feel enough?

The guy ducked and Kell found himself slammed back against the wall with the waiter right in his face, stealing his air. *We're duelling!* Kell took a deep breath. The scent of this guy made his head spin. He needed to retake the initiative but he could feel hands busy unfastening his bow tie, then the buttons of his shirt. When fingertips grazed his bare flesh, and fluttered over his nipples, Kell shuddered with longing. He wasn't sure where the goose bumps came from.

"Nice abs, rich boy," the guy said.

70

"Completely natural."

That won Kell another laugh.

The guy's fingers dropped to Kell's waist making short work of unbuttoning, unzipping, and spreading open his trousers while Kell stood frozen in place. He didn't look down. They still stared at each other, the guy's warm exhales caressing Kell's lips. *I want to kiss him and I don't kiss.*

Christ, he really is good looking. And not a pushover. Which was good and bad. Kell might behave like a slut with Marek, but that was all pretence. It made it even more important to Kell that when he chose to fuck someone, he was true to himself. He was too dominant to easily accept another alpha, yet one part of him didn't appear to be too concerned this was *not* a guy who'd call him sir.

"You look...decadent," the waiter whispered. "Bow tie hanging around your neck, shirt open, trousers undone, cock straining to get free. Wild. Hot. Sexy."

The guy groaned as he slipped his hands into Kell's shorts, fingers straying tantalizingly close to his dick before sliding over his hips and pulling Kell away from the wall in order to cup his butt cheeks. One hard squeeze and Kell's gasp almost leapt from his lungs.

"You slumming it, rich boy?" the guy asked.

"I'm not rich. If you're not going to call me sir, master or prince, call me Kell."

The guy gave a brief smile. "You think you're such hot stuff you can have whoever you like?"

"Only if they're interested. *Are* you interested?"

The guy leaned into him, pulling Kell against him and when Kell felt the size of the dick pressing alongside his, he gave a low moan. "No, sorry. You're not interested. I made a mistake."

Actually, he was beginning to wonder if he *had* made a mistake, bitten off more than he could chew. Maybe literally. That felt like a bloody big cock.

"Not sure this is going to work," Kell said.

"You can't dump me yet. We haven't had chance to do anything."

The guy flexed his pelvis, their cocks rubbed together and they both grunted.

"Oh fuck, fuck, fuck." Kell exhaled the words. "Maybe we should take this indoors, somewhere private. I've got a room."

"Why move? We're out of sight here and you don't seem the silk sheets type. But I suppose there could be a frisky horse or a belligerent poet you might collide with out here to bruise your other cheek."

Kell smiled. "Is that what happened to your forehead?"

"Yeah, there are a lot of frisky horses around. So were you hit or are you going to make up something else especially for me?"

"A fist."

"I hope he came off worse."

"He will." Kell lived for the day Marek went to jail. "What about you? That mark on your forehead?"

"As I said. Bloody frisky horses get everywhere."

Kell laughed. There were plenty of reasons why they shouldn't be doing this outside, but when the guy rocked against him, pushing their cocks together, Kell's ability to think faltered, then failed.

They switched positions again, Kell spinning the guy round, reaching to unfasten his bowtie, waistcoat, shirt, those tight, black trousers. He swallowed hard — twice — when he registered the lack of underwear. Another swallow when he felt the heat of the guy's cock against his fingers, the hardness of it. *Long and uncut. God, he is big. And he shaves.* Kell tugged the trousers down and let his thumb graze the sensitive cockhead, smearing precome over the slit. He was rewarded by an intake of breath and hips arching toward his.

They wrapped their hands around each other's dicks and held them together, still not breaking eye contact. This guy was into it as much as him, but would he let Kell fuck him? *Is he expecting to fuck me?* Kell's stomach roiled. *Christ, I want to fuck him.* So why

72

was part of him thinking—why not let himself be fucked? Apart from the fact that his arse was sore from Marek's rough handling.

This time when he turned the waiter, the guy allowed it. Kell groaned at the sight of such a perfect backside. It was smooth and firm and trim, dimpled at the sides, and the temptation to sink his teeth into it almost made his knees buckle.

"Your arse," Kell whispered, his voice croaky. "God, it's beautiful."

"Right. Er…thanks."

Kell chuckled. "I should have thought that. Not said it."

He bent his knees and slid his cock up and down the crease of the guy's butt, precome easing his way as Kell surged harder against him. Kell slipped his hands beneath the shirt, then under the guy's arms and finally laid his palms on gently rounded pecs, small puckered nipples pushing into the centre of his hands.

"Oh Christ," Kell whispered. "You going to let me fuck you?"

The guy let out a choked laugh. "Let's see."

Kell wasn't sure what that meant. He was too befuddled by lust to work it out. He flexed his hips to press harder against that perfect backside and bit down through material into the man's shoulder which brought a muffled curse and a stiffening of the body he leaned against. Need rampaged through Kell's veins. When he'd followed the waiter, planning to fuck him—assuming the guy agreed, Kell thought he'd have come and gone by now, and instead he wanted to make this last which was crazy. Someone could appear around the corner at any moment. He knew better than to take this sort of risk, but he couldn't deny it added to the thrill.

Condom, condom, condom. Kell dragged his mind back into gear, his hands from the guy's chest and fumbled in his pocket. He took out a condom and the tube of coconut lotion from the party bag. Part of him still worried the guy would change his mind, break away. So while Kell put on the condom and covered his dick with the cream, he leaned against his back, keeping him still, inhaling the scent of him.

73

He was so fucking hard, he hurt, but all the time in his head he kept thinking *hurry before someone walks around that corner.*

Kell shook as he slid his dick up and down the crack of the guy's butt, pausing over his hole, nudging not pushing, ignoring his protesting balls. The ache was sweet.

Do it. Do it. Do it.

Chapter Eight

Gethin's heart was pounding so hard he felt lightheaded, almost sick. He wasn't sure what he was doing. *Christ, you know what you're doing, you stupid wanker.* Taking a dick up the arse and he couldn't remember the last time that had happened. *Yes you can.* Gethin blanked the memory before he freaked out. Every time he felt the guy's cock slide over his hole, Gethin shook harder, and tried to force his fists through stone.

Not going to fit. Do it. Too big. Do it. Get the fuck off. Do it. Leave me alone. Changed my mind. Fucking do it!

But he said nothing, made no sound and didn't move when the rounded cockhead stopped sliding and lodged against what would most definitely be highly reluctant muscles. Then followed the nudging, pushing, urging them to stop resisting. *Good luck with that.*

This would hurt. It had been so fucking long. Well over a year. But at that moment, he was in more pain from fingers digging into his hips, and palms holding open his butt cheeks than from the pressure on the entrance to his body. He told himself to stop clenching, but his arse hole had a mind of its own.

The guy — Kell — panted against his neck. "Going to let me in or not?"

Gethin couldn't speak. His muscles said no, he tried to get *no* out of his mouth but his brain didn't seem to agree. *Why the fuck am I doing this? Letting this be done?*

Because you're lonely. Because you just want to feel something. *Because you love sex. You need sex. And this is all you can have without feeling guilty. And let's be honest, you're still going to feel guilty. But this way, the guilt will be less. Fuck and walk away. Easy.*

The man's whisper broke into his silent monologue. "You want me to huff and puff and blow your house down? Or crawl away with my tail between my legs?" He rubbed his chin on the back of Gethin's neck. "Fuck, you are so sexy. Your body, your skin, your voice, your arse. But if you don't want me to do this, tell me now before I disgrace myself and come before I get inside you."

Gethin made an effort to bear down and push back at the same time, and the guy's cock slid into him. Likely only an inch but it felt like twenty. *Shit, shit, shit.* The stretch, that inner straining of delicate tissue had Gethin holding his breath because it *did* fucking hurt.

"Oh fuck. You're tight. Tight and so…perfect. You smell good." Kell buried his face between Gethin's shoulder blades, breathing heat through his clothes, and setting fire to Gethin's arse as he pressed deeper.

Gethin's thighs widened. Had he consciously done that? He didn't think so. He imagined the long, hard dick of the blue-eyed devil disappearing inside him and bit back a moan. Gethin had thought of himself as being capable of resisting, of going without sex, without being touched, and all this time he'd been living a lie. He'd just not met the guy who could push through his defences until now.

A brush of his prostate as Kell thrust home and Gethin's world plunged into darkness before he saw stars explode. *Oh GodGodGodGodGod.*

"I get you then?" Kell whispered breathlessly. "Yeah, I did. Fuck. Sweet."

Don't stop was on repeat in Gethin's head but he wouldn't allow himself to speak. It was bad enough that he was letting himself be fucked by a stranger let alone permitting himself to beg for it. But then he didn't need to beg. He was getting nailed, the guy driving his cock in and out so hard, so deep, he was shunting Gethin into the wall. Gethin slid a hand down to protect his dick, for some reason not wanting to stroke himself, not wanting to acknowledge how deeply receptive he was to this. He braced his other arm against the stone work, fist clenched. A tiny part of him wished for a hand covering his, fingers entwining, some show of affection.

He was a fool. He knew what this was. Two horny guys getting off. *He* was the one who hadn't wanted to give his name. *This* was what he'd asked for. A cold hard fuck with no meaning other than the provision of a few moments of raw mutual pleasure. The guy held up Gethin's shirt, bunching it in his fists in a deathlike grip as he increased his speed.

Gethin's thoughts of coming drifted under the onslaught of delight brought by the cock ramming into him. It felt good, that delicious inner press, the sensation of being filled, the caress of his prostate.

I'm not a fucking bottom.

So what are you doing?

I'm never going to see this guy again. What does it matter?

He heard a change in the guy's breathing, a stuttered gasp, then his cock jerked in Gethin's arse as his mouth pressed harder against Gethin's shoulder. Kell's hands still lodged on Gethin's hips, not even reaching for his dick.

Gethin switched from being okay to not being okay in an instant. What had gotten into him? What the fuck had he been thinking? When Kell finally reached for Gethin's cock he pushed his hand away. *Not Kell. A nameless man. It makes it easier.*

"Get out of me," Gethin muttered.

The moment the cock slid from his arse, Gethin yanked up his trousers and forced his still hard cock back behind his zipper. He stared at the wall as he pulled his shirt into place, buttoned it up, smoothed it down, sorted out his waistcoat and fumbled with his bowtie, putting himself back together. Regaining control of his emotions wasn't so easy.

"Are you okay?" the guy asked in a tone that said he knew Gethin wasn't.

"Fine." Gethin stalked off, disgusted with himself. When he felt the hand on his shoulder, he spun round and planted his fist in a firm stomach. *Oh shit.*

Kell doubled over, gasping. "What the fuck was that for?"

Gethin deserved the punch he received in return. He should have walked away, but he didn't. He made a grab for the guy's open shirt and then they were fighting, fists clenched, muscles tensed as they exchanged half-hearted blows before wrapping themselves around each other, heads pressed together.

"What the fuck are we fighting about?" Kell panted.

Because Gethin had given in when he shouldn't have. Because he had a point to prove, though he wasn't sure what that point was or who he was trying to prove it to. Then they were down on the grass, in each other's arms, each trying to pin the other down, part laughing, part not. Gethin managed to grab the guy's leg and flipped him onto his back but the next moment, *he* was the one on his back, jerking his head aside to avoid the fist coming for his nose.

"Stop it," Kell hissed. "Okay, I get you're pissed off, but just tell me why. What did I do? Not do? Say? Not say? Touch? Not touch? I'm sorry, okay? Just stop fighting."

Gethin lay on his back, his chest heaving. *Now* what was he supposed to do? Kell had him pinned down, his hands on Gethin's forearms, his knees and most of his body weight on Gethin's thighs. *And I'm still fucking hard. Shit.*

"If I'm going to have to kill you, I'd like to know your name," Kell said.

Gethin exhaled. "We're not going to see each other again, so why does it matter?"

"It matters to me. I don't want to remember you as the fucking nutter who made me come so hard I saw stars."

"Gethin." *Why did I tell him?*

"Gethin. Right. Cool name. Not heard it before. So what the fuck was that about, *Gethin*? Everything was great, more than great. Your turn and you flip out. Why? What did I do wrong?"

"Nothing. Sorry."

Kell didn't move from on top of him. "I pushed you into it. Is that what it is? You didn't say no but…you were tight. Oh Christ, you have done it before?" He looked stricken.

"You didn't push me into it. And yes, I've done it before."
Kell rolled on one side and lay next to him.

"You're going to wreck your shirt," Gethin said.

"Fuck the shirt." He put his hand to Gethin's face then didn't touch it. "If it makes any difference, I'd have flipped out if I'd been where you were."

Then he *did* touch and for a moment Gethin turned into the caress before he sprang to his feet. Kell pushed to his at his side.

"I've got to get back to work," Gethin muttered and strode off, brushing himself down, his cock already giving up in disgust.

It wasn't difficult for Gethin to keep busy. The kata had to be stripped back, everything made ready for collection the next day. Gethin could hear the heavy beat of music coming from the old banqueting hall inside the castle and wondered if Kell was dancing, if the guy had found someone else to fuck. *Why should I care? I don't.* What had he meant that he'd have flipped out? The guy didn't take cocks up his arse? Two tops wasn't going to work, but then Gethin hadn't behaved like a top and it wasn't as if it was going to happen again.

He was annoyed not just because he'd let Kell take him, but for zipping up before he'd come. Did it make him any less guilty that he'd not spurted all over the wall? Did he *feel* less guilty? Jonnie wasn't going to find out. It wasn't as if Gethin would tell him. Jonnie wasn't even his boyfriend, he just thought he was. *I don't need to feel guilty. Shit.*

When he'd completed the jobs Angel had earlier tasked him with, he retrieved his leathers from the room used by the staff and headed for his bike. At least at this time of night there wouldn't be much traffic on the road.

As he headed away from the castle, he felt better. He wasn't running. He had to come back because Angel needed him here tomorrow, but space from what had happened earlier seemed like a good idea. The vibration in his balls increased with his speed and

Gethin crouched low over his machine, enjoying the ride. He took a sharp corner too fast, let his knee drop perilously close to the ground and eased upright just in time as he came out of the bend. His heart pounded. He didn't want to kill himself, though he did like flying close to the edge. Once he was out on the main road he eased up on the throttle. He also didn't want to get nailed by the police.

Kell didn't bother to rejoin the party. He'd lost his bowtie and his shirt was ripped and dirty. It was easier to slope off to bed and avoid questions. He grabbed his jacket and made his way to the room he'd sometimes slept in as a boy. He was touched that Quin's mother had done that for him, though the bed still had the same hard mattress.

He stripped and showered, then sat in the window seat looking out onto the front of the castle remembering how he used to wish this was his home, that Quin's parents were *his* parents, that Quin was his brother instead of Oliver. Even thinking Oliver's name made the hairs stand up on Kell's arms.

As he stared out the window, he saw a figure accelerate away on a black and silver Kawasaki. The guy looked like he was part of the machine, lying in an almost horizontal position, curled around the bike like a lover and Kell found himself wishing Gethin was curled around him. They had unfinished business. He was fairly certain the guy hadn't come. Kell felt bad about that.

On the other hand, Gethin was clearly mixed up and Kell wasn't sure that was entirely down to being topped when he wasn't used to it. *Fuck it*. He had to stop thinking about the waiter because there was no point. They weren't going to see each other again. Kell ought not to want to see him again. He couldn't afford to get entangled with anyone, let alone someone who was fucked up.

Yet…

Kell found himself still thinking about him, wondering if he could find a way to get in touch with him. He could ask Quin for the name of the party planner, ask *him* for Gethin's number or give the guy *his* number to give Gethin.

Why?

What for?

What's the point?

Fast fucks. That was all he could have. Anonymous fucks. So he had to forget that face, that body, that arse, that awkward roughness.

Right after he'd jacked off thinking about it. He wrapped his hand around his cock and closed his eyes.

It took Gethin most of the ride to Wellbrook Manor to calm down. If this was what happened when he had sex then it was just as well he'd been doing without. He hadn't come. Christ, he'd been close but no cigar. His body had been overruled by his brain. Just.

He had to talk his way in to see Jonnie. It was far too late, he knew it was, but the staff felt sorry Gethin was the only one who came to see their most severely disabled guest, as they called them, not patient. Guest implied you were only there for a while and that it was your choice. Jonnie wasn't a guest.

Jonnie was in bed but his light was on. He beamed at Gethin when he slipped in.

"Dart. Waiting for you." Jonnie used his nickname.

"Were you planning on going somewhere?"

"Nightclub."

Gethin smiled. This was Jonnie in a good mood.

"You okay?" Jonnie asked.

"Tired."

"Lie next to me?"

Gethin settled on his side at the edge of the bed. He ran through what he'd been doing all day and an edited version of what he'd done that evening. It was uncharacteristic of Jonnie to ask how he was. Gethin was always careful not to complain too much about anything, yet he couldn't guard every comment.

"You smell different," Jonnie said.

Oh fuck. "Yorkshire pudding? Fish and chips? Champagne?"

"Different." His voice was subdued.

"That will be the wrestling. Two guys got into an argument about a girlfriend and Angel asked me to step in. I had a bit of a tussle with the bigger one."

"Did they have a band?"

Don't ask if I got hurt. "Yeah, there was a group playing."

"Good as us?"

"No. Not as good as us."

"Will you stay tonight?"

"I can't sleep on the bed with you. There's not enough room."

"The chair? Just want to wake and see you."

Shit. But Gethin was tired. He didn't want to have to disturb the owner of the hotel Angel had booked him into. "Okay. I have to leave early though. Everything I spent the morning putting up, I need to take down."

"Tell me about what we used to be like."

Gethin sucked in his cheeks. He knew Jonnie meant the band. "You could play the guitar better than anyone I've ever known. Too good for the group really, but then you were the star. They used to scream, the girls. It was you they wanted. Fuck the rest of us. Even after they found out you were gay, they still loved you."

He kept talking until Jonnie was asleep, then retreated to the chair, tried to get comfortable and resigned himself to that not happening.

Chapter Nine

Kell might have managed to avoid Quin's mother at the party, but he had to sit next to her at breakfast the next morning.

She patted the chair on her left. "Kellan. Come sit with me."

He carried his plate of food to the far end of the long table. Quin sat slumped on her other side looking as if he'd not been to sleep, eyes wide, hair messed up but a goofy grin on his face that said he'd got lucky. Hopefully with his girlfriend because Quin's middle name was not Faithful.

Kell had always enjoyed meals at the castle, particularly breakfast. At home, he'd be lucky if there was cereal. His mother had never eaten before noon. She wouldn't be allowed that luxury now.

"Did you enjoy yourself last night?" Quin's mother smiled at him.

"Yes, thank you. I forgot to ask though, is my Aston Martin parked next to Quin's?"

She laughed. "So what are you up to these days?"

There it was, the question he didn't want to answer.

"Kell's in security," Quin said.

"Trading?" she asked.

Her son chuckled. "Not securities. Security. Making things secure. Tight. Safe from zombies."

Shut up, Quin.

She frowned at her son and turned to Kell. "And do you like it?"

"Some of the time."

"You decided nuclear physics was not for you, then," she said.

Kell winced.

"Nor astrophysics, marine biology, veterinary science, chemical engineering or golf course management?" She raised her eyebrows.

"Did you memorize everything I thought about doing?" Kell asked.

"I just wanted you to do a job you loved."

He hoped she didn't press for details. Quin knew he was a cop but was sworn to secrecy about that and Kell knew he'd probably guess he was working undercover.

"I was thinking Kell could advise the business as to whether we're secure enough," Quin said. "Well, not Kell. Someone who works for him. One of his many minions."

Oh God. If the idiot began to elaborate, Kell was doomed to spill lie after lie.

"Goodness. Are we under attack from zombies?" she asked. "I have to remove their heads to finish them off. Right?"

Kell laughed.

"If you *can* use Kellan, you should. Talk to your father." She turned to Kell. "And how's your family? Your…brother?"

"Well." *Please leave it at that.* Oliver had seemed well enough though Kell wished Oliver nothing but the worst. The pause when Quin's mother mentioned him indicated she knew how Kell felt. Not that Kell had ever said anything, or needed to when Quin had never hidden how *he* felt about Kell's brother.

"I often think about your mother." Quin's mother sighed. "So sad."

"Don't," Quin warned.

She patted Kell's hand. "Sorry. Give my best wishes to your father when you see him."

Kell somehow managed to eat what he had in front of him. Quin changed the subject to the activities that were planned for the day and the rest of the table joined in the conversation. Only a limited number of guests had stayed in the castle. The rest of those invited for the whole weekend had been put up in bed and breakfast accommodation nearby and would be joining them later.

"What do you have your name down for?" Quin asked him.

"Flower arranging and cake decorating," Kell said.

Quin's mother tsked. "I wanted you on my paintball team."

Everyone laughed but Kell knew she was probably serious. If he ended up playing paintball he hoped he *was* on her team. She'd won an Olympic medal for shooting.

"No," Gethin said. "I am *not* fucking doing it."

Angel stood in front of him with his arms crossed. "Ninety minutes, that's all."

"No."

"It's not as if you'd be naked."

Gethin gaped at him, then dangled the short black apron Angel had pushed into his hand right in the guy's face. "What's this supposed to cover?"

Angel smirked. "Well, in your case, darling, it will probably only *just* hide your important bits."

"You complete and utter bastard."

"Yes, I am." Angel sighed. "Look, all you have to do is serve them cocktails, flirt, and play a few games."

"I have no idea how to make cocktails or how to flirt with women and I do not like the idea of playing games while I'm practically naked."

Gethin shuddered. He had the sneaky suspicion that having him as a butler in the buff had been Angel's plan from the moment he'd talked him into helping this weekend. The fucker probably hadn't even needed him yesterday.

"I'm relying on you," Angel said. "These women are expecting a good-looking, semi-naked guy to serve drinks and my usual chap's got a horrible rash on his backside."

"So have I."

"Liar."

"I'm not."

"Show me. Prove it."

Gethin sagged.

"The crib sheets for the cocktails are behind the bar. Everything you need is there. You could have fun if you tried."

Gethin cast him an incredulous look. "Fun? You have remembered I'm gay? You didn't need me at all yesterday, did you? Don't lie or I'm out of here."

Angel winced. "Not really. But I *do* need you now. These are the women who don't want to mess up their hair building a raft or dodging paintballs. I had to find something to entertain them. Any of them could be a lead to further business. Impress them and I'll be booked up years in advance."

"You're already booked up years in advance."

Angel scowled. "These people *know* people. Important people. All I need is one famous name and I can pick and choose who I work for."

"Why didn't you just tell me what you wanted me to do?"

"Because you'd have said no. I really do need you to do this, Gethin. I didn't have anyone else I could ask."

Gethin glared at him. "An agency? Or are spotty butts spreading like Ebola?"

"I tried. They were all booked. I needed someone I could trust not to behave inappropriately."

"I could still behave plenty inappropriately."

"But you wouldn't." Angel put on his mistreated puppy face. "Please, darling."

"Just women, right?" Gethin asked.

Angel nodded.

Gethin sighed. "Okay, then we're done. We're even and I stay in my office one month rent free."

"Agreed." Angel turned to go.

"No, no, no. Wait right there. You're escorting me to the room and telling them not to touch."

Gethin undressed in front of him and Angel whined. "This isn't fair."

"It's not like you haven't seen me naked."

"Yes, but then you were bleeding all over the floor. I wasn't looking at that part of you. Oooh you're hung like a…"

"Like a what? Cobra, donkey, sperm whale, duck?" Gethin folded his clothes into a neat pile before he tied the apron around his hips.

"Duck?" Angel gaped at him.

"Look it up." Gethin strode for the door.

"Your arse." Angel groaned. "Your gorgeous arse. That tattoo. You're teasing me. Arrghh."

"Why yes I am. And it serves you right. Let's get this over with."

"Try and smile. Please."

Gethin clenched his jaw. He was pissed off with Angel but if he left the guy in the lurch, Angel might decide sharing office space was no longer an option. Gethin had seen Angel in T-rex mode and he was scary. Gethin didn't have many friends, but Angel was one of them, and doing this wasn't going to kill him, just embarrass him.

Angel walked into the room ahead of him and all Gethin could see were women staring, jaws dropping before grins formed.

"Good morning, ladies," Angel said. "I'd like to introduce you to…Drake." Angel turned and winked at him. "He'll be serving you cocktails of your choice and playing a few games. Have fun but no ruffling his feathers. He has a sharp beak."

What? Angel walked out before Gethin could find out what games he was supposed to play.

"Who's first for a drink?" he asked.

"Me. My name's Belinda." She leaned over the bar and stared at his groin. "I'd like a Screaming Orgasm."

Thank fuck for the crib sheet. Gethin was tempted to increase the amount of alcohol, but then maybe a room full of drunk women would cause him even more problems.

He soon realised he didn't need to do anything to get them drunk, they were doing it all by themselves. No sooner had he finished making the last woman a cocktail, than Belinda wanted another. He began to make double quantities. Gethin fended off their hands — mostly, fended off their questions by lying, but despite his request that they not take his photo, he knew several had.

Gethin coped and smiled until the games started. He knew to the minute how much longer he had to do this and he'd never known time pass so slowly. The birthday boy's girlfriend, who'd introduced herself as Dakota, was clearly the one in charge and the first one who'd tried to grope him. Gethin was tempted to offer to strip and let each of them touch for twenty seconds if they'd let him leave alone afterward. They were all trying to get a rise out of him — literally — and at least he found that amusing because there was no way he'd get an erection.

Dakota produced a box of plasters. "First game. Drake stands in the middle of the room. I'm going to stick a plaster somewhere on his body, then blindfold the one who has to find it. I've got a stopwatch. Winner's the one with the quickest time."

"This is one game I want to lose." Belinda licked her lips and everyone laughed. Apart from Gethin.

Oh Jesus Christ. I'm going to kill Angel.

"No using hands." Dakota grinned. "Only your mouth."

Fucking hell. "Not under the apron," he said. "Or over. Or anywhere near my butt."

From the squeals of excitement he doubted anyone was listening.

The first woman to be blindfolded was nervous and started at Gethin's toes. Dakota had slapped the plaster on his knee. All the women were shouting encouragement and he stuck a wry smile on his face and imagined all the things he was going do to Angel.

"Ellis is going to kill me," the woman wailed as she gingerly mouthed her way up Gethin's shin.

"He's not going to know," Belinda said.

"I tell him everything."

Belinda snorted. Gethin was dreading her turn.

He had to grab one woman's head when her mouth strayed too close to his balls. He didn't like having their lips all over him but he pretended as though he did. His face ached from smiling, though he wondered how successful he'd been at fooling them when he didn't end up with a stiff cock. That seemed to be the aim of the whole thing and had turned into a competition. Dakota had the penultimate turn. Belinda was determined to be the last. Belinda stuck Dakota's plaster over his mouth and she took ages to find it.

After Belinda had been blindfolded, Dakota put her finger to her lips, and looked round at everyone. The plaster was still in her hand.

"Ready. Steady. Go," Dakota said.

As Belinda leaned in toward his stomach, Dakota quickly pressed the plaster onto the place she'd first touch and everyone, including Gethin, gave a heavy sigh when her mouth landed straight on it.

"Oh bad luck," Dakota said.

Belinda pulled off her blindfold and glared. The others were laughing, but Gethin could see she had no idea she'd been tricked.

Eleven minutes to go.

"Time for a game of Twister," Belinda said. "Me first."

Killing Angel was too good for him. Gethin wanted to take him apart bit by bit, as slowly and painfully as possible while he read Shakespeare to him, badly.

"Three spins each," Dakota said.

Within two spins Gethin was on his hands and knees at one end of the plastic play mat with Belinda glaring from the other end. He'd given up worrying about being almost naked. By the time two other women were on the mat as well and they were all entangled, he was actually laughing. Partly because time was almost up but even more because Belinda still hadn't got her hands on him.

When the door opened and Angel came in, Gethin wanted to kiss him for being on time, then kill him for persuading him into this. The women trooped out to some other activity, probably to throw pots with some other poor naked sod, though Belinda didn't leave without sliding her palm across Gethin's bum. Angel must have seen the look on Gethin's face because he muttered something about Gethin tidying up, then rushed out after them.

Thirty minutes more. That was all Gethin would give him. The bad news was that he couldn't even go straight home. Earlier that morning, Jonnie had pleaded with him to come back later. He piled up the glasses in the sink behind the bar. Wiped down and tidied up the bottles he'd used, then put the cushions straight on the couches and chairs. The used plasters went in the bin and he folded up the Twister game and put it back in the box. When the door opened, he wished he'd gone to change before he did any of that.

Kell walked in. "Am I too late to play?"

Oh shit. "I should warn you I have black belts in judo, karate and taekwondo."

Kell laughed. "You take it easy on me last night or is your black belt in bullshit?"

He stared at the apron and slowly let his gaze rise over Gethin's chest. Gethin felt his cock begin to fill. *Fuck.*

"Did you forget to get dressed this morning?"

"Something like that."

If ever Gethin needed confirmation he was gay, the last hour had surely confirmed it. Women's hands all over him and not a peep from his cock. One guy staring and his dick was trying to lift the apron to take a look.

"I need to get my clothes," Gethin said but made no move to walk past Kell, knowing his arse would be on display.

"Must you?" Kell stepped toward him. "I've just worked up an appetite playing paintball. All that aggression, surges of adrenaline and nowhere for them to go."

"You lost, did you?"

Kell frowned. "No, I fucking didn't." He took a step closer to Gethin. "I owe you."

"Owe me what?" But he knew what Kell meant.

Of course the sensible thing for Kell to do would be to walk away. He was breaking his own rule, but he didn't care. Gethin's cock tented the apron. One small piece of fabric stopped him seeing the guy naked in broad daylight and he *wanted* to see him naked. He'd already spotted scars he hadn't noticed last night and there was an elaborate well drawn dragon tattoo on his leg. He tried to ignore the not minor consideration that the castle was milling with people, any of whom could walk in at any moment. *Oh God, now I'm even hotter.*

"My clothes are in a room across the hallway," Gethin said quietly.

In the periphery of his hearing, which happened to be very sharp, Kell heard the sound of people outside the room. It was an opportunity and he took it. He grabbed Gethin's arm, propelled him behind the large couch and pulled him down.

"What the—?"

A hand over Gethin's mouth shut him up. Then the door opened and they both froze.

"Want a drink?" someone asked. Kell didn't recognize the voice.

The couch was large enough to keep them unseen, unless someone leaned over the back and they'd only do that if they made a noise. Kell smirked. Gethin sprawled on his back, Kell at his side, Kell's hand still over his mouth. He kept it there. Gethin stared at him without blinking. There were at least four people the other side of the couch, three men and one woman, their conversation punctuated by the sounds of glasses and bottles clinking.

When Kell pushed the apron up over Gethin's stomach, Gethin wrapped a hand around his wrist. Kell moved his other hand from Gethin's mouth and put his lips there instead, swallowing Gethin's startled splutter. Kell had intended only to distract him before he trailed his tongue down the guy's body, but when Gethin opened his mouth Kell was lost, swept straight out to sea, no lifeboat in sight.

I don't kiss. But Gethin tasted of pineapple and coconut and some sort of liqueur, and Kell's head swam. He dragged his nails through Gethin's hair and speared Gethin's mouth with his tongue, deepening the kiss, exploring his teeth, his palate.

I don't kiss.

But the world hadn't ended in a blaze of fire. Kell's cock had hardened, not gone soft. A kiss wouldn't kill him. One kiss didn't mean he was going to start thinking about rings — not wedding rings anyway. *Fucking stop thinking.*

Stop kissing. This is not about kissing a guy.

A loud laugh snapped him out of the moment and Kell jerked his head up, but they'd not been discovered. Gethin looked at him, his cheeks flushed, his eyes half-lidded. Kell lowered his head and licked Gethin's mouth. *Is he going to stop me?* He licked over Gethin's stubbled chin and down his neck, smiling as the ridged Adam's apple shifted under his lips. He trailed his tongue down the centre of Gethin's heaving chest while the guy lay tense beneath him, hands balled at his sides.

Kell was so turned on it was hard to breathe, so intoxicated that everyone in the room could have been leaning over the couch watching them and he couldn't have stopped. He wanted Gethin completely naked. He fumbled for the tie on the apron, pulled it undone, then dragged it away. Last night, he'd not been able to see much, now he could take his fill.

He bit back his groan. Long, silky, hard, thickly veined — how many ways to describe a cock? Kell wrapped his hand around it, felt the heat of it and heard Gethin quietly exhale. The shaft swelled in his grip and when he pumped, just once, the sensation of silken skin shifting over the steel core made his own cock press insistently behind his zipper.

A glance at Gethin's face told Kell the guy knew what he planned. The conversation was loud enough to cover any slight noises they might make, but it was still risky. Though the risk was all on Gethin's side. He might get the sack. Kell would just get outed to a few more people he'd never see again and Quin would likely dine off the story for months. But Kell didn't want Gethin to get fired, so they had to be silent. Gethin's hand brushed his face and Kell caught his thumb in his mouth and sucked. While he sucked, he dragged his hand up and down Gethin's dick, and gently pumped.

When he tried to move his head down to where his hand was busy, Gethin didn't let him. So Kell slipped his hand to Gethin's swollen balls, cupping them gently before he squeezed around the base of the cock. Maybe Gethin thought he'd call out if Kell used his mouth. Maybe he just wasn't into being sucked off. Kell didn't believe that. But if he couldn't use his mouth, he'd use his hand to milk him. It had once been done to Kell by a much older guy. Kell had always been in too much of a hurry to bother doing it since, but he wanted to torment Gethin, wanted to see him struggle to keep quiet and still.

Kell wrapped his hand around the base of Gethin's cock and squeezed almost to the point that it would hurt, signalled by the tensing of Gethin's stomach, before he moved his hand a little way toward the head and squeezed again. He kept going inch by inch until he reached the head and then pressed with his thumb and forefinger until pearls of precome formed at the slit. Kell licked his lips, slid his hand to the base and repeated what he'd just done— squeeze, slide up, squeeze, slide up.

By the time he'd done it three or four times, his hand and Gethin's stomach were glistening with moisture. Gethin's chest heaved and his eyes kept opening and closing as if he was trying to watch but struggling. His muscles were rigid. Kell blew on his cockhead and as Gethin's hips began to lift, he tightened his grip around the base of his cock and pressed the knuckles of his other hand onto the strip of flesh beyond. Gethin silently mouthed obscenities and Kell smiled and took both his hands away.

Gethin frowned, gave Kell a questioning look and Kell shook his head. Gethin scowled but he got it. Gethin wrapped his hand around his own cock and jerked himself off. It didn't take long and Kell stared at him unblinking. He watched Gethin's cock swell, then pulse. His balls changed shape, drawing up to the base of his cock then he was coming all over his stomach — *fuck it, right up his chest* — long streams of milky come spattering his skin and not a sound from his mouth. *Wow.*

Gethin ached with the strain of keeping quiet, ached with the pleasure of coming. His heart was still racing. When Kell dropped his head and licked come from his chest, Gethin slid his fingers into his hair and relished every fucking second of it. He lay motionless while Kell laved him, sucked his nipples, explored scars with his tongue. No one had ever done that before. Gethin hadn't let them. Knowing Kell couldn't ask about them made it easier.

The room emptied and Gethin braced himself for the question about the marks on his body.

"Want to do this again?" Kell asked.

That hadn't been what he'd expected. "Fuck behind a couch?"

"Maybe. Or something different next time. Maybe behind a bus shelter." He grinned. "You live in London?"

Gethin nodded.

"With anyone?"

"No." *Oh God. No, but…*

"Neither do I. Interested in occasional, casual hook ups if I can find a secluded couch or an isolated bus shelter well away from frisky horses and belligerent poets?"

Gethin's heart thumped hard.

"I really fancy you," Kell whispered. "But I'm only interested in no strings attached sex. If you want more than that, I'll walk away now."

"Keep talking."

Kell's face lit up. "I thought…we could have our own personal version of Grindr. If I text you and you're free and up for it then great. If not, fine. And vice versa. I have a job that means I work most nights, but I don't start until late. We can find places to meet. Doesn't have to be a couch involved. Or a bed. Or a wall. Or a bus shelter. Though…" He shook his head. "Either of us can call a halt any time we like. Every time we meet can be like the first. We could pretend we're strangers. What do you think?"

Gethin took a deep breath. "Will you go and get my clothes for me? They're in the room across the hall."

Kell sighed. "Okay."

Gethin exhaled when Kell left. No strings attached sex. Didn't that sound like the perfect solution? They were either available or they weren't. It wasn't being unfaithful to Jonnie. Jonnie might not remember he'd cheated on Gethin, but that's what had happened. If Jonnie hadn't had the accident, Gethin would never have had any more to do with him. Kell would never need to know about Jonnie. There'd never be any need for complicated explanations as to why Gethin wasn't around when Kell wanted to see him. It sounded too good to be true.

Kell dropped his clothes behind the couch and Gethin put them on. Once he was decent, he stood up.

"By any chance do you have a bike? A Kawasaki?" Kell asked.

"Yeah."

"So it was you I saw zooming out of here last night."

"Probably."

"You looked sexy, hugging that machine with your thighs. I jacked off thinking about that and our earlier encounter."

Gethin pushed his hands in his pockets.

"What's your answer?" Kell asked. "Want to play or not?"

Gethin took out his phone. "What's your number?"

Chapter Ten

On the train to London, Kell took out his phone and changed the opening screen back to the picture Marek had taken. He scrolled to Gethin's number, stored under the letter G and his finger hovered for several seconds before he put the phone away. Calls to chat were not a good idea. Neither were flirty texts. Having Gethin's number on a phone Marek might grab and check wasn't a good idea either. But it wasn't as if Marek used Kell for anything more than a quick fuck. They weren't in a relationship. It had nothing to do with Marek who Kell saw.

Christ. Was that just wishful thinking? Kell sighed. He knew nothing for sure. The sensible thing to do would be to never call Gethin. Delete his number so he *couldn't* call. But Kell had never been sensible, not as far as sex with a guy he fancied was concerned. Maybe not over sex with a guy he definitely *didn't* fancy. He'd crossed the line with Marek. He was fooling himself that he had a choice. He'd been drawn into quicksand. Kell clenched his jaw.

His life would be much better if he could stop thinking about that prick and instead think about Gethin. How long before Gethin called him? Who'd break first? But then after one or two more hook ups with the guy, Kell would have to stop the thing in its tracks.

Probably.

It was too risky.

Probably.

It was weird how much better he felt—brighter, cheerful, more hopeful, and he didn't think it was only due to having had a weekend away. Finding a guy he'd like to see again hadn't been part of his game plan, but there was a spark inside him now, another reason to put up with all Marek's crap, an antidote to his poison. Even if there *were* only one or two more fucks with Gethin on the horizon.

Probably.

What the fuck am I thinking? A spark? Feeling something for Gethin was a bad idea. Worse than a bad idea because it could get both of them into trouble. Kell hadn't yet lied to the guy but he'd have to. Whatever this was between them *had* to stay casual and any feelings Kell allowed to develop should be left behind when he walked away from their last encounter.

Maybe three more times.

Or four.

Shit.

Doctor Umar Khan, one of the doctors Jonnie liked, stopped Gethin before he went into Jonnie's room. Gethin tensed because doctors were rarely seen at Wellbrook. They only came from the nearby hospital when there was a problem.

"Is Jonnie okay?" Gethin asked.

"He's not having a good day."

"Has something happened?"

"He was convinced his toes were moving. He refused to believe the nurses when they said they weren't. He became distressed and I was called. There was no movement."

"Right."

"He's rather depressed."

Gethin bit his lip. "That's nothing new."

"More depressed than usual."

"Okay. Thanks for the warning."

How could Jonnie be anything *but* depressed? He wasn't going to get better unless there was a sudden medical breakthrough and even then it would be years before any treatment was rolled out through the NHS.

When Gethin walked into his room, Jonnie sat in his wheelchair facing a blank wall.

"Hi," Gethin said.

The chair didn't turn and Gethin moved to a spot where Jonnie could see him. His eyes were open but he didn't acknowledge Gethin's presence.

"Not having a good day?" Gethin asked.

Jonnie huffed.

Gethin took a deep breath. "Sorry I had to leave early this morning. But I told you I'd come back and here I am."

"Why?" Jonnie muttered.

"Why what?"

"Why come? What's point? Why bother?"

Because without me you'd have no one visiting you. Gethin struggled to find something to say, something that wasn't going to upset Jonnie further.

"Who else is going to listen to me moan?" Gethin leaned against the wall in front of him. "I had to be a butler in the buff today. All I wore was a skimpy apron. Angel tricked me into it. He'd told me he needed me to set things up and serve drinks, then he half-blackmailed me into making cocktails for a room full of drunken women who were desperate to get their hands on my cock."

He'd hoped Jonnie would laugh or show some interest but he stayed silent. Gethin told him about the plaster game and Twister, making it sound funnier than it was. "I was glad they didn't get round to pin the tail on the donkey."

"Shut up," Jonnie said. "Not like I can ever play like that."

Gethin swallowed. It was impossible to get this right. What could anyone say to a quadriplegic guy without upsetting him? Everything that came from Gethin's mouth was a reminder to Jonnie of what he'd lost. The official advice was to be normal, speak normally and that's what Gethin tried to do, but...

"You told me you were working," Jonnie said.

"It *was* work. Angel paid me." Sort of. "I need the money. Investigative work's only trickling in."

"Yeah, well wouldn't have been doing that if you'd stayed with the band."

Gethin counted to ten.

"Use my money," Jonnie said. "Not like I need it."

Gethin clenched his fists. The only reason Jonnie had money in his account was because Gethin was putting it there.

"There's no point in anything," Jonnie said. "Had enough. Tried and tried and nothing changes. Toes don't move. Nor does my cock." He swivelled the chair so he could look Gethin in the face. "Don't want to do this anymore. Need you to help me end it."

Bile surged into Gethin's throat. It wasn't the first time Jonnie had asked. "You *have* improved. You can breathe on your own. Move your fingers. You have to be patient."

"No. Want to die. Want you to help me."

"I can't. You can't ask me to do it."

"I *am* asking you."

"I'd go to prison. Is that what you want?"

"No."

Gethin wrapped his arms around him and pressed his face into Jonnie's thin hair.

"You're clever. Could find way," Jonnie said.

Gethin took a shuddering breath, then stepped back. "I can't." His heart pounded.

"Please," Jonnie said.

"I couldn't cope after." Gethin slid down the wall and sat on the floor. He hoped it looked as though he just wanted to sit, not that his legs refused to support him.

"I can't cope now. Don't want to live like this… No one should have to live like this if they don't want to."

It was as though Jonnie was making a special effort to speak clearly, because every word burned into Gethin's brain.

"You've felt like this before and got over it," Gethin mumbled.

Jonnie let out a strangled laugh. "Got over it? Never got over it. Always thinking it. Go to sleep and hope I don't wake up. *Pray* I don't wake. I want to die. Why can't I have what I want? This is my life. No one else's. *This* is not what I want."

"I know." Gethin was choked by emotions clawing their way to the surface like skeletal hands reaching to pull him down. "But I can't kill you."

"Don't want more pep talks, more medication. Don't want anything but this to finish. Had enough… Can't do it anymore… You wouldn't want this life, would you?"

"No."

"I'd do it for you… I'd do it because I love you. If you love me, you'll help me."

Shit, shit, shit.

"Know what's so crap about my life, Dart? Not just loneliness… Humiliation. Can't fucking do anything. Not wipe my backside. Not wipe away my snot." He gasped for breath. "I have no control, no choices except over what I want to eat… They wheel me into room next door to sit and stare at a guy with no legs so we can talk. At least he can walk when they make him legs. I can never walk again."

Jonnie's cheeks flushed. "They ask me about what I did before." He gave a strangled laugh. "Why would I want to think about what I've lost? My memories aren't good things… They torture me… I. Want. This. To. Stop."

Gethin dragged his fingers through his hair, then pushed to his feet. "I can't… I have to go."

"Think about it," Jonnie said. "Promise."

Gethin nodded. He couldn't breathe. He had to get out. He rushed down the corridor, took the stairs without registering the treads under his feet and bolted outside to his bike. *No fucking car to sit in and cry*. He pulled his helmet on, started the engine and released his scream under cover of the noise.

His phone rang and he switched it off without checking who it was. There was no one he wanted to talk to. He powered the phone down and pushed it into his pocket. No temptation to call Kell. No need to answer Jonnie. No one pressuring him to do anything. He didn't care about lost work. Jonnie wasn't the only one who wanted everything to stop, nor the only one whose memories were painful.

When he opened his eyes, he saw Dr. Khan hurrying toward him. Gethin switched off the engine, removed his helmet and blinked the tears from his eyes before the guy reached him.

"Bat out of hell?" the doctor asked.

Gethin let out a strangled groan. "Something like that."

"He asked you."

Gethin saw no point in denying it and nodded. "Did he ask *you*?"

"Jonnie's talked about dying before. He insisted he didn't want to be resuscitated in the event of a catastrophic incident and as you know, as he named you his next-of-kin, that's now in his notes. He's said to various health professionals that he wishes he was dead, but that's not unusual for someone in his situation. And there's a difference between wishing he was dead and actively asking for help in dying." The doctor sighed. "I should have had this conversation before you spoke to him this morning, but I hoped he wouldn't ask you."

"Who else does he have to ask? No one comes to see him. Do his parents even call to see how he is?"

"They email."

"Fucking hell." Gethin rolled his eyes.

"Everyone deals with tragedy in a different way."

"They're his *parents*. They could have had Jonnie living with them in Portugal. Given him a home. Some degree of normalcy. They turned their backs on him and fucked off to play golf in the sun while their son lies paralysed from the neck down."

The doctor said nothing, but then Gethin hadn't expected him to.

"I said no when he asked," Gethin whispered. "I said I'd think about it, but it was an excuse to leave."

The young doctor nodded. "It's not an easy conversation to have. Assisted suicide is illegal in the UK. Medical staff would face professional and legal sanctions if we did anything to hasten death. But it's important to Jonnie that he's able to talk about wanting to die. We're trained in how to respond, but you're not. I understand how hard it must be to listen to your friend ask you to help him end his life, but you can't do it."

I could, but I won't. There's a difference.

"Would you want to die if you were him?" Gethin asked. "Did Jonnie ask you that?

"Yes, he asked me."

"Did you answer him?"

"I told him I'd want to live. I'd try to make the best of my life that I could. I'd continue to work in some capacity. I could still see patients. Maybe study psychiatry because it doesn't require doing physical examinations. Jonnie could still be involved with music, not performing but writing songs. He *can* have meaning in his life. There will be improvements though it will never be the life he'd expected to have. Maybe you could talk to him about working when you next come in. There must be a program he could use on his computer that would enable him to write music."

Gethin had installed it and as far as he knew Jonnie had never used it, but then it hadn't been Jonnie who'd been the most creative one in the group.

The doctor took a deep breath. "Jonnie's asked me for information about organizations that are sympathetic to assisted suicide."

Gethin's heart thumped hard.

"I'm professionally bound not to provide that information or to contact such an organization on his behalf."

"He can look it up online."

"I'm sure he has. I just wanted you to know what was in his head. It's important he feels communication paths are open, that he can tell us how he feels, what he wants, what he's worried about. Many of those who look into assisted suicide either change their minds or never actually make specific plans. We're trying to show him there *is* hope, there *is* a future for him. I'd like to think you'd support us in that."

Gethin said nothing. He was wondering what he'd say if Jonnie asked him to take him to Switzerland.

"Jonnie's lucky to have you."

But Gethin wasn't lucky to have Jonnie.

"I've arranged for someone to come and talk to him. We need to reassess his care plan. Patients with Jonnie's degree of spinal damage almost always have times when they feel like this. I know how hard it must be to see someone you love suffering."

"I don't love him," Gethin blurted. "He thinks I do and I don't."

"Don't feel guilty about that. You still come to see him. You spend time with him, talk to him, you even make him laugh. He thinks the world of you. So do the staff here. There are not many relationships that can withstand these sorts of pressures. You can care for someone without loving them. This has had a huge impact on your life too. Jonnie can't yet see that."

More likely he didn't want to see it. "Is his memory likely to come back?"

"Hard to say."

"Because one thing he doesn't remember is that six months before he had his accident I found him in our bed being fucked by two guys he'd picked up in a bar. I packed my gear, said I never wanted to see him again and walked out. The next time I saw him was the day he ended up in intensive care. He doesn't remember our relationship was over, and I can't tell him, can I? Wreck another corner of his world? What would that do to him?"

"Ah. Sorry."

Gethin pulled at his hair, a nervous habit he'd tried to stop and failed. He wished he'd not revealed that history to the doctor. He didn't want sympathy.

"You feel trapped too," the doctor said.

"But I have a choice. I could stop coming to see him. Jonnie has no choice. His world is what it is and if I were him, I'd want to die too, but don't worry, I'm not going to kill him."

Gethin put on his helmet and rode away. What was he going to say if Jonnie brought up the subject of going to Switzerland? At least Gethin had time to think about it, thanks to the doctor. But thanks to the doctor, that was yet another thing to fret over.

Instead of going back to his bedsit, he went to the office. While he was in such a bad mood, he might as well work on decrypting the rest of the data from Charlton's computer and have another think about why, out of all the PIs in London, Izabela had chosen him. Just because of the advert or not?

It was only when he took his phone from his pocket as he sat at his desk that he remembered he'd turned it off. He had a load of missed calls and several messages. None from Kell. Gethin's cock stirred. *I'm not fucking calling him this quickly. No flirty texts. No calling to chat.* He switched on his computer, and while it warmed up, he started to read.

Dieter's photo hadn't stuck a chord with any of his contacts, but at least they'd now keep a look out for the teenager, though Gethin knew it was needle in a haystack stuff. Izabela had called him four times and left two messages.

"Hi there. Sorry. I panic. He hit me again and I just… I change my mind. I want you to follow him. Sunday night at seven he's meeting a client at the Dorchester. Tomorrow morning he leave at seven thirty for his office in Blackheath. He told me he'd be late back. He's having a meal with clients at the OXO Tower. Please don't do anything with that stuff off computer. There'll be pictures of me. I…forgot. I'll keep it in case I need lawyer. Drop it off tomorrow and I pay amount we agreed and a thousand as bonus. Thanks."

A thousand? It was already after seven but Gethin wouldn't have gone to the Dorchester. He was suspicious about the whole set up. There had to be something on this stick that was the key to everything. A less scrupulous PI would have taken the money and run. Gethin really needed the money but...

Izabela's second message started with her crying. "Please, please. I need that information off computer. I'm going to be in so much trouble if I don't have it. If he find out what I did, what we did, he kill me. He kill you."

Oh God. In trouble with who? Gethin put his elbows on the desk and rubbed his temples. Truth or more lies? He could just hand over the memory stick and forget he'd ever done the job, but...

Gethin clicked onto the last message which was from Jonnie.

"Gethin. Shit. Did I come on too strong? Sorry... Wasn't asking you to cut my throat...but won't change my mind... If you won't help, I'll find another way... But I need you with me on this. Love you."

He tossed the phone aside with a groan, turned to the computer and started to work.

It was four in the morning before Gethin pushed back in his chair. Brian Charlton appeared to be the accountant he claimed he was. Fully qualified, no strikes against his name. The guy was *not* a computer expert. The decryption hadn't been difficult, though Gethin had learned from experts and become more proficient than many of them. Most of the files and spreadsheets appeared to be legitimate accounts for a variety of businesses — shops, nightclubs in London and elsewhere, a photographer, a specialty cake business, hairdressers. Gethin googled each business and found they existed, but had no idea whether their declared revenues were true or false.

There were other spreadsheets where there was no company name, just a series of codes that Gethin had failed to break, assuming they actually hid something and weren't just random numbers and letters. Large sums of money had been moved from one bank account to another, out of the UK and back again. Gethin wasn't a financial expert. He couldn't make sense of it but it did look suspicious, and reinforced his theory that Charlton could be laundering money.

The guy's personal UK bank account showed the usual activity: direct debits to utility companies and his mortgage provider. Payments to credit card companies and generous amounts transferred from his account to that of Izabela Dushku. Charlton took a salary that seemed reasonable to Gethin. The guy paid tax and national insurance. But he also had more than one offshore account holding a lot of money. Millions.

It was easy to see illegal activity where there was none. For all Gethin knew Charlton had won the lottery, or been left money when his parents died.

Gethin looked again at the photos of the women. Could there be a reasonable explanation? If the amounts below the photos were what the woman had been paid rather than payment *for* the women, he was going to look an idiot if he went to the police. If it hadn't been that Izabela was so desperate to get her hands on the information, and that *fucking* gun, he might have just given her the memory stick and taken the money.

Getting into Charlton's emails would be easy. But although Gethin had already broken the law, doing more could land him in serious trouble. He decided to drive back to his flat, get some sleep, then decide what to do.

Gethin had hoped for inspiration to strike while he was unconscious, but it hadn't. He rolled out of bed with his thoughts still dominated by worry over whether Izabela had picked him for a particular reason. If there was any way she could have known about his past. It was still possible he could go to prison for what he'd done as a teenager and in his early twenties. He'd covered his tracks but even so.

He spent the rest of the day spying on a woman who lived in Islington. Once he had the photos her husband probably didn't want, Gethin went to the guy's office and showed him the snaps he'd taken on his phone.

The guy slumped at his desk. "Fuck. I knew, but I still hoped."

"Do you want hard copies of the pictures?" Gethin asked.

"Email them to me."

"Sorry," Gethin said.

The guy looked up at him. "Not as sorry as me."

He took a cheque book out of his drawer and wrote out a cheque. Gethin went straight to a bank and paid it in. There had been no more calls from Izabela, no more people enquiring about his services, nothing from Jonnie and nothing from Kell. Gethin nearly sent a text. An hour forgetting about his shitty life held a lot of attraction, but as he started to compose a message, Jonnie called him and Gethin let Kell go.

Chapter Eleven

Two days on the trot, Kell crawled into bed at four in the morning. From the moment he'd arrived at work, he'd hardly had time to draw breath. Carting supplies for the bar up from the basement stockroom, pacing outside in the freezing cold while Alec, the guy on the door—who had a frigging coat—took a long break, fetching food for Warner and his guests, babysitting the young guy Warner had taken a shine to in case anyone else took a shine to him, collecting glasses and bottles—the teen had helped with that, and getting fucked in the mouth in Warner's office by Marek who gripped Kell's beaded necklace so tight, he'd left a red line on his skin.

All that and nothing to give his boss. The guys with Warner were Eastern European, but that was as much as Kell could ascertain. The youngster had sat with them for a while and Kell had hoped to tease some information out of him, but he'd not had the chance to talk to him privately.

He lay on his back in his pokey bedsit and looked up at the ceiling. The street light stood right outside his window, the thin curtains providing no barrier to the amber illumination. The dingy room was depressing. Stains on the ceiling had spread to join the marks creeping up the walls. The floor was rough, just bare board, and though he'd covered as much of it as he could with cheap rugs, he still kept wondering what had caused the stains he'd hidden. Vomit? Piss? Blood? Some guy jacking off? A lot of guys jacking off?

The bathroom was basic—three bottles of bleach and an hour's scrubbing the day he moved in had helped, but no amount of work, apart from a complete refurb, could make it somewhere he'd like to linger. The shower was barely big enough to fit inside and the supply of hot water unreliable.

It was better not to think of the life he'd once had, not quite the castle Quin had lived in, but a big, luxurious house, or even the flat he'd left to live here. It was hard to believe he'd ever move back into his old place. He'd put it with a rental agent and a couple had snapped it up the same day. Kell's belongings sat in storage awaiting the end of this job, though if anything went wrong he might have to leave London. If he could bring Warner, Marek and the rest of them down, they'd go to prison and Kell would be safe — theoretically — because he'd appear to fall with them. But if they discovered he was a cop, they'd kill him.

Kell rolled over, knowing he was going to have problems sleeping even though he was exhausted. He didn't like starting work late and not going to bed until early in the morning. It had thrown out his body clock and it was taking a long time for him to get used to the odd hours. He wasn't sure he'd ever adjust.

In his first undercover job, he'd lived homeless on the streets for a couple of weeks growing an impressive but itchy beard and a set of filthy clothes before he'd moved into a squat run by violent eco-activists. He'd joined them on a couple of their expeditions but when they planned to free dogs from a testing centre, he reported them to his boss, even though he had a sneaking admiration for what they wanted to do. The night of the action, Kell had been arrested with the others. The officer that took him down had been rougher than Kell had expected and he'd ended up with a broken rib.

His other undercover work had been as part of a gang planning a series of robberies. But they'd carried out a raid and misled Kell on timing. A lot of money had been spent on a police operation which achieved nothing and Kell's boss was still pissed off with him.

This was Kell's chance to redeem himself and leave the force on a high. Spying on Silas Warner was a big deal, except Kell was reaching breaking point with Marek. The guy was *too* interested in him. Kell's ability to convince himself he was doing this for the right reasons was unravelling faster and faster. He'd thought going away for the weekend would help, but it had just reminded him of what he was missing, of what he'd let himself be drawn into.

His nerves were starting to shred. He wasn't cut out for this. He'd joined the police because he wanted to make the world fair — at least a small part of the world, but maybe the price he was paying was too high. His father had been quite clear about his disapproval. Kell knew he was worrying him.

Fuck it. If he started to think about his family, he'd get no sleep at all. A fragile mother in la la land who didn't recognize him, a father who thought more of him than he should and a brother who relished tormenting him. Oliver had left him alone for a while so it could only be a matter of time before he restarted his campaign of terror.

Maybe on my birthday. Kell shuddered. He knew no one would believe him about Oliver. Oliver and his wife had friends in high places, and it only seemed to be Kell who realised his brother was a hateful, vindictive, sadistic, homophobic dickhead. Kell hoped Oliver didn't fuck up his kids because he'd fucked Kell up. He'd killed Kell's hamster by feeding it to their father's dog, regularly stole Kell's pocket money and made sure Kell got the blame for almost every bad thing that happened when they were youngsters. His mother, who'd still had all her marbles when they were young, thought Oliver was perfect. Kell snorted. No, he was wrong. She'd been crazy then too.

If Oliver came into the club, he'd out Kell without a second thought, probably with a smile plastered on his face, then as Oliver and his father stood at Kell's grave, Oliver would likely manage to convince him it had been an accident or even better, Kell's fault. Luckily the chance of Oliver walking into a gay club was zero. Kell wished he could blame the way Oliver treated him on his brother's homophobia, but it went much deeper than that. Back to when Kell was born.

Kell battered his pillow into submission, then rolled the other way. It was almost six. Too early to text Gethin. *Oh shit.* Kell didn't want to be the first to make contact. *Christ. I can't last forty-eight hours?* He groaned as he buried his head under the pillow and tried to blank his racing mind, knowing that when he did sleep he'd slide into a nightmare about Marek fisting him. If not that, then one about Oliver betraying him. Kell made a concerted effort to replay what he and Gethin had done behind the couch, pictured Gethin in his head, those wide green eyes, and slid his hand to his cock.

Gethin's contact at the Met, Detective Chief Inspector Tom Beckwith, was the cop Gethin had spoken to about the paedophile. Despite Gethin thinking he was doing everyone a favour, apart from the guilty party, Beckwith had threatened to arrest Gethin. He didn't approve of private investigators cocking up crime scenes — not that Gethin had. Gethin had arranged to meet him that morning in a café at Tower Hill. He knew Beckwith would be purposely late but Gethin arrived on time and worked on his laptop.

After he'd talked to Beckwith, he intended to search for Dieter, starting with a squat in north-east London he knew welcomed teens, assuming the place was still in operation. It had been set up in a commercial property where squatting wasn't illegal, whereas squatting in residential homes was a criminal offense. He clicked onto several websites checking for groups giving information about how to inhabit empty properties, then opened TOR to get onto the Deep Web to see if he could spot any new addresses.

When he'd compiled a list, he returned to his usual search engine to see what else he could find. Trying to persuade anyone in a squat to admit they'd even *seen* Dieter would be hard. At seventeen, he was old enough to leave home. Squatters took in the homeless when they could, as long as they didn't cause trouble and played their part in the set up. Gethin would have his work cut out persuading people *he* wasn't going to cause trouble.

111

He glanced up when Beckwith pulled out the chair at his side, the metal feet grating on the tiled floor.

The stocky, grey-haired detective sat down and glared at Gethin. "I'll have a cappuccino and a bacon buttie. Then at least this won't have been a complete waste of my time."

Gethin closed the lid of his laptop and went over to the counter to place the order. When he came back, Beckwith had opened Gethin's computer and was looking at the screen.

"Been thrown out of your nest?" Beckwith chuckled. "Looking for somewhere to live? Try Iceland."

Gethin closed his laptop.

"Start talking," Beckwith snapped.

Gethin told him everything from when he'd had the first call from Izabela.

Mention of the gun made Beckwith sit up. "A Beretta? You sure?"

"Yes."

"Go on."

"One moment she's telling me to forget it, the next to bring the memory stick and she'll pay me more. I suspect she's either being bribed or threatened or maybe even in cahoots with whoever wants the information. Charlton doesn't know how to keep himself safe."

He put a folded sheet of paper and two memory sticks on the table. "The silver one holds what I copied directly from his computer. The blue one has the same information, but where necessary and where I could, I've decrypted the files. I've written Charlton's address and Izabela's telephone number on the paper along with a rough drawing of the layout of the house downstairs showing the location of the computer."

Two coffees and Beckwith's bacon sandwich arrived. They stayed silent until the waiter had gone.

"Why did she choose you?" Beckwith bit into the bread.

Gethin curled his toes in his shoes. "An ad in the Metro."

"Do you get much work like that?"

"It was the first time I've tried it. I have a missing teen I'm searching for and his mother found me the same way."

"Hmm. Show me what you have."

"Before you say it, I know I broke the law. But bear in mind I could have kept quiet, handed her the data and walked away significantly richer." Gethin put the blue stick into the laptop and opened the document with the women's photos. He turned the screen so Beckwith could see but no one else.

"I thought the amounts might be the price to buy them, but it could be the money they were paid for doing...whatever. It's just that the shots look awkward, the women uncomfortable."

Beckwith didn't say anything as he ran his gaze over the images.

"Now the spreadsheets," Beckwith said.

Gethin opened one of them. "Considerable sums of money being moved between many places. The guy's an accountant, but again, it feels as though there's more to it than that. Details of ships too and bills of lading."

"You figure out what those codes mean?"

"No. Maybe I could eventually, but it's not my job and I've spent enough of my time on it. I've overstepped the mark, stumbled into something that looks shady and I'm stepping right out of it. I'm sure your guys can decrypt what I haven't." Actually, they probably couldn't, but Gethin had done more than enough. "Is Charlton known to you?"

Beckwith smiled without showing his teeth. The same smile Gethin had seen before Beckwith had threatened to arrest him.

"You know I'm not going to tell you that."

"What do you want me to do?" Gethin asked.

Beckwith pulled the stick out of the computer without going through the proper removal procedure and Gethin winced. Both memory sticks and the sheet of paper went into Beckwith's pocket. He bit into his sandwich and chewed as he stared at Gethin.

Gethin took a swallow of his coffee which was now lukewarm.

"When did you learn how to hack?" Beckwith asked.

Oh shit. "When I was a teenager."

"Are you known in the hacking world?"

Fuck. "Once upon a time. Not now."

Beckwith turned his sharp gaze on him. "Are you concerned that this Izabela or whoever's behind her knew what you could do?"

"It had crossed my mind."

"Worried you, you mean."

Gethin nodded.

"More likely you were chosen because you're a single inexperienced operator. Not hard to find out how long you've been in operation. Maybe they were aware you drive a beat up car, live in a small flat, look…scruffy. *They* were the reasons you were picked, not because you could decrypt the data on his computer."

Gethin wasn't convinced.

"Leave everything to us." Beckwith wiped his mouth with a paper napkin, screwed it up and dropped it on the plate.

"What am I supposed to tell Izabela when she phones?"

"Delay her. Tell her you've been busy, invent some family emergency, say you'll get the stick back to her as soon as you can. Wait until I tell you, then give it her. She won't know you've decrypted it." Beckwith sipped his drink. "Lucky that Charlton turned up when he did."

Gethin glared. "So he could pull a gun on me? How was that lucky?"

"Lucky for us. Because if he hadn't come home, she'd have told you she'd changed her mind, asked you for the memory stick, you'd have given it her and that would have been that. She used you."

You think I don't know that?

"You should be more careful. Illegally hacking into people's accounts, ferreting out their passwords, while supposedly checking for cheating partners? You're treading a fine line. I'm keeping my eye on you."

114

Beckwith pushed to his feet. Gethin didn't expect a thank you, which was just as well because the detective walked out without saying another word. Gethin's phone vibrated in his pocket and he pulled it out hoping it wasn't Izabela or Jonnie. He smiled when he read the message and tapped in his reply.

Kell glanced round when a dark-haired guy in his thirties, lanky as a colt, with stubble on his cheeks and shadows under gorgeous green eyes settled on the seat next to him. Gethin wore black jeans and a mid-length grey pea coat that fell open to reveal a white shirt, and he had a computer bag over his shoulder. Kell adjusted his position on the bar stool and took another sip of his beer. He schooled his respiration, though it was impossible to calm the blood rushing through his veins. Looking too keen was a mistake.

Gethin groaned as he leaned against the bar and pulled his fingers through his hair.

"You sound like you need a drink," Kell said.

"I need...something." Gethin grinned.

The smile hit Kell like a punch. The next breath he took was shaky.

"What can I get you?" the barman asked.

"Whatever he's drinking."

The barman opened a bottle of Dos Equis. Gethin took a long swallow and out of the corner of his eye, Kell watched his Adam's apple move up and down.

"Hard day?" Kell asked.

"Yep."

"You look tired."

"I'm okay." He smiled again, dimples in his cheeks and Kell's surge of lust took him by surprise.

"Only two percent of the world's population have green eyes." Kell said it so Gethin would turn and look at him full on. He did. *Moss green. Lagoon green. A tiger's eyes.* He wished he had the perfect words to describe the colour. *Exotic. Exciting. Sexy.*

"And two percent have red hair," Gethin said.

"You lucked out there." Kell stared at him, glad his own hair was dark.

"You don't like red hair?"

"Not much."

"What else don't you like?" Gethin asked.

Kell leaned a little closer. "Maybe I should tell you what I *do* like."

"Maybe I can guess."

Kell cocked his head on one side. "You can try."

"Scruffy short black hair, green eyes, the odd scar, tattoos, bitten fingernails. Black jeans sitting low on the hips, a white shirt not all the way tucked in, gray coat, casual black shoes, no socks…no shorts."

Kell chuckled. "Uncanny."

Soft lips quirked in a smile. "I have a talent."

"And what do *you* like?" Kell's heart hammered.

Gethin pinned Kell with his gaze. "Untidy dark hair, blue eyes, the odd scar or two, perfect fingernails, no tattoos. Jeans sitting low on the hips, a T-shirt that's ridden up at the back to show a strip of flesh, Converse trainers, no socks…no shorts. A guy who's maybe not quite what he seems."

Oh fuck. What has he seen? "Damn. They're not Converse."

"Shit. I've gone right off you now." He took another slug of his beer.

Kell stared at the long fingers encircling the bottle, and watched condensation slide down the glass and drip onto the bar. "That's a shame. You're just my type." He imagined those fingers gripping his cock and shivered with anticipation.

Gethin glanced at Kell's crotch where his cock had swelled behind his zipper. "So I see."

"Want to come to my place?" Kell surprised himself. He'd been intending to lure Gethin to the washroom.

There was an uncomfortably long pause before he had an answer. "Are you sure?"

Not now, no, after that pause. "Yep."

When Gethin looked at his watch, Kell felt a surge of irritation.

"We *could* fuck in the washroom, but my place is just around the corner." Kell kept it cool, but he was annoyed.

"Okay. Your place."

Excitement replaced irritation. *I am so shallow.* Kell paid for their drinks, pulled on his jacket and they walked out of the bar together.

It was a cool afternoon, the sun lukewarm in a faded October sky. Kell shivered. He should have worn more layers. They walked side by side, more or less matched in height and size, though Kell liked being slightly taller. Their little fingers accidentally brushed — was it accidental? — and the breath caught in his throat. *Shit.* All he could think about now was sex, having another man's hands on him, putting his hands on another man. Not *any* man. *This* man.

"How far around the corner?"

"About half a mile."

Kell thought that would make Gethin laugh and it did.

"I didn't say which corner."

The walk gave Kell plenty of time to think about threading his fingers through that short, silky hair, using his fingers and mouth on velvet-sheathed steel, pulling on Gethin's cock, sucking it, licking it, letting it slide through his lips and press against the inside of his cheek. He'd draw it down toward his throat, swallowing against it before he — *Shit. Stop it.*

Kell walked faster.

"In a hurry?"

"You were looking at your watch." Kell hated the undercurrent of petulance in his voice. Why had he revealed he'd noticed?

"I have somewhere I need to be later. I didn't want to waste time. I assumed we'd have a quick fuck in the bathroom — like strangers. Wasn't that what you wanted?"

Now Kell was annoyed again and he didn't quite understand why.

"You commented on me being tired," Gethin said. "But you look tired too."

Kell shrugged. "Goes with the job."

"Being a good-looking guy? Yeah. It must be a terrible strain trying not to look in every mirror you pass."

Kell laughed, flipped into a better mood. Or was that because his bedsit was coming up fast. He pulled his keys from his pocket and twirled them around his fingers. But at the thought of opening the door, his pleasure slid south. He cared what Gethin thought and the only good thing his place had was a big bed where Kell could lie and listen to the rumble of London traffic and congratulate himself on still being alive.

He pushed open the outer door, weaved through the lines of bikes chained up either side of the hallway and headed for the stairs. They passed no one on the way up. His fingers shook as he pushed the key into the lock. They weren't here for the décor. At least he'd left the place tidy.

The door was barely closed when Kell was spun round and shoved against it. The computer bag slid to the floor and hit Kell's foot as a warm mouth pressed against his. They clutched at each other, yanking their bodies together yet Kell still felt they were not close enough. He wanted to touch bare flesh, taste the soft skin at the crook of the elbow, slide his cock between those parted lips.

A tongue forced its way into Kell's mouth in an act of rough possession that overwhelmed Kell like a lightning strike. If he hadn't had his back to the door, he'd have fallen. *Christ, this guy can kiss.* Kell felt as if he'd been waiting his entire life for a kiss like this, for someone who could kiss like this. A kiss that could light up his body, fire every neuron, make his nerve endings sing.

But the kiss wasn't enough. Kell needed more. Now.

"Fucking hell," Gethin panted. "Desperate much?"

"Me?" Kell sounded as indignant as he could. "What about you?"

"You're like the nicest possible highly infectious disease. One touch and my resistance has gone."

"A disease called lust."

That comment earned a chuckle. "Yeah, so what *did* happen to fucking around with a stranger?"

"You'll do. You're strange enough."

Gethin laughed and kissed him again. They moaned into each other's mouths, grunts and gasps escaping between the kisses. Kell kissed him back just as harshly, suckling his tongue as he reached for the back of Gethin's neck.

But his fingers never made it. Both his wrists were held tight and Kell was forced so hard against the door he could almost feel himself sinking into it.

"Fuck." One word from Gethin's lips washed over Kell's mouth like a sugar rush before their lips were back together.

They kissed with the desperation of horny teenagers, and while they did, they stripped themselves and each other, their mouths barely moving apart as they toed off shoes and fumbled with zippers, tossing clothes aside. Kell didn't want to be this needy — had he *ever* been this needy? — but something about this guy made his head spin and his heart lurch behind his ribs. Their tongues rolled together and the taste of beer tripped more switches, the feel of a hard cock pressed against his sending him electric with excitement. Then they were tussling, a struggle of tongues, then hands, and Kell didn't know what he wanted anymore. To fuck or be fucked. To suck or be sucked. He didn't care because he wanted everything.

They broke apart only to take harsh breaths before their mouths joined again. His wrists had been released and he wrapped a hand around their cocks, Gethin's hand joining his. As they rubbed themselves off together, Kell could have died with the pleasure of it.

"Oh Christ." Gethin pressed his face against Kell's neck, licked, then kissed, then licked him again, smiling against him, and that one moment of tenderness almost made Kell lose control.

Their hearts thundered at the same pace, their hands frantically shifting in an identical rhythm. Kell wanted more than this, wanted to be lying down, fucking, but he was incapable of doing anything other than continue this race to completion. He only had to think the word *harder* and the hand that gripped him tightened. Precome covered his fingers as faster, harder, tighter blurred into a race that locked his lungs, made his heartbeat blend into one long, hard throb. Coming was all he could think about, apart from a wish they'd cross the line at the same time.

They came together, maybe a second apart; a warm, wet mess erupting between them as they gasped and gulped and stole each other's air. Kell kept moving his hand, letting their cocks slide in the slick heat, and he loved the way they stayed hard then softened together.

Kell pulled his mouth away. "Christ."

"Yeah." Gethin laughed. "You change the rules, take me to your place and we don't even make it to the bed?"

"Whose fault was that?"

"Shower?"

"Over there. It's kind of small."

Kell stayed where he was, propped up by the wall as Gethin headed for the bathroom. The sight of that taut arse and a well-inked dragon tattoo curling over one butt cheek and down the leg was almost enough to make him hard again. Kell wished the shower was big enough for the two of them to share. He flattened his hand over his belly, rubbed their come into his skin and because he knew Gethin wasn't looking, he lifted a finger to his mouth and sucked. He wasn't sure if it would freak Gethin out and the last thing he wanted to do was make him bolt.

Seeing him a couple more times wasn't going to work. Kell wanted to make this non-relationship last, draw it out as long as he could, but he was the one who'd made the rules. Part of him wished he'd never used the word casual. But one thought about Marek turned that on its head. He and Gethin might have a beer together but that would be the limit of their interaction outside sex. Showing any expectation of more would be the kiss of death — maybe literally. But fucking someplace safe like Kell's bedsit was better than risking getting caught in a public place. Their conversation would be simple. They'd fuck more than they'd talk. Kell had it all planned out.

He laughed. One fuck and he'd shifted from one last time to how many more times could they do it? Maybe they could fuck their way out of each other's head — assuming Gethin was feeling the same as him.

Gethin walked back into the bedroom, his dark hair wet, his eyelashes spikey. "Your turn."

When Kell emerged from the shower, he thought he'd be facing an empty room, but Gethin lay naked on the bed. His shock must have shown on his face because Gethin pushed himself up on his elbows.

"Want me to go?"

"No." Kell suspected he should have said yes, but he dropped down next to Gethin.

"I was surprised you brought me here," Gethin said.

"You can see why I didn't want to. I live in a dump."

"Your reason for not wanting me here has nothing to do with the condition of the place. But this place isn't you."

Kell's heart thumped hard. "You thought I was a rich boy?"

"You're friends with rich boys."

"Sometimes I make poor decisions." He shrugged and glanced around.

Gethin gave a brief smile. "This isn't what we agreed. We're not strangers if I know where you live. The game didn't last long."

"I'm bending the rules."

"Are we allowed conversation then?"

"A small amount." Kell stared into Gethin's startling eyes, let his gaze drift to his lips and wanted to kiss him again.

"Your place is no different to mine," Gethin said.

"Really?"

"Maybe the pattern of mould on the wall's a bit more interesting here. Patches of *aspergillus, cladosporium* and *stachybotrys atra.*"

Kell choked out a laugh. "Am I allowed to ask what you do apart from working for an event company?"

"Mould inspector. What about you?"

"I'm a Catholic priest."

Gethin smiled. "I'm damned then, and you with me."

"I'm a security guard." Kell paused. Telling him that wouldn't hurt.

"I think I'll pretend you're a priest. I like the idea of that. Next time, yeah? I'll play a straight guy, wear my glasses, and you can seduce me."

Kell smothered his moan. Gethin raised his eyebrows.

"Damn. I didn't quite manage to disguise that moan, did I?"

"Nope."

"Would you have phoned?" Kell wished he'd not asked the moment he had and to cover his embarrassment, he kept talking. "I wanted you to call me first but I thought, I'm going to be drawing my pension by the time he gets around to it. So I just cut out all that unnecessary *will he – won't he* crap."

"Yeah, I'd have phoned. I've had a busy couple of days."

Kell was about to reach for him when Gethin sat up.

"I should go," Gethin said. "Still have work to do."

Kell watched as he dressed, willing his cock to stay down but watching Gethin put his clothes on was so erotic he grabbed a pillow and dragged it over his crotch. Gethin turned and looked at him, dropped his gaze to the pillow and then lifted it to Kell's face.

"Forgive me father for I have sinned," Kell said.

"You only get forgiven if you sin again, my son."

Kell chuckled. "Good. See you."

Gethin walked out and Kell sighed.

This was all they'd ever have. A fun non-relationship. No commitment but hot sex. Kell didn't like that niggle in his belly that told him it was already no longer enough.

I want to know him. I want to know what he likes, what he doesn't like. I want to know what kind of man he is. I want to know if he could like me for more than sex.

Chapter Twelve

Gethin had been surprised by Kell's place. He'd expected something better from a guy who'd been a guest at a party attended by the rich and privileged. The birthday boy had talked about Kell as his best friend. It just went to prove Gethin had been right to think again when he'd made a judgment about the guests he was serving.

He made his way back to the tube, disappointed their encounter hadn't lasted longer, but knowing he'd done the right thing because the questions bubbling in his head were driving him crazy. Questions that would likely never be answered.

Was Kell happy being a security guard? What did he guard? Who did he guard? What bad decisions Kell had made that shifted him from moving in circles that encompassed Denborough Castle to living in a mouldy bedsit in London? Even if Kell had lost his money, what about his family? Did he have parents or siblings?

Gethin groaned. *Think about something else.*

What music did he listen to? *Oh shit. What am I doing?* Where did Kell go on holiday? Had he had adventures? Did he want to have them? Who had he been out with before? Before what? *Me? He isn't going out with me.* Why didn't Kell want more than zipless fucks? Because the guy was hurting? Why?

Shut the fuck up. Since Gethin didn't want to answer any questions of that sort, there was no point even *thinking* them. He walked faster. He should have known there was no way he could have a casual relationship. Maybe he'd have managed it if he'd been able to turn off the investigator in him. Their own personal Grindr was great in theory, but it didn't feel right. Gethin was already too interested, too invested.

A small selection of clothes hung in Kell's wardrobe, nothing expensive, there was a pile of paperbacks under the bed and a cupboard full of ready meals next to a small hob and microwave. But the furniture was old and tired, there were no photos, none of the paraphernalia he'd expected to see apart from the newish looking TV. The place was clean, ignoring the mould, but...soulless. A place Kell could leave in an instant. That was what had felt wrong, though Gethin sensed it was deliberate and suspected it had something to do with Kell's wish for sex without strings. What was he running from apart from commitment? *Who had hurt him?*

A security guard's pay wouldn't be high, so that explained the bedsit, but something still felt off. Gethin hadn't survived as long as he had by not listening to his intuition. Gethin didn't think Kell had a problem with drugs or alcohol. He had far better muscle definition than Gethin. Toned as if he spent time at the gym.

Gethin pattered down the steps of the tube station with questions still bubbling and was so distracted, he almost stepped onto the wrong train. He moved across to the other platform and leaned against the wall.

Why did Kell want nothing more than quick fucks?

Shit, I'm such a hypocrite when that's all I can have. After Jonnie cheated on him, Gethin had been too hurt to risk his heart again, then after the accident...a whole load of emotions had gotten in the way of everything and he'd done without sex. He thought there was almost no chance of Jonnie hearing about Kell, but what if he did? That fucking six degrees of separation. *Anything* was possible. Except not Jonnie walking again. Gethin couldn't bear to cause him more pain.

What about your pain?

I don't count.

He dropped into a seat on the train. Gethin's sense of guilt had wrapped wings about swirling resentment and the pair hung like twin albatrosses around his neck. It would be easy to lessen the load. Make that the last time he'd see Kell. He took out his phone, blocked Kell's calls and deleted his number, hoping it would make him feel better.

Instead, Gethin spent the rest of the day in a sullen mood, traipsing around London between various squats getting spat on, sworn at, and mocked. He'd handed out more than a hundred quid to persuade people to talk and keep a look out for Dieter. Maybe one of them would help him. It was difficult to get anyone to look properly at the photo. He'd hoped seeing Dieter in his school uniform might tug at a few heart strings. Gethin was respectful and polite, offered his card and said if they ever *did* see Dieter to please ask the teenager to phone home. There wasn't much more he could do.

What he'd not had by the end of the day was a call from Izabela and he wasn't sure what to make about that. A small part of him worried about her safety. While he no longer knew what to believe of what she'd told him, his gut said she was being coerced. But it was out of his hands now. He hoped Beckwith seized Charlton's computer while it was still intact and found the gun before it ended up in the Thames.

Since he was close to his office, Gethin decided to call in and collect his mail. He was hoping for a cheque from a job he'd completed last week. As he approached his building, he spotted the light on in his room. Gethin's pace didn't falter and he dropped his gaze back to the pavement. He stayed on the opposite side of the road and kept going, crossing much farther down before doubling back. He had a pass card for Clayton and Saunders, an architect partnership three buildings away, cloned from one he'd stolen then returned, and he let himself in. Gethin's pulse raced as he hurried up the stairs to the roof.

He looped the strap of his computer bag around his neck and rested for a moment before he approached the edge. He'd only used this route once, *before* he'd accepted Angel's offer of office space. Although Gethin knew Angel's suggestion was an opportunity he shouldn't turn down, making sure he had a safe exit was too ingrained in him to ignore. A childhood spent in care, being abused and beaten, had left him messed up. He'd run away more than any other kid he knew.

Gethin lowered himself to a gutter then crept up a slope. With a series of jumps and no small amount of inelegant scrambling he eventually reached the neighbouring roof, from where he could drop down onto his building. Not exactly parkour, that wasn't his specialty, but getting out of tight scrapes was.

Once he'd made it to the final roof, he left his bag tucked behind an air-conditioning unit, then silently headed down the stairs. He felt as though a scorpion was crawling over his skin, that prickle of dread telling him he could be in trouble or pain at any moment.

The door to Celebrations was closed, but the one to his office stood slightly ajar. Gethin remained motionless for several minutes, just listening, but heard nothing to alarm him. He tried the handle on the Celebrations door, found it locked, and walked down the corridor to his office where he shoved the door open with enough force to startle those inside and hit anyone standing behind.

No one was there. They'd trashed the place and gone. He didn't have to even think hard about who might be responsible. Whoever had paid, persuaded or threatened Izabela to get data from the computer. Or Charlton if he'd found out what Gethin had done. Gethin stood in the doorway and looked around, checking for anything added as well as items removed.

He didn't see any trip wires, cameras, explosives, but that didn't mean they weren't there. *Paranoid much?* Gethin shook his head at his idiocy but he was still careful. He took a few pictures with his phone. His computers were in pieces, the contents of his filing cabinet lay strewn over the floor, but the skirting board didn't appear to have been tampered with. Gethin was surprised he wasn't more pissed off. He wondered if part of him had expected it and the other part of him knew that in the grand scale of things, worse could have happened.

Calling the police wasn't something he particularly wanted to do. So much hassle when whoever did this was long gone, but his insurance wouldn't pay out if he didn't make the call. Plus he ought to tell Beckwith. As he stepped deeper into the room he spotted a note on his desk.

IF YOU CALL THE POLICE IT WON'T JUST BE YOUR
OFFICE THAT'S TRASHED. YOU KNOW WHAT WE WANT.
WE'LL BE IN TOUCH.

Gethin slid around the edge of the room, keeping away from
the window, wary of throwing a shadow. He crouched behind his
desk. The memory stick was still there. He left it, pushed the
skirting back into place and exited the room, setting the door
exactly as he'd found it. Why had the light been left on?
Carelessness? Was there any way they'd been able to see him in
there? Just in case, he hurried back to the roof.

 It wasn't a shock that his office had been discovered. He
didn't broadcast its location, but with a bit of judicious searching
of company records it could be found. Izabela knew the name of
his business, and *his* name though he'd only given Charlton his
middle name — Rhys, plus she had his telephone number. Finding
out where he *lived* was a different matter.

It wasn't an unreasonable assumption that whoever had
trashed his office might be waiting for him close by, either to
persuade him to give up the memory stick or to follow him to
where he might have stashed it. Gethin wondered if they'd
checked his computers before they destroyed them. But there was
no way they could open anything without his passwords.

Ten minutes later, after reversing the way he'd reached the
building, Gethin was walking down the street with his bag over
his shoulder. He hadn't even wanted to retrieve his bike in case it
was being watched. He called Beckwith but the guy didn't answer
so he left a message. Gethin returned to his bedsit by tube, getting
on and off trains at the last minute to make extra sure there was no
one following.

He walked past where he'd parked his car two streets away
from his flat. Even with a resident's permit a parking place was
hard to find. He couldn't see anyone watching so he returned to
his vehicle. He wasn't worried someone could be waiting for him
in his flat, but he *was* worried about a risk to Angel and Tilda, and
this was something better explained face to face.

Gethin stopped only to buy a bottle of red wine before he drove to Islington via a roundabout route. Parking was just as much as a nightmare there.

When he knocked on the door of Angel's house, a carefully restored early Georgian Grade Two listed townhouse, it was Henry who opened the door, a yapping dachshund under each arm.

Gethin brandished the bottle.

Henry gaped at him. "He didn't tell me he'd invited you for supper. I'll kill him. He's not back from his mother's. When he is, *then* I'll kill him."

"He didn't invite me to supper. I need a word with him."

"Ah right. Come in."

Once Henry had closed the door, he put the dogs down and Gethin bent to make a fuss of them. They rolled onto their backs, their tails wagging so furiously their bodies rotated on the smooth floor.

"They'd have you stroking their stomachs all day, the little tarts." Henry tsked. "Winston, Kennedy, leave the poor guy alone."

Gethin followed Henry to the kitchen. The house was magnificent. No muddle of styles, or garish features, the walls were shades of Farrow and Ball with splashes of colour coming from paintings and several expensive rugs scattered on the beautiful oak floor. Gethin suspected Henry had put his foot down on Angel's rainbow exuberance when it came to their home.

"The house is a tip," Henry said.

It wasn't. Henry swept up a pile of papers from the table and thrust a mug in the dishwasher. "Now it's not."

Gethin laughed.

"You can stay for supper. Lasagne's in the oven and there's plenty, but the price is you have to serve it as a butler in the buff. Every conversation I've had with Angel, he's managed to bring your arse into it. And your tattoo. I feel utterly deprived I haven't had the pleasure."

Gethin groaned. "He conned me into that."

Henry raised one eyebrow. "He can be very persuasive when it comes to backsides. Want a cup of tea or a glass of wine?"

Gethin wanted wine, but needed to keep his head clear. "Tea would great, thank you."

"Have a seat."

Gethin hung his bag and coat on the back of a chair and settled at the big oak table.

"How are you?" Henry asked.

"I've been better."

"Ah, that sounds ominous. How's business?"

"That could be better." Gethin sighed.

"Your website stats are healthy."

"Probably boosted by people admiring your creative work, rather than contemplating hiring me to catch their husbands having sex with another woman…or man."

Henry winced. "Is that the only type of work you're getting?"

"Mostly. It's what I expected, though I've just been hired to look for a missing teenager. Sadly, I'm not having much success."

Henry put the drinks on the table and sat down. "Tell me about it."

Gethin was glad to be distracted and went through what he knew about Dieter and where he'd looked so far.

"No inappropriate internet friends?" Henry asked.

"I had a look at his computer. There was nothing that worried me. He has four hundred friends on Facebook. No way can I check all those."

"What would you have done as a boy of his age if you'd needed to run?"

Gethin curled his toes in his shoes and made sure his face showed nothing. "Stayed in as cheap a place as I could find until I ran out of money. Gone to a hostel. Looked for a job. Been too easily persuaded that some old guy wanted to help me and not fuck me." *Shut up.*

Henry gave him a sharp look. "He might seek out others like him."

"I checked the squats I know of."

"No, I didn't mean runaways or the homeless. I was thinking of gay teenage boys. Maybe anyone gay. He'd feel safer in that environment even though he wouldn't be."

"He's too young for a bar or a club. He looks younger than he is." Gethin showed Henry his photo. "Jail bait."

Henry nodded. "Hmm. They'd still let him in a club. You said he likes to dance?"

Gethin groaned. "Yeah. You think I should check out all the gay clubs in London? I don't even know if he's in the city."

The dogs started to bark and Gethin tensed.

Henry put his hand on his shoulder. "It'll be Angel."

The door slammed. "I'm home," Angel called. "Get down, Winston. Yes, I love you too, Kennedy. Henry? Why aren't you here sniffing me as well? Are the dogs more pleased to see me than you are?"

"Yes, they always are and we have a visitor," Henry called back. "Watch what you say."

"I know it's not my mother." Angel's eyes widened when he came to the study. "Quick, Henry. Get your clothes off, and we'll tie him up. Damn, I got that the wrong way round."

Henry laughed.

"I'm serious," Angel said. "Alternatively, I need you upstairs. Now." He purred.

"Have some wine." Henry poured him a glass.

"To what do we owe this pleasure?" Angel sat at the table.

"My office has been ransacked."

"What?" Henry gasped.

Angel put his wine down without tasting it. "Good grief."

"I wasn't followed here," Gethin said. "I made sure of that."

"Followed? What the fuck?" Angel straightened. "Henry, sit down. Gethin's going to tell us what's happened, but knowing him it will be like extracting blood from a stone."

131

Not this time. *This* they needed to hear. "Someone broke in, smashed all my equipment, tipped over the filing cabinet and scattered the contents. They also left a message suggesting it won't just be my office that's trashed if I go to the police."

"Oh my God." Angel drank half his glass at one go. "*Cry woe, destruction, ruin and decay.*"

Henry glared at Angel. "Richard II. Not appropriate."

"Why not?" Gethin asked.

"The next line is *The worst is death, and death will have his day.*" Henry sucked his cheeks. "What have you done?"

"It's better you don't know."

Angel frowned. "Something illegal?"

"I came across something…shady when I was downloading data from a guy's computer."

"Was that when Tilda had the phone call?" Angel asked.

Gethin nodded. "I've handed a couple of memory sticks to the police, but whoever the bad guys are, they want the information, and they didn't find it in my office. I'm hoping the police will sort it out, but in the meantime you need to be careful."

He pinned his gaze on Angel. "I don't know how much the guy or guys who wrecked the office know about me. I used an imaginary party company as cover but my office is next to the real thing, next to you. They might figure out you know me, and it could put you in danger. Tilda needs to switch off that phone, take out the SIM card and chuck it away. You and she are the only ones who know about our arrangement, right?"

"Yes," Angel said.

"There's no point anyone denying I'm the PI down the corridor if people come asking, but you should stick to just being my landlord. If they mention Party Solutions, deny all knowledge and look outraged."

"I'm good at looking outraged," Angel said.

Henry nodded. "He is."

The two exchanged a smile.

"I had a gun pulled on me." Gethin needed Angel to understand how serious this was.

"Oh my God." Angel gaped at him.

"The guy thought I was having sex with his girlfriend, but even so… Now all this has happened, it's clear there's something—"

"*Rotten in the state of Denmark,*" Angel muttered.

Even Gethin knew that one. Hamlet. "Macbeth."

Angel glared and Henry chuckled. "He's winding you up."

"It's Romeo and Juliet, isn't it?" Gethin said.

"Please." Angel put his head in his hands.

"I called the police about the damage to my office. I'm waiting for them to call back. It might be helpful if you discovered what had happened tomorrow and called them too. The door's ajar. Yours was still locked by the way."

"Christ." Angel's shoulders slumped even further.

Gethin pushed to his feet.

"Sit down," Henry said. "You're not going anywhere until you've at least eaten."

Gethin sat again. "I've brought trouble to your door, Angel, and I'm sorry. I'll find an office somewhere else."

"No you won't." Angel straightened and poured more wine. "You're not the bad person here. It might be wise to lie low for a while, but the moment this is over, business as usual."

Gethin started when his mobile vibrated and he pulled it out. He wanted it to be Beckwith, but it was Zena Hoehn, Dieter's mother.

"I hope I'm not disturbing you," she said. "I just had a call from Sam's mum. She was about to wash one of Sam's jackets and found a card in the pocket for a nightclub in Vauxhall called No Escape."

Gethin tensed. That was one of the clubs Charlton did the accounts for.

"Sam's admitted he and Dieter have been there twice, once when Sam's mother thought Sam was staying with us and the other when I thought Dieter was staying with them. I know it's a long shot, but maybe you could look there?"

"Okay. Leave it with me." It *had* to be a coincidence Charlton was linked to No Escape. Gethin did *not* like coincidences.

Henry put the lasagne on the table and passed out the plates. "Not the police?"

"No, it was the mother of the teenager I'm looking for. Apparently the boys have been twice to a club called No Escape. She wants me to check it out. You could be right, Henry. Maybe Dieter's found a place to dance."

"No Escape?" Angel blew out a breath. "Have you ever been there?"

"No, have you?" Gethin asked.

"Once upon a time, darling. I don't need to trawl now." He winked at Henry. "I've caught my big fish. The club's in Vauxhall. Changed hands a couple of times since I last went and from what I hear it's gone upmarket, though that wouldn't be difficult. I wonder if it retained the Back Passage."

"What the hell is that?" Henry asked.

Angel raised his eyebrows. "It's not hard to guess. A corridor at the rear of the club with rooms where almost anything goes. At least it *was*. It was very seedy twenty years ago. A man called Silas Warner owns it now. I went to the same school as him. Up to fifteen years ago I knew him…quite well. He had a preference for young boys, though not too young. When I no longer looked youthful enough, he turned his back on me. I used to be a bit of a drama queen and he had a mean streak."

"Used to be?" Henry said. "You're not still?"

"*Faith, he has gone unto the taming school.*" Angel gave him a coy look.

"Taming of the Shrew?" Henry said.

Angel beamed.

"I don't recall you mentioning Warner," Henry said.

"Because he's someone to forget. He's arrogant, ruthless and I…" Angel took a deep breath. "The last time I spoke to him was a couple of years ago. He asked me to arrange a party. I lied and said I was far too busy."

Henry raised his eyebrows. "You really *don't* like him then."

"He's the type who'd step on the backs of women and children, and kick them in the teeth if it meant he could be the first onto a lifeboat. I hope your boy's *not* there, not if he's come to the attention of Warner. He's rather…possessive with his toys. Well, he was."

Gethin thought about Dieter's innocent appeal and swallowed hard. "I better go and look."

"Tonight?" Henry asked.

"If they're open."

Angel tapped buttons on his phone. "Seems they have themed nights. Sunday it's… leather." He put out his tongue and panted. "You…in chaps…bare chest…bare arse… Henry and I will go with you. Eat fast, darling."

"We're not going," Henry said.

"No, you're not." Gethin forked up a mouthful of lasagne.

"Spoilsport." Angel glowered, then his face brightened. "We can at least get you dressed in the right gear."

"I'm not taking my trousers off."

Angel sighed. "You suck the fun out of everything."

Chapter Thirteen

While Angel searched for what he claimed was the perfect outfit, hopefully some not too garish leather vest—plain black with no chains, studs or sequins—Gethin Googled No Escape and its owner. He found plenty of images of Warner who was a good-looking guy, tall and thin with lupine features, a sharp toothed grin and hooded eyes. His thick hair was slicked back in most shots, smooth and dark as seal skin. Warner had bought the club five years ago and had apparently spent vast sums on it.

He owned another venue in Manchester with the same name, one in Leeds called Hell's Mouth and another in Newcastle named Heaven's Gate. None of Warner's clubs used DJs or live music, instead play lists were streamed from the business headquarters in Isleworth. Gethin had thought bands and DJs would always be an integral part of the club scene but obviously not in Warner's venues. *Shame.*

All the clubs were on Charlton's spreadsheets. As were Warner's other businesses. The gay and straight porn websites, an online 'adult' store selling everything to do with sex: clothing, toys, DVDs, and a whole range of equipment from St Andrew's crosses to nipple clamps. Warner was also named as a director of a handful of X-rated gay movies.

None of that meant he was a crook, but from what Angel had said about him, it appeared to be a good match between an unpleasant nightclub owner and an equally unpleasant accountant. Gethin was worried to have two jobs with connections to the same nightclub, but he couldn't see any way that this was a set up.

The last thing he felt like doing was going to a noisy club to ask questions about Dieter, but returning to his bedsit held even less attraction. Though when he saw what Angel wanted him to put on, he changed his mind.

"That is *not* an outfit." Gethin stared at the strips of leather in Angel's hand. "And you can forget that." He pointed to a leather jockstrap.

"Fine." Angel tossed the latter aside but advanced on Gethin with the rest. "You need to blend in."

"I can go in my normal clothes."

Angel huffed. "And speak to Warner, show him this boy's picture and ask if he's seen him?"

"That was the plan."

"What sort of PI does that?" Angel looked aghast. "Subterfuge, darling. Know what the word means? You need to wander round the club looking for him, and if the young man is there, have a quiet word in his ear and whisk him out without Warner seeing, because if Warner has his eye on him, he won't let him just leave even if he wants to."

Gethin had the feeling there was something he wasn't getting here. Henry had his arm around Angel's shoulders, hugging him. What had they been talking about upstairs?

"Really, Gethin, don't go dressed as you are now," Angel said. "You won't get into the club let alone grab a chance to talk to anyone."

It was a good point.

Gethin parked a couple of streets away from No Escape. He was lucky to find a spot so close and it made it less of a hardship to leave his coat in the car on the basis that if he had to leave in a hurry, he might not have chance to get it back from the cloakroom. But he shivered with cold as he walked to the club. If it had been any farther, there was no way he'd be walking around in this fucking harness, but maybe he should be grateful it wasn't naked dance night.

Well, I wouldn't have come then, would I?

He was already regretting letting Angel fasten him into this black leather contraption. He hoped it was easier to take off than put on or he'd be banging on Angel's door and waking the bastard up in a couple of hours.

He'd protested as Angel had wrapped it around him, but had accepted that wearing something to help him blend in was a good idea. Though the way the leather crossed his chest and back reminded him of a dog harness. When he'd caught his reflection in the mirror as he was being fastened into it, he had a sudden vision of Kell fucking him from behind, hanging onto the straps, and his stomach had lurched. Angel *and* Henry's open-mouthed gazes when he was finally clipped into it had Gethin's stomach lurching again. The pair couldn't get him out of the house quickly enough. Not hard to guess why.

When he saw there was a queue to get into the club, he groaned. Luckily he didn't have to wait long and the moment he stepped inside, his shivers subsided under the blast of heat. He paid the entry fee, had his hand stamped, paid more to cover all the extras including the Back Passage and had his hand stamped again. If he was going to look for Dieter, he might as well check everywhere. He hoped one visit would be enough, but even if Dieter *had* come to the attention of Warner, there was no guarantee he'd be in the club that night. Gethin suddenly felt as if he was on a fool's errand.

He bought an expensive beer from one of the bare-chested, good looking barmen who all wore collars with sharp metal spikes, then headed for a gloomy corner of the club where he could stand with his back to the wall. He let his gaze roam over the main dance floor as he sipped from the bottle, telling himself to make the drink last. The other club employees wore a uniform of black jeans and black T-shirts with the words No Escape in white letters on the back and front. They were mostly big bulky guys who didn't smile, unlike those working on the bar who smiled all the time and looked as though every moment they weren't working was spent at the gym creating perfect abs and pecs.

Leather night hadn't sounded too bad, uncomfortable as this harness was, but Gethin wondered if Angel had either made a mistake or tricked him because there was a lot more than leather trousers, studded belts and spikey collars on show this evening. He'd spotted a couple of naked guys — well, naked apart from cages around their cocks — being led around the club by chains attached to the only other thing they wore — silver bars through their nipples. Their backsides were covered with red wheals. Close to Gethin a guy kneeling at the feet of another had his chest and arms restrained by rope that was intricately knotted. It looked tight enough to be painful, but even if it wasn't, Gethin would panic if he was tied up like that, unable to move his arms. He didn't cope well with restraints, particularly anything over his head.

Gethin turned down three invitations to dance. None of the three guys recognized Dieter. This was *not* Gethin's scene and it was hard to pretend it was. He took out his phone, Googled the club again and this time clicked onto the schedule of events. He gritted his teeth when he saw Angel *had* lied. *Angel, you fucking bastard.* He sent him a text. *Can't w8 2 show U how much I've learned about BDSM. I'll bring my new whip and demonstrate.*

There was a real mix of ages in the club and the older guys weren't always the dominant ones. He saw a couple of cocky young men leading submissive fifty year olds around. This somehow didn't seem like the night he'd find the teen. There had been no sign on his computer of an interest in BDSM. Some gay porn in the history but vanilla stuff and no saved downloads. He mentally groaned at the idea of returning for several nights to make sure the kid wasn't here. If Warner had taken a shine to him, it might be easier to watch the man's home.

Gethin thought about what he'd been like in his teens. Unloved, uncared for and easily flattered by the attention of older men. Dieter wasn't unloved or uncared for, but if he was just finding his wings, places like this that attracted a mix of cultures and a wide social range, young and old guys and those in between, were an almost irresistible lure. Gethin had always hoped for a prince, but they'd all been frogs. Almost everyone here wanted the same thing in one form or another. A blow job, a fuck or some fumbling in the bathroom, cocks rubbed together, mouths pressed together, a few moments of mutual delight. Gethin doubted much had changed except now the venues were less seedy and he was older and wiser.

A guy his age with a bushy beard stepped in front of Gethin. "Dance?"

"No."

"Fuck?"

"No."

"Recognize him?" Gethin held up his phone.

"No."

The guy moved on. Cool indifference was part of the tango, though not part of Gethin's. He couldn't see the point in playing hard to get when he had no interest in being got, but in in any case, he was working, not here to pick someone up, despite Angel pressing him to make the most of the opportunity. Gethin wondered if he could tell Jonnie about this, how he felt like a trussed up chicken, whether it would make the guy laugh or upset him. It was getting harder and harder to strike the right balance when he visited and now the subject of helping him die had reared its ugly head, Gethin dreaded going even more.

The combination of the music and frantic light show was on the way to giving Gethin a headache. The beat made the walls and floor vibrate, and multi-coloured circles spun and collided on every surface and body. The dance floor heaved, dozens of sweaty men writhing against each other, some with lips locked, many with hands clutching butts or fondling groins. Gethin vaguely thought it should have turned him on, but it didn't. Many of the glistening male torsos were impressive, but those guys knew how good they looked and that sort of arrogance left him cold. He preferred builds like…Kell's.

"Haven't seen you in here before," someone said.

Gethin took a small swig from his beer and didn't answer the shorter — older — guy in front of him.

"You look hot," the man said.

I am, but not in the way you mean.

"Can I buy you a drink?"

"No." He took out his phone and showed the picture of Dieter. "Seen him in here?"

"No. You looking to sub? I can—"

"No."

"Pity."

Gethin watched him walk away. Short, stocky, fair and forty, not his type. Not that he was looking. Even if he wasn't going to see Kell anymore—and he wasn't, he couldn't now he'd deleted his number—he had no space in his life for another guy. It would get too complicated, too distracting. But casual sex wasn't as easy as it sounded, not for him.

You've still got his number in your texts.

I don't have to look at it.

Just reminding you.

Gethin gritted his teeth. *I can't even fool myself.*

He turned his attention to the sides of the room where groups of men were gathered, heads together, mouths opening and closing as they tried to talk above the heavy music pulsing from the speakers. In a few minutes, he'd have a wander and see if he could spot Dieter.

"Wanna dance?" A bare chested, barely legal youngster with nipple piercings and a wonky smile swayed in front of him.

"No." Gethin showed him the photo. "Seen him?"

"Why bother with him? You can fuck me."

"Have you seen him?"

"Might have. Want me to suck you?"

"No."

"Dickhead." He staggered off.

Gethin took another pull from his beer and realised he'd drunk it all. He went back to the bar and bought another that he definitely wouldn't drink. The same barman served him—went out of his way to serve him.

He smiled at Gethin. "You made that last."

"I'm driving."

"You look good in that harness."

"You look good in that collar."

The guy laughed.

"Seen this kid around?" Gethin held up his phone.

The barman's gaze flittered to the left. "Yeah. Put that away. Don't let Warner know you're looking for him."

Gethin's pulse jumped. The guy turned to serve someone else.

When the barman finished he came back to Gethin. "If you're around when we close, want to get breakfast?"

"Maybe. Is Warner here tonight?"

The guy sighed. "Standing next to a booth on the far left. Sharp suit, dark hair, red tie. And don't tell him I told you."

Gethin wandered to a point from which he could see the booth without looking obvious and spotted Dieter. That was the good news. The bad was that club owner had a possessive hand on the boy's shoulder and Dieter was looking at Warner as if all his Christmases and birthdays had come at once. Judging by the designer gear and the chunky watch on Dieter's arm maybe they had.

Warner was gripping Dieter's shoulder with sharp, bony fingers, laughing at something one of the guys with them was saying. Gethin didn't think much of his chances of getting Dieter on his own so he could talk to him let alone persuade him to leave his sugar daddy and return to his anxious mother, but he had to try.

He scanned the heaving dance floor, keeping Dieter in the periphery of his vision, hoping the club wasn't going to live up to its name. Why had Warner called it No Escape? No escape once you were in the guy's clutches? No escape without paying a fortune for drinks? No escape if you were stupid enough to try and wrangle a kid away from the club owner? Maybe the best Gethin would manage was whispering to Dieter to call his mother and let her know he was still alive. *Better than nothing.*

Watching Warner with Dieter, Gethin found it increasingly difficult to imagine a scenario in which he'd spirit the kid away and return him to the family home at which point Dieter would burst into tears and admit what an idiot he'd been. Unless Dieter *wanted* to leave, there was little Gethin could do except confirm he was still breathing.

"No," Gethin said before the guy who'd slid in front of him had opened his mouth.

The guy glared and stomped off.

Well, there was *something* Gethin could do. Dieter was only seventeen. Old enough to leave home, but too young to be in an over-eighteens club and too young to be drinking, though Gethin hadn't seen him drink anything. The police would remove Dieter from the premises, but they'd be ineffective at keeping him out, especially if Warner wanted him. Sadly, Dieter *wasn't* too young to get into bed with the club owner.

When Warner patted Dieter on the backside and Dieter moved away, Gethin straightened, wondering if this was his chance to catch him on his own. But Dieter headed for the centre of the dance floor and climbed onto a small stage with a pole. A roar went up when he toed off his shoes, then shimmied out of his jeans and T-shirt to leave himself wearing nothing but his watch and tight silver shorts, his semi-hard cock clearly outlined beneath the material. He took hold of the pole and slowly turned around it as he waited for the music to change. Warner had followed Dieter to the stage, his gaze fixed on him. Everyone stopped to watch, and Gethin quickly understood why.

Dieter was talented. With pale, smooth, shining skin and a shy smile on his face, he wrapped himself around the pole like a snake, curving, arching and twisting his body. He hung upside down, held in place by one leg, then supported his weight using one hand. He bent so far back he looked as if he'd snap in two. Gethin wondered if he'd ever been that supple. This kid was made of rubber. The transition from one position to another, from one move to another was seamless, in perfect time with the music. Sexy, graceful and beautiful.

Gethin had to remind himself Dieter was only seventeen and this was not appropriate. Having him dance like this was like throwing chum into a sea of sharks. Gethin could almost feel the testosterone filling the air. Dieter's mother had proudly showed Gethin her son's medals for gymnastics. She wouldn't be impressed to see him twerking, rolling and bucking his hips, simulating sex, dragging his hands down his body, teasing with every breath, every move. This kid didn't lack confidence. Gethin had rarely moved away from the wall at his age. Not dissimilar to his current position.

Dieter ended his routine by slithering into Warner's arms and the guy laughed, but when Dieter reached for Warner's drink, probably scotch, the guy moved it out of reach and tsked. Gethin lost sight of them as the dance floor refilled with men grinding and bumping to the pounding beat. He took a sip of the beer he'd been nursing and almost spat the warm liquid back into the bottle. Engineering a chance to talk to Dieter without getting his face kicked in by one of Warner's men would be tricky, but first he needed to find him again. Leaving the safety of the corner, he sidled around the room. When he spotted Dieter, he wished he hadn't.

The club owner had his guys positioned around him but it wasn't enough to disguise what was happening. Dieter on his knees, Warner's cock in his mouth, Warner's hand behind his head, shoving Dieter down hard. They might have been partially obscured by a pillar, but this was risky. Though who was going to report them? Gethin sucked in his cheeks as Warner's head went back, his teeth bared in a grimace.

"Hi, gorgeous," someone said at Gethin's ear.

Oh fuck, not again.

A tall black guy wearing virtually nothing nudged Gethin's hip with his own and fluttered false eyelashes. "Dance with me?"

"No," Gethin said.

"Want to fuck?"

"No."

"Why not?"

"You're not my type."

"Is it 'cos I is black?"

Gethin glanced at him, but the guy was smiling.

"Hey, the line sometimes works. I'm good. What do you say?"

"No."

The guy scowled and stamped. "Why not?"

"I'm not in the mood," Gethin said.

He glared and walked away.

When Gethin looked for Dieter, he had his clothes back on and had moved to a booth with Warner, two guys sitting opposite. The biceps of one were bigger than Dieter's waist. Gethin wondered if he was the minder of the other guy who wore a sharp suit and had an Eastern European look to him. Wasn't hard to imagine the sort of business they were discussing. Nothing legal.

If this was Gethin's lucky night, Dieter would at some point need the bathroom and he could follow. If no chance to talk to him arose, then he'd tell his mother where he was and maybe offer to come here with her.

Chapter Fourteen

As Marek shoved Kell against the wall in Warner's office, his head collided with the edge of the door and Kell sucked in a breath at the bite of pain.

"What have I done now?" Kell asked.

Marek's rage worried him. Though Marek in a good mood worried him too.

"Nothing. You not cause. You cure."

Being the cure *should* be less painful than being the cause, but Kell still shivered. Marek grabbed him around the back of the neck, pressing his fingers into the tender flesh and at the same time thrust one his legs between Kell's, forcing him back so he was immobilized. The pressure against Kell's balls increased to the point of pain as Marek ground his thigh against him.

Struggling to get free was a mistake. Marek crushed more of him with his weight until Kell thought his ribs would crack under the strain.

"What's wrong?" Kell forced out the words hoping Marek might let something slip.

"Something easy turned into something difficult."

"Can I help?"

"Yeah. Suck my cock," Marek snarled.

Kell had known that was coming. Because the sooner he cooperated, the quicker it would be over, he made no protest as he was pushed to his knees. The sound of Marek unzipping his trousers sent shudders rippling down his spine, but he did what Marek wanted, pulled out the guy's cock and started sucking. Kell turned off as best he could. This wasn't him. This was his job—sort of. Just like any horrible job people had to do. Unblocking toilets, wading through sewers, testing cat food. *A few more weeks and I'm done. If not. I will be done.*

"Look at me," Marek said.

Marek stared down as Kell looked up. At least when Kell had the guy's cock in his mouth, he didn't have to say anything, call Marek sir or express gratitude for being used.

It didn't take long for Marek to come, but Kell had no idea whether than was what the guy had wanted or not.

"I like to see you struggle to swallow," Marek said.

Kell would have liked to see Marek struggle too, with that big black dildo rammed into his mouth. When Kell had licked him clean, tucked his cock in his shorts and zipped him up, he pushed to his feet.

"Better now?" Kell risked saying. "Or do you need an aspirin?"

His answer was a snort.

"You still look angry," Kell said. "Can I help?" *Give me something. Tell me something to make what I did worth it.*

"Stupid people make me angry."

"Did I tell you I have a degree?"

Marek's lips twitched.

"Astrology. Went straight for the hard stuff. I bet you're a Virgo."

Marek laughed and Kell breathed a sigh of relief that he got the joke.

"Anything else I can do?" Kell asked. Maybe one day something useful would slide from this guy's mouth. "Shoulder massage? Rub your back? Do your horoscope?" *Threaten to chop someone's nuts off?* Hopefully not that.

"What did I tell you about being kind?"

Kell shrugged. "You haven't had one of my massages."

Marek threaded his fingers in Kell's hair. "Your smart mouth condemns then saves you. You better make sure it keeps saving you." He yanked at Kell's hair and Kell yelped. "Relieve Josef, then Alec while they take breaks."

By the time Kell came back inside, he was half-frozen. He leaned against the long, curved bar, and stared out over the heaving dance floor keeping his eyes peeled for trouble and faces he recognized. He let his gaze drift past the dancers and settle on the booth where Warner, the sick, conniving fucktard, sat with his arm around his latest toy, playing with the young guy's flyaway hair, occasionally tugging hard enough to make the teen wince. Kell sighed.

He checked to see where Marek was before he let his gaze return to the booth. Two men sat opposite Warner, and Kell managed to get a photo of them. He sent it straight to his boss, then deleted it from his phone. As Kell stared at the booth, Dieter glanced up as if he sensed his attention, and Kell turned the other way. *Ignore me, kid, or you'll land both of us in the shit.*

"Hi," said a guy at Kell's side. "Can I buy you a drink?"

"Get lost."

"Well fuck you," the man snapped and stormed off.

No, thanks.

"You're not being nice." The voice and hot breath against his ear set every nerve in Kell's body tingling, the air suddenly electric with the fear of discovery, the threat of violence. *Fuck!* Had Marek seen him take the picture?

"I'm not nice." Kell turned to face him.

Marek stared at him with no expression on his face. "Warner is paying you to be nice."

"Warner is paying me to make sure everyone plays by the rules, not for me to be nice."

"You should have more respect for customers."

"I'm not paid to dance with them. I don't like dancing. But for you I'd make an exception. Tango?" Kell held out his hand.

Marek's cheek twitched. "Careful, smart mouth." He walked away.

I'm an idiot. Pissing off Marek would never end well. The guy wasn't jealous, was he? Kell shivered. He hoped that wasn't the case. He turned back to the room and began scanning, letting his attention fleetingly settle on every guy, making a snap judgment before he checked out the next. But unlike the rest of those in here

148

appearing to be doing the same thing, Kell didn't have the same motive. He wasn't looking for a possible hook up, or his one true love—*as if*—but for faces he recognized, both known villains as well as guys who might say the wrong thing and cause trouble for him or for Warner for entirely different reasons.

"Like to dance?" Someone slipped a hand over his thigh and squeezed. Kell grabbed the slender wrist.

"No."

Kell turned to face Tula, the Kenyan, who as usual was dressed in some slip of bright coloured material arranged around his hips and showing a clear outline of his oversized cock. In the country legally. Now working for Warner. But he'd just taken something illegal considering his dilated pupils. Hooked in more ways than one.

"I'm working," Kell said.

"I've never seen you dance." Tula pouted.

"So you know there's no point asking me. Was it Marek's suggestion?"

The guy huffed and sashayed off. It was part of Tula's job to get patrons to dance and buy drinks, to use the back rooms, roof terrace, video room, and dungeon, anything to persuade them to part with more of their cash. Not technically part of Kell's job but still expected of him. Kell swept his gaze over the dance floor while ensuring Warner, Dieter and the two men stayed in his peripheral vision.

A kid as young as Dieter shouldn't be in here, let alone be the plaything of a bastard like Warner. Kell knew he'd already shown too much interest in the teen who was currently out of bounds to everyone, but he wouldn't stay that way if Warner was true to form, according to what one of the barmen had told him. Once he tired of his toys, he passed them to others. Kell would have liked to whisk the kid out of there but he couldn't—not yet.

Kell took a slow stroll around the room. As he turned to glance back at the booth, he froze in shock. What the fuck was Gethin doing in the club? *Did he follow me?* What the hell was he

149

wearing? *Christ.* Hip-hugging tight black trousers and a black leather studded chest harness, the strips of leather framing his pecs and shoulders.

For a long moment, Kell forgot the heavy beat pummelling his eardrums, forgot why he was here, forgot everything because his head was filled with a desire to drag the guy into the alley at the rear of the club, grip the leather straps, and fuck him through the wall. *Jesus. Get a grip.* He squashed the flare of lust, wondering how he should play this. Maybe pretend to not know him, to be unconcerned by his presence? Then he registered Gethin was staring at the booth *he* was watching. Staring at Dieter and Warner. *Oh shit. What the fuck was happening?*

Kell didn't *know* Gethin was going to cause a problem, but he sensed it. As Dieter stood up, Gethin moved forward and Kell strode straight through the middle of the dance floor, knocking men aside to intercept Gethin before he reached the booth. Kell registered Warner had pulled a sulky-looking Dieter down onto the seat and it belatedly occurred to him that Gethin could have simply been heading for the Back Passage, but Kell couldn't take the risk.

"Need help?" Kell asked.

Gethin swivelled to face him, looked him up and down, and said, "No."

A shocked awareness that he'd been judged and found wanting had Kell hesitating long enough for Gethin to pass the booth and continue toward the rooms at the rear. Kell watched him go. Gethin was pissed off. He couldn't blame him. Not that Kell had said *where* he was a security guard, but still. The leather straps crossing Gethin's back looked like a spider's web and Kell's cock went fully hard behind his zipper. *Fuck it.*

"Everything okay?" Marek materialized at Kell's side.

Shit. Storming across the dance floor like that, shoving guys out of the way had sent antennae twirling. Marek was like a shark sensing blood in the water—and probably blood in Kell's dick—from miles away.

"Yep," Kell said.

"Is he trouble?" Marek asked.

"Neh." Kell turned his head, hiding his erection, and pasted a grin on his face. "Just going to ask him where he bought that harness."

"You thought he was trouble," Marek said. "So did I. Check him out. Just in case."

Cursing Marek's keen eyes, Kell did as he was told. He spotted Gethin showing his wrist to Huginn. Kell followed and nodded to the bouncer who pulled open the door.

The Back Passage was lined on either side with rooms anyone could use if they paid extra and had the stamp to prove it. Most of the rooms had large viewing windows for those who preferred to watch rather than play. A quick glance at the men huddled around the windows and open doors revealed no sign of Gethin, and Kell was surprised. Unless he'd already arranged to play, it was a bit fast to have entered a room. Even in this dark world there were courtesies to be observed.

Hoarse grunts, groans and the sounds of whips cracking punched through the dampened music as Kell started along the polished concrete floor of the dimly lit black tiled corridor. He tensed at a sudden shrill cry of pain. It was impossible to tell whether anyone was really in trouble. He just had to accept guys came to these rooms by choice. And on BDSM night, if they screamed, it was because they wanted to be made to scream.

Stairs at the far end were guarded by Muninn who was just as broad, just as sullen, and had nuts and bolts tattooed either side of his thick neck. The guys weren't really called Huginn and Muninn. Those were the names of Odin's ravens, but it sort of fit in Kell's head. They were Warner's eyes and ears. The stairs led up to rooms to rent for private parties and up another level there was a roof terrace that gave passengers on passing trains an occasional thrill. Kell had sussed out alternate exits should he ever need them. If this place caught fire, he wanted to know which way to run.

But no rooms had been booked upstairs tonight so Gethin couldn't have gone up there, and the way into the dungeon was at the other side of the club. Which meant he had to be inside one of these rooms where men of all ages, shapes and sizes indulged in everything you could imagine and whole lot you likely couldn't. The air stank of sweat, come and piss with an underlying sickly odour of whatever air freshener the cleaners had sprayed. Sometimes Kell could smell the coppery tang of blood.

His eyes adjusted to the low light as he kept moving down the corridor, going from side to side, pushing his way to the front to check each room in turn, waiting until he could see the face of every participant before he moved on. When he got back to the door and hadn't seen Gethin, he was puzzled. He went through to the main dance floor.

"A guy in a leather harness come out?" Kell asked Huginn.

Huginn shook his head, though that didn't mean he was telling the truth. Kell went back inside and took a closer look in each room on the second pass but didn't spot Gethin. Back on the other side of the door, Warner had moved out of the booth and now stood at the bar with Tula hanging off his arm. Dieter and the two guys had gone. Had Warner given Dieter to the two men to play with? And where the fuck was Gethin?

What the fuck was Kell doing in here? Even as Gethin had walked away, he knew he was being unreasonable. Why shouldn't Kell be in here? Not quite the security guard job Gethin had imagined, but so what? Plus they weren't anything to each other but a convenience, and not even that because they'd met for the last time. Not that Kell knew.

Seeing Kell had thrown him, and Gethin had been rude, but what was done was done. He didn't want to talk to Kell. He didn't want to risk losing a chance to talk to Dieter. Suspecting Kell would follow him into the back rooms, Gethin slipped behind the door. When Kell moved inside, Gethin edged out again hidden at the back of an entering group before the door closed.

He bought another beer and found a place to stand with a reasonable view of the dance floor. What was he supposed to say if Kell approached him again? *Fuck off, I'm working?* He was supposed to be a party planner. *Fuck off, I'm looking for a hook up?* Maybe he should just tell him he didn't want to see him anymore. Maybe Kell had already got that message from Gethin's curt dismissal and there'd be no need to say anything.

When Dieter leaned against the wall next to Gethin, his face glistening under a thin sheen of perspiration, Gethin only just managed to smother his gasp of astonishment. Close up, the teen was even better looking, his soft brown eyes flecked with gold and framed by mascara covered lashes, his smile genuine because he hadn't yet been sucked in too deep by the company he was keeping. It could only be a matter of time.

"Not seen you in here before." Dieter stared at Gethin's chest. "Cool harness."

"Thanks."

"*Have* you been here before?"

"No," Gethin said.

"Why tonight?"

He sounded genuinely curious and Gethin shrugged. "Book club was cancelled."

In Dieter's giggle, Gethin caught a glimpse of the teenager he really was.

"You read then?" Dieter asked.

"I try. Not the long words obviously."

The kid laughed again and moved a little closer. Gethin edged the other way. Dieter's attention kept straying toward the bar where Warner stood with his hand on the backside of the tall black guy in the mini sarong who'd earlier approached Gethin.

"A friend of yours?" Gethin asked.

"Who?" Dieter spun to face him.

"Warner or the black kid?"

"Tula?" Dieter sneered. "Not my friend. I'm with Warner. Just so you know."

Gethin heard the defensive tone and wondered if seeing Warner touching Tula was upsetting him. *Is Dieter flirting with me to try and make Warner jealous? Christ, that's not a good idea for either of us.*

"I saw you dancing," Gethin said. "You're very good."

"Thanks. I made nearly two hundred pounds."

"You get to keep it all?"

"Yep." He frowned. "Shouldn't I?"

"Sometimes club owners take a cut."

"Oh."

"You look like a gymnast." Gethin resisted the impulse to rush this. If he said the wrong thing, Dieter might run deeper into what he didn't yet recognize was a prison.

"I am." Dieter moved closer and Gethin shifted away again.

"Close enough," Gethin said. "I don't want anyone to get the wrong idea."

He saw Dieter glance again at Warner and a look passed between them.

Ah, not what I thought. "Did Warner ask you to flirt with me?" Gethin asked.

"I'm supposed to encourage guys to pay for the other rooms."

"I already have." Gethin showed him the stamps.

"Oh. Well, you want to go somewhere else? The roof terrace? The video room? Buy another drink and I'll show you round."

"No thanks."

"You need…anything else?"

Gethin assumed he meant dope. "No, do you?"

Dieter gave him a startled look and in that moment looked so young that Gethin wanted to throw him over his shoulder and run. He wouldn't get far.

"No, I don't take drugs."

Dieter made a move to leave and Gethin tugged on his hand. "Keep me company?"

Dieter hesitated. "You need to buy something."

"You?"

154

Even in the dim light, he saw the blush steal over Dieter's face.

"I thought you were with Warner," Gethin said.

"I am, but I do what he tells me."

Gethin glanced at the bar to see Warner jerking the black guy off under the cover of the material around his hips while at the same time conducting a conversation with a bald guy standing next to him. Dieter turned so his back was to the tableau.

"What are you doing in a place like this?" Gethin asked. "You hardly look old enough to have left school."

"I'm old enough."

"Are you really offering yourself to me? Is that what Warner told you to do?"

"I need to earn my keep," Dieter said quietly. "I chose you. This first time, he let me choose. Anyone in here, he said, and I chose you."

Oh Jesus Christ. "Is this what you want?"

Dieter stared into his eyes. "You can fuck me. I'd *like* you to fuck me."

"You know what I'd rather do?"

"What?" There was a wary look on Dieter's face.

"Take you home to your mother, to your friend Sam. They miss you."

Chapter Fifteen

Gethin hadn't intended to shock Dieter to the point that he keeled over, but the teen would have done if Gethin hadn't caught his arm. The moment he knew Dieter wasn't going to faint or run he let go.

"I'm not here to make you go back," Gethin said quickly. "Your mother hired me to look for you, but you're old enough to decide for yourself whether you'd rather get paid to pretend to have sex with a pole, fuck guys you don't fancy, or let a guy stick his fist up your arse just because Warner tells you to. I hope you'd rather give your previous life another try. But if you don't want to go home, I can find somewhere for you to stay, somewhere safe. You can go to school, take your A Levels, maybe go to college, dance school if you like, get a proper job."

Gethin expected more resistance. Anger maybe. Or denial that he needed help. He got tears. *Fuck.*

"He'll hurt me," Dieter whispered.

"I won't let him. Stop crying or someone will come over to see what I've done to upset you."

"There was another boy who tried to leave. Tula said they didn't let him. They—"

"Shut up. Not now. Smile at me." Out of sight of anyone, Gethin pressed his spare car key into Dieter's hand. "Put that in your pocket. My car isn't far away. Turn left out of here then take the first road on the right, first turn on the left. Twenty yards. A black Peugeot. Press the key and the lights will flash. Lie down on the back seat under the blanket. Lock the door. I can't leave here straight away in case they connect us. You need to stay in the car. No matter how long. Okay?"

Dieter sucked in a ragged breath. "My stuff."

"Forget it. You have to be careful how you leave. Warner will be having you watched. I'll cause a distraction."

"Have you…have you seen my mum?"

156

"Yes."

"She—"

"We can talk later. You need to walk away from me now and act as though you're pissed off. Try to stay near the entrance, wait until things flare up, and when you're sure you're not being watched—get out of here."

Dieter moved away from Gethin then turned and gave him the finger. But when he headed straight back toward Warner, adrenaline surged until Gethin registered Dieter was responding to the guy's beckoning gesture. Gethin worried Dieter would say the wrong thing. The distraction had to happen sooner rather than later. He strolled to the rear of the club to the Back Passage, and showed his hand stamp. He'd seen a red fire alarm box on the wall the other side of the door close to the first viewing window.

He joined the group ogling a young guy tied in a rope swing who was being fucked in the mouth and the arse by two big hairy guys. Gethin checked out the box. Press in the centre, the glass would break and the alarm would sound. He just didn't want to be seen doing it. So he started shoving as if he was trying to get to the front, deliberately elbowing a couple of men. As he'd hoped, he was elbowed back. People grew stroppy, voices were raised and fists started to swing. Gethin was able to punch the alarm with his bottle and be nowhere near it moments later.

The noise was so loud and overpowering for a moment everyone seemed to freeze, then there was a mad rush toward the main room. Those farther down the corridor propelled Gethin and the men around him out onto the dance floor. There was a lot of yelling and shouting as everyone pushed to get to the exit. When he saw Dieter trying to get away from Warner and not succeeding, Gethin dropped his shoulders and shoved his way sideways through the crowd.

He didn't have much of a plan and it depended on there still being people milling close to Warner. When he was near the bar, Gethin lurched as if he'd been pushed, threw himself at Warner's legs and brought him down.

"Shit, I'm sorry," Gethin gasped. He flailed as if he was trying to get himself up and help Warner up while he was actually keeping him down as long as he could.

"Get the fuck off me," Warner snapped.

Gethin was yanked to his feet and thrust out of the way by a muscular dark-haired guy. A quick glance around showed no sign of Dieter.

"I'm sorry," Gethin said. "Someone shoved me."

"Get out of here," Warner barked.

Gethin joined the exodus from the club, hoping Dieter was well on the way to the car. He heard sirens as he stepped onto the pavement. Warner must know by now there was no fire and when he couldn't find Dieter he might put two and two together. Gethin thought about hanging around in case Dieter hadn't managed to get out, but he'd pressed his luck far enough.

He headed down the street, past lines of cars whose windows refracted the night's colours into a shimmering range of red and blue and yellow. The hair prickled on the back of his neck and he glanced back to see Kell staring after him. *Shit.* As desperate as he was to get out of the cold, Gethin didn't go anywhere near his vehicle until he was certain there was no one on his tail. He breathed a silent sigh of relief when he spotted the raised mass on the back seat. Once he was sure no one was watching, he unlocked the door.

Dieter's head popped up as Gethin climbed in.

"Keep down," Gethin snapped.

"Okay. Where are we going?"

Oh kid, you could have climbed into the car of a killer. You trust too easily. How many guys travel around with a spare car key?

"Did Warner give you a phone?"

"Yes. I've got it here. He just called me. I didn't answer."

"Power it down. Does he know where you live?" Gethin pulled out.

"I never told him."

"Did you give him your full name? Mention where you went to school? Tell him anything about your gymnastics?"

Dieter sighed. "Yeah."

"Then he knows where you live." Gethin took out his phone and tossed it on the back seat. "Call your mother. Tell her you're with me, that she needs to pack to stay away for a week and be out of the house inside twenty minutes. We'll meet her at Toddington services on the M1. She mustn't tell anyone what she's doing or where she's going."

This was almost a test of how much she loved her son, because Gethin knew how crazy this sounded.

There was a loud groan from the backseat. "You think he'd hurt my mum?"

"If Warner wants you back, he might threaten your mother to persuade you to go with him. Better not to give him that opportunity."

"He might just let me go."

"Like the boy Tula told you about? What happened to him?"

Dieter let out a ragged gasp. "He had his face cut."

"Then we play safe, okay?"

"Okay."

Gethin had taken in what Angel had told him, and what he'd not. He'd seen the way Warner looked at Dieter, like a sweet he enjoyed sucking. What worried him was that Dieter had picked Gethin to be his first paying customer. Warner had seen Gethin reject him, which meant he'd be remembered for that and for knocking Warner over. Gethin had the sneaky suspicion telling Dieter to find a guy was a test, that no way would Warner allow anyone to touch the kid yet. If Gethin had tried to take Dieter up on his offer, the big guy who'd glared when he'd toppled Warner would have stepped in to persuade Gethin he'd been mistaken.

Dieter was too valuable to be allowed to walk away. Maybe telling Zena Hoehn to leave her home was an overreaction, but experience had taught him to play safe. Assume the worst. Same with the twenty minute window. He couldn't get anywhere near

Dieter's house in less than an hour's driving but Warner might know someone who lived nearby. Even twenty minutes might be too long. Pointless calling the police when no offence had been committed.

"You don't think he'll let me go." Dieter's voice was subdued.

"It's better to be cautious. You and your mum can stay somewhere else while I find out whether Warner is still looking for you."

Gethin made his way out of London heading toward the motorway, listening as Dieter talked to his mum. There was a lot of crying and apologizing before Dieter said goodbye.

"She'll do it."

"Good," Gethin said. "I'm going to pull over now and you can get in the front."

When Dieter was sitting beside him, Gethin held out his hand. "Phones."

Gethin put his back in his pocket. Dieter had the latest iPhone. Gethin checked it was switched off, then put it in the glove compartment.

"You know why you can't have it?" Gethin asked.

"Yeah. I can be tracked."

Once Dieter was buckled in, and Gethin had retrieved a T-shirt from the boot and pulled it on over his harness, he headed back into the traffic.

"You all right about going home?" Gethin asked.

Dieter twisted his hands on his lap and said nothing.

Interesting that he didn't want to answer. Gethin would make sure he did before they reached the service station. If Dieter gave him any reason to worry, he'd be having words with his mother and might even end up taking the teen back to his place for what was left of the night.

"How did you know where I was?" Dieter asked.

"Sam's mum told your mum she'd found a card for No Escape in Sam's pocket. Sam said you'd danced there. Your mum thought it was worth a try."

"I can't believe she paid you to look for me."

Yeah, well she hasn't paid me yet. "She was worried sick. She wants you to finish school, pass your exams, get a good job. Same as all mums want." Most of them.

"So is this what you do? Look for missing people?"

"Some of what I do. I spend most of my time following people suspected of cheating."

"And are they?"

"Usually, and if their partners are abusing them, I do what I can to help."

"Sounds like social work."

Gethin gave a short laugh. "Some of it is."

"I thought being a private detective would be exciting."

"I can spend hours sitting in my car waiting for something to happen and even if it does, it's rarely exciting."

"You set off that fire alarm and knocked Warner over. That was brilliant."

"My heart's still pounding."

"Nah. You're cool. So are you into guys or were you pretending?"

"I'm into guys."

There was a short pause before Dieter spoke again. "Not into me?"

"You're too young for me. Plus Warner was watching you. I don't think he'd have let me take you anywhere. Or if he had, that big guy with him would have been right behind us."

"Marek."

Gethin heard fear in Dieter's voice.

"What does Marek do?"

"He's Warner's second in command. He's from Albania. If bad things need doing, Marek does them. I've seen him in the bathroom covered in blood."

"Has he touched you?"

"No. Kell's his thing."

Even as Gethin was thinking — what did it matter? — he knew it did. "Kell?"

"One of the security guards. He's nice. I feel sorry for him."

"Why?" Gethin couldn't help ask the question.

"Because of Marek. Marek scares me. I think he scares Kell too. Marek only has to look at me and I feel like I'm going to piss myself. Kell's kind to me. He's funny. I don't get why he and Marek have a thing. You think Warner is too old for me?"

Gethin wasn't sure whether he wanted the subject to change or not. "I don't think age matters if love's involved. But this isn't love. It's just sex. Warner likes young men. You could do so much better than him. Why did you run away from home?"

Gethin wasn't sure Dieter would answer. He was beginning to feel sure he wouldn't when Dieter finally spoke. "I was on my own in the house when my mum's boyfriend came in. He was drunk and he tried to make me give him a blow job. Mum arrived home just in time, and he said if I told her, he'd say I came onto him. I laughed. But when I *did* tell her, she wouldn't believe me. She said if I said it again, she'd send me to my dad."

Shit. "You think she does now?"

"She just said she did."

"You didn't make it up because you didn't want him to take the place of your dad?"

"No. I *want* someone to take the place of my dad. Mum just told me she loves me, that I should have never doubted she loves me more than anyone. She's sorry she didn't believe me."

"This guy's not still around?"

"She said he left not long after me."

"Why didn't you take your phone?" Gethin asked.

"Because I'd have been tempted to use it and I know you can be traced. I thought when I'd earned enough by dancing at the club I'd buy another but Warner gave me one. He was decent. He gave me somewhere to live, a flat with Tula, and he bought me clothes, and this watch. I know he doesn't love me, but I didn't mind him fucking me."

162

Gethin winced. "Sex is supposed to be about more than not minding. It should be something special between you and the other guy." Unless your name was Gethin Jones.

"I suppose."

"You told me you didn't take drugs. Is that the truth?"

"Marek gave me a couple of pills once when I was nervous about dancing. No big deal."

"Yes it is. Don't take anything."

"Right, Dad."

Gethin glared. "Don't be a smartarse. It's easy to get hooked on drugs. Tula takes them."

"I spent most nights with Warner."

Gethin tightened his grip on the wheel. "It would only have been a matter of time before you were on drugs too."

"I don't want to get addicted."

"Then don't start taking anything. What about alcohol?"

"Warner wouldn't let me even have a beer." Dieter sounded disgusted.

Gethin almost laughed. Drugs and sex were fine, but not booze.

To Gethin's relief, Dieter's mum was sitting in her car in the service station car park. He pulled up next to her and Dieter leapt from the car. She sprang from hers and as they hugged each other, Gethin felt a brief satisfaction in having made someone happy — for a while at least. He got out of his car and leaned against the driver's door, shivering in the cold air.

"Thank you," she said to him, still holding tight to her son. "I was frightened I'd never see him again. I can't believe he's here."

"Where's Tigga?" Dieter looked in his mother's car.

"I couldn't find him. You know what he's like at night. Doing his circuit of the females in the neighbourhood. He can get in through the cat flap. I left food. I'll go back and get him."

Gethin mentally groaned.

"You should have found him," Dieter said, his voice surly.

163

"Hey," Gethin snapped. "Your mum did exactly the right thing. You woke her in the middle of the night and she did what you asked and left the house quickly. How many mothers do you think would have followed those instructions?"

"I want my cat," Dieter whispered.

For Christ's sake. "You *left* your cat," Gethin said.

Dieter's shoulders slumped.

Gethin sighed, reconciled to fetching the damn thing. "How am I going to know it's your cat?"

"He's ginger," Dieter said. "A white tip at the end of his tail. He wears a collar with his name and our postcode. He comes if you call him. There's a carrying case under the stairs."

"Okay. I'll look for him. Sit in your mum's car while I have a word with her."

She and Gethin sat in Gethin's car.

"Thank you so much. I can't believe you found him."

"He's told you why he ran?"

She nodded. "Vic's gone. He lasted less than a week after Dieter disappeared. The bastard. I should have believed Dieter. But he's played up before about guys I've dated."

"Said they touched him?"

She shook her head. "No, he'd never said that until Vic. I feel so guilty. He said you found him in a club, but what happened? Why have we had to leave the house?"

"Warner, the guy who owns the club where Dieter's been dancing, is a hard man. I might be making more of this than I need to, but from what I've heard and seen, I don't think Warner will just let Dieter go. It makes him look weak. There's a risk he or his men might come to your house. Dieter didn't tell Warner where he lived, but he told him enough that Warner could find out."

"But he can't *make* Dieter go with him."

"What if he threatened to hurt you if Dieter didn't go back? Or said he'd tell people lies about you or Dieter? That you hit him, made him fuck you?"

She sucked in a breath.

"He might wreck your house. Kill your cat. I have no idea whether he'd do any of that or nothing but I've learned it's better to assume the very worst thing."

"That can't make for a happy life, imagining mothers having sex with their sons." She glared at him and Gethin's cheeks heated.

"The point I was trying to make was that Warner won't care what he has to do or say to get what he wants. Dieter knows that another teen who tried to leave did so with a scar on his face. He's scared. I didn't have to say much to persuade him to come with me."

"How long do we have to stay away from the house? I can't afford to live indefinitely in a motel, and I have a job in the city."

"Give me one week to find out if Warner is looking for him. Can you take a vacation or ask for compassionate leave? Maybe send Dieter to his father and you live with a friend for a while?"

"Dieter and his father don't get on. I'll call my boss, arrange something. It'll do me and Dieter good to get away."

"You can't tell anyone where you are. Nor can Dieter."

"All right."

"No one. I mean that. Not even the school to say he's coming back, or any of his friends. If you brought his phone, don't give it him. Switch yours off when you're not using it."

She stared at him. "Should I call the police?"

"Warner's not broken the law in a way that would get you police protection. Not yet. Warner didn't… Dieter was a willing participant."

"Oh God."

"Dieter was too young to be in the club, but Warner would likely only get his fingers rapped, and pissing him off is not the way to get him to let Dieter go. You have my number. Any problems, call me. Do *not* go home until I tell you it's safe. Check into the motel in this service station and I'll find the cat and bring it here."

Gethin drove back to Edgware, suspecting he was overreacting and knowing he'd just landed himself with more work he wouldn't get paid for. He thought about Kell, tried to stop thinking about Kell, and failed. There was nothing he could do. Kell hadn't lied. He was working in security and from what Dieter had said, it didn't sound as though Marek was much different from Warner. But why stay there? Why work in a place like that? Was there something about Kell he hadn't seen?

What did it matter? That was the last time he'd see him. He had far more important things to worry about. Such as rescuing a cat. *Shit.*

Chapter Sixteen

"Where the fuck is he?" Warner screamed the words, spittle flying from his mouth.

Kell stood with the other employees in front of Warner and Marek. The club was empty of patrons. Closing early meant lost revenue which no doubt added to Warner's rage. He'd ordered all of them onto the streets to look for Dieter, but the kid was long gone.

"Someone must have seen something. The little shit either ran or someone took him. His phone's off." Warner paced. "That guy he was talking to, the one in the harness, the one who fucking tripped me up… He set off the alarm, then knocked me over as a distraction."

Was he right? "That might have been an accident," Kell said, then wondered what the fuck he was doing. Gethin had walked away from him, Kell owed him nothing. The guy hadn't even answered his phone. Kell had tried three times and each time it had gone to voice mail, and on every occasion he'd deleted his call history just in case.

Marek stared at him. "You don't set off a fire alarm by accident."

"I meant tripping up the boss was an accident. It was chaos in here, everyone fighting to get out. A lot of people got knocked over. Me included. We all thought there was a fire. Dieter ran like everyone else."

Marek came right up to him and put his mouth against Kell's ear. "You have that guy waiting at your place?"

Oh fuck. Kell poured indignation into his voice. "No. The only contact we had was me asking him where he bought his harness."

Reuben was checking the cameras. Kell was relieved they'd back up what he'd said.

"You followed him," Marek said.

"You told me to. I went into the Back Passage and I couldn't see him. Next time I did, he was on his own in here, leaning against the wall, talking to Dieter. Then Dieter went back to the boss."

Alec came into the room and approached Warner.

"Anything?" Warner asked.

"The camera in the Back Passage isn't working," Alec said.

Warner clenched his fists. "Why the fuck not?"

"I don't know. I'll have to call someone in to check. The camera on the exterior caught Dieter leaving after the alarm went off. He was the middle of a load of guys, part of a group that turned left, then the camera lost him."

"What about the guy who knocked me over?"

"He was pushed toward you by the crowd. He tripped and brought you down. Looked like an accident. He was one of the last ones out and turned right."

Kell was relieved Gethin hadn't been caught doing something he shouldn't have. Maybe he'd arranged to meet Dieter and had the sense not to do it right outside the club. But that didn't sit comfortably in Kell's stomach.

"The kid thought there was fire, and ran. Tula ran too," Marek said.

"But I came back." Tula sidled up to Warner and was pushed away.

"Could he be trying to get your house?" Marek asked Warner.

"It's possible. He doesn't have a key, but he might be hanging around outside. Take Kell and check. If he's not there, try his mother's place."

For fuck's sake. Let the boy go.

"You have a problem with that?" Warner stepped right into Kell's space.

Kell's thoughts must have shown on his face. *Careless.* "No." The only answer he could give. Had that been the only answer Gethin could give when Kell had confronted him in the club? How was Gethin involved in this?

Warner owned an attractive looking place in Holland Park that had to have cost millions.

"There are lights on," Kell said.

"Warner leaves them on. I'll go inside and through to back. You look around out here."

Kell wasn't going to miss the opportunity to see inside. He waited, then followed Marek. The post was still on the floor. Kell picked it up and checked it. Nothing of obvious interest. Marek was clattering around upstairs. Kell slipped into the room on the left... Dining room. It annoyed him that Warner had good taste. Big oak table with a glass centrepiece. The room on the right was a drawing room, cream couches, cream carpet, blue curtains. A pile of books on the coffee table, the top one about medieval warfare. When Kell came out, Marek was at the bottom of the stairs.

"What you doing?" Marek asked.

"Thought I'd help you look in here."

Marek wrapped his hand around Kell's throat and squeezed as he pushed him back against the wall. "When I tell you to do something, you do it, understand?"

"Sorry," Kell choked out.

By the time they'd reached the Hoehns' house, it was four in the morning. Kell really hoped there was no one home. If Dieter had made it all the way here, the idea of 'persuading' him to go back with them gave Kell a big problem. Months of work down the drain, but really, would he have a choice? He had to help Dieter. He knew the teen had run away from home, knew his mother had reported him. It had been a hard enough decision to keep the knowledge of where he was to themselves. Kell's boss could get into trouble for that.

Marek drove past the house, a small semi on a quiet road. There was no car in the drive, though that didn't mean there was no one home.

"Ring the bell." Marek pulled up. "Talk your way in and find out if kid is there or been there."

"What if there's no answer?"

"Go round the back. Get inside and let me in front."

"And when she or a neighbour calls the police, because who'd be ringing the bell at this time in the morning, you're going to drive away and leave me?"

Marek grinned. It wasn't pleasant. "Get on with it and we can go home and get some sleep."

Kell slipped out of the car and hurried up the path to the front door wondering if he could use his phone without Marek seeing. As he reached for the doorbell, he let his finger slide to the side. If anyone *was* home, did he really want them to come to the door? If he went around the back, he had a chance to warn them, get *them* to call the police. He pretended to press the bell again, then set off around the back of the house only to stumble to a halt when he found Gethin wrestling a pissed off ginger cat into a carry case.

"What the fuck?" Kell whispered.

Gethin jammed the cat inside and fastened the flap. The animal hissed and wriggled, and the case jerked violently.

"What the hell are you doing here?" Kell whispered. "Is Dieter here? Or his mum?"

"No."

"Shit." Kell could see no way of escape for Gethin except for the way Kell had come. There was no time for a discussion. "Don't go round the front until I've let Marek into the house, then get lost—fast." Kell walked in through the open kitchen door.

His heart was thundering in his chest while his mind raced trying to make sense of what was happening. The only conclusion he could draw was that Gethin had gone to the club specifically to look for Dieter, found him, snatched him and had come here to get his mother and his cat, and if Gethin had been a little quicker, or he and Marek been a little slower, Kell wouldn't have known.

As he walked down the hall, the flap lifted on the letterbox.

"Hurry," Marek snapped.

Kell made a meal out of opening the door trying to give Gethin as much time as he could.

"Haven't checked to see if anyone's upstairs," Kell whispered as he closed the door.

"Do it now," Marek said. "No lights."

Kell took the stairs two at a time, went into the front bedroom and straight over to the window. Gethin jogged up the road, tossed the wriggling carry case onto the backseat of a car and drove away. Kell sighed and looked around the bedroom. Dieter's room. Bed neatly made. All the kid's trophies lined up a shelf with his books. The room looked tidy, undisturbed. No sign he'd been back.

The second bedroom was little more than a storage space filled with suitcases, boxes and Christmas decorations. The third was the mother's. The duvet was askew on the bed, drawers open, and wardrobe door ajar. Kell considered the merits of putting the bed to rights and pushing the drawers back in and was lifting the edge of the duvet when Marek came in. Kell noticed he was wearing gloves.

"What the fuck you doing? She's not hiding under there."

"Seeing if it was still warm," Kell said.

"Ah. Smart. Is it?"

"No. Doesn't look as though Dieter's been back. His room's too tidy."

"Warner is going to be pissed off."

Kell glanced into the bathroom on the way past. No toothbrush or paste. He followed Marek downstairs.

Marek opened the fridge and checked the contents. "Stuff's fresh. She's been here until recently. Maybe until tonight. Dieter must have phoned her."

"She might be staying the night with a friend."

"Or Dieter told his mum to come get him. They could be back any minute."

Kell hoped the missing toothbrush indicated that wasn't going to happen. "It looked as though she packed. Those drawers

171

open in her bedroom. Duvet off the bed. Dieter might have asked her to meet him somewhere. Or she might be the untidy type and gone to stay with a friend."

"They have a cat. Fresh shit in litter box. She'll be back."

"Unless they asked a neighbour to feed it."

"You a fucking ray of sunshine." Marek glared at him, then sighed. "Better give boss the bad news." He took out his phone. "No one here," he said into his phone. "She might have run. Drawers are open in her room. Kid's room is tidy, hers not... Yeah... Okay... But not at this time in the morning. We knock on neighbours' doors and they'll call the cops... Okay. We can do that. You could put a trace on his phone, report it missing... Oh right. Yeah. He must have switched it off."

"Or someone switched it off for him," Kell said. "What if he's been kidnapped?"

Marek stared at him as he spoke into the phone. "Yeah. I'll see to it. Bye." He put his phone away and walked over to the door. "Where did you find key?"

It was still in the door. Gethin had left it. *Thank God.*

"I checked all the usual places people hide keys," Kell said. "No point making a noise getting in if the home owner's stupid enough to leave a key under a plant pot."

"Warner wants us to trash the place," Marek said and Kell's heart sank.

"And that's going to make Dieter want to go back to the club?"

"What kid wants, doesn't matter." Marek lifted a bottle of olive oil and dropped it on the floor. It shattered and oil splashed everywhere.

"I hate to spoil the party," Kell said. "But if we start making a noise, we'll wake the neighbours and then we'll be explaining what we're doing to the police. Plus, we don't know she isn't in bed with a boyfriend. We don't even know Dieter wants to come back home. He ran from here didn't he?"

Marek stared him. "You're right."

172

Kell swallowed his shock.

"Warner is pissed off. He's thinking with his dick. Let's go."

Kell locked the door and to his horror saw no sign of a plant pot. Maybe Marek wouldn't notice.

"Where was key then? I thought you said it was under plant pot?"

Kell tucked it at the back of the wheelie bin. "I meant generally. Most times when I've had to get in somewhere that's locked, the key's under something outside the back door. Most often a flower pot, but wheelie bins too, behind slabs, under rocks. I once found one inside a mouse trap."

When Marek said nothing more, Kell heaved a silent sigh of relief. Back in the car, they headed down the road, and Kell tried to look relaxed when he was feeling anything but. That could have all gone to hell if Marek had seen Gethin.

"How long you been working for Warner?" Marek asked.

Kell was sure the guy knew to the day. "About five months."

"Where were you before?"

"In jail." Marek knew that too.

"Oh yeah, in Paris."

"Fleury-Mérogis."

"Never heard of it," Marek said and Kell suspected he was lying.

"Nor had I till I landed up there. It's the biggest prison in Europe. Thirty-five percent of prisoners are foreign." *Thanks, Google.*

"What's it like compared to British jail?"

"I never been inside in the UK, but Fleury-Mérogis was a shithole. Overcrowded. Bad food. Hard beds."

"What did you do to get put in there?"

"I skinned a guy who asked too many questions, then ate him."

Marek laughed so hard he ended up coughing.

"I have work for you tomorrow. Thursday your night off, right? You interested?"

173

"Is it legal?"

Marek chortled again. "I'm beginning to like you."

After all this time, Kell was finally getting somewhere.

Gethin was usually quick to assess situations, but he was having trouble working out what Kell was up to. It was obvious Warner had sent Kell and Marek to Dieter's house to find Dieter and presumably take him back, but Kell had helped Gethin get away when it was clear Gethin knew where Dieter was.

Why? Because of their…arrangement? Kell didn't yet know Gethin had backed out of that. There was no sign that came up your phone saying 'your number has been blocked by this person.' Gethin had snubbed him in the club, so maybe Kell had got the message. It wasn't hard to conclude Kell helping him had something to do with Kell not wanting Dieter to be found. Which made Kell a good guy not a bad one.

Coming at this from the other side, what might Kell think Gethin was up to? In Kell's position, he'd have assumed Gethin had come to the club to look for Dieter, found him, and created a diversion to enable Dieter to get away. Then he'd either brought Dieter home and persuaded his mother to leave, or he'd left Dieter somewhere and told his mother to drive there. But she'd not taken the cat so Gethin had to come back. Gethin was either a Samaritan who'd acted quickly and decisively when Dieter appealed to him in the club, or he was a friend of the family, or he was a private investigator.

But what did it matter? They wouldn't be seeing each other again. *Probably.*

Before he reached the motorway, he drew up at the side of the road, retrieved Kell's number from a text message and put it back in his contacts.

The cat yowled as Gethin pulled back into the traffic. He could hear it scratching at the inside of the carrier. He'd never had a pet as a kid though he'd lived in foster homes that had dogs. No cats. Gethin never bothered getting attached to anything or anyone. After his parents died, nothing had been permanent in his life.

He hadn't realised the cat was out of the bag until the damn thing leapt onto his lap with an outraged snarl and sank its claws into his thigh. He almost drove off the road.

"Jesus Christ. Get off." He tried to grab the thing by the scruff of the neck and it scratched his hand. "Ouch."

Gethin was on the motorway, not supposed to pull onto the hard shoulder unless it was an emergency. Unexpectedly sharing a car with a wild animal counted as an emergency. The cat hissed like a pissed off snake and jumped onto the top of the dashboard. Gethin flicked his indicator, pulled off and put on his hazard lights.

No way was he opening a door and risking the animal making a break for it. He unfastened his seatbelt and reached to grab the carrier from the backseat. He had no idea how the thing had escaped.

"Should have called you Houdini," he muttered.

Wrestling the animal back to safety proved tricky. The cat braced its legs to try and stop Gethin sliding him in, gripping the outside of the carrier with sharp claws. A moment later, Gethin had more scratches and the cat lay sprawled in the footwell, its malevolent stare making its feelings quite clear.

"Nice, kitty." *Vile, spitting, fucking bastard.* His hand was bleeding.

Subtlety and speed were called for. Gethin distracted with one hand while he made a grab with the other, and managed to get a firm grip on the back of the cat's neck.

"There. That wasn't so bad. Just calm down."

He stroked it a couple of times, and the cat growled. Before it could wriggle free, he shoved it backward into the carrier and breathed a sigh of relief when he'd pushed the metal gate closed. He clipped the fastening in place. *Oh fuck. Two fastenings.* That's what he'd done wrong. The cat's yowls and hisses increased in volume.

"I love you too."

He resisted the impulse to toss the carrier on the backseat, and instead put it there carefully before switching off his warning lights and pulling onto the carriageway.

When he'd parked outside the motel, he called Dieter's mother. "I'm outside. Bring something to cover the cat. They might not allow them in the room."

"I'll be out in a minute."

Gethin was desperate for a coffee. He was shattered. He yawned and rubbed at the scratch marks on his hands.

Zena opened the car door and slipped into the passenger seat. She glanced in the back and sighed. "That's not Tigga."

"What? He was outside your house. It says Tigger on his collar."

"That's Miranda's cat. He's called Tigger with an er not an a, and there's no white tip at the end of his tail."

"Oh fuck," Gethin muttered.

Chapter Seventeen

"Hey, sleeping beauty."

Kell jerked upright in the car to see they were parked down the road from his place. He'd never told Marek or Warner where he lived though wasn't surprised it was known.

"Thanks for the lift." Kell unclipped his seatbelt and climbed out of the car.

"Going to invite me in?"

"No."

"Try again."

"Want to come in?" *Please don't.*

"Sure."

Fuck. As Marek followed him up the stairs, Kell felt himself slowing, his arse tensing. He opened the door and switched on the light. Marek stepped in after him and pushed the door closed. Kell watched as Marek checked out a pile of books, looked in his cupboards, his wardrobe and the bathroom. He had no idea what the guy was looking for. Signs he was an undercover cop? He wouldn't find them.

"You don't have much," Marek said. "And this place is dump."

"I just came out of prison. Everything I had, I lost. And I know it's a dump. I don't earn enough to afford anywhere better."

"Apart from big TV."

Kell snorted. "First thing I bought with my wages."

Marek held out his hand. "Your phone."

"Why?"

"You want me to fuck you with it?" Marek snapped.

"No, sir."

"Then give it me."

Kell took it from his pocket and handed it over. *What have I done? Why's he suspicious?* Kell's heart pounded so hard, he could feel the beat throbbing throughout his body.

"Uncle Bob?" Marek asked.

"My mother's brother. He's not well. I keep an eye on him."
Ring him. Kell quite liked the idea of his boss being woken at this
time in the morning.

"Who's G?"

"G for guy I met at my friend's party."

"*Fancy a fuck? Scissors Paper Stone. Two this afternoon.*" Marek
read the text Kell had sent to Gethin.

Too late to wish he'd deleted that.

"No answer?"

No because that *had* been deleted. "Guess he wasn't as
interested as I was."

"I'm not enough for you?" Marek tossed the phone on the bed
and stepped into his space.

Kell held his ground. "Are you jealous?" *You fucking idiot,
Kell.*

But Marek laughed. "Mr. Smart mouth. Tell me what beats
scissors, paper *and* stone?"

Kell didn't get the word *you* out before Marek was on him,
holding him tight, his mouth spewing filth into Kell's ear. "I going
to shove my cock deep inside your arse and ride you so hard it
fucking hurts to sit down. You feel me inside you for hours after I
walk away. I make you come until you can't breathe. I make you
beg for more. Tell me what you want and call me sir."

"Fuck off and let me sleep, sir." *Oh fuck, did I say that, not think
it?*

Marek gaped at him in astonishment, then smiled. Kell
fought. He couldn't help himself, but Marek was too strong to
tussle with for long, plus he liked it when Kell resisted, so Kell
gave in. He wanted to be able to walk straight when the guy had
done. He didn't want to think about Gethin, but he did. That
added guilt to the pile of crap already circulating in his head. How
could anyone want a guy who was prepared to let Marek do
whatever the fuck he wanted?

Almost.

Marek bit him and Kell yelped. *Find a place in your head and hide there. This* will *end.* But Kell was haunted by thoughts of having let this happen for nothing, of never getting the information his boss wanted, and that somehow in the process of trying to do the right thing, he'd been drawn in too deep and was losing part of himself he'd never get back.

No one would ever want him.

Gethin would never want him.

Maybe he wouldn't be comfortable in his skin ever again.

He fought again, struggled, and paid for his resistance with pain that pushed him to the brink. When Marek finally stood up and dressed, Kell lay on the bed, bloody, bruised and bitten, his breathing shaky. But not completely broken.

"You shouldn't have fought," Marek said.

Kell said nothing. It hurt to speak or move. *I can't do this anymore.* Though that was what he thought every time this happened. Though never as bad as this.

Marek lay at his side and rubbed his thumb over Kell's lips. "I go too far. Sorry."

If Kell hadn't been lying down, he'd have fainted in shock.

"Tomorrow," Marek said. "Come to club at seven. Warm clothes. Make good money." He heaved himself up, and closed the door quietly on the way out.

And those few words pushed Kell into continuing. He rolled to his feet with a groan, locked the door, and padded over to the window. After he'd watched Marek drive away, he exhaled.

At least at this time in the morning there was plenty of hot water. He stood under it a long time wondering how he'd explain the bites and bruises to Gethin. Whether he'd get the chance. Whether he wanted the chance.

He went over what had happened from the moment of shock when they'd seen each other in the club, up to where he and Marek had driven away from Dieter's house. Kell didn't need to think beyond that. Gethin had somehow gotten Dieter away from

No Escape, grabbed his mum then gone back for the cat. Kell had helped him and if Marek found out, Kell was dead.

By the time Kell stepped from the shower, he was exhausted, but wired. He threw painkillers down his throat and before he could talk himself out of it, called Gethin.

"What?" Gethin snapped.

There was a loud yowl.

Kell stiffened. "Are you okay?"

"No."

"Is that the cat?"

"The wrong fucking cat."

Kell laughed and winced.

"It's not funny."

"We need to talk," Kell said.

"You think? All we need to say can be covered in one sentence. Thanks for not giving me up, but forget you ever met me." Gethin cut him off.

No, Kell wasn't going to do that. He made another call as he struggled into his clothes.

Gethin parked in the same spot near the Hoehns' house. He pulled the carrier onto his lap, opened the car door then unfastened the clips so the cat could get out. It didn't move.

"For fuck's sake." Gethin tipped the carrier upside down and the cat stayed inside, presumably clinging on for grim death with those razor-sharp claws.

Dawn was about to break. If he wasn't careful he'd end up getting arrested for cat rustling. He was reluctant to put his hand inside the carrier and instead gave the thing a hard bang. To his intense relief, the cat dropped out, swivelled and landed on all fours on the pavement. It hissed at Gethin before loping up the road, tail in the air. Gethin locked his car and hurried to the house.

He'd had to abandon the key Zena had given him so if it hadn't been left in the door, he'd need to break in, unless he was lucky enough to find the cat outside. He slid through the shadows down the side of the house, turned the corner and froze. Kell sat on the back doorstep, a large ginger cat purring contentedly in his arms, a key in his hand.

"Name's Tigga," Kell said.

"You told me your name was Kell."

Kell gave a quiet laugh. Gethin put the carrier down and pocketed the key.

"In you go," Kell said and the cat jumped from his lap, went straight inside the container and curled up. Kell fastened both catches—of course he did—and pushed to his feet. *Is he wincing?*

"How the fuck did you manage that?" Gethin asked.

"Animal magnetism. Where are we going?"

"What do you mean *we*?"

Kell picked up the carrier and set off toward the road. Gethin opened his mouth to argue, then gritted his teeth and followed. The last thing he needed was to draw more attention.

"Where's your car?" Gethin asked as they reached the pavement.

"I got a lift."

Not hard to conclude Kell had been dropped off by Marek with orders to wait for Dieter's return.

"You're not coming with me." Gethin made a grab for the carrier, and Kell moved it out of reach.

"Yes I am."

"Going to use the cat as a bargaining chip to get Dieter back into Warner's clutches?"

"No."

"Realised you made a mistake helping me and now you're trying to put things right with your boss?"

"Going to make any more stupid assumptions?" Kell snapped.

Gethin sighed and headed for his vehicle. He unlocked his car and held out his hand for the carrier.

"I'm on your side," Kell said.

"What does that mean?"

"Exactly what it says on the tin."

Gethin hesitated, then climbed in. "I'll give you a lift."

Kell put the carrier in the back and dropped onto the passenger seat.

Gethin set off toward the motorway, not yet sure what he was going to do. At least they weren't being followed. There was so little traffic, a tail was easy to spot. But then if Kell intended to tell his boss where Dieter was, there was no need for a tail.

"So what are you?" Kell asked. "Cat thief, friend of the family, or private detective?"

"What are you?" Gethin retorted.

"I told you I worked in security. I'm not the one who fucking lied."

"I didn't fucking lie."

Kell huffed. "You let me assume you worked for that party company."

"I *was* working for them. You think I wore nothing but that apron and let women put their hands all over me for fun? I was helping out a friend who was short staffed."

"That's why you were such a crap waiter."

Gethin sucked in his cheeks. "Yeah, that's right."

"I don't know why you're acting like I've pissed you off. We made an arrangement, had fun, then you turn up at the place where I work in *security* and treat me like I'm something you stepped in."

"I... Sorry. But I had to be careful."

"You're not a waiter. What are you?"

"Cat thief."

"A private investigator." Kell glanced at him. "You came to the club looking for Dieter."

"His mother reported him missing, but the police aren't interested in a runaway seventeen-year-old so she contacted me. I was as shocked as you when I saw you in there."

"Why did he run?" Kell asked.

"A problem at home, but that problem no longer exists. Dieter saw No Escape as a refuge instead of the prison it actually was. He was flattered by Warner's attention, charmed by his lies, excited to have gifts like that watch, thrilled to make money dancing, but he doesn't belong in a place like that, nor in Warner's bed. He's little more than a child. Dieter told me he didn't *mind* Warner fucking him. Shit, that's not what I want to hear coming out of the mouth of anyone, let alone a teenager."

Kell sucked in a breath. "No. You're right."

Gethin caught an undertone in that quiet response that worried him. He wanted and didn't want to ask Kell about Marek.

"If Dieter spends too long with a man like Warner, he'll end up broken," Gethin said. "You work for the guy. You know what he's like. Dieter was destined to end up on drugs, pimped out, Christ knows what else. He offered himself to me because Warner told him to choose someone."

"Warner wouldn't have let you touch him."

"I guessed not, but I've been told he eventually gets bored of his toys. I want Warner to leave Dieter the fuck alone."

"So do I."

Gethin pressed his lips together.

"You don't believe me?" Kell snapped. "Why the hell do you think I told you to get out of there with that cat?"

"Because you knew it was the wrong cat?"

Kell gave a short laugh. "I didn't want to watch Marek *persuade* you to tell him where Dieter was. He's not a guy who listens to no."

"Marek?" Gethin decided to pretend he didn't know who Kell was talking about.

"Big guy. Buzz cut. Couple of inches taller than me. A lot broader. Warner's second in command."

Gethin waited for him to tell him the rest, but Kell said nothing.

"Why the hell are you working for a shit like Warner?"

"The money's good."

Gethin frowned. What was he spending his money on? He lived in a tiny place and had nothing except that TV.

"I'm saving to get the deposit for a bigger flat."

"How long have you been working for him?"

"Few months."

"What did you do before?"

"I was in prison."

What? "What for?"

"Theft."

Gethin was shocked and disappointed. "Which jail?"

"Fleury-Mérogis. In Paris. What sort of job could I get after that? I was tailor-made for No Escape and Warner."

Gethin was realizing he knew next to nothing about this guy. He tried to tell himself it didn't matter because that had never been the intention, but it *did* matter.

"You're okay with what Warner does?" Gethin turned onto the slip road to the motorway and put his foot down on.

"No, but I've done nothing illegal."

Kell wasn't stupid. He knew that wouldn't save him if Warner went down.

"What were you and Marek planning to do at Dieter's house? Ask him to go back with you and walk away when he said no? What did you do when you found he wasn't there? Come up with this plan?"

"I'm on your side." Kell's voice was subdued, as if he sensed Gethin didn't believe him. "Warner told Marek we were to trash the place but I convinced him it was a bad idea. That was *after* Marek tipped oil on the kitchen floor. I locked up, put the key behind the wheelie bin and told Marek that's where I'd found it."

"Then what did you do?"

"You don't trust me?"

"I have no fucking idea whose side you're on." Gethin wished he did.

"Warner has no reason to suspect I know where Dieter is. I'm not giving the kid up to him."

"Christ, Kell. What the hell are you doing working there?"

"Because it's all I can do."

"No, it's not. You've chosen to work for a guy who makes his living from gay clubs, and porn. A guy who pushed a teenager into sucking him off in public. A guy who told that teenager to pick whoever he liked in the club and persuade them to pay for sex with him. He was lucky he picked me."

"You're right that it was probably a test."

"Doesn't matter. Next time it might not have been."

"I'm on your side," Kell said. "It's the truth. I'll do whatever I can to keep Dieter away from Warner. He's a good kid."

"You think I'm going to drive you to Dieter so you can phone your boss and impress him with your cunning?"

"No," Kell snapped. "Have my fucking phone if you're worried. How many times do I have to tell you I won't give him up to Warner?"

In any case, neither Gethin nor Kell would know where Dieter and his mother went once they left the motel.

"Okay," Gethin said. "I believe you." Though he wasn't sure he did. He still had the feeling there was something he wasn't getting and not just about Kell's relationship with Marek.

"Dieter and his mum are in a motel," Gethin said. "I told her she'd have to stay away from home until I was sure Warner was no longer interested in her son. I'm thinking a week. Any chance?"

"I'm not sure. That kid can really dance. It's like he's made of elastic. The club has been getting busier as word's spread. Warner *does* get easily bored, but Dieter's different and Warner's a control freak. He won't like someone taking one of his toys. He'll want Dieter back to prove a point *before* he throws him to the dogs."

Gethin exhaled. "So a week's not long enough and living anywhere in the vicinity is a bad idea."

"Yep."

"Right."

"I could keep you up to date with what was going on," Kell said. "Call you when Warner moves onto someone new."

Gethin doubted Warner was the type to forgive and forget. But Dieter and his mother would be safe as long as they'd did what Gethin told them.

"Does Warner think I had anything to do with Dieter's disappearance?" Gethin asked.

"Marek spotted me scything my way across the dance floor to get you. He thought you were trouble, and that I'd recognized trouble in you too. I told him I asked you where you bought that harness."

"You didn't tell him you fancied me?" Gethin made himself laugh. *Tell me about you and him. What is he to you?*

"Because that would have gone down *so* well." Kell shook his head. "It would have been better if you hadn't come to Marek's attention. Now you have, he won't forget. But they don't know who set off the alarm. Lucky for you the camera wasn't working in the Back Passage. Knocking Warner over made him suspicious, but I pointed out everyone was panicking and the camera that caught it happening *was* working. You managed to make it look like an accident. I got knocked over too. You didn't leave with Dieter and the cameras show that as well. The two of you went in opposite directions. I don't think Warner has access to any of the street cameras. As long as he doesn't find out you're a PI, I think you're okay."

Kell hadn't taken the opportunity to open up about Marek and Gethin was disappointed. "Maybe I should come back to the club another night. If I had anything to hide, I wouldn't do that."

"I think you should stay as far away from the place as you can."

"Why? Because Marek won't like it?" Gethin wanted the words back but it was too late.

Kell gave a heavy sigh. "What did Dieter say?"

"What do you think he said?"

Kell shifted in his seat. "We agreed this was going to be casual. All we are is fuck buddies."

Gethin bristled. "I asked if you were in a relationship."

"You asked if I lived with someone. I don't."

Gethin felt as if he'd stepped into freezing water in leaky shoes and the cold was creeping up his legs. His life had been wrecked by cheating. First Jonnie, and now he spent his days gathering evidence of unfaithful partners. He was angry Kell had let him think he wasn't involved with anyone.

"You don't live with him but you're in a relationship," Gethin said.

"Not a relationship. It's complicated. Fuck, I hate that word."

Gethin could feel his hope for something more with Kell sliding out of reach. "You're with him, but wanted to mess around with me on the side."

"No," Kell snapped out. "It's not like that."

"Marek's your boyfriend."

"Stop fucking guessing," Kell shouted. "I hate him. I hate it every time he touches me. He doesn't give a shit about me and I don't give a shit about him. He uses me when he feels like it."

Kell sounded so angry, Gethin was taken aback, but he couldn't stop poking. "Isn't that what you wanted us to do? Use each other when we felt like it? Text when we were in the mood for a fuck?"

"Nothing like that. I *can't* say no to Marek. I don't *want* to say no to you."

Gethin swallowed hard. *Can't?*

"Shit," Kell mumbled. "I know how it makes me look. But I need this job. I *have* to have this job."

"And you're letting yourself be fucked to keep it." Gethin dug his nails into the steering wheel. "I hope you play safe."

"Yes, I fucking play safe. I always play safe. I'm not that much of an idiot."

The services were coming up fast. Gethin wasn't sure whether to drive past and drop Kell at the next junction. *What am I not getting here? Kell's being coerced? Threatened?*

He pulled off the motorway into the services and brought the car to a halt in front of the motel. He took out his phone and called

187

Dieter's mother. "I'm outside with the cat. I'll be at your door in a couple of minutes."

After he'd finished the call he turned to look at Kell. "I—"

"Why don't we get a room?" Kell asked quietly.

Gethin felt a tightening in his gut. *How can I still want him?* But Gethin's life was complicated too. Jonnie was his secret. Why shouldn't Kell have secrets too? Whatever he was doing with Marek, Gethin *did* believe it wasn't something Kell was happy about.

"We've both been up all night," Kell whispered. "Just…be with me for a few hours."

After a long moment, Gethin nodded. At least while Kell was with him, he wasn't telling his boss about Dieter. Though maybe Kell just wanted to delay him until Warner got there.

"There's a towel in the back Dieter's mum brought out to cover the carrier last time. Bring the cat inside."

Gethin retrieved a bag and his coat from the boot. He always carried toiletries and a spare set of clothes. When he'd paid for a room, he led Kell to the first floor and swapped his bag and coat for the carrier. "Stay here." *Where I can see you but they can't.*

When Dieter's mother opened the door, he handed her the container and the key to her house.

"Thank you," she whispered.

"Have you thought where to go?"

"Yes, I—"

"Don't tell me. Don't tell anyone."

Chapter Eighteen

Kell clung to Gethin's coat. It smelled of him and that stupidly made Kell feel better — safer. Except he didn't deserve to feel either. *He doesn't trust me. I'm not sure he believes me.* That hurt and yet how could he blame him? He wanted to tell Gethin he was an undercover cop, but it went against everything that had been drilled into him. It would put them both in danger.

Gethin came back down the corridor and Kell followed him up the stairs.

"The tiger delivered safely?" Kell asked.

"Yep."

Gethin unlocked the door and gestured for Kell to go in. Kell dropped the coat and bag on a chair, took off his jacket and sat on the bed. A double — had that been intentional? He groaned and put his head in his hands. He was desperate to tell Gethin the truth. He didn't like Gethin thinking he was a slut, letting himself get fucked just to keep his job.

Fuck it, I am a slut. I've just got out of bed with Marek and now I want to get into bed with Gethin. His chest ached as much as his battered body.

He startled then straightened when Gethin sat next to him. *Christ. My nerves are shot.*

"This casual thing isn't working out, is it?" Gethin said. "We're getting to know one another whether we like it or not. I must admit, I hadn't expected to hear you'd been in prison."

Kell gritted his teeth, then sagged and turned to look at him. "I shouldn't have started this. I'm sorry. It's just that...I like you. It felt good to be with someone I liked."

Gethin stared straight into his eyes. "I like you too."

"How can you?" Kell's voice shook. "I told you what I'm doing. What I'm...letting Marek do."

"I'm guessing you have your reasons. Going to share them?"

"I can't," Kell whispered. "God, I want to tell you, but I really can't." The lump in his throat grew big enough to choke him. "I know what we agreed, keeping it casual, and it can't be more than that, but you made me... You made me smile when I thought I'd forgotten how. You made me see life could be different. I don't want this to end, yet I don't see how it can continue, don't see why you'd want it to. I swear I'll never tell Warner about Dieter, but I know you have no reason to trust me."

"I could have left you at Dieter's house. I didn't. I've brought you to where Dieter and his mother are hiding. I *am* trusting you. I don't like whatever's going on between you and Marek. That should be reason enough to stop this now, yet I find myself not taking that path."

A flare of hope burned in Kell's chest. "I'm looking for another job." It was sort of true. *What would I say or do to make this not end now?*

"Not easy when you're an ex-con. Do you have any qualifications? Is there something you *want* to do?"

Kell couldn't continue that conversation without spilling more lies. Gethin's hand lay on the bed next to his and Kell shifted until he could interlace his fingers with Gethin's.

"I need you to help me forget, not remember," Kell whispered. "Can we just have that? For a few hours? One last time. Forget everything. Please?"

Gethin seemed to stare at him for an impossibly long time before he nodded. Kell stood and tugged Gethin to his feet. When he felt the harness under the T-shirt, he shuddered. "Still wearing this?" Kell curled his hands around the bottom of Gethin's T-shirt. By the time Kell had pulled it off, his cock was rock hard. He trailed a finger down the leather where it crossed Gethin's chest, tracing the route it took over his slender torso.

Kell smiled. "When I saw you in the club, I wanted to grab hold of the straps and fuck you where you stood."

Gethin raised his eyebrows. "Funnily enough, when I put it on, I had this image in my head of you fucking me from behind, holding onto the harness."

"Christ. So you're not going to freak out if that's just what I do."

"Not as long as you don't say giddy-up, doggie."

Kell tried and failed to stop the stupid grin breaking out on his face. "I'll try not to."

"Or giddy-up, horsie."

Kell laughed. This guy had no idea how great it felt to laugh and mean it. Kell could hardly believe Gethin hadn't dumped him at the side of the motorway. *How can he still want me?*

One last fuck, stupid. That's what you agreed.

I don't care.

Kell pulled him close and slid his hands up his back, wrapping his fingers around the leather and yanking him in tight. Their kiss was deep, wild, intoxicating. Gethin danced his fingers down Kell's back to his trousers, and slid his thumbs under the waistband before sweeping his hands round and over Kell's flies. *Undo them. My zipper is strangling my cock.* Gethin slid his fingers between Kell's legs, cupped his dick and balls, and Kell arched into his grip, rocking so that Gethin gripped him harder.

I am on fire. Blood pounded in his head as Gethin peeled him out of his T-shirt. Now their chests were only separated by strips of leather. Kell moved back to take a better look, his mouth watering at the way the harness shaped and framed Gethin's pecs. He was like some exotic warrior. *One who's on my side, though he doesn't know it.*

"He bit you?" Gethin snarled.

Three words wrecked the moment. Kell tensed, wondering if Gethin was going to hit him, but all he did was rub his thumb over the bite mark on Kell's shoulder, then over the one at the left side of his nipple. Still…Kell's heart had sunk to his toes. He was pulling away as Gethin jerked him back.

"He bit you," Gethin repeated. The belligerence had gone, though the disappointment that replaced it hurt more.

"I don't mind being bitten," Kell muttered. "But I mind him doing it."

"It's a good thing he isn't here," Gethin whispered. "Because I'd fucking kill him."

Kell's heart lost a little weight. Gethin slid his hands over Kell's backside and they both groaned. Gethin managed to open Kell's trousers with one hand and wrapped his fingers around Kell's cock. *I wish I didn't want him so much. This is so fucking hard.*

"You okay?" Gethin asked.

"Forgotten my name."

"So long as you haven't forgotten what to do."

"Buy bread and milk. Oh God, and eggs."

Gethin slid his hands around to Kell's butt, dipped inside his shorts and squeezed. Kell fumbled with Gethin's trousers, the long, rigid cock making them difficult to open, then Gethin's dick was in his hand, hot and hard and heavy. Kell kept telling himself this would be all right, that at least he could have this.

"That feels good," Gethin whispered.

"Don't you ever wear shorts?"

"Sometimes."

A few words exchanged, then they were kissing again, taking turns to plunder each other's mouth, nipping at lips, sucking. Whenever they broke for air, Kell stared into Gethin's face, drinking in his eyes, still struggling to believe Gethin was still here with him. Before thinking could stop him, he ran the tip of his tongue along Gethin's thick dark lashes.

"Weirdo," Gethin said.

"Yeah, sorry. It's just your face. I want to eat it."

"There's other parts of me that are tastier."

Kell shoved at Gethin's trousers, and Gethin shoved at his until their cocks were kissing, the wet heads melded together by their hands. They kicked out of their rest of their clothes until they were naked in each other's arms—apart from that harness.

Gethin's fingers were digging into Kell's backside and Kell had his fingers under the lowest strap across Gethin's back. Stifled moans and gasps burst from their lips as they writhed together.

Kell pressed his face against Gethin's neck. *I wish I could tell you who I really am.*

Gethin eased away. "I need one minute. Get the lube and condoms out of the bag."

Kell watched him disappear into the bathroom and groaned. Not going fast was torture of the sweetest kind. His cock was yelling at him to shove Gethin on the bed and fuck him hard. His head was telling him to take it slow. He grabbed what they needed and pulled back the cover on the bed. When he turned, Gethin stood in the doorway of the bathroom watching him. *Oh fuck, his cock, that harness.* Kell shuddered.

"Promise me something?" Gethin asked.

"What?" His heart thumped.

"Before you fall asleep, help me get out this harness."

"Damn, I was hoping you'd never take it off." Kell paused. "How did you get it on?"

"Remember the party organizer? He and his partner fastened me into it. I put my foot down about the leather chaps."

"Whoa. You'd have had a bare arse?"

"Yep." Gethin smiled from the doorway.

Kell wrapped his hand around his cock and pressed down his balls. "Ask to borrow them. And a cowboy hat. Maybe not the whip, but then again… Shut me up now." *Shut me up because I'm never going to see you again, am I?*

Gethin walked into his arms, aligned his hot body against Kell's, and brushed his lips so gently over Kell's bruised cheek, that Kell's heart twisted in pain. Gethin kissed his way down his neck and along his shoulder, lingering on the bite mark while at the same time letting his hand drift down Kell's chest and onto his cock. Kell hadn't expected Gethin to press his teeth into the bite and he gasped at the sharp pain.

"Now it's *my* bite," Gethin whispered, the hot wash of his breath sending goose bumps skittering over Kell's skin.

Gethin wrapped his hand around the base of Kell's cock, and stroked up to squeeze the swollen, sensitive head.

"Fuck, fuck, fuck." Kell shivered.

Propelled onto his back on the bed, Kell lay with his legs hanging over the side, Gethin looming over him, his mouth quirked in a smile. He took Kell's balls in his hand, rolled them in his palm, rubbed them with his thumb and Kell forgot how to breathe.

"Shit, shit, shit." Kell bit back his whimper.

"Why are you saying everything three times?"

"Are you fucking counting, counting, counting?"

Gethin smiled.

"You're supposed to be insane with lust," Kell said.

"I am." Gethin kissed and licked and sucked his way down Kell's body, tracing the line of his hips with his tongue, until his mouth joined his hand.

"Oh God," Kell groaned. "See, that was only once. Arrgh, fuck no. God, God, God."

Gethin ran the tip of his tongue down Kell's shaft, following the length of the long dark vein. He breathed on him, blew air over the wet trail he'd left, lapped up the little pearls of precome sliding from the slit before nuzzling his balls, pulling one, then the other into his mouth. He teased, tugged and sucked until Kell thought he was going to die. He could hear himself talking rubbish, pleading, groaning, begging and he couldn't shut up.

"Yeahyeahyeah…fuck…God…more…Gethin…please…Jesus! No more…more…oh fuck."

Kell lifted his head so he could watch, then threaded his fingers in Gethin's hair, and stopped watching. *Too much.* He tugged at the strands, trying not to pull too hard, not to buck into his face, not to *fucking* come. Not yet. Gethin wrapped one hand tight around Kell's cock and pressed his tongue behind his balls. The sensation of Gethin's hair against his thighs made Kell shiver.

Then Gethin licked the uber-sensitive strip of skin that led to his anus, and gasps changed to whimpers. Gethin swept his tongue back and forth, tormenting until Kell yanked him off by his hair.

"No more," Kell pleaded.

Gethin grinned. "I've only just started."

But Gethin didn't protest when Kell grabbed his shoulders and reversed their positions so that *he* was the one kneeling on the floor and Gethin lay on his back with his knees bent, legs spread—waiting. Kell wrapped his lips around the head of Gethin's cock and sucked, tangy precome fizzing in his mouth. He nuzzled and tongued his way down Gethin's groin, the taste of salt and sweat, musk and soap adding fuel to an already blazing fire.

When he reached the taint and sucked, it drew a deep grunt from Gethin. One tentative lick over his hole and Gethin clenched his thighs around Kell's shoulders. Kell reached up to push his fingers into Gethin's mouth and once they were wet, brought them down to feather around the entrance to Gethin's body. When his tongue joined them, fluttering over Gethin's hole, it was Gethin's turn for incomprehensible muttering.

Wet tongue, wet fingers, rough chin, silky hair—Kell knew exactly how that felt. *Fucking brilliant.* He wanted to drive Gethin wild, wanted him to buck and thrust and yell—but not too loudly when they were in a thin-walled motel bedroom. He wasn't going to be saying giddy up *anything* but he loved the idea of holding that harness as he fucked him, the illusion of control it would give.

Kell licked and kissed, his tongue pushing into Gethin's body while one hand pumped Gethin's cock and the other fumbled for the lube.

"Sorry, I can't wait," Kell gasped. "Well, *I* could, obviously. But my cock can't and I always listen to my cock."

Gethin gave a strangled laugh as Kell expertly flipped him over and pulled him up on all fours. Slick fingers speared the cleft of his backside, and Gethin rested his forehead on the bed, giving a soft moan. Would Kell let himself be fucked? If Gethin managed

195

not to come, he'd have a chance to find out. Fingers circled his arse hole, an insistent push and press, before Gethin's muscles allowed them in. The burn was sharp, strong, so good he heard himself whine and snapped it off.

While Kell pushed his fingers in and out of Gethin's arse, he kissed his way up his back, the wet heat of his mouth making Gethin squirm. When Kell reached the neck, he nipped the skin, breathing hard as he rocked against him. Kell's cock replaced his fingers, the rounded crown nudging and pressing against the entrance to his body. Gethin tensed and stopped breathing, telling himself to push back. Speared by the thick cock, pain replaced pleasure. He gritted his teeth, groaning as he bore down and took Kell inside him, pain before the ache faded and all he could feel was pleasure.

Kell wrapped his hands around the straps crossing Gethin's back and tugged.

"No 'ride 'em, cowboy' either," Gethin forced the words out.

But as Kell thrust into him, Gethin's mind shut down to whatever Kell might say. All he could concentrate on was *this*, the deep-seated delight of being filled by a cock. Gethin wanted it hard, wanted Kell to fuck him through the bed. And Kell did. He shoved his dick deeper and faster, clinging on to the harness, dragging Gethin up as he powered into him.

A change of angle and Kell's shaft glanced off his prostate. Gethin cried out, throwing his hips back against Kell's forward thrust. He could feel Kell's balls slapping against him, feel Kell's rise toward orgasm. Kell jerked him up time after time until Gethin felt as though the guy *was* riding him, the pair of them joined in some strange counterbalanced movement that maintained the rhythm, but pushed Gethin toward what he was trying to delay. *Not yet.*

Then Kell was coming, the force and speed of his thrusts slipping out of tempo into frantic coupling.

"Gethin," Kell gasped.

196

The sound of his name almost tipped Gethin over the edge but as Kell's cock swelled and pulsed inside him, he just managed to pull back from the brink. Kell let go of the harness and Gethin sank onto the bed with Kell's sweaty body draped on top of him.

Gethin waited for guilt to strike but it didn't. Even if he and Jonnie *could* do this, Gethin wouldn't. Just because Jonnie was living in the past, didn't mean he had to keep Gethin there with him. *Will Jonnie guess what I've done? Do I want him to?* Not while he was contemplating assisted suicide. If Jonnie went through with it, life would be a lot less complicated. Gethin deserved the painful stab of guilt that followed that thought.

He waited for resentment to strike, and that *did* hit hard, but not hard enough to give him regrets. Gethin wasn't happy about what Kell was doing with Marek. He didn't want to share Kell with anyone, particularly someone who abused him. Kell wouldn't tell him why he continued to let himself be used, but what excuse could there be that Gethin would be able to accept? Gethin's hopes that whatever he and Kell had might grow roots and shoots and leaves, and turn into something more than lust had withered and were dying. His hopes that Kell might be someone he *could* tell about Jonnie were dying too.

"Stop thinking," Kell muttered against his neck, "and fuck me."

Gethin's cock sprang back to life at the thought of fucking Kell. One last fuck. One last fuck that Kell would remember forever. He gave Kell long enough to get rid of the condom and grabbed one himself before pushing Kell onto his back. Gethin fumbled with the lube and accidentally squirted it all over Kell's chest.

Kell laughed. "That was fast."

"Hey, no laughing. I just wanted to sure my monster cock didn't split you in half."

Kell rolled his eyes and Gethin wiped the excess lube onto the sheet. He positioned his cock at the entrance to Kell's body, and despite his intention to go slow, pushed hard into him. Kell's muscles tightened around his dick to the point of pain and Gethin sucked in a breath. Kell grinned.

Gethin grunted. "Smug isn't an attractive look."

Kell chuckled and Gethin groaned as the sound vibrated through him. When he began to move, Kell stopped laughing and began making little cries of pleasure. *Does Marek make you feel like this? Why do you have to let him fuck you?* Kell wound his arms and legs around Gethin, buried his fingers in his hair and dragged him down for a lingering kiss. When Gethin pulled back, Kell's eyes were glazed. *Is that all this is? Fucking?* Gethin rocked his pelvis and began to drive harder, shoving Kell across the bed. Firm, strong thrusts wound his balls toward explosion and Gethin forced himself to slow, change to short, snappy jabs, then gentle pushes. Anything to make this last, drag out the pleasure as long as he could.

"Shit, shit, shit," Kell mumbled.

"Back with the threes?"

Kell's hands dropped from Gethin's head. One clasped the sheet, the other his half-limp cock. His cheeks were flushed, his mouth open and he looked so sexy, Gethin found himself picking up speed again.

"I need an hour of this," Kell said.

"You must have been asleep. I've been going for fifty-eight minutes."

Kell's smile split his face. Gethin circled his hips, didn't just thrust but made his cock dance, twist and corkscrew. He drove in hard, slid in slow, plunged in fast until his balls ached with need. So long since he'd felt like this. Had he *ever* felt like this?

"Oh fuck," Kell groaned. "That's so good." He paused. "Good, good, good."

He reached for the harness with both hands, wrapped his legs around Gethin's hips and pulled him down for a kiss.

Tension coiled at the back of Gethin's head, shot down his spine and electrified his balls. Synapses snapped, crackled and popped. His balls knotted up tight against his dick then come erupted from him in pyroclastic blasts. *All* of Gethin came, not just his cock. His entire body tensed and arched, his toes curled, his hands clenched on Kell's shoulders as he filled the condom.

When the last spasm had faded, he slumped on top of Kell, his heart still galloping out of control. If he'd had a pacemaker, he suspected it would have exploded.

"Jesus," Kell whispered. "You are *good*."

No one had ever complained, but Gethin knew he'd wanted Kell to think that, had done what he could to ensure Kell enjoyed being fucked by him. To wipe Marek from his mind. Both their minds. *That didn't last long.*

"*Really* good," Kell said. "*Really, really* good. *Really —* "

"Yeah, I got it." *Fucking Marek.* Gethin gripped the condom and eased out of him.

"Wait." Kell reached to unbuckle the harness. He manoeuvred Gethin free of the leather straps and tossed them onto the floor.

Gethin padded to the bathroom, got rid of the condom and stared at himself in the mirror. Cheeks flushed, eyes bright, hair a mess. He was shocked to see the smile on his face. It faded fast. It wasn't that he didn't want Kell anymore, but Marek was too big an issue for Gethin to ignore.

When he emerged, Kell was asleep, lying the right way round on the bed, head on the pillow. Gethin lay next to him and pulled up the covers. He hesitated, then turned to face the other way. He felt the moment he did it that Kell *wasn't* sleeping, that he'd just pissed him off and he rolled over to see Kell staring at him, his face blank.

"Do you agree with assisted suicide?" Gethin asked.

Kell started. Maybe that shouldn't have been the first thing that came from Gethin's mouth, but it had worked as a distraction.

"That wasn't what you were thinking." Kell's mouth tightened into a thin line.

Shit. Not a distraction at all.

"Marek," Kell said.

Gethin stiffened. He didn't want to discuss what Kell was doing. He didn't get why, would *never* get why he'd let a guy hurt him, and knew he was fooling himself if he thought he and Kell could go anywhere while he was still fucking around elsewhere. *So tell him.*

Gethin sat up. "Look. This was fun. I wish you weren't messing with another guy but you are. You don't want to share your reasons — fine."

"It's not because I want to," Kell said.

Gethin raised his eyebrows. "And that makes it okay?"

Kell pushed himself up. "No." He moaned. "I can't do it. I can't not tell you. I'm not letting Marek fuck me just so I don't get fired. I'm working undercover."

It took a moment for Kell's words to sink in. Gethin groaned. "Christ. You're a cop?" That explained so much.

"Yes."

Gethin sighed. "I should have guessed." *I really should have guessed.*

"That wouldn't have made me much of an undercover cop if you had."

"Is your name even Kell?"

"Kellan DeMornay. If you tell anyone I'm a cop, I'm dead."

"I'm not going to tell anyone." Gethin struggled to work out how he felt. Glad that Kell wasn't a thief, hadn't been in jail but... There was a but.

"I hadn't planned this... thing with Marek. I'm not supposed... Ah Christ, I don't know what I was supposed to do or not do. Follow my instincts. Except..." Kell flopped back on the bed and threw his arm over his eyes.

"Except what?"

"The first time it happened, he raped me."

Gethin pressed his lips together as he settled back at Kell's side.

"After that, there didn't seem much point resisting. But I do. He likes me to fight. Shit. I don't want to talk about this. He's standing between us like some fucking psycho, wondering which one to kill first. But I've gone so far, if I stop now, it's all been for nothing."

"Hey. You don't need to explain. Sometimes we have to do stuff we'd prefer not to. The greater good, yeah?"

Kell moved his arm and gaped at him.

"Now you're thinking what you do with Marek doesn't matter to me," Gethin said, "that I don't care. It matters, and I care. I don't like it, and I wish he'd never touched you. I still want to kill the bastard, but I *do* understand. Nothing's black or white."

"This *is*. I want out. I've had enough. I'm on the edge. Every time he touches me I want to throw up. I want—"

"Hush." Gethin stroked his cheek. "Maybe the end is closer than you think."

"I've got fuck all to tell my boss."

"Maybe I can help you out with that. Do you know Detective Chief Superintendent Tom Beckwith?"

Kell frowned. "Yeah. He's my boss's boss. Do *you* know him?"

Gethin nodded. "I got my hands on some information off a computer belonging to an accountant who does the books for Warner's businesses, including No Escape. Apart from spreadsheets that might indicate money laundering, there was a document with photos of naked women, and amounts in euros underneath. I gave a memory stick with all the data on to Beckwith."

Kell pushed up on one elbow. "Christ. What do you mean—got your hands on? How?"

"I was tricked. I thought I was downloading information for a potential divorce, but the woman who hired me isn't married to the accountant. I have no idea who's pulling her strings, but she's desperate to get her hands on the data I downloaded. So desperate, my office was broken into. I'm waiting for Beckwith to tell me what he wants me to do."

Kell gave a choked laugh. "Our lives are more entwined than we thought. You might as well tell me where you like to go on holiday, if you have an obnoxious brother and whether you're allergic to anything."

He made it sound like a joke but Gethin sensed it wasn't. Their non-relationship *was* changing whether they liked it not. When Gethin wasn't sexed-up from wanting to come, sexed-up from having just come, it was easier to think straight. This was already more than stringless sex. No matter how important it was for Kell's job, Gethin didn't want Marek to fuck him. He wanted Kell out of the club and maybe the information he'd taken from Charlton's computer would help that happen.

His heart beat faster at the thought that he'd been on the point of walking away. Kell shouldn't have told him he was cop but he was glad he had.

A phone started to buzz and Gethin realised it was his. He got up and fumbled in his clothes until he found it. *Oh shit*. He knew Kell was listening but he didn't want to disappear into the bathroom. He took a risk and answered.

"Needed to hear your voice," Jonnie said.

"It's a bit early." Gethin glanced at the bedside clock. Just after six.

"Wake you?"

"I wasn't asleep."

"Don't feel well. Hot."

Gethin leaned against the wall with his back to Kell. "Have you told anyone?"

"Yes. Need you though."

"I can't come now."

"Want to see you. Please. Love you."

"Jonnie." Exasperated, the word slipped out unbidden and Gethin winced, knowing Kell would have heard.

"Where are you?" Jonnie asked.

"Working."

"Where?"

"Toddington."

"Need you."

"I'll see you soon." Gethin ended the call.

He switched off the phone and tossed it onto his trousers.

"Somewhere you need to be?" Kell asked.

"No." Gethin wasn't ready to reveal that part of his life. They'd had enough revelations for one night. He dropped back on the bed.

Kell wrapped himself around him. "I want this to work, but I don't know how it can."

Neither did Gethin. "I rarely take holidays. I don't have a brother or a sister. I'm not allergic to anything."

"Cornwall. Obnoxious brother four years older than me. Anchovies. Though that might be because I don't like the idea of eating bones." Kell rested his head on Gethin's shoulder. "My mother's insane. My father thinks the sun shines out of my arse."

"What's your father doing checking out your arse?"

Kell chuckled.

"Is your mother *really* insane?"

"Yep, really. Not just a figure of speech. She's in a secure place. My brother Oliver is insane too, but he's better at hiding it. He tries to kill me every now and again."

Gethin pulled back to look at him to see if he was joking.

"I'm serious. He's a twisted fuck who made my life a misery in any way he could when were young. Still does when he gets the chance."

"How did he try to kill you?"

"Which time?" Kell gave a quiet laugh. "Once, we were at the seaside digging holes and Oliver convinced me to tunnel between them. He usually never played with me without there being some sort of trouble and I should have said no, but I didn't. I was enjoying myself. Oliver said I could be the one to break through from my side to his. I'd managed to get my head and shoulders out into the other hole when the tunnel collapsed. The weight of the sand…" He sighed. "I was crushed. Oliver did nothing. I could see his feet. He sat on the edge of the hole swinging them backward and forward. If my dad hadn't come, I'd have died."

"Shit."

"Oliver hates me."

"Because you're gay?"

"I wasn't gay when I was seven. Well, I probably was, but I didn't know it then. He just hates that I was born, that he had to share our mother. Every birthday, he does everything he can to wreck the day for me. He's a complete bastard. Are your parents still alive?"

"No. Long dead."

"Tell me something interesting about you."

Gethin exhaled. "I used to be in a band."

"Wow. Anyone I'd have heard of?"

"No." Gethin regretted saying that much. He left it a long time before he spoke again and wondered if Kell had just been waiting for him to add a little more than no. "What are we doing?" he whispered.

Kell didn't answer. Was he asleep? Gethin didn't move, just lay there and thought of what he might have said if Kell had asked that question of him.

I don't know what we're doing apart from fucking each other.

You're a crap liar. You're doing more than fucking.

You're taking a chance.

Chapter Nineteen

When Kell woke, Gethin wasn't beside him, but he could hear the shower running. He groaned as he stretched, then rolled out of bed to get his phone and make a call.

"Hi, Uncle Bob. Can I ask a favour?"

"You didn't die in the fire then?" Lane snapped.

Kell cringed. "That seems years ago."

"Well it wasn't."

"Okay. Brief summary." He glanced at the bathroom door. "Remember that teenager, Dieter, Warner took a shine to?"

"Of course I remember. You made enough fuss about him. A runaway. But he's seventeen. He can do what he wants."

"His mother hired a private investigator. The guy had a tip about Dieter being at the club, and set off the alarm to get him out of there. Dieter's now with his mum and they're away from their house in a safe location."

"Shit. So you'll get nothing else from him."

"No." *You selfish wanker.* Kell waited for his boss to make the connection.

"How would you be aware of all that?"

There we go. "It's…complicated, but I happen to know the PI."

Lane's exasperated sucking of teeth made Kell clench his jaw. "So your cover's blown?"

Kell could have said yes, and that would have been it, but he'd done too much to walk away now. "No. The PI knows I'm a cop, but he won't say anything." No need for Lane to know Kell had *told* Gethin he was undercover.

"Your life might depend on him keeping quiet."

"I trust him."

"And how long have you known him?"

"Long enough. There's something else you need to know." Kell told him what Gethin had discovered on the accountant's computer. "The PI gave the information to DCI Beckwith."

Lane let out an exasperated snort. "Beckwith knows you're undercover at the club and he's said nothing to me. I'll talk to him.

"Marek's asked me to go in tonight. Early. Should be my night off. Something's up."

"Excellent. Send details when you can. I'll pull a team together just in case."

Kell ended the call as Gethin came out of the bathroom. "You're dressed." He didn't try to hide his disappointment.

"I have somewhere I need to be." Gethin's voice was flat and he didn't look at Kell.

"Fine." Kell grabbed his clothes from the floor and pushed past. He only just managed to stop himself slamming the bathroom door.

That was that then. Even knowing he was working undercover wasn't going to make Gethin get over Marek. Kell didn't blame him. He knew how he'd have reacted if someone he liked was doing the same. Gethin might have said he understood and maybe he did, but there was a difference between understanding and accepting.

As he stood under the shower, it occurred to him that he had no way of getting back to London unless he hitched a lift. *How stupid was I to think this meant something?* A hot session in bed and a few confessions did *not* make a relationship. When he thought about it, *he* was the one who'd opened his heart, talked about his family, not Gethin. How did his parents die? When? Who brought him up? What about this band? Why couldn't Gethin tell him?

Kell regretted talking about Oliver now, though he knew *why* he'd done it. To show Gethin he was a survivor, more than an undercover cop who'd crossed the line. Kell had a life. He had a family. Dysfunctional as it was. And all he got from Gethin was that he'd been in a band. Great, but the guy had closed that conversation straight down.

When they'd lain in bed and Gethin had muttered the question — what are we doing? — Kell had been too choked to reply because didn't asking that say everything? All they were doing

206

was fucking. That's what they'd agreed. Except now Kell had the feeling Gethin didn't even want that anymore.

Would Gethin wait for him? Maybe tonight it would all be over. No more Marek. But who was Jonnie? *Fuck.*

When Kell came out of the bathroom, he was shocked to see Gethin still there. "You haven't gone?"

"You need a lift, don't you?"

Kell bristled. "You don't have to bother. I can get back." *That is so mature.*

"Going to hitch a ride? You should know better. Anyway no one picks up hitchhikers these days. Even hot ones."

Kell's mood lightened at the teasing. "I find sticking my dick out works every time."

"Well, keep it in your trousers or you'll get arrested."

They padded down the stairs.

"Could we get breakfast first?" Kell asked, hope back in his heart.

"I don't have time." Gethin dropped the two keys on the unattended desk, took a step toward the glass exit door then shoved Kell to one side with a hard thrust. "Shit. Don't move."

"What the fuck?"

Gethin dropped his bag and coat. "Marek and Warner are in the car park with Dieter and his mother."

Kell took a step toward him.

"Don't you dare. You're not wrecking months of undercover work. Hide in case they come in here."

Gethin ran out before Kell could stop him. Kell pulled his phone from his pocket and called his boss. "I need assistance at the M1 services at Toddington, north side. Warner and Marek are trying to grab Dieter from his mother and the PI."

"Right… Okay…" There was long pause before Lane spoke again. "Help's on its way. Have you been seen?"

"No."

"Keep out of sight and stay on the line."

Kell picked up one of the keys from the desk and ran back up the stairs. The room they'd been in overlooked the car park. Hidden by the curtain, he stood and watched. Surely Marek and Warner wouldn't do anything stupid in broad daylight in the middle of a parking lot covered by security cameras.

Would they?

Gethin sprinted across to where Dieter was struggling with Marek. Dieter's mother was screaming at him to let Dieter go. Warner sat in the car with the window down.

"What the hell are you doing?" Gethin snapped.

Marek turned to him and gave a surprised snort.

"Let Dieter go."

Marek wrapped his arm around the teen's shoulders. "He wants to come back with us, isn't that right, Dieter?"

The boy's eyes were wide with shock. He glanced at his mother and nodded. "Yeah. I want to go back."

His mother pulled her phone from her bag. "I'm calling the police."

"Dieter wants to come with us," Marek said. "They won't stop him."

"What have they threatened to do?" Gethin asked Dieter. "Hurt your mum?"

"Don't go with them," she said.

Gethin stepped toward Marek. It made him sick to think of Kell letting this guy fuck him, bite him. "Let him go." *Give me an excuse to hit you. Please.*

"What the fuck does it have to do with you?"

Warner got out of the car. "You know this man?" he asked Dieter.

Gethin had two ways to jump. What risk was there in denial? "You told him he could choose anyone he liked. He chose me. I said I didn't have much money. He shot me the finger and walked back to you." He sent a silent plea for Dieter to go along with this

208

and for his mother to keep quiet. But if Marek knew who he was, he was wasting his time.

"You set off the alarm." Warner glared at him. "Cost me a lot of money."

"Not me. I panicked when it went off, got pushed over and knocked you over too. I was so confused I couldn't remember where I'd parked." He gave a shaky laugh. "I found Dieter shivering in a doorway. Promised I'd draw out cash and I drove him here. He'd gone when I got out the bathroom. He doesn't want to go back to the club. So what's your problem?"

Warner grabbed Dieter's arm and tugged him away from Marek. "Dieter chose to work for me. I didn't force him. He still owes me for his accommodation. When he's paid his debt, he can go home."

"He's only seventeen years old." His mother was crying.

"How much money does he owe you?" Gethin asked.

"Why?" Warner looked him up and down. "You're not going to pay it."

"How much?"

"Ten thousand."

Dieter and his mother gasped.

"You're going to be a good boy and dance for me." Warner stroked Dieter's arm.

"Leave me alone." Dieter tried to jerk free and Warner smacked his hand across the teen's face. "Get him in the car," he told Marek.

As Marek pulled at Dieter, Gethin moved in, kicking Marek's leg and yanking Dieter free. He pushed the boy behind him and toward his mother. Marek landed a fist in Gethin's stomach and he doubled over in pain. But when the second fist flew toward him, Gethin caught Marek's wrist and flipped him so he sprawled on the tarmac.

"You fucking cunt." Marek sprang to his feet.

The pair of them grappled, trading blows and kicks. Gethin knew this wasn't going to end well for him. He wasn't a street

209

fighter and Marek was much bigger and tougher. Marek wrapped an arm around his throat and Gethin slammed his elbows back into his chest. He worried that if he didn't stay on his feet, Kell would come outside.

"Leave him alone," Dieter's mum shouted. "I've called the police."

A sharp blow to his lower back made Gethin cry out in pain. Marek brought him down, a foot hit his ribs and as Gethin curled up and protected his head, he heard a siren.

"Shit. Grab the kid, and get in the car," Warner called.

Got to get up. Delay them till the police arrived. He was on his knees, panting, when two police cars roared up. Gethin glanced at Dieter who was clinging to his mother.

"What's happening here?" one of the policemen asked.

"A misunderstanding." Warner smiled.

"What's your name?" the policeman asked.

"Silas Warner."

Gethin's mouth felt wet. He rubbed his lips and saw blood on his fingers. He felt as if he'd been knocked down by a tank. He groaned as he stood up.

"This young man works for me," Warner said. "As does this gentleman." He gestured to Marek who stared at Gethin as if he wanted to stamp him into the ground like an annoying bug.

Gethin's chest was heaving and his ribs hurt. He wasn't sure he could get a sentence out yet. He was interested to hear what Warner would say. How had he known Dieter was here? He'd avoided telling Warner he was a private investigator because he hadn't forgotten the guy's link to Charlton. But if the police asked for his name, the game might be up. He glanced at Marek. Maybe it was anyway.

"Dieter's seventeen years old," his mother said. "He ran away from home and I reported him missing. I had a call from him to say he was here with this man and I drove to get him."

Warner gasped in mock-astonishment. "Oh my word. I thought he'd kidnapped Dieter." He pointed to Gethin. "He was seen by my staff watching Dieter in the club last night. Someone set off the fire alarm. Dieter disappeared in the confusion. I was worried sick. I tried to ring his mother but she didn't answer. So I contacted his father. He told me Dieter was here. You can ask him."

Gethin mentally groaned. *What did I say? Don't tell anyone where you are.*

"We were just discussing Dieter's return when this man came up and attacked my employee."

Why hadn't the cops asked Gethin his name? Or Marek his? He began to wonder if Kell was behind their speedy arrival rather than Dieter's mother.

One of the policemen walked over to Dieter. "You want to stay with your mum or go with your employer?"

"Stay with my mum," Dieter whispered. "I don't want them to hurt her."

The policeman turned to Warner. "Hurt her?"

Warner put up his hands, palms out. "What Dieter does is entirely up to him. No one wants anyone to be hurt. This has just been a misunderstanding. I was worried about him."

Dieter pulled the watch off his arm, walked over to Warner and handed it to him. "Thank you for this. I didn't know you wanted payment for my food and accommodation. That was stupid of me. Maybe you can sell the watch for what I owe you. Or was that not a present?" He stepped back to his mother's side.

Gethin was impressed. He hadn't thought Dieter would stand up to Warner.

"What about you?" one of the policeman said to Gethin. "*Did you start it?*"

Gethin almost laughed. He'd kicked at Marek's leg if that counted as starting it. He wished he'd kicked him in the nuts. "I was trying to help Dieter."

"Look, we don't want to press charges," Warner said. "It's a misunderstanding. We can all go our own way."

"I don't—" Dieter's mother began to speak.

211

Gethin shot her a warning glance and she closed her mouth.

"So everyone's okay about this?" one of the cops asked.

When no one disagreed, Warner and Marek drove off, followed a couple of minutes later by the police cars. *Well that had been fucking strange.*

"Oh God," Dieter's mother sagged. "I told my ex-husband. He'd been worried. I never thought…"

"Give him a call," Gethin said. "Find out what he said."

A few minutes later, they had their answer. Someone who'd claimed to be a cop had gone to her ex's house, woken him up and persuaded him Dieter was in danger.

She put the phone back in her pocket. "I'm so sorry."

"Maybe it's not entirely a bad thing. Warner gave the police his name. They took the registration of his car. It's far less likely he'd try to get Dieter back now." *Getting even with me, however…*

"Why didn't you tell him you were a PI?" Dieter asked.

"It wouldn't have made any difference and the fewer people who know what I do, the better. Thanks for keeping quiet about that. You did well."

"So we can go home?" Dieter's mother asked.

"Maybe give it a few days. Just to be certain."

Gethin waited until they'd driven away, then limped back to the motel. Kell was waiting in the lobby. He pulled Gethin into his arms and Gethin flinched in pain.

"Shit. Sorry," Kell whispered. "Don't ever do that again."

"What? Shove you out of the way so you don't wreck your cover?"

"No. Worry me like that."

A shiver of…something…raced through Gethin's veins. "I assume you called the police?"

"Yep. Thank God they came fast."

"Are you implying I couldn't have taken Marek?" Gethin pretended to be affronted.

"I was worried he'd ruin your good looks. Who'd fancy you then?"

Gethin laughed and sucked in a breath at the ache in his ribs. "Do you want a lift?"

"I don't think I should. I've got a ride coming."

"Okay. Listen—take my number out of your contacts, just in case."

Kell's cheek twitched.

"You could memorize it first." Gethin gave him a little smile. "I didn't tell them I was a PI. As long as Warner doesn't register the police didn't even ask my name, I should be okay." Though he still worried about Marek.

"I told my boss to make sure the police didn't ask Marek for his name either."

"Good thinking. I wish I could tell you I'd kicked the shit out of him, but it would be a lie."

"You're not hurt too badly, are you?"

"I'll survive." Gethin picked up his bag and coat and walked out. His phone rang as he approached his car. He pulled it out and checked the caller. "Miss me already?"

"I deleted the number, but thought I'd better test what I'd remembered in case I found myself calling a Catholic priest."

Gethin laughed. "Take care."

"You too. Gethin?"

"Yeah?"

"You can't keep me safe, but you *can* keep me strong."

Gethin's stomach clenched. "Good."

Kell ended the call.

Gethin plugged his phone into the hands free unit in the car and headed back to the motorway.

He'd only gone a couple of miles before he had another call. *Angel.*

"Hi, person I'm going to punish very hard," Gethin said.

"Darling, you make that sound such a treat."

"Well, it won't be."

"Your office. Oh my God. It's such a mess. It looks like someone went wild with a hammer."

"Probably."

"I didn't need to pretend to be shocked. Everyone is upset. I called the police, but they don't appear to be in a hurry to get here. Are you coming in?"

"Not yet. Do me a favour and arrange for the door to be repaired. I'll pay you."

"The insurance will pay. Tell me how you got on at the club."

"Didn't the threat of demonstrating the whip I bought tell you everything?"

Angel purred. *Damn him.*

"I needed to blend in. In that get up, I attracted the attention of everyone in there."

"Because you're fucking gorgeous, you idiot. Anyone interesting?"

"I was *not* there to pick someone up."

"Wasted opportunity. Did — er — you need help to get out of the harness?"

The conniving... Gethin cut him off and made another call.

"DCI Beckwith," the cop said.

"Thank you for actually answering." Gethin didn't bother to keep the snap out of his voice.

"I hear you were involved in a little fracas this morning. I need you to step right away from this, right away from Warner and No Escape. You got the boy back. You did your job. Now leave things alone."

"What about that memory stick? Anything useful? What if Izabela calls me again?"

"Give it back to her. Pretend you couldn't read it. I'd choose a public place if I were you. Goodbye, Mr. Jones."

The cop ended the call and Gethin sighed. He was happy to leave things alone but would things leave *him* alone?

When he reached Wellbrook Manor, he checked his face in the mirror before he got out of the car. A lick of his fingers and a quick wipe rid his mouth of the trace of blood. He climbed out of the car with a heavy sigh and headed for the entrance.

Kell sat in the back of his boss's car looking out through darkened windows. He was unbalanced, and that was worrying because it made him vulnerable.

"Do I need to pull you out?" asked his boss from the driver's seat.

Kell fidgeted. He hadn't expected the Detective Superintendent to come himself. He should say yes, but there was something going down tonight with Marek and he wanted to at least have something to show. "I'm not at risk. Gethin didn't tell them he was a PI. Letting Marek and Warner think he'd brought Dieter to the motel shifts attention from me."

When he'd seen Marek lay into Gethin, Kell had run back down into the lobby. How far would these guys go in a public area *and* in front of two witnesses? If the police hadn't turned up when they had, Kell would have gone to Gethin's aid. Gethin had risked his own safety to keep Kell safe and Kell was more touched by that than he could say.

"What were the pair of you doing at the motel—apart from the obvious?"

Kell clenched his fists. The only sign of annoyance he'd allow himself because Lane couldn't see his hands. "I told you Warner sent me and Marek to Dieter's house to see if he was there. I went around the back and found Gethin. I made sure Marek didn't spot him. After Marek dropped me off at my place I called in and got a ride to the motel. I wanted to be sure Dieter was safe and that Gethin didn't land me in trouble."

That was weak. Kell waited for Lane to laugh.

"And you find out not only has this guy pissed off Warner by snatching his star attraction, but he's also stolen information about Warner's businesses from his accountant's computer. A fucking tangled web. We don't yet know who's behind that. It's even possible it's Warner wanting to know he's not being cheated by Charlton."

215

Kell doubted that. "Warner's more likely to go for brute force than subterfuge."

"The PI's office was broken into and his computers trashed by people looking for what he'd taken. They didn't find it. They presumably don't know we already have it."

Kell straightened. "They trashed his computers?"

"Someone went to a lot of trouble to get that information. Why did they choose Gethin Jones?"

"I don't know him that well."

Lane snorted. "That's not what you told me. He's aware you're working undercover. Is that where you met him? Under the covers?"

Fucking bastard. "I met him at a party. Okay? Not that it has anything to do with you."

"Yes it does. If you're to stay safe I need to know everything. I don't like coincidences. I don't like that Jones is linked to Warner in two different ways — through his accountant and through Dieter — and you're right in the middle. Drop him. Now."

Kell curled his toes.

"If Warner discovers someone has copied files and spreadsheets from his accountant's computer, and then finds out you know who took it, you're in serious trouble."

"You better hurry up and find out who's behind it then."

Dieter and his mother weren't the only ones who needed to lay low. Kell wanted Gethin to do the same.

"What information was there on the computer?" Kell asked.

"Look in that folder in the back of the seat."

Kell pulled it out and started to read.

Chapter Twenty

Gethin walked into Jonnie's room to find him crying. His stomach cramped and he sucked in his cheeks as he crouched down at the side of the wheelchair.

"You don't cry." Well that was stupid considering what he was seeing. He pulled a tissue from the box on the bed and gently wiped Jonnie's face.

"Thought I'd used up lifetime's quota of tears," Jonnie said. "Wrong."

Gethin pulled the armchair across the room and sat next to him. He put his index finger on the finger Jonnie used to control his life and stroked it gently.

"Face," Jonnie said.

"Your tears are gone, mate."

"Not mine. Yours."

"Ah. I got hit. Big guy. Albanian... We brawled in a car park," Gethin said before Jonnie got the wrong idea. "You remember that teenager I told you about? Dieter? I found him in a nightclub. The owner had taken a fancy to him but Dieter wanted to leave. I drove him to a motel to meet his mother, and the club owner found out he was there. It was lucky I'd decided to stay the night in the motel or it'd have been all on his mother to have stopped him getting snatched this morning."

"What happened?"

"She called the police. I don't think she and Dieter will have any more trouble."

"Pay you?"

Gethin huffed. "Not yet. Maybe I'll get four hundred. But if I was actually invoicing for the full amount it would be more like a thousand. She can't afford that."

"Scratched."

Gethin looked at his hand. "Yeah. Dieter wanted their cat. I got the wrong one." Gethin embellished the story but he could see Jonnie wasn't really listening.

"Emailed them," Jonnie said.

Gethin didn't have to ask what he meant. Blood thundered in his head.

"Read it." Jonnie clicked a couple of times and Gethin read what was on the screen.

"Had to join," Jonnie said. "So I joined."

Gethin sighed.

"Need help," Jonnie said. "Need you."

Gethin looked at the sites Jonnie had accessed. The price of an assisted death in Switzerland plus cremation, medical costs, fees and transport. Between ten and fifteen thousand pounds.

"Have that much?" Jonnie asked. "Not yet maybe, but royalties? Lend it?"

Lend it? It served Gethin right. He'd been putting regular sums into Jonnie's account and told him they were royalties. While Gethin and the rest of the band *should* be receiving royalties, there was an ongoing dispute between lawyers since Gethin left and another after the band dissolved following Jonnie's accident. Add in the crooked agent and nothing had yet been paid. What was due would likely get swallowed up in legal fees.

"Help me. Please. Need send copies of medical records and letter explaining why this life is not…what I want." Jonnie took a shaky breath. "Written letter but need doctors here to give me records… Need written assessment from doctor saying…I'm of sound mind."

"Jonnie…"

"Can't talk me out of this. One thing in life I want…more than you."

Jonnie's speech was less slurred, as though this was too important for him to not be fully understood.

"Please, please. Death isn't worse thing… *This* is. Death is easy…but I have to have help. Need someone to take me…arrange everything…*be* with me."

"Oh God, Jonnie." Gethin sucked air and caught nothing in his lungs. "Look. Give life another chance. I know this isn't what you want. But you could still compose music, write lyrics."

"Miserable fucking songs about not being able to swim in sea, play in snow, wrap myself around guy I love… Songs about wanting to die. No one's interested… No one wants me."

"What about me?"

Jonnie gave him a sad smile. "Better for you if I'm dead."

"Don't say that. What about your parents?"

"Better for them."

"You don't kill yourself to make life better for someone else."

"I want it for me." He blinked. "You always said I was a selfish git… I need this soon. Fast. Please… If you won't help, I'll have to ask stranger."

How are you going to do that? You don't even have the fucking money to pay for it.

Gethin put his head in his hands and closed his eyes.

"Know it's hard to ask but I need you to help. I asked staff here. Won't even talk about it… Sent fucking psychiatrist… Dr. Tolly. Need him to say I'm of sound mind… Said he could talk to you about me. Call him."

"How about if I took you on holiday? Maybe we could get you in the sea or out in the snow."

A shadow crossed Jonnie's face. "Not this Jonnie."

Oh fuck.

"Last thing I ever ask of you."

Gethin took a deep breath. "What about your parents?"

"Don't want to see them again."

"You have to tell them what you want to do."

Jonnie stayed silent for a moment. "Think about it. Will you help? Will you get medical records? Ask doctor to say I'm not crazy?"

Gethin's throat seized up. He looked at the guy at his side and remembered the old Jonnie. The pain in the neck Jonnie, the sexy Jonnie and even the cheating Jonnie, and Gethin knew the guy hadn't meant to hurt him. It was just the way he was. Careless, carefree, thoughtless. And Gethin was aware of what Jonnie *wasn't* saying. Not that his accident had been Gethin's fault. Jonnie had never blamed him, not exactly, but…

"Please."

"Okay. I'll help." Gethin could barely believe he'd uttered the words. He had to force them past the hard lump in his throat. But Jonnie smiled in a way Gethin hadn't seen since before the accident. His eyes shone and there was a kind of peace in his expression that Gethin had *never* seen before. What right did he have to prevent Jonnie doing what he wanted?

Though that didn't mean he wouldn't keep trying to get him to change his mind.

When Gethin finally left, he went to get the number of Jonnie's psychiatrist, Dr. Tolly, from Candy on the reception desk. Gethin stood by a window in the lobby and first phoned Dr. Khan, Jonnie's personal physician. He'd expected the doctor to be difficult about discussing what Jonnie had said, but he wasn't — just disappointed. Jonnie was entitled to have access to his medical records and the doctor agreed to email them.

"I'm sorry," Gethin said. "I've tried to talk him out of it. I'll keep trying but…" He choked up.

"I can't discuss this any further with you."

"Okay." Gethin ended the call.

When Gethin looked up he saw Candy staring at him, no smile on her face.

"You okay?" she asked.

"I wanted to say no to him."

"Don't beat yourself up," she said quietly. "There's no right or wrong thing to do here. Jonnie's a sad young man. I see him when they wheel him to the movie room. He never talks to anyone. The nurses say he doesn't complain anymore. He used to moan about everything. He's lost the will to care. You have to do the caring for him."

Gethin left before he broke down. He wasn't a guy who cried, but he was being pushed beyond his limits. He phoned the psychiatrist before he got in his car.

"Dr. Tolly?"

"Yes."

"This is Gethin Jones. A friend of Jonnie Miller, a patient at Wellbrook. Is it convenient to talk?"

"Yes."

"I'm guessing you know why I'm calling."

"Yes."

Don't give me any help here. Gethin took a deep breath. "Jonnie says he's given you permission to talk to me about his health."

"Yes."

Do you ever use more than one word? Was the guy worried Gethin was going to psychoanalyze him? "He wants me to help him go to Switzerland where he intends to take his own life." Even saying the words made Gethin feel sick. "To do that he needs to be declared of sound mind. Do you feel he *is* of sound mind?"

"Assessing mental capacity is a complex process."

The one time Gethin wanted a one word answer—though he wasn't sure which word he wanted to hear. Now he was going to get a lecture.

"It's not something that can be easily judged like whether a tap is on or off."

I'm not a fucking moron. "But you've been his psychiatrist right from the start. You know him as well as anyone. I appreciate there are ramifications to your judgment, but I want the best for Jonnie. I want him to have the right to choose his own future. That doesn't mean I agree with him. But he deserves the chance to make the decision knowing that he *can* make it. I hope you won't take that away from him."

"The situation requires analysis. I—"

221

"There's nothing to analyse." Gethin tried to keep his temper. "He's paralysed from the neck down with no hope of significant improvement. He doesn't want to live like that."

"Even so, I have a duty of care. Jonnie's depressed. He—"

"Wouldn't you be depressed?" Gethin raked his fingers through his hair in frustration.

"He's refused medication."

"Because antidepressants can't make him better, can't make him walk. Look… Please just consider it. If you won't declare him sane, I'll have to find someone who will. I absolutely understand you respect the sanctity of life, but Jonnie doesn't want the life he has. He wants the life he *had* and he knows that can't happen. Just think about it and if you can't help, please consider giving me the name of someone who will."

Gethin ended the call before the guy could say no.

He climbed into his car and rested his head against the steering wheel. It was hard to think straight with worries about Jonnie swirling in his head. Things weren't sorted between him and Kell, but now Jonnie took priority.

Kell arrived at the club as ordered just before seven. When he stepped inside, Marek was talking to Warner on one side of the room. Huginn and Josef, one of the bouncers, leaned against the bar on the other. Josef waved to him and Kell headed to their side. Leo one of the barmen came out of the bathroom and joined them.

"How's it going?" Kell asked.

Huginn didn't answer, just stared at him with his sharp, raven-black eyes.

Josef shrugged. "The boss and Marek are pissed off."

"Why? What's happened?"

Josef shrugged again. "Dunno."

"Know what we're doing tonight?" Because the sooner he found out, the better the chance of giving his boss a heads up, though Kell's location would be constantly monitored via his phone.

"No," Josef said.

Warner disappeared in the direction of his office and Marek walked over. "Josef, you and Leo in one vehicle. Kell and I will take other. Come."

Kell followed them out of the club and around the corner to where two old white vans were parked. He memorized the registration of the first but couldn't see the second.

"Want to drive?" Marek asked.

"Not really." He preferred Marek to have his hands on the wheel and not on him.

Marek climbed in on the driver's side.

"Where are we going?" Kell asked as he sat beside him.

"Seaside."

Kell fastened his seatbelt. Now he had to be careful. Look too interested and he could fuck this up.

"What you get up to today?" Marek asked.

"Went to an exhibition of twigs in the Tate Gallery."

Marek chuckled, but Kell wasn't joking. He'd needed space to think. Staring at twigs hadn't helped.

"Are we going after Dieter?" *Please say no.*

"That little prick? He's done."

"What's that mean?" Kell's heart jumped into his throat.

"Warner found out he was in motel on motorway and we went there this morning. But his mother hired private dick and he was there too. Things got heated. Cops arrived."

"Shit."

"Warner decided Dieter's too much trouble."

Kell was relieved to hear it.

"That guy in club *was* trouble," Marek said.

"What guy?"

"The one you liked."

Kell tensed. "The one in the harness? I liked his harness, not him. What's he got to do with this?"

223

"You were wrong it was accident. He set off alarm. Pushed Warner over."

"*He* was the private investigator?" Kell thought it was safe to make the jump.

"Yeah."

"Christ. So he snatched Dieter?"

"Took back to mother. He'll run again. Kids like him always do."

Kell changed the subject. Lack of interest was safest. "What are we up to at the seaside? Building sandcastles?"

"Collection and delivery."

"Is this a job for Warner or you?" Kell asked.

"Why?" Marek glanced at him.

"Just wondered."

"Don't."

That question had got him nowhere. The next might. "Will we have time to stop for a burger? I'm hungry."

"You can suck my cock."

"Can I have fries and ketchup with that?"

Marek laughed. "Take paper from my jacket and put directions into sat nav."

Pett Level Road. Winchelsea Beach. Kell was fairly certain that was in the middle of nowhere.

"Know it?" Marek asked.

"No." Kell stretched his legs and groaned, then became aware of Marek's interest in his groin and stopped moving.

"You have family?" Marek asked. "Apart from Uncle Bob."

Kell's background had been prepared for him. "My parents live in Scotland. They're not happy about me being gay. I have a brother who hates me, but not because I'm gay." Kell had insisted that be put in. He could talk truthfully for hours about Oliver.

"What did you do to make him hate you?"

"Be born. He wanted to be an only child. My mother told me he almost suffocated me when I was a baby. She said it was an accident, but I don't think it was."

He hoped Marek would open up about himself because Lane hadn't been able to find out anything about him.

"How come you have a Slovakian name when you're from Albania?" Kell asked.

"My mother was Polish."

"She still alive?"

"No."

"Brothers and sisters?"

"I have a sister. Fourteen years younger than me. I've always protected her. I'd kill anyone who tried to hurt her."

"Does she live in the UK?"

Marek nodded. Kell didn't push. He'd asked enough.

"How you feel about moving in with me?" Marek asked.

Kell was so shocked he didn't say anything for a moment. Not just shocked. Horrified. He knew his boss would be delighted. "I don't think so," he muttered. "I already have a brother trying to kill me. You go too far sometimes."

Marek chuckled.

Kell struggled to get his head around Marek asking him that. No way would he tell his boss. *I'm not moving in with this guy.* Kell wanted this over so he had a chance with Gethin.

"You move in this weekend. You live in a shit hole. Why you want to stay there?"

"Okay. If you like. I'll be allowed to make coffee, will I?" *No way.* He closed his eyes and leaned against the window.

He hadn't intended to fall asleep and jerked upright when the van juddered to a halt.

"Still want burger?" Marek asked.

They were in the line for the drive through.

"Please. I'm just going to nip inside and have a piss." Kell pulled out his wallet and Marek pushed his hand away. "Thanks."

Kell hurried around to the entrance, went straight to the bathroom, checked it was empty and shut himself in a stall. He pulled out his phone and called his boss.

"Uncle Bob. Can I ask a favour?" Kell whispered.

"Go ahead."

"Collection from Pett Level Road, Winchelsea Beach. TN36 3NQ. Delivery afterwards. Two vans. No idea what's involved."

He rattled off the van registration then froze. Someone had come into the bathroom. Kell flushed the toilet and stuffed his phone into his pocket. When he emerged, Josef stood at a urinal.

Kell washed his hands and stuck them under the drier. "I hope Marek's bought me a Happy Meal."

Josef snorted.

"Any idea what we're collecting?" Kell asked.

"Nothing of interest to us." Josef zipped up, rubbed his crotch and winked.

Women?

By the time Kell climbed back in the van, it had moved to the collection point. Marek handed him the food and drove to the far end of the car park. The other van pulled in next to them. Kell hadn't realised how hungry he was until he began to eat. He finished his burger in a couple of bites and an idea occurred to him.

"I need another. You want something else?" he asked Marek.

"Chicken nuggets. Tomato sauce."

Kell tapped on the window of the other van to ask if they wanted anything, but more to stop either of the guys following him. They shook their heads and Kell headed for the restaurant. He was fairly certain he couldn't be seen at the counter, but he was still careful. When he pulled out his wallet, he took out his phone at the same time.

"Uncle Bob. Can I ask a favour?" Kell nodded to the woman serving. "A Big Mac and a nine chicken nugget Happy Meal."

Lane laughed. "Not sure I can manage that."

"Could be women we're collecting."

"Pett Level Road runs along the coast. Whatever you're there for will be coming from the sea. We can't put a team in ahead of you because the vehicles would be seen. We're considering grabbing one van and letting yours go."

"Okay."

Kell ended the call, pushed the phone in his pocket and left with the food. Everyone was where he expected them to be when he got back to the van. Marek rolled his eyes when he handed him the Happy Meal.

"You get a toy dog." Kell handed it to him.

Marek tossed it back.

Kell put his hand on his heart. "I'm crushed. First gift I give you and you throw it back." Kell stroked the dog with his finger. "Don't take it personally. He's like that with everyone."

Marek snorted. The moment he'd finished eating, he set off again. Kell kept quiet until they reached the coastal road. According to the sat nav they were ten minutes from their destination.

"We collecting shells?" Kell asked. "Bit dark."

"Keep your mouth shut."

When Marek pulled into a small layby, Kell was sure the guy been there before. It wasn't easy to spot from the road. The other van parked behind. Marek switched off the engine and climbed out. Kell followed him.

Marek opened the back of the van and handed them all dark jackets and dark hats. "Put them on, and stay quiet."

He led them across the road, up over a sandy ridge and down onto a shingle beach, the stones slipping beneath their feet. The tide was in. Kell could hear waves breaking, the sea sucking at the pebbles. Marek was talking on his phone, but too quietly for Kell to hear what he was saying.

"Now we wait." Marek put his phone away, sat down and lit a cigarette.

Josef and Leo settled a few yards away.

"You next to me." Marek patted the shingle.

Kell tucked his hands in his pockets and dropped down by his side. The horizon was little more than a faint line in the night sky. Too much cloud to see stars. Kell liked looking at stars. He'd taught himself to recognize constellations when he was a kid. When he wasn't at school, he spent as much time as he could away from the house and on warm summer nights, he used to lie on the grass at the far end of the garden and look up into the sky. He wondered if Gethin liked looking at stars, whether he'd get the chance to find out.

"Suck me off," Marek said.

What? Kell glanced around. "Out here?"

"Who's watching?"

"Josef and Leo for a start." *But hopefully not my boss.* He had mental image of some satellite homing in on them, broadcasting their image to a room full of goggling cops.

"You two keep eyes peeled for boat," Marek called, then tugged at Kell's hair. "See? No problem. *They* do as I tell them."

Kell kept his back to Leo and Josef, came up on his knees and unzipped Marek's jacket so he could get at his trousers. Fortunately, Marek was already hard. Kell eased the guy's cock out of his shorts and wrapped his hand around the base. He never wanted to do this, but he particularly didn't want to do it now he and Gethin were getting somewhere. *So do it fast. Don't think.*

He dropped his head into Marek's crotch and enveloped the crest of his dick with his mouth, sweeping his tongue over the top. He knew how to make Marek come fast and he concentrated on the head, doing every trick he knew. Marek's breathing faltered.

Kell blanked his mind except for the thought that *maybe* he'd never ever have to do this again. He sucked harder, twisted the base with his fist as he pumped and felt Marek's dick heat and swell. Then Marek was coming, spurting into his mouth. Kell swallowed the salty-sweet come and wondered who he hated the most, Marek or himself.

Chapter Twenty-One

"Over there," Leo said.

Kell saw a light blink out at sea. Marek stood and tossed his cigarette aside. He took out his phone and flashed an answering signal.

"They come in two batches," Marek said. "Josef, you and Leo take first group. Go back via Hastings. Don't stop."

Kell stayed quiet. It was a while before he could see anything. He focused on a boat that didn't appear to be moving, then spotted an inflatable heading toward them, the sound of its engine carrying over the water. Marek looked back toward the road as if he'd heard someone and Kell wondered if Lane had decided to take *all* of them out now, but nothing happened. Though if Lane did have a team ready, they'd wait until the boat was ashore.

"Persuade them not to make noise," Marek said.

The boat was full of young women, all of whom looked cold and frightened. Two guys jumped out of the boat into the surf and pulled the craft up onto the shingle. Apart from Marek, they all helped get the women and their bags onto the shore. When one of the women spoke, Marek snapped something in Albanian — well, Kell thought it was probably Albanian — and she shut up. Kell helped a slender blonde over the stones and up the ridge to the road. He carried her bag and held her hand. Her fingers were freezing. He wondered what they'd been told, what they were expecting.

"Where you from?" he whispered in English.

"Albania. This really England?"

"Yeah."

She looked relieved. There were seven girls. None looked older than twenty and probably weren't even that, but at least they weren't children. Kell tried to link their faces to the photos from the file in his boss's car but it was so dark, it was hard to be sure. When he returned to the beach, he saw one of the guys from the boat hand Marek two shrink-wrapped packages, and then the craft was off again, back out to sea.

Kell strode over the shingle to Marek's side. "What do the women think they're doing here?"

"They know what they doing. Working."

There was no sign of the packages and Kell wondered if Marek had stuffed them in his jacket.

The boat came back with more women and Kell helped them out of the boat. Marek was rough when he handled them and gruff when he spoke. Kell carried the cases of two up the beach and over the ridge while Marek carried nothing. Kell had the feeling that if the guy had a whip, he'd have used it.

The women seemed happy once they reached the van and Kell felt bad about that. This time he thought he *did* recognize a couple of the faces. Was Lane going to let this vehicle reach its destination? If so, it prolonged Kell's agony because it meant they weren't pulling him out yet. But technically, what evidence was there to link Warner to any of this?

When the women were locked in the back, Kell took off his jacket and beanie, and climbed in the front next to Marek.

"No trouble tonight," Marek said. "Last time they all fell out of boat. Shrieking and wailing." He tsked.

Kell pushed the jacket into the footwell and saw one of the packages Marek had been handed. *Where's the other?* "What's in there?"

"Coke."

"Oh."

Marek glanced at him. "Oh?"

"Yeah. *Oh shit* I don't want to get caught with that. Still, it has your prints on it, not mine."

Marek sniggered. "I like that about you."

"That I'm always right?" Kell couldn't help it.

"You don't touch drugs. You don't drink too much. You talk too much but I know how to shut you up."

"Yeah." Kell pressed his lips together.

Marek pulled up outside a house in Deptford and took out his phone. Whoever he was calling didn't answer and Marek's forehead creased.

"What's wrong?" Kell asked.

Marek tried another number, waited then cut off the call. "Fuck."

Kell opened his mouth and changed his mind. Marek pissed off was never good news.

"No answer from Josef or Leo. They had less distance to travel. They should have arrived thirty minutes before us." He sighed. "Let's get girls into house. Pass me the coke."

Kell handed the package to him.

"Your fingerprints on it now." Marek chuckled.

Fucker.

When they let the women out of the van, Kell wanted to yell at them not to be so docile, so accepting. But they picked up their luggage and walked down the garden path and in through the door of the terraced house at 72 Vincent Drive as if they were arriving on holiday. Kell hoped all this was being recorded. They handed over the girls to a couple of guys Kell had never seen before and Marek also gave them the coke. They exchanged a few words in another language and Kell wished he knew what they were saying. Not speaking Albanian put him at a huge disadvantage.

"Can I use the bathroom?" Kell asked.

One of the guys pointed up the stairs. Kell shuddered when he saw the state of it—stained bath, filthy toilet. He locked the door and texted Lane. *7 Albanian girls delivered 72 Vincent Drive Deptford plus packet coke. Marek still has one packet.* Then he deleted the text, flushed the toilet and came back downstairs. Marek glanced at him, his face red with fury.

Kell clutched the banister. "What's wrong?"

Marek grabbed the sleeve of his jacket and tugged him out of the house. When Kell moved toward the van, Marek jerked him away. The lights flashed on an old BMW parked further down the road. Kell was shaking when he climbed in. He wasn't sure why he was so anxious. He was constantly on edge while he was undercover, but this was something different. Maybe it was because he knew things might happen quickly tonight and he needed to be ready. Or maybe it was because Marek was so unpredictable especially when he was angry.

After he'd fastened his seat belt, he crossed his arms so Marek wouldn't see his hands shaking. He watched the van they'd come in do a three point turn and head down the road. Marek pulled away in the opposite direction.

"What's happened?" Kell asked.

"No word from Josef or Leo. Both phones going to voice mail. I don't like it."

"Maybe they had an accident."

"Maybe. Warner will be pissed."

That answered one of Kell's earlier questions. Warner *was* behind this. "Where are we going?"

"Another job. Small one. This one you keep quiet about. *My* job, not Warner's, understand?"

"Yeah."

Less than ten minutes later, Marek pulled up outside an apartment building with scaffolding at one side. A big guy in a black leather jacket approached the car as they got out and as he drew nearer and Kell saw his face, he gasped. *Marek's brother? Twins?* Marek nodded to the man, exchanged a greeting and hugged him.

"Pav meet Kell," Marek said.

Kell nodded. The guy smelled rancid, of sweat and cigarettes and something else Kell didn't even want to try to identify. It unnerved Kell that he looked so much like Marek. *A multiplying nightmare.*

The three of them walked up four flights of stairs and along an open landing. Marek signalled to Kell and Pav to stand to the side, then knocked on the door of flat fifty-eight.

Whoever was in there opened it with the chain attached, but Marek kicked the door open and they all piled in. Kell's heart was pounding like crazy, but when he saw whose flat it was, it stopped beating. Gethin was backing away through an open plan space and ended up against the wall next to a grey couch.

Fuck, fuck, fuck, fuck, fuck, fuck. Not enough fucks to say how Kell was feeling.

"I don't believe it," Marek said with a laugh. "Small world."

What? It sounded as if Marek was as surprised to see Gethin as he was. Kell didn't understand what was happening.

"I don't recall inviting you in," Gethin said.

Marek stepped forward and drove his fist into Gethin's stomach. As Gethin doubled over with a grunt, Pav grabbed his wrists and wrenched them behind his back. *I can't do this. I can't stand by and watch.*

But as Kell moved, Gethin gasped, "Three against one. That's sporting."

Kell got the message.

"Sporting?" Marek smirked. "This my sort of sport. That first hit was for this morning." He hit him again, and Gethin cried out. "That was for taking what doesn't belong to you."

What? Christ. "What's this about?" Kell glanced around. "Is Dieter here?"

"I'm not talking about that little pricktease. Where's memory stick?"

Oh shit. "What memory stick?" Kell asked.

"Shut the fuck up," Marek snarled.

"I need the bathroom," Kell mumbled. *I need to text my boss.*

"Stay where you are." Marek didn't take his eyes off Gethin. "Where is it?"

"Fuck off," Gethin gasped.

Pav did something behind Gethin's back and Gethin sucked in a breath.

Marek hit him again in the stomach. "Where?"

"In my office," Gethin said.

"We looked in your office."

"Well hidden."

"Where?"

"If I tell you…you let me go?"

"Promise." Marek smiled.

God, don't believe him.

"Take me and I'll *show* you." Gethin stared at Marek.

"Maybe we should just start cutting until you talk." Marek grinned, Pav laughed and Kell fought not to throw up.

"The data's encrypted. You won't be able to read it."

"Have you read it?"

"No."

"Liar." Marek hit him again and Kell clenched his jaw.

"I read some of it…" Gethin took a deep breath. "I can decrypt it. You need me."

Marek was silent for a moment. "Okay. We go to your office."

Kell's restarted heart was in a race with his brain. Marek had been behind Gethin stealing that data from Warner's accountant? On Warner's behalf or for himself? Kell didn't have to think too hard about that. Marek didn't want Warner to know about this.

At least Gethin had talked himself out of his flat which was a good thing because it gave him a better chance to get away, and Kell would do everything he could to help.

"Fasten his hands." Marek handed Kell a cable tie. "In front."

Gethin clenched his fists with his thumbs together, palms facing down. Kell knew that would give him the best chance of slipping free. He didn't look into Gethin's face as he wrapped the tie and tugged. Not tight.

Marek smacked Kell's head. "Fucking useless. Tighter. Turn his wrists."

Gethin put his wrists together and Kell pulled on the tie, making sure the fastening was in front. Did Gethin know the trick to get loose? Not that it always worked, but Kell had practiced it, just in case. Arms up, slam them down and to the sides, over the hips.

Marek pulled Gethin's phone from his pocket, tossed it on the couch, then threw his coat at him. "Carry coat. Hide wrists. Call for help and I kill person you speak to."

Gethin nodded.

"Office keys?" Marek asked.

"Pocket of my coat."

"Pav, pick up his laptop."

Kell dragged the door closed as they left, relieved Marek's kick hadn't stopped it locking. *Useless piece of crap.* They didn't pass anyone on their way downstairs. Marek opened the car and Pav pushed Gethin into the back.

"Sit with him." Marek told Kell.

Kell slid in and fastened Gethin's seat belt.

"What you doing?" Marek asked.

"Fastening his seat belt."

Kell thought Marek and Pavel would choke themselves laughing. *I wish you fucking would.* Kell pressed his knee against Gethin's, felt Gethin's answering press, and mentally smiled. But when Kell's phone vibrated, he froze. He pulled it out. *Warner.*

Marek glanced in the mirror. "Who is it?"

"Warner."

"Careful what you say."

Kell took a deep breath. "Hi."

"Where are you?" Warner asked.

"With Marek. You want to talk to him?"

"No. Can he hear?"

"No."

"Keep this between us. I'm going to tell you what happened tonight and I want you to say yes or no if I get any of it wrong. Okay?"

"Yes." *Oh Christ, what's going on?*

"You arrived in Deptford before the other van."

"Yes."

"Are Leo or Josef answering their phone?"

"No."

235

"Was Marek worried by that?"

"Yes."

"Did he deliver a packet to the house?"

"Yes."

"One?"

"Yes."

"Not two?"

"No."

Warner sighed. "Are you coming back to the club? Ask him."

"Warner says are we going back to the club?"

"Not yet," Marek said. "Checking about Leo and Josef."

"You hear that?" Kell asked.

"Yes." Warner ended the call.

"What he want?" Marek asked.

"He's worried about Leo and Josef. I said there were no problems. They set off in the direction you said. There was no sign of anyone watching. They hadn't arrived before us at the house though you'd expected them to. Why didn't he ask you all that?"

"He did. You sure that all he ask?"

Choose sides. Fast. "He asked if you delivered a packet. I said yes. Is that okay?"

"Yes."

"Is Warner checking up on you?" Kell put as much incredulity into his voice as he could manage.

"No. He's checking up on you."

Kell didn't think so.

Gethin stiffened when he heard Marek say Warner was checking up on Kell. Kell's presence had been reassuring, but maybe Kell was in trouble too. He'd been shocked when Marek kicked his door down but when Kell had appeared, he'd felt relieved. Except he didn't want Kell to get hurt trying to help him.

Gethin thought he'd worked things out. "Izabela Dushku is your sister."

"Pav's too." Marek chuckled.

236

Well, duh. The pair were obviously brothers. Very similar features.

Pav turned and grinned at him. "My sister good actress. Her tears fool you. And bruises. She makeup artist."

"What are you talking about?" Kell asked.

"Keep your mouth and ears shut," Marek said. "You don't need to know this."

Then why bring him?

"At least tell me why you chose me." Gethin still worried there was some link to his past he'd not severed.

But the rest of the journey passed in silence. Kell rubbed his knee against his and Gethin wished he found it more reassuring.

The office building was deserted. They went up on the lift and Kell stroked his butt. *Don't get caught.* Gethin stepped out first and headed down the corridor. Marek took the keys from Gethin's pocket but it was only when the door didn't open that Gethin remembered the lock had been changed.

Marek nodded to his brother and one hard kick from Pav worked. Marek switched on the light. Angel must had asked someone to tidy up. The remains of his computers had been swept into a heap, his paperwork was stacked on his desk and the boxes of cables and parts had been piled up in the corner.

"Get it," Marek said.

"Unfasten my wrists?"

"Do I look stupid?"

Gethin moved behind his desk and bent down. For one heart-stopping moment, he thought the memory stick had gone before he touched it with his fingers and pulled it out. After he stood, Marek shoved him down onto the chair.

"Now you tell me what's on it."

"I need my hands free. I can't work like this."

Marek pulled out a knife and cut him loose. Finally, Gethin had a plan and a chance. The knife went back into the left pocket

237

of Marek's jacket. Gethin switched on his laptop and waited for it to power up.

"If you move the desk out you can see better," Gethin said.

"Pav." Marek nodded to his brother.

Pav and Kell dragged the desk away from the side of the room which now gave Gethin two ways of getting from behind it. He tapped at the keyboard and pulled up the data from his laptop, hoping Marek wouldn't notice what source he used.

"Money's going into banks, companies, investment businesses, markets, then brought back into the UK." Gethin's heart rate increased. "A complicated trail. Look."

Gethin swivelled aside to give Marek room. As the man bent to check the screen, Gethin pulled the knife from the guy's pocket, leapt around the desk and grabbed Kell. He flicked open the blade and held it at Kell's throat. For a long moment no one spoke.

"Drop the fucking knife," Marek snarled.

"You have what you want," Gethin said. "I'm leaving. Get your brother to move away from the door."

He could feel Kell trembling against him.

"Let him go," Marek said.

Gethin pressed the knife against Kell's skin and heard Kell gasp. *Christ, it's sharper than I thought.* Blood trickled over his fingers and the necklace snapped. Beads bounced onto the floor. *Sorry, Kell.* Gethin was relying on Marek having *some* interest in keeping Kell alive.

"Pav—move," Marek snapped.

The guy stepped away from the door and Gethin edged around the room holding Kell. He felt behind him for the door handle, spotted the look the two brothers exchanged and knew they were going to make a move. Gethin sent a silent apology to Kell, shoved him hard into Pav and fled.

They'd expect him to make for the stairs down and Gethin went up. It gave him a few precious seconds, maybe minutes if they checked each office. He'd made it onto the roof before he heard them coming.

"Fucking get back here," Marek yelled.

Gethin dropped to the next level, ran along the gulley and jumped into the night sky.

Chapter Twenty-Two

Marek sent Kell down the stairs to look for Gethin while he and Pav went up. Kell's neck had stopped bleeding, but there was blood on his jacket and T-shirt. He wasn't sure whether Gethin had meant to cut him or slit his necklace, but he wouldn't have killed him. Kell was surprised Marek hadn't said – "Do it. See if I care." Kell didn't want him to care.

He stayed inside the building and leaned against the wall by the exit. If Gethin came this way Kell would ask Gethin to hit him. While he had the chance, Kell took out his phone.

"Hi Uncle Bob. Can I ask a favour?" he whispered.

"Where are you?"

"In the PI's office building with Marek who has a fucking brother. Pavel. Why didn't we know about him? Marek wanted the USB stick. I think he's after Warner's money. The PI's made a run for it. What happened tonight? Speak fast."

"We intercepted the first van. Everyone's in custody. The house is under observation. Few more days, maybe not even that, and this will be done."

Kell switched off his phone and stuffed it in his pocket. Maybe he ought not to be waiting. Maybe he should be checking Gethin was okay because if Marek got his hands on him, he'd kill him. But if Kell moved away from the door, *he'd* be the one in trouble. He was reassured by the fact that Gethin knew this building and Marek didn't. Hopefully Gethin had an exit route planned.

When he heard footsteps, Kell straightened. Marek appeared in the hallway.

"He's not come this way," Kell said.

"He jumped off the fucking roof." Marek gave a frustrated grunt.

Kell's stomach roiled. "What?"

"I'm not jumping after him. Next time I see him, I'll kill him."

Still alive then. Thank fuck.

Pav came into the foyer and shook his head.

Marek nodded to Kell. "Go home."

"On our next date, you think we could do something less exciting?" Kell asked.

Marek grabbed Kell's hair and chuckled as he pulled him close. "You did okay."

"Okay? Well at least I didn't lose my head."

Marek rubbed his thumb across Kell's throat. "He will for marking you."

They split up outside and Kell watched them drive off. He waited to sag until the car had turned the corner.

"Worried about me?"

Kell spun at the sound of Gethin's voice. He stood in the doorway of the building, propping the door open behind him with his foot.

Kell ran up the steps. "You jumped off the roof?"

"I'd just cut your throat. I felt terrible."

Kell gave a choked laugh.

"Come inside." Gethin held the door open.

Kell stepped into the light and Gethin ran his finger across Kell's neck. "Are you okay? Not traumatized for life? The knife was sharper than I'd thought."

"Maybe that was a good thing. The blood convinced Marek you meant it."

"But not you?"

"I never thought you'd hurt me."

Gethin pulled him into his arms. "But I did and I'm sorry."

Kell let himself melt for a moment, then pulled back. "Now he *really* wants to kill you. You need to hide someplace until this is done. Outer Mongolia *might* be safe. Definitely not your flat, though I did manage to jam the door shut so no one should be able to steal your collection of Royal Doulton figurines."

"Come back upstairs with me. I hope they've left my keys."

Kell went after him. "So...you jumped?"

241

"I have a way of moving between this building and one farther down the road via the roofs."

"What are you? Spiderman?"

When they reached his office the door stood ajar. Gethin walked over to his desk, bent and picked up the keys from the floor. "I hoped he wouldn't notice when I knocked them off. The memory stick's gone."

"But he left the laptop."

Gethin picked it up. "He didn't realise the information on the stick hasn't been decrypted. What I showed him was on this."

"He'll know as soon as he plugs the stick in."

"Yep." Gethin threw Kell his coat. "Put that on. You'll have everyone thinking it's a zombie apocalypse." He walked over and touched Kell's neck again. "I nearly dropped the knife when I realised I'd cut you."

"It's just a scratch."

Gethin pulled an old leather jacket out of a cupboard and handed Kell a helmet.

"You wanted a ride on my bike. Now's your chance."

Kell tucked up behind Gethin wondering if he could be any colder. He held onto the bike with one hand and onto Gethin with the other. His fingers were frozen. His toes were frozen. His whole fucking body was frozen. Except for his cock. That was hot. Pressed up against Gethin's arse, how could it be anything else? But it felt as if the wind was cutting straight through Gethin even though Kell knew that was impossible.

As Gethin manoeuvered through traffic, Kell learned to lean with him. He was seriously turned on. A powerful machine between his thighs, the growling revs of its engine vibrating through his body, a sexy guy to hang onto, who was at least keeping one part of him—the most important part—warm, the streets of London flashing past—Kell was tripping on adrenaline.

Gethin zipped through gaps that made Kell suck in a breath, and wove around cars, buses and pedestrians. He wondered where they were going. Not to his place, nor Gethin's. Part of him wished Gethin would keep going, take them out of London, out of the country. Not to Outer Mongolia but to some warm beach where the most dangerous thing that could happen was getting sand somewhere uncomfortable. Kell's undercover job had grown doubly dangerous now he knew Marek was working against Warner. It was like walking a slippery tightrope with crocodiles on one side and alligators the other.

When Gethin finally pulled between two cars, and switched off the engine, they were in Islington outside a smart Georgian townhouse.

Gethin took off his gloves, turned and flipped up his visor. "You can get off now."

"You're assuming I can move."

"What did you say?"

Kell couldn't unclench his fingers to lift his visor. Gethin took his own helmet off and then helped Kell with his. He held both helmets in one hand and grabbed the laptop from the box. Kell was trying to convince his muscles to cooperate.

Gethin brushed his fingers against Kell's. "Shit, you're cold. Let's get inside."

Kell struggled off the bike and followed Gethin to the door. "Where are we?" Kell asked.

"Somewhere safe."

The door was opened by a good-looking guy in his forties. He had short dark hair, wore jeans with holes in the knees and a soft-looking, baggy grey sweater. A big smile blossomed on his face when he saw Gethin.

"Here again?" the guy said.

"Yeah. Henry this is Kell. Kell meet Henry."

Henry shook Kell's hand and winced. "You're like ice. You didn't give the poor guy gloves? Come on in."

Two dachshunds came running up, tails wagging. Kell bent to stroke them. "Sorry for the cold hands, guys."

"Winston and Kennedy," Henry said. "Our vicious guard dogs. Angel! Guests! Go through, you two."

"Angel runs the party business," Gethin said but Kell had remembered the name.

Henry ushered them into a room with a wood burning stove and Kell's jaw dropped when he saw the huge, part-decorated Christmas tree in the corner. *In October?* Angel had the strings of several small wooden reindeer hanging from his mouth. They dropped to the carpet when he gaped at Kell and Gethin.

"You're here with someone." Angel clutched his heart. "*Oh joyful day.* Not Macbeth. There are no joyful days in that play. Henry IV part two. Then he frowned. "You look familiar."

"This is Kell. He was at that party."

"He was the one watching you." Angel beamed. "My butler in the buff worked. Can I jump to conclusions?"

"No." Gethin turned to Kell. "Why don't you get warm?"

Kell moved closer to the fire and took off his coat.

"What the…?" Henry gasped.

Ah, the blood. "Gethin tried to cut off my head," Kell said. "Failed, obviously." He dropped down on the rug and held his hands up in front of the fire. The dogs curled up next to him.

"You need to clean up or have a drink first?" Henry asked. "I need one. I gave up arguing about the tree and I've had to listen to carols for the past hour."

"I'd like hot chocolate and marshmallows," Angel said. "The pink ones."

Henry rolled his eyes. "I didn't buy pink ones. We have almost everything drinks-wise. Including mulled wine. You can have what you like."

"Hot chocolate sounds great," Kell said. "Thank you."

Gethin put the helmets in a corner and tossed his jacket and laptop on top of them. He retrieved Kell's coat and put that there as well and Henry stared at the pile pointedly.

"Okay, I'll move them." Gethin picked them up.

"What would you like to drink?" Henry asked Gethin.

244

"Coffee please."

"Right. Give me a few minutes and don't tell Angel anything until I get back," Henry said.

Gethin took the helmets and coats out of the room.

"It's a lovely tree." Kell tried to think when he'd last hung a decoration on a Christmas tree.

"The theme is rustic." Angel retrieved the reindeers he'd dropped and hung them on the branches. "I'm going for silver in the dining room, red and gold in the kitchen and white in the bedroom."

"Four trees?" Kell raised his eyebrows.

"Five. Red *and* gold in the kitchen. No, six. I forgot the hall. Multi-coloured in there. Good practice for my Christmas parties."

Gethin came back in and slouched on the sofa, his face pale.

"I had a moment of déjà vu there," Angel said. "Reminded me of the first time we met when you dropped at my feet covered in blood. Gethin's first job as a private investigator and he was beaten up. I bundled him into a taxi and we've been friends ever since. I told him he ought to rethink his profession, but he's stubborn."

Gethin raised his eyebrows. "I *am* sitting here."

"Do you think you could help again this year?" Angel asked him.

"With what?" Kell glanced between the two of them.

"Putting up Christmas trees at my parties."

"If I live that long. The lock needs changing again on the office."

Angel frowned. "I haven't even given you the new key yet."

"I know."

Henry walked in with a tray and put it on a side table. He gave Kell his drink first and Kell cradled the mug in his still cold hands. He was exhausted. The adrenaline had finally seeped away. Good thing it *was* his night off because after everything that had happened, he had no energy. Henry sat opposite Gethin, and Angel perched almost on top of Henry. Kell managed a smile.

"Can we stay the night?" Gethin asked.

"Of course," Henry said.

"Start at the beginning. Don't leave anything out." Angel leaned forward.

"You can have a brief version." Gethin dragged his fingers through his hair. "Dieter is back with his mother and I think—safe from Warner. Kell works at No Escape. The guys who trashed my office didn't find what they were looking for so they came looking again tonight. This time they brought Kell. I had to pretend to threaten Kell so I could make a run for it. The bad guys left with what they think they came for but they'll need someone to decrypt it. Kell left with me. They're not aware that Kell and I…"

"That Kell and you are what?" Angel asked. "You can't stop. I didn't follow the rest at all but now it's getting interesting."

Henry glared at him before turning to Gethin. "So you can't go back to your place."

Gethin shook his head. "I'm hoping all this will be resolved in a few days. The police are involved. It's a matter of waiting."

"You think I could have a shower?" Kell asked.

"Course you can." Henry started to get up and Angel pulled him down.

"Gethin knows where it is." Angel smiled.

Once they were out of the room, Gethin took Kell's hand and a lump sprang up in Kell's throat.

"Okay?" Gethin asked.

"Yeah. I like your friends. Christmas trees though?"

"Angel loves Christmas."

He led Kell through a high-ceilinged bedroom and into a spectacular bathroom. There was free-standing tub as well as a huge walk in shower, and fluffy white towels hung on wing-shaped radiators.

"Okay?" Gethin let go of his hand.

"You're not leaving? What if I slip and bang my head? What if I start bleeding again? What if I lose the soap?"

"That would be a disaster."

Kell stripped quickly, tossed his clothes into a pile in the corner and turned to see Gethin staring at him. All Gethin had done was pull off his sweater and unbutton his shirt.

"You're beautiful." Gethin spoke quietly but the words echoed around Kell's body and settled in his heart. *Oh and in my cock*. Could cocks preen? His was trying to.

Gethin stripped quickly. "Check in the cupboard for shampoo and body wash."

"Are they euphemisms for lube and condoms?"

Kell heard Gethin laughing as he searched in the cupboard under the twin wash basins. *Thank you, Angel and Henry*. He tossed everything into the shower and as he turned it on, Gethin came up behind him. Kell groaned in bliss. He felt as though more than two hands were touching him and forced his eyes open just to check they hadn't been joined by Angel and Henry. *Just Gethin the octopus.*

Gethin kissed his way down Kell's spine and Kell arched his back, his head tipped to take the full force of the water. He braced his arms on the glass and spread his legs as Gethin knelt behind him, his face against Kell's butt, kissing and licking. And while Kell could have had him do that for hours, he wanted Gethin inside him now or his cock in Gethin's mouth. He didn't care. He just needed to come.

A long blink and Gethin was in him in one eye-watering, breath-stealing thrust. If Kell hadn't seen the torn packet on the floor of the shower, he might have worried. Then he worried himself anyway by wishing Gethin wasn't wearing a condom, wishing could *feel* him, have his come inside him, filling him, coating him. *Fuck, stop thinking.*

Gethin sank his teeth into Kell's shoulder. "Okay?"

"Are you in yet?"

Gethin rotated his hips and Kell hissed.

"Yeah, yeah, I'm okay," Kell blurted.

Gethin pulled back, then fucked him so hard Kell's knees almost buckled. Every thrust hit that perfect little spot and stars burst in Kell's head. *Oh God…fuck…Christ.* He reached for his cock to jerk himself off but Gethin swatted his hand away and fisted it himself, stroking…just right.

Tension coiled at the base of Kell's dick and sent lightning shooting up his shaft. He spurted all over the glass, air shuddering out of his lungs, his muscles clamping down on the cock lodged inside him. Gethin stopped moving and stood pressed against him, his cock lodged deep inside Kell's body.

"Jesus," Gethin whispered.

As the last aftershock twisted Kell's gut, Gethin wound up again, pulling almost all the way out before he thrust deep, the force of the movement shoving Kell forward until he hit the shower wall. Gethin put a hand on Kell's shoulder to hold him in place as he drove into him. Kell threw back his hips to meet Gethin's lunge and heard Gethin's breathing grow choppy. Kell smiled, knowing he was driving Gethin wild.

"You better not be looking smug," Gethin forced out. "You came first."

"I won, right?"

"Only just."

"Get a prize?"

"Me."

Kell felt the dick inside him swell and Gethin moved faster, his hips shifting in a wild dance, his fingers digging into Kell's hips and neck. Kell couldn't match the speed of Gethin's thrusts so he leaned against the glass and took what Gethin gave, enjoyed it, *owned* it. Gethin cried out as he came, shoved up tight against Kell and Kell felt him shake as he filled the condom. Kell didn't have time to take another breath before Gethin had pulled out and spun him round to kiss him.

They poured everything into that kiss, ate at each other, told each other how they felt without saying a word. Kell had waited all his life for this guy, and every shitty thing that had ever happened to him had been worth it if Gethin was his reward. This job would be over soon. Kell wouldn't take more undercover work, wasn't even sure if he wanted to stay in the police. This might have started out as something casual but they'd moved further away from that every time they'd met.

Too soon for that four letter word but there was a chance for it to develop. Kell wanted to go out with Gethin properly, go on dates, talk about something other than Warner or Marek or Charlton. He wanted this job done, over, finished so that he and Gethin could enjoy the present, and make a future.

Gethin stepped from the shower and tossed him a towel. Kell snagged it and rubbed his hair. He heard a phone ringing and Gethin bent to the pile of clothing. When he looked at it, it was as if a shutter came down over his face.

"Who is it?" Kell asked.

"I have to take this." Gethin walked into the bedroom.

Kell didn't intend to listen but he heard anyway.

"Is Jonnie…? Okay. Yeah I'll come now… No, it's fine."

Maybe there was no future while this Jonnie could make Gethin go running to him. Why hadn't Gethin told him who he was? Kell put on his shorts and jeans, slipped his feet into his shoes. Maybe Angel or Henry would lend him a T-shirt. He looked in the mirror, touched the red mark on his neck and tried not to think about who Gethin had been talking to.

Gethin came back into the bathroom and dressed quickly. "I have to go out. Someone I need to see."

"Okay."

"I might have to stay overnight," Gethin said.

"Right."

"He's…an old friend. Needs my help."

"Can I go with you?"

"No."

He walked out and took Kell's splintered heart with him.

Chapter Twenty-Three

Kell sat on the bed clutching his bloody T-shirt. It was eleven thirty. He'd been looking forward to spending the night in bed with Gethin, looking forward to feeling safe, looking forward to talking, and now Gethin had gone. *Thank fuck I didn't say anything stupid.* Kell was annoyed to find he had a painful lump in his throat. Why had he tried to fool himself this was going anywhere?

Maybe if he'd told Gethin he wasn't going to work undercover again? His fingers tightened on the T-shirt. Why would he care? It was Kell's thirtieth birthday tomorrow, but why would Gethin care about that either? He was glad he hadn't told him. Kell needed to get his mind-set back to where it had originally been. On emotionless fucks. On doing his job. He jumped at the knock on the door.

Angel popped his head around. "Everything all right?"

Kell nodded. "Do you have a T-shirt I could borrow? I need to chuck this one away."

"I'll find you something." Angel disappeared.

Kell jumped again when his phone rang. He dragged it out of his pocket, but it wasn't Gethin.

"Hi." Kell wondered what the hell Warner wanted.

"I know it's your night off but Pete's called in sick and Charlie's cut his hand slicing lemons and had to go to the hospital. I need you to work behind the bar. I'll pay you double."

Kell sagged. "Okay. I'll be there as soon as I can."

When Angel came in carrying three different T-shirts, Kell picked the grey one.

"Can you call me a cab, please? I have to go into work. They're short-staffed."

Angel took his phone from his pocket. "Ivan, darling… Yes, please. For a friend. Quick as you can. Thanks." He put his phone back. "Five minutes. They're just around the corner. Are you sure you're all right?"

Kell plastered a smile on his face. "Yeah, fine. Thanks for the hot chocolate and the shower and everything. I love your tree. It's been an early birthday present being somewhere warm and comfortable."

"Your birthday?"

Kell's chest clenched tight. "Tomorrow. Don't tell Gethin."

"Aren't you coming back? It sounded from what Gethin said as if you were in danger."

"Gethin is, I'm not." Kell made his way out of the room and padded down the stairs, Angel on his heels.

Kell pulled his jacket out from under Gethin's laptop, tempted for just a moment, to see what was on it. As far as he knew Gethin hadn't switched it off so maybe Kell wouldn't need a password to get into his files. But what was the point? He pulled the jacket on, grimacing at the blood stains.

"Gethin must really like you," Angel said.

He had a funny way of showing it.

"In all the time we've known him, he's never brought anyone here, never introduced us to anyone. He's a very private person."

"Does he already have a boyfriend?" *I'm not a fucking boyfriend.* Kell tightened his fists and pressed his nails into his palms. "Tell me because I'm not going to waste my time on someone who…" His voice dried up. *Not just my time, my heart.*

Angel hesitated too long. "There's a guy called Jonnie, but their relationship seems complicated. I suspect Jonnie's married and Gethin is his bit on the side."

Oh God.

"Does he open up to you?" Angel asked.

"Not really."

"Gethin jumps when Jonnie calls, but he's never talked about him and he shuts me down if I try. I've offered Gethin tickets for all sorts of events he could take the guy to, but he's never accepted any which makes me think he can't risk being seen with him. I've tried to set Gethin up on dates and he's never interested. So you see why I'm surprised he brought you here. I don't think he has any friends and he needs someone. We all need someone. Gethin's…fragile."

And I'm not?

"Give him another chance, darling." Angel grabbed his hand. "I can tell you're pissed off with him."

Kell pulled his hand away. "It's Jonnie he's rushed off to see. He said he might have to stay the night. Maybe the guy's wife is out of town." *Try not to sound bitter.*

Angel fluttered his hands. "I was only guessing he was married. He might not be. It drives Henry mad when I guess."

"Whatever. You're wrong about Gethin needing me. He doesn't need anyone."

Kell heard the sound of a car pulling up outside. "It was nice to meet you," he said and headed for the door.

Gethin ran up the steps of Wellbrook Manor and when he found the door locked, he rang the buzzer. A woman he'd not met before let him in and Gethin took the stairs two at a time to Jonnie's room. If this was a false alarm… But there were a couple of nurses in there with him. Gethin stepped to his side. Jonnie was back on the ventilator. His eyes were closed, his face whiter than usual.

"How is he?" What a stupid question.

"Stable now. But it was…" The nurse shook her head.

Oh God, why didn't you let him die? His notes say Do Not Resuscitate.

Gethin took Jonnie's hand. "Hey, mate."

Jonnie opened his eyes and looked straight at Gethin. *What the fuck do I say to him?* Jonnie blinked four times which was a sign he wanted to use his computer. Gethin set it up and attached the specially adapted mouse to Jonnie's finger.

"Go away," Jonnie typed.

"I've only just got here."

"Go the fuck away."

One of the nurses put her hand on Gethin's shoulder. "Come back tomorrow. We should have him off the ventilator again by then."

Gethin bit back his irritation at having come all the way here only to go all the way back, but it wasn't the first time. He leaned over Jonnie and put his mouth right next to his ear. "I'm working on it. I promise."

It was only when Gethin parked outside Angel's house that he registered he should have taken a key. He called Kell's phone and when he didn't answer, tried Angel.

"This better be important," Angel said.

"I'm outside."

Angel cut him off and a moment later flung open the door. Gethin walked in.

"Kell's gone," Angel said.

Gethin spun round. "What?"

"He had a call to say they were short-staffed at the club so he took a taxi there not long after you left."

"Fuck."

Angel glared at him. "Where have you been? What the hell was so important you had to waltz out of here in the middle of the night? Kell was… You *hurt* him. *Art thou not ashamed to wrong him with thy importunacy?* Two Gentlemen of Verona, and not fucking Macbeth. I'm ashamed of you. You used him."

Gethin shifted straight from confused to annoyed. "You're imagining something that doesn't exist. We fuck. End of story."

"You are *not* just fucking him. You're blind if you think that. For a PI you're not very observant."

"What are you two arguing about?" Henry called from upstairs.

The dogs bounded down and jumped up at Angel.

"See, even Winston and Kennedy are pissed off with you."

"What have I done?"

253

"You let him hope," Angel said through gritted teeth. "You. Let. Him. Hope."

Gethin sagged. "It's complicated."

"Jonnie." Angel snarled the word.

"Off limits."

"Kell thinks that where you went. To see Jonnie. Is it true? Is Kell your bit on the side while you have a guy somewhere else you can't be with maybe because he's married?"

"I…" Gethin couldn't make the word *don't* come out of his mouth. He couldn't deny Jonnie tonight, didn't want to tell Angel the truth until he'd told Kell, but he could set one thing straight. "Jonnie's not married. I need to go to the club."

"You can't. Kell said it was too dangerous for you."

"It might be more dangerous for Kell. I'll wear a disguise. Is it a special event tonight? Werewolf night?" He pulled out his phone and checked. "Fetish. Fuck." He huffed. "Okay. I need a paper bag."

"For fuck's sake. You can't put a paper bag over your head. Wait there."

Angel stamped up the stairs pursued by the dogs. Gethin was well aware going to the club was more than risky. If Marek recognized him, he was a dead man. But Gethin didn't want Kell anywhere near that maniac. He'd assumed Kell wouldn't go back. *I'm an idiot.*

"Strip to your waist," Angel said as he came back down the stairs.

Gethin put his helmet down and unzipped his jacket. "What have you got?" He eyed the shiny material in Angel's hands with no small amount of unease.

"An assassin hood. Try it."

Gethin pulled the hood over his head. It left only his mouth exposed, his eyes covered by a strip of perforated material. Gethin hated it. He felt as if he couldn't breathe and tugged it off.

"No one would recognize you in that," Angel said. "You look scary. Take off your T-shirt and put this on."

He helped Gethin into vinyl sleeves that exposed only the tips of his fingers. The material crossed above his pecs and fastened together with a zip up his throat.

"Those trousers will do. They're black. The boots are good." Angel glared at him. "Put the mask in your pocket. You *have* to wear it or you'll be recognized."

"How come you have all this stuff?"

"Henry and I like to dress up, not that it has anything to do with you. Good thing for you that we do. Now go and get Kell. Grovel and bring him back."

Gethin left his T-shirt and sweater on the floor and put his jacket back on. He zipped the mask into a pocket.

"Oh by the way," Angel said. "Kell told me not to tell you, but I'm not going to let that stop me. It's his thirtieth birthday tomo—today now. Don't fuck this up."

Gethin covered the four miles in just over ten minutes, but it took him another five to find somewhere to park. He took off his helmet and pulled on the hood before he removed his jacket. *I hate this.* He could feel panic building inside him and sucked in air. *Christ, I can't even take a deep breath.* He almost pulled the hood off again but Angel was right. He *had* to wear it. He crammed his helmet and jacket into the bike box and hurried to the club. Marek's knife was tucked down the side of his boot under his trousers. He hoped he wouldn't need it.

Even as he paid the entry fee and had his ribs stamped, since his hands and arms were covered, he wondered what he was doing. Kell was working. He wouldn't just walk out because Gethin wanted him to. Gethin needed to explain about Jonnie, but not now. Though he could tell him enough to make Kell not mad with him anymore.

Something else was niggling at him too. What Kell had said about his birthday and how his brother always did something to spoil it. Gethin wanted to make this birthday special, take Kell somewhere and spoil *him.*

Kell's mouth hurt from smiling, his back ached from standing, his body ached from Gethin's hard fuck, and the spiked collar was chafing his sore neck, but he'd pleased Warner by coming in and so far, he'd seen no sign of Marek. *That* was enough to keep him smiling. He'd debated whether to tell Warner what had happened. It came down to who Kell would rather have on his side. Both guys were dangerous, but Marek worried him more.

The club was busy. Kell usually missed Fetish night. The range of outfits was amazing. Guys wearing PVC zipped thongs, cock rings, cock cages, cock and ball dividers, leather harnesses similar to the one Gethin had worn—and nothing else on their bodies, apart from shoes, some of them high-heeled. At the other extreme there were slinky body suits that covered everything but the mouth, and there was even a zipper to pull over that—Kell shuddered—military gear, blindfolds, and one guy wore a tight pink PVC dress with his tackle sticking out through a hole in the front. Not Kell's scene but everyone seemed to be having a good time, they were well-behaved, and that was all that mattered.

As Kell wiped down the bar a guy put his hand in front of him holding a twenty pound note. Kell recognized the elaborate signet ring. *Shit.*

"I'd like a dirty vodka martini."

Kell looked up. Oliver's voice sounded like breaking glass and made Kell feel as if he'd dived into a mess of jagged shards.

"Don't you know how to make one?" his brother asked. "Not much of a bartender, are you? Pathetic at that as you are at everything else. Three parts vodka to one part dry vermouth. Splash of olive brine. Pour into a cocktail shaker half-filled with crushed ice. Shake well, strain, garnish with a black olive and serve. With a fucking smile."

"You forgot the dash of cyanide." Kell reached for a beer without looking which one he'd selected, flipped off the cap and slammed it on the bar. It frothed over.

"Staff these days." Oliver tsked but picked up the beer. "Like my outfit?"

He was wearing a bandana eye-mask, simple black leather harness and tight black trousers.

"Didn't think they'd let me in if I didn't look the part." He chuckled.

"What do you want?" How had Oliver found out he worked here? Kell's heart was thumping uncomfortably fast. He almost wished he could have a heart attack. Was it worth pretending?

"What do I want? Well, to wish you happy birthday, of course, brother mine." Oliver sipped the beer and grimaced. "You know how much I look forward to it. I've not missed a year since the day you were born." He leaned over the bar. "Wondering how I knew where you were? Your boss told me."

Which boss? Lane? Oh God. Why? I'll kill him. No, Lane wouldn't. Then who? Warner? Marek? Lane's boss Beckwith? Someone higher? Kell's mind swirled like a tornado but he made sure he showed nothing on his face. He moved to serve another customer, aware of his brother's unswerving, unnerving attention. There was going to be trouble. The only way to avoid it was to leave with Oliver which was not going to go down well with Warner, but Kell had no choice. Oliver only had to say a couple of words and Kell was finished. Not just finished. Dead.

Try asking him. Kell moved back in front of him. "Oliver. Please don't say anything. This job is important."

His brother laughed. Kell almost expected to hear one of those maniacal cackles rising above the level of the music so that everyone would stop dancing and turn to look at him.

Try a threat. "Okay. If you're not going to be nice…you say or do anything to fuck this up for me and I'll call your wife and tell her you're into kink."

Oliver sniggered. "She knows."

"Then I'll announce to the room that you're looking for a master who'd shove food up your arse."

"Don't be so pathetic. You really are a waste of oxygen. I find it hard to believe we're related. I think Mother must have done a Lady Chatterley and fucked the gardener."

"Is this guy bothering you?" asked a gruff voice.

Kell looked at the man in the hood who'd come up at his brother's side. He wanted to say yes, but feared the consequences.

"I'm his brother," Oliver said. "So get fucking lost."

Oliver gasped as a flash went off in his face. The guy in the hood had taken Oliver's picture with his phone.

"Oliver DeMornay," said the guy. "Member of parliament for North Grinstead. On the Justice Select Committee. Which newspaper do you *not* want to publish your photo dressed like that? You're still recognizable even with that mask."

"Give me your phone," Oliver snarled.

The guy passed it to Kell.

"Kell, give it to me," his brother snapped.

"Leave without saying a word and the photo will be deleted," said the stranger who wasn't a stranger. *Gethin.* "Open your mouth and you'll be all over Twitter before you get through the door."

Oliver glared. "This is not over."

"Yes it is," said the guy.

Gethin grabbed Oliver's arm and tugged him away from the bar. Kell thought it was one of the best things anyone had ever done for him and one of the stupidest.

When Gethin came back, Kell moved to the quieter end of the bar, Gethin's phone in his hand. "You need to get out of here," Kell said.

"Not without you. I should have told you where I was going but it was an emergency and Jonnie is a long story."

I don't want to hear about Jonnie.

I want you to tell me everything about Jonnie.

"Gethin *leave. Now.*" Kell could see Marek walking toward them and he knew by the raw anger on Marek's face that this time it *was* directed at him and that put Gethin in danger too. "Run," he barked.

There was no time for Kell to get out from behind the bar. No time for Gethin to get out of the club. Only time for Kell to press 9-9-9 on Gethin's phone and tuck it out of sight behind a container of lemon slices. The bouncer Kell knew as Muninn was one side of Marek and Big Sev was on the other. Gethin flinched as they pressed against him.

Marek's eyes glittered with malice as he glared at Kell. "You fucking cunt." He turned to Gethin, dragged his hood off and spat in his face.

Kell had been so busy being anxious about the scene unfolding in front of him, he failed to notice danger approaching his side of the bar. He gasped as Alec poked a knife into his lower back.

"Either of you shout, or try to run, then I castrate the other." Marek nodded to one of the barmen and two half full shot glasses appeared on the bar. Marek picked one up and held it to Gethin's lips. "Drink or Alec will remove Kell's balls."

"What's in it?" Gethin asked.

"It doesn't fucking matter," Marek snapped. "Drink it. Now. Or I'll tell Alec to cut dick off as well."

Gethin hesitated, then drank and when the same threats were repeated, Kell drank too. He tried to hold the liquid in his mouth, but Alec pinched his nose and held his lips together. Kell spluttered and the vodka went down. *Not just vodka.* Kell knew they'd been drugged.

"Now we wait," Marek said.

"I'm sorry." Kell stared at Gethin.

"Oh, how touching." Marek leaned over the bar. "I cannot fucking wait to get my hands on you. I promise you my fist, yes?" He sniggered. "I do you both and you watch."

Even as Kell was formulating a plan, his head swam and he wobbled. His stomach was empty. The last thing he'd eaten had been that burger. Felt like days ago. Whatever drug was in the vodka was racing through his system. Kell's knees shook and Alec grabbed him as he fell.

"Help," Kell whispered. He should have shouted sooner, not just accepted.

Dimly aware of being moved across the dance floor toward the exit, he flailed trying to get free, but his limbs felt boneless. As he was half-dragged through the door, he saw Oliver watching.

"Oliver. Help." Kell tried one last time and as he passed out, all he could see was his brother's smile.

Chapter Twenty-Four

Kell gasped awake when he was hit by a deluge of cold water. "Finally," Marek said.

Kell's hair dripped water down his face and he blinked. He was tied to a chair, his arms secured behind him with rope. Gethin sat tied to a chair a few yards away, his gaze fixed on Kell, breathing heavily, his face bloody. *Oh God.* Kell shivered. He was soaked. There was water all over the floor around him but Gethin didn't appear to be wet. Marek paced between them. Kell could see Muninn behind Gethin and could *feel* someone behind him.

"I thought you weren't going to wake," Marek said. "You miss the fun."

Kell took a quick look around. They weren't in the club. Maybe a warehouse. A dark transit van sat in front of large double doors, a loading bay at the side.

Marek stepped in front of Kell, leaning in until his face was right in front of Kell's. "You have anything to say?"

"I knew I shouldn't have bought you that Happy Meal."

Marek laughed and stood upright. "Hard to persuade your friend to talk. Hard to shut you up."

Kell was thinking frantically, trying to come up with something that would at least get them out of these ropes. Marek backhanded Kell across the face and his head snapped to the side.

"Ouch," Kell mumbled. *Fucking bastard.*

Marek nodded to Muninn who took out a gun and held it against Gethin's knee.

"Right," Marek said. "Start talking. How do you two know one another?"

"I met Gethin at that party. You saw his number on my phone. G for guy, remember? We got talking and he told me he was a private investigator looking for a kid called Dieter Hoehn. Dieter's such an unusual name, I thought it had to be Warner's

261

Dieter. Gethin paid me two hundred quid to tell him where Dieter was. Maybe I shouldn't have taken it but I needed the money."

"Go on," Marek said.

"Gethin came to the club, triggered the alarm, tripped up Warner and ran with Dieter. That was the last time I saw him until you took me to his flat."

Marek hit him again, a blow that rattled his teeth and made him bite his tongue. The coppery tang of blood seeped into his mouth, dripped over his lip.

"All right," Kell gasped. "We fucked. Okay? Once. I told him never to come to the club again, but the idiot did." Kell glared at Gethin.

"You let me think he going to cut your throat."

Marek put his hand on Kell's cock and squeezed through the material — hard. Kell squirmed and sucked in a breath.

"You allow him to get away from his office. You knew I didn't have what I needed."

"He didn't tell me anything about a memory stick. I only knew he wanted to find Dieter, nothing else. I was shocked when we burst into his flat. I didn't know he lived there. Christ, if I'd known, if I was plotting something with him, you think I'd have just gone there with you? I'd have called him, warned him. I thought I was going to throw up. I asked you if I could go to the bathroom. Remember? And I didn't *pretend* he was going to cut my throat. I thought he would. That knife was fucking sharp."

Marek paced around him and Gethin. Kell was beginning to hope. All he needed was for Marek to believe him. Marek still didn't know he was working undercover, didn't know it was Kell's fault the other van hadn't reached its destination.

Marek walked over to Gethin. "I want all information from memory stick or I get crazy. Understand?" He nodded to Muninn. "Take him into office."

When they cut you free — run. But Muninn still had his gun out and Alec was there too, untying Gethin. Maybe Gethin wouldn't do anything that risked Kell's safety.

"There's no need to hurt anyone," Gethin said.

Marek smirked. "You have thirty minutes to get details I can read before I start. I begin with fist up his arse."

They led Gethin away and Kell wondered if he'd see him again.

"What's on the memory stick?" Kell thought it'd look strange if he didn't ask.

"Warner's business accounts. Prepared by Brian Charlton, my sister's boyfriend."

"Actual boyfriend or pretend?" While Marek was in front of him and couldn't see his hands, Kell wriggled his fingers, trying to loosen the rope.

"She like him. He has money and he spend it on her. Let her decorate his house. Buy her jewellery. But maybe she shouldn't have liked him."

"You think Charlton is cheating Warner?"

Marek didn't answer.

"I don't know why you're so pissed off with me." Kell put a whine into his voice. "I haven't done anything."

Marek flew at him, knocked him and the chair over, and landed on top of him. Kell cried out at the pain in his arms.

"You don't fucking know?" Marek screamed at him. "I ask you to move in with me. You think I ask that of every guy I fuck? Then you let him fuck you."

Kell thought his arms were going to break. "He didn't fuck me. I fucked *him*." He seized his chance. "You made it clear I was never going to get to fuck you, but I like to switch. That's not going to happen with you. And you never said this was exclusive. You don't treat me like a boyfriend, just like a whore."

Marek stared at him for a moment. Kell had tears in his eyes. *My fucking arms.*

"He told me you were a cop," Marek whispered.

Fuck. "What? That's crap." Gethin would never do that. *Oh Christ, but my brother would.*

"I see in your eyes. Your brother."

"I told you the arsehole hates me. Throughout my entire life he's done everything he could to make my existence as miserable as possible. He's tried to kill me more times than I can count."

He groaned when Marek climbed off him and heaved the chair upright.

"How?" Marek asked.

"We dug a tunnel on the beach and when it collapsed on me, he sat and watched. My father dug me out. Another time Oliver tried to drown me in the sea and my mother rescued me. When I was twelve, he put a poisonous snake in my room. He fed me poisonous mushrooms. He pushed me off a cliff. How much more do you want?"

Marek probably thought that was all normal. Kell's arms were killing him. He wriggled his fingers and shooting pains flashed to his shoulders.

"Why?" Marek asked.

"He hated me from the moment I was born. He liked being the only child, getting all the attention. He thought when I came out as gay that my parents would hate me but they didn't. My mother's in a mental hospital in Scotland. I think what Oliver did drove her there."

"Why did he come to club?"

"Because today it's my thirtieth birthday. Oliver likes to do something special for birthdays. Something particularly cruel. That's why he told you I was a cop. I'm not." Kell could see Marek didn't believe him. *Shit, I wouldn't have believed me.* "I bet he slipped it into the conversation, pretended he shouldn't have said anything, asked you not to say anything."

That scored a hit. Marek looked less certain. Kell tried not to swallow, not to show any sign of nerves, but he was fighting for his life. And Gethin's.

A phone rang and Marek pulled it from his pocket. Kell wondered where his phone was, wondered if help was coming, if anyone knew where they were. Marek moved away from Kell to talk and Kell kept trying to get free even though he knew it was hopeless. Even if Marek believed what he'd said, he wasn't going to let Gethin walk away and Kell wouldn't walk away from Gethin.

When Marek had finished his call, he came back to Kell and put a cable tie around his wrists before he cut off the ropes.

"Into office," Marek snapped.

Still in trouble then. He stumbled when Marek shoved him forward and unable to break his fall, Kell twisted so that he didn't land on his face. Marek hauled him to his feet.

The printer was whirring. Gethin didn't even turn to look at him. His fingers flew across the keys, the screen filling with line after line of code. Muninn stood pointing a gun at his head.

Gethin reached for the bottom sheet of those being churned out by the printer and offered it to Marek. "That's the list of all the files on the stick. If you want everything printed out you'll need another ink cartridge. I'm copying all the financial stuff but there's books worth of emails and files from the recycle bin."

"Save it to computer," Marek said. "Show me where you put it."

Gethin clicked. "There. It's copying into the file called Consequences." He turned in the swivel chair. "Going to let me go now?"

"Did Kell fuck you?" Marek asked.

Gethin glanced at Kell. "Yes."

Marek stared at Kell. "Did you fuck Kell?"

Oh God, oh God.

"No," Gethin said.

How did he know that was the right answer? Kell tried not to look relieved. He tried not to look anything.

"Let me go," Gethin said. "I've done what you wanted. I haven't even been paid. What you do with the information has nothing to do with me. I'd be happy to pretend we never met."

"Until you decide you need money."

"I'd prefer to die in my bed of old age."

Marek sneered. "Wise but not wise enough when it mattered."

Marek nodded to Muninn and he brought the gun down on Gethin's head. Kell couldn't stop the gasp sliding from his mouth. A moment later, there was a sharp pain at the back of his own head and he was falling.

Gethin came round with a start, a sharp pain slicing into his skull. *Where am I? Where's Kell?* There was a gag around his mouth, nothing over his eyes. He kept them closed. There was no tell-tale light the other side of his eyelids so he knew it must be dark. Though not necessarily night time because he was *inside* something, gagged with a cloth that smelled of oil and tasted slimy, cable ties around his wrists and ankles, lying on his side on a hard, rippled metal surface. He still wore his trousers and boots but that was all and he was cold. Very cold. He could hear nothing, feel nothing except the aches of his body. Everywhere hurt, even his toes.

Kell. His stomach lurched and he opened his eyes into almost complete darkness. He looked toward splinters of light on his left and thought he was in some sort of box or maybe the back of a van. He rubbed his face against the floor until he'd pulled the gag away from his mouth.

"Kell?" he whispered.

There was no response and his heart cramped. But as he shuffled across the floor he heard a groan. Gethin kept shuffling until his shoulder collided with bare flesh. *A chest.* He squirmed until his face was next to Kell's, then turned and used his fingers to pull at Kell's gag until he'd dragged it down. Gethin rolled over and lay on his side facing Kell, though he could barely see him.

"Wake up, Sleeping Beauty," Gethin whispered.

"Need kiss," Kell mumbled and the pang in Gethin's chest hit like a knife. *Oh fuck. The knife! Is it still in my boot?* It felt like it could be, but he hurt all over so it was hard to tell if the pressure against his ankle was from being kicked or because of the knife he'd stashed there.

Gethin kissed Kell's dry lips. "*Now* wake up."

"Where are we?" Kell choked out.

They lurched suddenly as an engine started and the floor shifted beneath them.

"In a vehicle of some sort," Gethin said. "A truck, a van."

"Christ," Kell moaned.

"Did they hurt you?" Gethin asked.

"My head. Oh fuck. They hit you with a gun, then they hit me."

"Did they take your phone?"

"Yeah." He groaned. "I called for help with yours." Kell's voice was a whisper. "Left it on and hid it in the club."

Would the emergency services treat that as a crank call if no one spoke? Would they go to the trouble of locating the mobile? If they did, Warner or Marek would have an excuse.

The vehicle they were in was moving quickly. Gethin didn't want to get to where it was going. "We need to get free."

"I'm not sure I'm supple enough to get my hands in front of me."

"You don't need to. I think I still have Marek's knife in my boot. If you can get it, we can cut the cable ties."

Gethin squirmed until his legs were positioned close to Kell's hands. He could feel Kell fumbling with his lower leg, then his boots and when Kell whispered, "Bingo," Gethin sighed. Manoeuvring to get in the right position for Kell to use the knife wasn't easy with them bouncing around all over the place and Gethin winced as the blade slid into his wrist.

"Shit," Kell whispered. "I've cut you."

"Keep going."

When the tie fell and Gethin's hands were free he shuddered with relief. He wiped his bloody wrists on his trousers, then took the knife from Kell. After he'd freed Kell, he sliced through the tie around his ankles.

267

"We have an advantage now," Gethin whispered. "When they open the doors, we have to be ready. But let's see if we can find a way out of here before then. Crawl to the side and work your way round. Feel for anything we can use as a weapon or tool."

Gethin found only solid metal sides, roof and floor, and locked rear doors.

"Nothing," Kell whispered.

"Think we should try to break the lock with the knife? We might snap it but…"

"Yes," Kell said. "We know what's going to happen when the van stops and they open the doors. Even though we're free, they have guns."

Gethin felt for screws and began to undo them with the knife.

"Should we have a plan for what to do when they stop?" Kell asked.

"Go to the back of the van, pull the gags back over our faces and pretend we're still tied up. They'll have to come in to get us. I'll attack whoever comes in first whether they go for me or you."

"Are you any good with a knife? You need to cut deeper than you did at my neck."

Gethin gave a small laugh. He kept working at the panel covering the door mechanism and managed to wrench part off.

"Maybe we should just kick it," Kell said. "Break it open. If we fall, it has to be better than what's coming."

They tumbled as the van seemed to leave the road. Gethin tightened his grip on the knife as he and Kell fell away from the doors and slammed back into the partition that divided them from the driver.

"What the hell?" Kell gasped.

The front of the vehicle collided with something and they were flung back. Gethin desperately clung to the knife. The vehicle settled but didn't seem steady. *Why is it wobbling?*

"Shit. Are you okay?" Kell asked.

"Yeah."

"We must have hit—oh fuck. Are you bleeding? Am I bleeding? My hand's in…no…Christ, it's water. It's fucking water."

Gethin's heart tumbled out of his chest. "We have to get back to the doors. The van's going to tip engine first. We need to be at the other end."

They crawled to the back and clung to one of the panels Gethin had prized open. There was a sliver of daylight between the doors but the lock was still firm. Kell pushed to his feet and kicked at it. Gethin joined him but the rocking of the van made it difficult to stay upright.

"We're not going to drown," Kell said.

Gethin wished he could be sure that was true. The van hadn't gone into water by accident. It had been propelled in and it seemed more than likely the water would be deep because whoever had done this wanted them to be swallowed.

"Keep kicking," Gethin said.

He knew they didn't have long. Once the vehicle tipped, they'd have no way of staying upright, no way of exerting force on the only way out.

Kell could feel panic welling inside him, surging up his throat, threatening to choke him. "Kick together."

Time after time, they kicked at the lock until the angle of the vehicle made it impossible. There was more light coming in where they'd deformed the door panels but the lock was still in place. Kell felt himself sliding to the partition. He tried to scramble back to where Gethin clung on, still driving the knife into the lock, but there was nothing to hang onto. There was a foot of water where Kell crouched and it was getting deeper.

Kell kept trying to reach Gethin and failing. But when the vehicle seemed to slightly level out he was able to scramble back to the doors and he grabbed hold of a bent panel.

"Where've you been?" Gethin asked.

"Thought I'd have a quick swim while you were busy."

"Shit."

Kell heard the knife skittering away and realised what had happened.

"Leave it," Gethin said. "The lock's broken. I think if we push, we can open it."

The vehicle shifted again and water poured in through gap at the bottom of the door that Gethin had made.

"Fuck." The same word from both their mouths. They shoved as hard as they could, but the doors stayed closed.

"It's the pressure," Kell said. "We won't be able to get them open until the van's full of water."

"Maybe not even then."

"Maybe not." Kell reached for Gethin's face. "I'm sorry."

"What for?"

"Getting you into this."

Gethin kissed his forehead. "I got myself into it."

"This is my brother Oliver's fault."

"How come?"

"He told Marek I was a cop. "

Gethin gave a heavy sigh. "That might have landed *you* in here, but I'm here because of the memory stick. Though that fucker Marek will get a surprise. Apart from the not minor detail that when he opens the file, he'll lose every scrap of data, I also sent a message in code to a hacker friend of mine and asked him to contact the police."

Kell kissed him as the water rose around them.

"I don't like this," Gethin said.

"My kiss? Under the circumstances I think I did a good job."

"How deep do we have to go before the van fills? What if we hit the bottom and it's still not full?"

"Don't worry about things that haven't happened."

The water was getting deeper. They were standing in it up to their waists, shivering, their teeth chattering.

"Your birthday," Gethin said. "Angel told me. That was why I came. I thought if your brother turned up, I could protect you."

"Oh God."

"One time in my life I really wish I could say Happy Birthday." He gave a choked groan.

"The day's not over yet."

"I'm glad I met you," Gethin said.

"Even though we're standing in the dark, in freezing water, in a sinking van without any certainty we'll make it out *and* my cock's not hard?"

"Yeah."

"Me too," Kell said.

They clung to each other and by shoving Kell up to the door and him then hauling up Gethin, they managed to get to the back of the van. The water was chest high now.

"I'm pretty sure Marek was trying to get Warner's money," Kell said

"Probably."

As the water lapped at his neck, Kell realised he might never know. He hoped the bastards got what was coming to them.

"Can we try now?" Kell shivered.

"Make sure you take a lot of deep breaths. We don't know how long it'll take to get to the surface. Hopefully the van wasn't pushed off a boat and we're somewhere in the North Sea."

A deluge of adrenaline swamped Kell's body. "Better look out for sharks."

"We need to kick." Gethin pressed his face into the air pocket. "Keep kicking because there's not going to be much force behind it."

"Don't die," Kell blurted. "You haven't taken me on a date yet."

Gethin let out a choked laugh.

And they kicked and kicked and kicked.

Chapter Twenty-Five

When the doors of the van opened, for a moment Kell couldn't believe it. At the last moment, he'd taken a mouthful of air, but was already desperate for more. He clung to Gethin's arm and kicked out of the vehicle into black water. Once he was sure Gethin was swimming at his side, he let go and used both arms to power himself up. He was cold, tired and his lungs were on fire. *Where was the fucking surface?* He couldn't see anything and his arms ached, the muscles damaged by Marek landing on him.

Don't stop. Don't stop. He kept repeating that in his head but it was hard to keep going. His body was so heavy and the water seemed to be getting darker, colder. If he could just take a breath… Just one. But he couldn't.

This isn't fucking fair. Kell felt overwhelmed with sadness that when his life might actually have been going somewhere, instead it was about to end because he had…to… breathe. The pain at the top of his chest spread down, went deep. He was still kicking— just, though hardly moving his arms. He knew the moment he opened his mouth it would be over, but desperation was overwhelmed his common sense.

Don't stop. Gethin's voice he heard in his head. *One last push.* He kicked and his face broke the surface. He took a huge gulp of air. *Not dead. Where's Gethin?* Kell spun in a circle and choked out a gasp of relief when he saw Gethin a few yards away and heard him coughing. Coughing was good. You coughed when you were alive.

Dawn was breaking, a red tinge spreading in the eastern sky. A new day. *Oh God, we made it.* Kell splashed over to him, his lungs still on fire, his arms killing him.

"Happy Birthday," Gethin said.

"Where's my cake?"

"We need to get…out of this water." Gethin spun round.

"Keep quiet…just in case."

They swam to the side and hit a concrete wall.

"Find a ladder." Gethin's teeth chattered as they let the current carry them downstream.

When they brushed up against metal rungs, Kell grabbed hold, caught Gethin's arm and pulled him close. Gethin pushed him up first. It was all Kell could do to put one hand over the other. His teeth were rattling like a machinegun and he was shaking violently. Sheer force of will kept him moving up the rungs until he finally slithered onto the dock. When Gethin sprawled at his side, he pulled Kell into his arms.

"You think they're still around?" Gethin whispered.

"Don't know. They might have waited to make sure we didn't get out. Where the fuck are we?"

Gethin checked their surroundings. "Somewhere on the Thames. Better than *in* the Thames." He muffled his cough. "Oh fuck it. That was close."

"We need to get out of here and warm up. Stick to the shadows until we're sure we're okay."

They hadn't gone far before they were stopped by a pair of uniformed security guards. Kell almost collapsed with relief.

"What the hell have you two been doing?" the taller man asked.

"Escaping from a submerged vehicle. I'm a cop." Kell wrapped his arms around himself in a futile attempt to keep warm.

"Come into the office," the other man said.

The two guards shot each other a glance then took off their high-vis jackets and gave them to Kell and Gethin.

"Thank you. Can I borrow your phone?" Kell asked.

"Here." One of the men held his out.

Kell called his boss as he walked. "It's me," he said.

"Where the fuck have you been? We had—"

"Shut up and listen." Kell winced after he'd said that. "We nearly drowned. We're cold, soaked and need help right now."

"We?"

"Me and the PI."

"Where are you?"

"I'll pass the phone back to the guy who owns it. He can tell you."

Kell gave it to him and stepped into a warm prefabricated office. When he looked back at Gethin he was shocked by how white he was, the marks on his face standing out.

"I'll rustle up some blankets," said the shorter guy.

Kell sat on the floor and struggled out of his shoes, then his trousers and shorts. Gethin did the same and with the men's coats over their shoulders, they edged up to the fan heater pumping out hot air.

"Happy Birthday yet?" Gethin looked at him.

"I'm still waiting for my cake."

The blankets arrived and once they were enveloped by them, Kell began to warm up. Mugs of hot sweet tea were pressed into their shaking hands.

"There's a vehicle in the river then?" one of the security guards asked.

"Yes. Forensics will need to handle it. Not far from where you found us if you need to warn people."

"Take a wrong turn?" the other said.

"Something like that." Kell let the men think it was an accident. "The police are on their way."

Kell wasn't surprised his boss insisted they went to hospital. He *was* surprised they were taken to a private one. He didn't want Gethin out of his sight but he could hardly say that, plus Gethin had been uncharacteristically quiet which worried Kell.

He was allowed to shower, had his injuries treated, just minor cuts, bruises and strains. His arms weren't broken. They just felt like they were. He was given grey sweat pants and a hoodie to put on before the questions started. He told Lane everything he thought he needed to know, including the role Oliver had played.

Lane frowned. "Are you certain?"

"Yes, but I can't prove it, and I realise no one would believe me."

"You understand you're accusing him of —"

"Yes. It's his game. One he's played since I was born."

"But you almost died."

"That was the point. Now tell me your side."

"We had an alert about a 9-9-9 call from the club. As far as we knew, you were there. At least your phone was. Then we lost the signal. It was too risky to let things run any longer. Search warrants were issued for a number of premises and arrest warrants for almost thirty people including the accountant. They're all in custody."

"Including Warner and Marek?"

"Yes Including them."

Kell felt a rush of relief sweep over him and the last chill evaporated from his body.

"We're lifting the van out of the river. Forensic teams are working in the club, the houses where the women were detained and the warehouse where you were held — a guy called Alec can't seem to stop talking. Apparently, the plan was to take you to another location but Marek received a call, freaked out and said the van had to go into the river. Warner lawyered up and has said very little. Marek has said nothing. We've taken the other group of women into custody. Cocaine was found in several locations. We got them."

"I resign."

Lane laughed.

"I mean it. I've had enough."

"You need a rest. I know how stressful it is working undercover but take time to think about your future."

Kell didn't need time but he was too exhausted to argue. "Do you know if Marek was definitely working against Warner when he arranged for Gethin to hack into the accountant's computer?"

"I'm inclined to think Marek wanted a bigger share of the money, but now the business has collapsed, he might pretend he was just doing what he was told by Warner, or acting on his sister's suspicions before he told Warner. Either way, they'll all go down."

Which was what Kell wanted to hear.

"Is your relationship with Marek going to cause us any problems?" his boss asked.

Which was not what Kell wanted to talk about. "I'm not pregnant."

Lane glared.

"What do you want me to say?" Kell ground his teeth. "You wanted information. You chose me because I was gay. I let him fuck me. Okay? He didn't force me." Because admitting the rape was *not* going to happen.

Lane put his head in his hands. "Shit."

"He came after me. I never pursued him. I didn't trap him into anything. I played a role and he fell for it."

"You need to put everything in your report. We can't get caught out on it. I want the preliminary draft done before you leave the hospital. I'll have someone wait for it. It goes nowhere until I've read it and discussed it with you. Tomorrow I want you in the office to be thoroughly debriefed."

Lane walked out.

"I don't even get a fucking 'well done' or my wallet back?" Kell snapped at the closed door. He pulled the paper and pen closer. He very nearly started with 'once upon a time' but managed to control himself.

When he'd done, he handed the sealed envelope to the cop sitting outside his room, then went looking for Gethin. He was asleep, his face all banged up from the beating Marek had given him. He was beautiful even with the cuts and bruises. *My bloody brother almost got him killed too.* Not just Oliver's fault. *Mine as well.*

He was an idiot to think he could have kept this casual. He'd known the moment he looked at Gethin his interest ran deeper than that. Kell had lost the battle before he'd even followed him from the tent—fucking kata.

"Quit staring at me," Gethin said.

There was light back in his green eyes. A half-smile on his face.

"Where did you get your stylish outfit?" Gethin asked.

"There's one for you too."

Gethin pushed himself to a sitting position. "We can leave?"

"Did you give a statement?"

"Yeah. I'm not supposed to leave the country."

Kell gaped at him. "They didn't say that."

"No." He chuckled. "I...I do have to, though."

Kell's plans were crumbling to dust. "Go abroad?"

"Yeah. I'll tell you why, but not in here."

He threw back the cover, pulled off the gown and stood naked in front of Kell. Kell gave a quiet groan.

"You have the energy for that?" Gethin raised his eyebrows.

"God, if you'd have suggested it when we were sinking in that van I'd have been up for it. Probably."

Gethin laughed as he dressed. "What are we supposed to do for shoes?"

"Fuck knows. I don't have any money. No wallet, no phone."

"Me neither. I'll borrow a phone, call Angel and ask him to get someone to drive my car over here from the office. We can go to your bedsit and you can pick up some clothes. I suspect my bike's been impounded by now, but I'd like to check. If it hasn't, I can ride that back to my place while you drive the car."

"You sure you want me there?" Kell hated that he'd asked, hated that he'd sounded even faintly pathetic, the tiniest bit desperate.

"Yes."

Kell exhaled. There was no hesitation, no—if you *want* to come, no—yeah but only for tonight. Just a firm *yes*.

"My place isn't much, but it's better than yours," Gethin said. "I wish I could shell out for a smart hotel with room service, but I can't afford it."

Kell could, but Gethin's bed sounded perfect to him. Gethin borrowed a phone to make the call, then they went down to the entrance to wait.

As they sat next to each other on a couch in the foyer, Gethin put his hand over Kell's.

"You okay?" Gethin asked.

"As long as I'm not in a coma and dreaming this, yeah, I'm good. Well, every muscle in my body aches including my eyelids but apart from that I'm perfect. I'm just having trouble believing it's all over."

Gethin squeezed his fingers and Kell wished that in one way he'd got that wrong because he didn't want this part to be over. Would Gethin tell him about Jonnie? About why he needed to go abroad? *Do I know this guy at all?*

When Angel burst through the doors of the hospital, Gethin pulled Kell to his feet.

"Are you all right?" Angel clapped his hand to his heart. "Oh God, you're not. What in heaven's name are you wearing? *The soul of this man is his clothes.*"

"Macbeth?" Gethin asked.

Angel growled. "All's Well That Ends Well. I'll show you where I parked, but stay ten paces behind. I'm mortified someone might see me with you dressed like that. No shoes? They'll think I've picked up some homeless rent boys. Ah… two good-looking homeless rent boys. Walk either side of me and cast me adoring looks."

Kell sniggered.

"You're worried about my clothes and not my injuries?" Gethin asked as they set off.

"Are your important parts in working order?" Angel asked.

"Not tested them all yet." Gethin glanced at Kell and Kell's cheeks heated.

Angel pressed for details of what had happened but Gethin put him off, promising to tell him later. Kell's feet were frozen. He picked his way carefully along the pavement relieved when they reached the car.

"Do you want a lift?" Gethin asked Angel.

"I've a meeting to go to a couple of Tube stops away from here. I'm fine. Here's the keys and a hundred pounds. Is that going to be enough?"

"Thanks. That's great."

Angel wrapped his arms around Kell. "Happy Birthday," he whispered. "Next year, I'll throw you a party."

"You think—?"

Angel put his finger over Kell's lips. "Yes, darling. I *do* think." He winked as he walked away.

Kell slipped into the passenger seat and rubbed his feet on the mat and on his sweatpants to get rid of the bits of dirt and gravel he'd picked up. Gethin had the lid up on the boot and when he dropped into the driver's seat he was wearing shoes and a different sweater.

"You carry spares in case someone locks you a van and drives it into a river?" Kell asked.

"And I was proved right."

Kell smiled and once the heater was blasting warm air over his toes, he relaxed.

Gethin managed to slot the car into a small parking space right outside Kell's building.

"That was lucky," Kell said.

Gethin was beginning to think maybe he *was* a lucky guy.

But after they'd walked upstairs and reached the door, Kell groaned. "Shit. I don't have a key."

"Are you ever coming back here again?"

"That's true." Kell lifted one bare foot, kicked hard at the door and it sprang open. "Well look at that. All that practicing in a sinking van paid off."

Gethin wedged the door closed as Kell headed for his closet, stripping on the way.

"Not that I'm complaining," Gethin said, "but you could have stayed as you were."

"I want *my* clothes on." Kell slipped into jeans and Gethin wanted to strip them off again.

Kell wriggled into the T-shirt, stuffed his feet into shoes and began to pack.

Gethin hadn't thought this through. He wanted Kell to stay with him, but worried he was assuming too much. They'd agreed to keep this casual and it had moved far beyond that. He still had to explain about Jonnie.

Maybe Kell would understand.

Maybe he wouldn't.

He found himself swallowing as he watched Kell move around the room in jeans that showcased his taut arse. When Kell wriggled his backside, Gethin shot his gaze to his face.

"Now who's staring?" Kell pulled on a sweater and zipped up his bag. "That's all I need. The rest can stay. I'll contact my boss and tell him I've finished with the bedsit. I can find somewhere else to rent until my place comes vacant."

"Penthouse in the Shard?"

Kell laughed. He walked to the door and looked back. "Goodbye, too-small-shower. Goodbye, annoying lamppost light. Goodbye, asparagus mould... I can't remember the names of the others. Gladiator and stegosaurus?"

"*Aspergillus, cladosporium* and *stachybotrysatra*."

"You are so weird." Kell smiled at him. "But really useful in a pub quiz."

Gethin was surprised and relieved to see his bike where he'd left it. He pulled up behind it, retrieved his spare keys from a hidden compartment, unlocked the box, and took out his helmet and jacket.

"Going to be okay following me?" Gethin asked. "I know you've been to my place before but if you lose me, the address is in the sat nav under pizza. There's a lockup garage where I put the bike. Park the car anywhere. Shouldn't be a problem to find a spot at this time of day."

"Right."

As Gethin rode past No Escape, he saw police tape across the entrance and a cop standing guard outside. It seemed a lifetime ago he'd gone in there looking for Dieter. When he got back, he'd use his other phone to call Dieter's mother. He could see no reason why she and Dieter shouldn't go home. With a bit of luck, she'd tell him there'd be a cheque in the post.

Gethin kept Kell in sight all the way back and when he saw a spot for Kell to park, he pointed to it, then turned and pulled up alongside him. Kell lowered the window and Gethin handed him the key to his flat.

"You go up. I'll nip and buy some groceries."

"Okay."

After Gethin had unlocked the garage and pushed the bike in, he dropped the roller door while he was still inside and retrieved a spare phone and a wallet from a box hidden in the breeze-block wall. He left his helmet with the bike, locked up and set off on foot to the store at the bottom of the road.

By the time he'd reached it, he'd called Zena Hoehn and given her the good news. He cancelled his bank cards and called his phone provider and arranged for a new phone to be sent out. He always liked to have at least two of everything. Gethin bought what he needed from the store, then looked around to see if there was something he could get Kell as a present. He registered how little he knew about him and how he wanted to know everything.

Gethin picked up a selection of items including wrapping paper, then sweet-talked the assistant into making what he'd bought look nice. He chose a birthday cake, a box of candles and matches. The birthday cards were too soppy, so he bought one for a three year old with a sports car on the front. While the assistant was working wonders with paper, tape and scissors, Gethin borrowed a marker and added a big fat zero to the three, and wrote inside the card. It had crossed his mind that he could take Kell out for a meal, but if the guy was as exhausted as Gethin felt, they'd be better staying in.

Plus there was still the issue of Jonnie. Not the right time on Kell's birthday, but when would be the right time?

Chapter Twenty-Six

Gethin had to ring the bell three times before Kell opened the door, and he'd begun to worry. But when a smiling Kell stood in front of him, his slim-fit T-shirt clinging to the toned muscles of his torso, warmth flooded Gethin's veins.

"This better be important." Kell leaned on the door jam. "I'm expecting a very hot guy back any minute. So if you're selling overpriced household cleaning products or offering to introduce me to the Lord, I'm not interested, unless the end really *is* nigh, in which case come on in and sit really close."

Gethin laughed and pushed past him.

"I think you need to get someone to look at that door," Kell said. "It can be wedged shut and locked, but it's not very safe, is it?"

"I'll get it fixed."

"You were gone so long I taught myself to play the guitar. Listen."

When Kell picked up the instrument Gethin hadn't touched for more than a year, except to dust, his chest tightened. But the terrible, discordant strumming broke the spell and made him smile. "Wow, that's…quite inventive."

"Thank you. It's called 'Sad Song Sung Softly.' Note the alliteration." Kell put the guitar back on the stand.

"I didn't hear you sing." Gethin unpacked the groceries into the fridge and left the cake in a bag to hide it from Kell.

"I didn't get to that bit. Shall I play it again?"

Gethin shot him a look. "Maybe later. You hungry?"

"I *was*." Kell slid up behind him. "I'm so easily distracted."

The hard ridge of Kell's cock pressed into the seam of Gethin's butt, *rocked* into it, and the egg box slipped in his hand, but luckily didn't fall.

"Sex, food, sex…talk," Kell said. "Or maybe sex, food, sex, food, sex and then talk."

Gethin put the eggs down and held out the present. "Happy birthday."

Kell's eyes lit up. "Really? Thank you. Okay, revised plan. Open present, sex, food, sex then talk." He ripped the paper off lightning fast and took out the first item, a thriller by Jo Nesbo. "How did you know I liked him?"

"I looked under your bed."

"Snooping?"

"Checking for monsters. The CD's by a band I like so I hope you like them too."

"If they're anything like Abba, I'll love them."

Gethin felt as though his entire body was smiling. Kell made him happy. He couldn't remember when he'd last felt happy.

"Not seen this one." Kell brandished a sci fi DVD.

Neither had Gethin.

"Ah." Kell laughed at the mug with a red-nosed reindeer on the side, two packets of hot chocolate and mini marshmallows tucked inside. "I love it." He stacked up the ten boxes of condoms into a tower on the counter. "I'm never going into that store with you. You realise everyone in the neighbourhood will soon know how many boxes you bought at one go and will have you down as a sex maniac."

"I told the woman I was doing a science experiment."

Kell's eyes widened. "You didn't?"

Gethin laughed. "No."

Kell sucked his teeth. "Are you sure ten packets will be enough."

"We can buy more tomorrow. I went to a different shop for this." He put a large bottle of lube next to the condoms.

Kell grinned. He pulled Gethin into his arms. "Thank you for everything. But you're the best present of all." He pressed open the studs on Gethin's leather jacket and unzipped it. "I'm thinking sex, sex, sex, sex, sex now."

"That's amazing," Gethin said. "So am I."

"I washed my feet. Random thought but…"

284

Gethin nodded. "I better wash mine too."

When he tried to move away, Kell pulled him back. "Hey, presents aren't allowed to move until they've been fully opened."

Kell's smile was so filthy Gethin burst out laughing. Kell slipped the jacket from Gethin's shoulders and tossed it onto the couch, peeled the sweater over his head and threw it on top of the jacket. When he spread his hands on Gethin's bare chest and rubbed his nipples with his fingers and thumbs Gethin kept his groan inside but it felt as if Kell was stroking his cock.

"Arrgghh," Kell dropped his hands. "I'm touching *you* but it feels like you've taken hold of my dick."

Oh fuck, I like you. Gethin had never smiled as much. It was as if he'd been shut inside a box and Kell had hauled him into the sunshine.

Kell seized the back of Gethin's head, tugged him close until their faces were inches apart then gave him a sheepish look. "I'm blaming my irrepressible lust on the fact that we nearly died. Man's basic instinct. *I survived now I need sex.* Well, it's either that or it's your fault for being so bloody hot."

When Gethin finally felt the press of Kell's lips, it was as if he'd been swept up by a huge wave and carried out to sea. Each touch, every stroke of Kell's tongue made Gethin's heart beat faster. Kell started with a slow exploration, sweeping his tongue along Gethin's teeth, teasing, dipping, then his kisses grew hungrier, rougher, tinged with a touch of desperation. Hands that had danced over Gethin's back now clutched him tight as they writhed together and Gethin got lost in the scent and feel of the man in his arms.

By the time they pulled apart, panting, Gethin was dizzy with lust, blinded by longing. He slid his hand down to the front of Kell's jeans, felt the heat of the rigid cock under the material and squeezed gently.

Kell grabbed his wrist and wrenched his away. "God no. You'll make me come. And you're not even unwrapped yet."

Gethin toed off his shoes and Kell pushed down on the waistband of the sweatpants until they fell to the floor and Gethin could step out of them.

"Never wear those again. Promise." Kell shuddered.

"They're not that bad."

"I like you in…tight things. You're mine to play with, right?" Kell tugged off his T-shirt and tossed it aside. He fumbled with the fastening on his jeans and shoved them down his hips, kicking them off his feet.

"No shorts?" Gethin asked.

Kell gasped. "What? Did I forget?"

Kell's mouth landed on Gethin's nipple. The sharp bite made Gethin suck in a breath and flinch, but the pain also sent tremors of lust curling through his body.

"Hmm, you liked that." Kell looked up at him as he fluttered his tongue over Gethin's taut nub. "Pleasure and pain."

"Not too much pain."

"No whip tonight then." Kell wrapped his hand around Gethin's cock and sucked harder at his nipple.

Gethin groaned and his hips bucked, thrusting his cock into Kell's tight grip. He had one hand on Kell's shoulder, the other at the back of his neck, itching to push Kell down.

"Don't you dare come," Kell said. "Not until I've finished playing with you."

"We talking minutes?"

"Hours."

Gethin growled. "Oh no we're not."

Kell kissed him again, and Gethin melted against him. *This* kiss was slow, deep and gentle and something about it reassured Gethin they had a future.

"You taste so sweet," Kell whispered.

"Hospital antiseptic?"

Kell glared. "No. It's just you. I've got a serious case of desperation here. Coupled with a dollop of confusion. I don't know what to do first. I'm spoiled for choice."

"Just don't break me," Gethin said.

"I doubt I could break you. But I'd always put you back together. Super glue works wonders."

And wasn't that what Gethin had been looking for, albeit subconsciously? Someone who could put him back together, help him look forward to the future, help him live instead of just existing? Someone who'd listen to him explain about Jonnie and understand? Someone who'd teach him how to smile?

Kell grabbed a box of condoms and the lube, then turned and picked up another box before he grabbed Gethin's hand and pulled him into the bedroom. Gethin saw Kell had already drawn the curtains, turned back the cover on the bed, put what he guessed was a flower made of toilet tissue on the pillow, and switched on the bedside lamp.

"Too cheesy?" Kell asked.

"No." Gethin picked up the tissue and it fell flat. "A flower, right?"

"It was a dinosaur." Kell tossed the condoms and lube onto the bed. "Good thing you bought these because I had a look around and was thinking we'd have to make do with cling film and olive oil." He hesitated. "I guess you don't have guys back here often."

"I've never had a guy in this bed until now. I've never even brought a guy back here."

"You were worried about them playing your guitar better than you, weren't you?"

"Am I that obvious?"

"Lie down, lovely birthday present that might just be the best present I ever had if I don't count the Lego castle I was given when I was seven. I really wanted that. Bloody Oliver stole one of the crucial bricks and I had to write to Lego and get another."

Gethin lay on his back and Kell leaned over him, laying a trail of kisses from Gethin's lips, down the centre of his chest, in the crease of his groin, along the top of his thighs and finally down the length of his cock. Gethin clutched the sheets in his fists and willed his balls to behave. Kell slid his tongue over and around the tip of his dick, again and again, until Gethin couldn't stop the tremble from erupting in his limbs. He'd thought he was already at full hardness, but he seemed to grow even harder.

Kell ran his tongue around the ridge of Gethin's shaft, engulfed the head with his hot, tight mouth and Gethin gasped. *My balls. I need to come. Oh Christ.* "F-fuck." The word came out as a hoarse whisper.

"I love your dick," Kell pulled back to say. "Christ. How come I turn into a needy mess the moment we're together? Don't answer that."

Kell licked his palm then rubbed it over the head of Gethin's cock and Gethin's hips bucked off the bed. He only realised he had his fingers threaded in Kell's hair when Kell yelped.

"Hold the top of your bed and don't let go," Kell ordered.

Gethin wasn't a guy who took orders in bed — usually — but he wrapped his fingers around the headboard and held tight. Kell smiled at him before continuing the hot, wet, sucking, licking, teasing while Gethin's hips shifted ever more frantically trying to get Kell to work him harder, faster.

"Want you in my mouth," Gethin groaned out the words. Getting each other off at the same time seemed the only way of ending Kell's slow torture.

Kell looked up at him with his mouth still busy, still full, Gethin's cock bulging under his cheek.

"Now," Gethin said.

Kell moved lightning fast, shifting around until his dick appeared over Gethin's face. Gethin wrapped his hand around the base and pulled it into his mouth, sucked him in hard and tight, and Kell gave a muffled moan, his lips back around Gethin. The heady taste of precome fogged Gethin's head and he halted for a moment just to enjoy it, then they were sucking in the same rhythm, fisting each other's dicks at the same pace, doing the same thing with their tongues, teasing their slits, dipping inside, lapping at balls, licking down their lengths, swallowing entire cocks and trying to breathe at the same time.

Gethin took Kell's dick so far down, that for a moment Kell didn't move. Gethin contracted the muscles of his throat around the shaft and Kell whimpered. Gethin's whimper was blocked by what he had in his mouth. *Going to come.* Orgasm was on the rise all over his body, racing down his veins, jumping from neuron to neuron, every orgiastic little cell bursting with excitement as neural messages sprinted to his groin. Kell made a moaning sound around Gethin's cock and then they were both coming, flying into the sun. Kell spurted down Gethin's throat as Gethin jetted into his, the world exploding into a sky laden with fireworks, filled with promise and hope because of this man.

It felt as if Kell came forever into Gethin's mouth and Gethin kept swallowing until the last spasm had faded and Kell slumped against him, clutching Gethin's hips, his fingers digging in to the point of pain. When Kell's cock slipped free of his lips, Gethin sucked in air instead, and his heart began to slow.

Kell shifted round until his head was next to Gethin's on the pillow. Gethin reached to wipe a smear of come from the corner of Kell's mouth and when Kell grabbed his hand and licked his finger, Gethin growled.

"Hey, whose birthday is it?" Kell asked.

"Fuuuuck. That was good."

"I'd planned more but you distracted me. I didn't even get to use *one* of those condoms."

He snuggled up to Gethin and Gethin slid his arm around him. Cuddling was new for him but he liked it.

"Give me a few minutes and I'll be good to go again," Kell said. "I feel obliged to use *all* those boxes since they're for my birthday."

Gethin smiled as he stroked Kell's shoulder, trailing his fingers up and down his smooth skin.

"We nearly died because of my fucking brother," Kell whispered. "He's such a bastard. He's someone we have to talk about. Then we can fuck so I can forget him."

Gethin couldn't forget Jonnie. He had things to sort out and sooner rather than later.

"I told you about what happened on the beach," Kell babbled, "but that wasn't the first time he tried to kill me. He put a pillow over my face when I was three and tried to suffocate me. I can't see how I could possibly remember that but it's so clear in my head, I believe it's true. My mother came in and he told her he'd heard me cry and was trying to make me more comfortable. Fucking liar." Kell sighed. "I was desperate for Oliver to like me and he acted like I wasn't there. I should have been content with that, *happy* with that, but I was always trying to impress him, trying to make him notice me."

"Neither of your parents stepped in?"

"They didn't see how much Oliver hated me. Well not until he deliberately shoved me over a steep drop when we were skiing. My mother saw him do it. Luckily I fell onto a ledge and a rescue team were able to winch me to safety. Oliver said it was an accident but she didn't believe him. I think she thought back to all the times I'd told her what Oliver had done and she was so overwhelmed, she had some sort of psychotic episode. Whereas in the past she'd had them and recovered, this time she didn't. She was admitted to a psychiatric hospital in Scotland and she lives in her own little world, doesn't recognise any of us."

"And your brother is still tormenting you."

Kell spread his hand on Gethin's chest and rubbed his thumb over his nipple. "I should lock myself away on my birthday, somewhere Oliver can't find me. How the fuck *did* he find me? He said my boss told him, but Lane denied it and how would Oliver know I worked in the club, worked for Warner?"

"Maybe he talked to someone higher than Lane — Beckwith? Maybe told him he wanted to wish his brother a happy birthday — just quietly, obviously. He wouldn't want to interfere with an ongoing operation. But it would be morale booster for you. He knows the right things to say to get him what he wants. He's an MP. Supposedly on the side of law and order, someone who works for the people not just in his constituency, but for the whole country. Why would anyone worry he'd deliberately fuck things up for a brother who was risking his life to put the bad guys in jail?"

"That makes the most sense. Oliver can be persuasive. One of the cruellest things he ever did to me was fuck a boy I had a huge crush on. Oliver's not gay but he was willing to do that just to wreck my life."

"The photo I took is still on my phone. Of course, I don't have the phone anymore but he doesn't know that. Maybe the threat of giving it to the press will be enough to get him to leave you alone. Plus we have another year to think up a way to spoil his fun."

Oh shit. What did I just say?

Kell looked up at him, maybe feeling him tense. "Don't look so panicked. Maybe we *will* last that long. I know we said — I said — we'd make this casual but..." Kell swallowed hard. "I want more than that. I want to change my whole life. I don't want to work undercover anymore. Not sure I even want to be a cop. But the one thing I don't need to rethink is you. I want you. Not just for sex though you are pretty good at it."

Gethin laughed. "Only pretty good?"

"Ten boxes of condoms to prove you're better than that."

"I only need one."

"One box?"

"One condom."

Kell raised his eyebrows. "Okay." He chewed his lip. "So are you going to talk to me about Jonnie?"

Gethin exhaled. "Yes. Not an easy story."

"Just say it."

What else could he do? "After my parents died, I was brought up in care. Foster homes, local authority homes but nothing lasted. I was a loner. If I made friends, I moved and lost them. Or they let me down. Easier not to bother. I divided my time between the computer and guitar. Left school as soon as I could and worked in IT for a lot of different companies, including a detective agency. I was bored and I met Jonnie. He was in a band. He was charismatic, charming, full of life. They needed a new guitarist and I fit in."

"What was the band called?"

"Strip Jack."

Kell pushed himself up on his elbow. "I've heard of them. I don't remember anyone called Gethin."

"They called me Dart. Jonnie started it and it stuck. Three musketeers and D'Artagnan, me, though Jonnie was always the leader. The fearless one, the guy everyone loved. He was a complete bastard, to be honest, but you couldn't help liking him. We were an item, though no one knew. Not for a long while. He played at being straight for the fans. Though he came out eventually. I moved into his place. One day I came home to find him in bed with…yeah well. I just stood there. I couldn't believe it. He said he was sorry. Made up some crap excuse, but I walked out of his life and out of the band. That didn't go down well, the leaving the band part." He gave a hoarse laugh. "Jonnie was more bothered about that than me leaving him. I don't think he could quite accept I'd walked away. He thought he had me, that I'd forgive him anything."

"He hurt you."

"More than he realised which says it all. While I was with Strip Jack I calmed Jonnie down. He'd always been an exhibitionist, but I stopped him doing a lot of stuff I thought was dangerous. He pushed things too far. It was as if he thought he was invincible. He wasn't."

Kell gulped. "What happened?"

"About twelve months ago, he called to say he had a cheque for me. I didn't want him to know where I was living so I offered to collect it. It was all a ploy to get me to a place where I'd see the band rehearsing with their new guitarist. Jonnie wanted to prove they didn't need me. He didn't get that I no longer gave a shit. He climbed up onto one of the stage sets. The sort of stupid stunt I usually stopped him doing. He looked at me as if he was waiting for me to tell him to get down, but I didn't, and he jumped. The box he landed on tipped and he fell and hit his head and his back on a sharp edge. Now he's paralysed. He can move a couple of fingers, enough to drive his wheelchair, use his computer, put his light on or off. He can't wipe his own arse, feed himself or wank. He wants to die. He wants me to help him die."

"Oh fuck."

Gethin had to get it all out while could. "That's not all of it. We'd split up six months before his accident, but when he came round in the hospital, he didn't remember what he'd done. He thinks we're still an item. He says he loves me. I'm the only one who goes to see him. I'm paying part of the cost of his care. I've depleted my bank account buying him whatever he needs. He has no idea his money has gone. He thinks I love him and I fucking hate him."

Kell wrapped his arms around him and held him tight.

"He says if I love him, I'd help him die. How can it be right to do that when I wish he was already dead?"

Chapter Twenty-Seven

Kell threaded his fingers with Gethin's. That was a story he hadn't expected. What a mess. "What are you going to do? Can you help him die?"

"After saying no for a long time, doing my best to talk him out of it, I've finally given in."

"You can't actually…kill him." *Could he?*

"He wants to go to that clinic in Switzerland. He needs me to arrange everything."

"And pay for everything?"

Kell wanted that back the moment he'd said it, but Gethin gave a quiet laugh. "Yeah."

"How much will it cost?"

"At least fifteen thousand. I don't have it. There's money due to me from when I was with the band. I wrote some of the songs, but our agent was a crook and we're in dispute. Until it's settled I won't get a penny. I can borrow it. Angel would lend it to me. It's just…"

"I'll help you. I can lend you the money, help you arrange everything."

"No." Gethin shook his head. "I don't want you involved."

Kell clamped down on his disappointment.

"It's just that this is going to be difficult." Gethin turned to look at him. "When you said you wanted things to be casual, you can see why I thought that sounded perfect."

He was pulling away, Kell could *feel* it happening. "We're just heating up and you want to cool things down?"

"Hey, it's just for a while. Until it's over. I'd feel wrong if we were…"

"I get it." Kell sat up and Gethin pulled him down.

Kell didn't get it. Jonnie might think Gethin and he were still an item, but if the guy really loved Gethin, wouldn't he push him away, tell him to get on with his life?

"Are you blaming yourself?" Kell whispered. "In what fucked up world was it your fault he jumped and ended up paralysed? *His* decision. So what if he expected you to stop him. He jumped."

"Because he'd have lost face if he'd climbed down. He *wanted* me to stop him."

Kell rolled so that he lay over Gethin. "Are you sure? Maybe he'd have jumped anyway. Maybe he just wanted to hear you tell him to stop, but he was going to defy you to show he didn't need you controlling him. You're not responsible for what happened. It's his ego that's put him where he is. You say no one else goes to see him? Yeah, well that makes him even more desperate you keep going. What better way to ensure you continue to visit than to conveniently forget he cheated on you and that you walked out?"

Gethin clutched Kell's hips. "It doesn't alter the fact that Jonnie can't do this without help. I don't think I'm going to be a bundle of fun for the next few months."

"I'm *not* going to back off and wait," Kell said. "I know what we agreed, our own private version of Grindr but we've already gone beyond that. You mean more to me than a casual fuck." *I love you, you fucking idiot.* "I want a relationship with you. I want us to go out together and see where this leads." *I want a happy ever after.*

Kell waited for Gethin to agree with him and when he didn't, he wondered if anything he said would make a difference, but he was still going to try. "There is *no* reason why you have to do this alone. I don't have to meet the guy. He doesn't need to know I exist. I don't want to hurt him. I don't want *you* to hurt him, but we need each other right at this moment. Okay, *I* need you. Plus it's my birthday, you selfish bastard. You are not going to dump me on my birthday. You're not going to dump me before we've used all ten boxes of condoms *and* that entire bottle of lube." Kell held his breath.

"I wasn't going to dump you." Gethin slid his hands over Kell's arse and squeezed.

"You were going to put me on hold, like a telephone call? Still expect me to be there when you'd finished with your other call?"

295

"Yes."

"No. That's not going to happen. We're together and we stay together. If it goes wrong, then it goes wrong, but that won't be because of some selfish wanker who cheated on you and has now put you in an impossible position."

Kell waited and when Gethin didn't speak, he pushed himself up on his hands. "So do I go or stay?"

Gethin pulled him down. "Stay. Please."

Kell smothered his sigh of relief. "You don't have to tell me anything you do with him if you don't want to, just don't push me away. Okay?"

"Okay."

"I know I've done a lot of talking, but you *will* open up to me eventually, won't you? Tell me how you met Angel, why you decided to be a private detective, whether you like breakfast in bed, if you have any really annoying habits apart from those I've already noticed."

Gethin smiled. "Yep."

Kell slithered all the way down until his face was over Gethin's groin. Gethin's cock was semi-hard and Kell nuzzled it with his cheek.

"I want to fuck you," Kell said. "Then you can do me. Okay? Maybe we can do each other at the same time."

"I thought we just did." Gethin's eyes were heavy with lust.

"I have a party trick. Not that I've ever done it at a party." Kell ran the pad of his index finger over the glistening head of Gethin's cock and spread the precome around until the whole crest was shining.

He lifted his finger to his mouth and sucked it. "You taste good."

Gethin groaned. "If you talk to me, I've had it."

Kell grinned. "You taste *really* good. Sweet. Sour. Like a cocktail. Hah! Bad joke."

"I've gone off you now."

"Want me to stop?"

"Only with the jokes."

Kell sucked at the tip of Gethin's cock, sliding his tongue into the slit, his mouth watering at the taste.

Gethin groaned and Kell pushed up the guy's legs, nestling between his thighs. He pressed his mouth against the base of Gethin's dick, and rubbed his balls with his chin. When Kell fumbled for the lube and found the bottle pressed into his hand, he chuckled.

Kell squirted a dollop of the gel onto his fingers and while he enveloped Gethin's cock with his mouth, he tickled the underside of his balls, smearing the lube over the triangle of flesh beyond to tease his taint, circling his thumb but falling short of breaching the entrance to his body.

"Fuckfuckfuckfuck." Gethin was already gasping and Kell had hardly started.

He slid one lubed finger over Gethin's hole and Gethin's hips arched, shoving his cock deeper into Kell's mouth. Kell sucked harder enjoying the sensuous glide of hard, velvet flesh over his tongue, the sensation of raw energy pulsing below that smooth skin. He pushed in another finger, embedding them to the second knuckle.

"Christ." Gethin twisted Kell's hair in his fingers. "Arggh...arggh—"

Kell looked up over the expanse of Gethin's smooth abs and into those green eyes. *Oh fuck.* He reached for Gethin's mouth and slid two fingers in there as well, alternating the push and pull with those in his arse. It wasn't easy to do that *and* suck cock at the same time. Kell had never been good at multi-tasking. His own cock was back to full hardness and he felt increasingly desperate to drive it inside Gethin. He wanted to make this the best sex of Gethin's life.

Christ, how to fail before I start.

He worked his fingers deeper in Gethin's arse, curving them to find his prostate, registering Gethin's moan when he did, then stroking the small gland until Gethin jerked and bucked and writhed beneath him. Kell stroked Gethin's face to give him the chance to breathe.

"Kell." Gethin exhaled his name and dug his nails into Kell's shoulders. "More."

Kell turned the two fingers in Gethin's arse into three, pushed three fingers into Gethin's mouth and let his cock slide to the back of his throat. His own cock was throbbing more insistently, telling him to hurry, get to the good part, but Kell wanted to make this last. And if Kell needed to breathe, which he did, he had to pull back.

Gethin made a sobbing sound in his throat and Kell took his fingers from his mouth and leaned up to kiss him without taking his fingers out of his body. Kell undulated against him as their lips met, keeping up the rhythmic finger fuck while their cocks rubbed together, slick with lube and desire. As a gentle slide turned into a frantic rut, their mouths stayed joined, and Kell's heart pounded louder and harder in his head.

Gethin reached down Kell's back to the seam of his butt and ran his finger along the crack. If Gethin touched him there, Kell would come. He shifted out of reach, grabbed a condom but struggled to get it on because his fingers were so slippery. Frustrated, he tossed it aside and reached for another.

"Good thing I bought ten boxes," Gethin muttered. "Hurry the fuck up."

"Hey, Mr. Topping-from-the-bottom, who's in charge here?" Kell paused with his cock pressing against Gethin's anus.

"You."

"Then don't come."

"What?" Gethin blinked at him, those green eyes darkening.

"I can't do my party trick if you come."

Kell slid his aching, swollen cock straight into Gethin, one long, deep, smooth slide that sort of took him by surprise. Gethin clenched his muscles around him and Kell tried to tell him to stop or it would be over before he'd begun, but he couldn't form coherent words. He pulled back, thrust forward and Gethin sucked in a breath and wrapped his hand around his cock, pressing down at the base. *Doing what I asked him to.* Kell moved his hips faster, leaned on Gethin's legs and rocked hard into him, dragging his cock through nerve-rich tissue, shifting more quickly than he'd intended, but now unable to stop, racing for the finish line.

His balls drew up against the base of his cock and he slipped into hyper speed, ramming himself into Gethin until that tell-tale tingle flared in his skull and began to spread through his body. His eyes closed and he forced them open to see Gethin staring up at him.

"If you don't want me to come…" Gethin said between gasps, "then, hurry the fuck up."

Kell fell into ecstasy. His stomach wrenched with each rolling wave and he threw his head back as he came and came and came, tumbling into blackness that flashed in an instant to dazzling white light before the world returned.

"Oh fuck, that was so good," Kell blurted. "Get a condom on—quick."

He pulled out of Gethin, and let him straighten his legs. Kell turned and took off the condom he was wearing. Out of sight of Gethin, he wiped himself down, put on another condom and took a squirt of lube. He'd done this *once* before so he hoped he could still do it. He pushed Gethin's legs back against his chest, then positioned himself facing in the other direction. As he lowered himself down onto Gethin's dick, Gethin grabbed his hips and guided him. Kell groaned at the stretch and burn of the slow penetration, but watched every inch of cock slide into him with a smile on his face.

"Okay?" Gethin gasped.

"Fuck, yes."

Gethin's hands curled around Kell's hips, anchoring him and Kell took advantage of being pressed tight together to push his cock down toward Gethin's arse.

"What the fuck?" Gethin blurted.

Kell lifted his hips, managed to get part of his semi-hard dick into Gethin, then kept his hand in place to make sure it stayed put.

"We…you…shit…can…oh God." Gethin's breathing turned ragged. "Your party trick? Can you juggle plates at the same time?"

Kell laughed. It wasn't the easiest of positions and only possible if Kell's cock stayed partway erect. As they began to fuck, they instinctively shifted to keep each other in place. Gethin's fingers were biting into Kell's hips, and the pain kept Kell anchored. It wasn't long before Gethin stiffened beneath him, then he was coming and impossibly Kell felt his own cock work into some sort of dry orgasm that left him trembling with pleasure.

As his heart rate calmed, he extricated himself and flopped at Gethin's side.

"That was…" Gethin sighed. "How much time do you spend watching porn?"

"You mean I'm not the first to do that?" Kell gasped in mock-horror. "I thought I'd invented it."

Gethin gave a loud guffaw.

"It only works if you're not fully hard," Kell said.

"Plus you need an enormously long cock."

Kell sniggered. "I need to clean up."

"Lie still. Save your strength for round two. I'll get a cloth."

When Gethin came back into the bedroom, Kell was asleep. He didn't even wake when Gethin wiped him down. Gethin pulled the duvet over them and curled up at Kell's back. He hadn't wanted Kell to run despite what he'd said. Not that he was testing him, but Gethin had to know for certain how Kell felt. He was right—this had moved into new territory.

Kell made no demands on him which was supposed to be what Gethin wanted and it wasn't. Not any longer. The idea of Kell waiting for him to come home, meeting him in a restaurant, sitting beside him in the cinema—*that* was what Gethin wanted. Though guilt still swirled because he was thinking that when

Jonnie was dead, how much easier life would be. But even if Jonnie decided he wanted to live, Gethin wouldn't give Kell up.

Gethin woke the next morning and Kell was still sleeping, his dark hair mussed. He didn't have the heart to wake him. Kell's eyelids twitched and Gethin wondered what he was dreaming about. *Me?* He slid out of bed, showered, dressed, and decided to go out for a newspaper to see if there was anything about what had happened. He could pick up warm croissants at the same time. He scribbled a note, left it on the pillow and slipped out of his flat.

He ought to go and see Jonnie that afternoon, toyed with the idea of taking Kell and dismissed it. He hadn't given up on talking Jonnie out of assisted dying and if he brought Kell with him, it looked as if he was pushing Jonnie onto the plane.

He called Angel as he walked to the shop.

"Still alive?" Angel asked.

"Long story."

"Are you both okay?"

"Yes. Kell's fast asleep in my bed. *'Me thought I heard a voice cry 'sleep no more'.'*"

Angel laughed. "Have you been waiting to use that? But I'm not sure any use of the word 'sleep' in Macbeth is a good thing."

"Why?"

"It tends to herald death. *'Macbeth doth murder sleep.'* And *'Glamis hath murdered sleep'.*"

"We're fine. The bad guys are in custody."

"Glad to hear it."

"Angel, I know I already owe you a hundred quid, but I'd like to borrow more. It might be a while before I can pay you back."

"How much more?"

Gethin winced. "Fifteen thousand."

"Good Lord. Am I allowed to ask why?"

"I have a friend who wants to go to Switzerland to die."
Gethin wasn't going to lie. If Angel was against assisted suicide, Gethin would look elsewhere.

"Is this by any chance the Jonnie you keep going to see? The one who stopped you dating before now?"

"Yes. He's paralysed from the neck down after an accident. He won't get better and he's had enough. He wants to die. I've tried to talk him out of it. I'll continue to try but—"

"Yes, I'll lend you the money. You and Kell come for supper tomorrow and I'll give you a cheque."

"Thank you."

"You should have told me," Angel said quietly.

"I know."

Gethin had to walk another half mile to get the croissants because the closer shop had sold out. He was on his way back when he heard police sirens. For several yards, he managed to convince himself there was nothing to worry about before he began to walk faster. It was as if he'd found a slick puddle under his bike and known there was trouble ahead.

When he saw police vehicles and two ambulances at the foot of his building, he broke out into a run. He was overreacting. Kell was likely sleeping through the whole thing. It couldn't have anything to do with them because all the bad guys were in custody, right? *Oh shit…could someone have made bail?* The thought that the police could have missed someone and not told them… *No, no…* But these cops were armed. *Oh fuck.*

The newspaper and croissants fell from his hands as he sprinted toward the ambulance, but the vehicle pulled away before he reached it, the siren blaring. *That's a good thing, isn't it?* If Kell was inside it, it meant he was still alive. *I'm an idiot.* Why did he have to be inside it? He was probably up in the flat talking to the police. Or lying in bed fast asleep. But Gethin's stomach continued to churn.

He turned to the cops. "What's happened?"

"I'll have to ask you to step back, sir," said a uniformed constable.

"I live in flat fifty-eight."

The cop's face almost made Gethin crumple at the knees.

"Please tell me what's happened. Is Kell injured? Is it him in the ambulance?" Questions tumbled in Gethin's head. He pressed his lips together before he lost it completely.

The constable called over another officer, a more senior one. Gethin wanted to tear off after the ambulance, but maybe Kell wasn't even in it.

"This man says he's lives in flat fifty-eight," the constable said.

"Name?" asked the senior cop.

"Gethin Jones. I went out to get breakfast. I left Kell asleep. He's a policeman."

The constable's eyes widened. *What the fuck has happened?*

"Come with me," the senior guy said.

Gethin followed him.

"Detective Superintendent Nigel Lane is Kell's boss," Gethin said.

"I know him. I'm Detective Inspector Williams."

They walked in silence up the four flights of stairs and Gethin's steps grew heavier and heavier. When they reached his door, guarded by a policeman, Williams put his hand on Gethin's arm.

"There's a lot of blood. One guy survived. The other didn't. No identification on either of them. The dead man could be your boyfriend."

He handed Gethin covers for his shoes. "Don't touch anything. I want to know if you recognize this guy, that's all."

Gethin made a quiet moaning sound in his throat when he saw who was lying on the bedroom floor.

"Marek Dushku. He was supposed to be in police custody. The case Kell was working on involved a nightclub. This guy worked there. Lane has all the details. What happened to him?"

"He was shot. Same as your boyfriend."

303

The ground shifted beneath Gethin's feet. *Shot?*

"How bad?" Gethin was shocked he managed to get the words out.

Williams grimaced and Gethin felt the life drain out of him. *Oh God, no.*

"Which hospital?" Gethin croaked out.

"We need to talk—"

"Not now. Which fucking hospital?"

Gethin refused the offer of a lift and took his bike. He went too fast, nearly came off on one corner, and narrowly missed being clipped by a bus. He kept telling himself someone had made a mistake, Kell hadn't been shot and even if he had been, it wasn't serious. But his heart was pounding hard enough to burst out of his chest.

He wasn't next of kin. No one would tell him anything. He paced in the corridor outside the accident and emergency department and every fifteen minutes, he begged the man on reception to find out how Kell was. He called the Met to speak to Lane but the guy didn't answer. Tried to get hold of Beckwith and ended up leaving angrier and angrier messages for both of them.

One hour turned into two. Then a couple of men walked up to the reception desk and Gethin knew one of them. Kell's brother Oliver. He guessed the other was Kell's father. Gethin almost went up to them then thought again. Oliver hadn't seen him, or at least he hadn't recognized him which meant Gethin could follow them to Kell.

The pair ended up on the eighth floor in a visitors' room. Gethin stayed out of sight in the corridor. But he'd exhausted his patience. If they weren't going straight in to see Kell, he couldn't wait any longer. Oliver glanced at him then looked down again when Gethin walked in. Gethin belatedly remembered when he'd confronted Oliver in the club, he'd been wearing a mask.

"How is he?" Gethin asked.

Kell's father shook his head and the bottom fell out of Gethin's world.

Chapter Twenty-Eight

Gethin knew the moment Oliver recalled where he'd seen him before. Their gazes collided and understanding flowed like a torrent of raging water. The fury in Oliver's eyes made Gethin want to punch him. This was all *his* fault.

Oliver glanced at his father, then scowled at Gethin. "This man is not with the police."

"I didn't say I was." Gethin stepped forward and held out his hand to Kell's father. "Gethin Jones. I'm a friend of Kell's."

"Tobias DeMornay." He gave Gethin a wary look as they shook hands.

"Kell was in my flat when he was shot," Gethin said. "I'd popped out to get breakfast and a paper. I came back just as the ambulance pulled away."

"Do you know who shot him?" Kell's father asked.

"A man called Marek Dushku. Kell and I thought he was in police custody. I suspect it was his brother, Pavel, the police had arrested."

When Kell and the brothers had come to his flat, Gethin had *seen* how alike the pair were. He should have thought to check whether the police had arrested both of them.

"The police are blatantly incompetent," Oliver snapped. "My brother is dying because they didn't do their job."

Dying? Gethin's lungs locked and millions of needles pricked his skin.

"He's not going to die," his father said.

"He's been shot in the chest," Oliver snapped. "Be realistic."

Gethin's anger flared into life. He imagined heat radiating from him as if he was a blazing fire and he wanted Oliver to burn. "If he dies, it will be your fault."

"That's ridiculous," Oliver snapped. "The police failed to arrest a dangerous man."

"Don't you dare blame the police when you know full well what you did."

"What do you mean?" Tobias asked.

"I don't know how much the police told you, but Kell's been working undercover in a Vauxhall nightclub. The man who shot him is one of the men he worked for. Oliver came to the club and told Marek that Kell was working undercover."

"What?" Tobias spun to look at Oliver.

"Rubbish." Oliver clenched his teeth.

"Kell told me all about you, what you were like even as a small child. How every time he had a birthday, you ruined it in some way. I took a picture of you on my phone dressed in fetish gear. I threatened to go to the press with it if you didn't leave Kell alone. Minutes later, Marek came to Kell and he knew everything. You told him."

"You have no proof."

"Marek is my proof. He's in custody now and making a full statement." Gethin was relying on them not knowing Marek was dead.

"Did you tell this man about Kell?" his father asked.

"It was a…joke," Oliver blustered. "I didn't expect him to take me seriously."

You fucking bastard. "Well he did," Gethin snapped. "Kell and I were locked in the back of a van and it was pushed into the Thames. We were lucky we didn't die. Now Kell has been shot because you brought a long running undercover operation to a premature conclusion."

Gethin drew back his fist, smacked Oliver in the face and bloodied his nose. He hadn't even hit him as hard as he'd wanted to.

"How dare you!" Oliver screeched. He pulled a tissue from his pocket and pressed it to his nose.

"I dare because I fucking —" He took a deep breath. "I dare because I care about Kell and you don't. He's done nothing to you other than be born. You've tormented him all his life and it stops now." He turned to his father. "It's your fault too. You should have seen what was happening, done something."

A doctor appeared in the doorway of the room. "Mr. DeMornay?"

Kell's father stepped forward. "Yes."

Don't let Kell be dead. Don't…don't…don't.

"Your son came through the surgery with no further complications, though he's still critically ill. The first twenty-four hours are the most important. He's slipping in and out of consciousness, but you can see him for a few minutes. Don't worry about all the machines he's connected to. Everything is there to help him."

Tobias let out a shaky sigh. "Thank you." He turned to Oliver who'd moved to his side. "You. Go home." Then he turned to Gethin. "Come with me."

"Father—"

"I don't want you here," his father said.

Oliver stomped off like a petulant child. Gethin followed Tobias and the doctor, trying to force air into lungs that didn't remember how to work. When he saw Kell lying so still, so pale, his heart cramped. *Oh God.* He looked vulnerable. Like a child. There was a tube in his mouth and an IV in his arm, monitors attached to his chest. A big dressing over his chest. Gethin thought of how he'd lain with his head there, listening to Kell's heart beating, never thinking it might stop. It *can't* stop.

Tobias took Kell's hand. "Kell? Can you hear me?"

Kell made no response.

"I'm sorry," his father whispered. "I didn't realise Oliver was still hurting you. I thought… I thought he'd grown out of it. I should have protected you and I didn't." He glanced at Gethin. "But you have a champion. Gethin has just punched your brother. I don't think Oliver has ever had anyone stand up to him before apart from you. Your mother and I indulged him. It was a mistake. You need to get better, you hear me? I'll come and see you again tomorrow. I'll ensure Oliver is not allowed to visit you."

He stepped back from the bed and nodded to Gethin before he left the room.

Gethin took hold of Kell's hand and stroked his palm with his thumb. Each time he opened his mouth to say something, emotion choked him. *Whatever state he's in, I want him back.* If they had to be careful every day of their lives, Gethin wanted him back. His mind slipped to Jonnie, who lay there just as motionless as Kell. If Gethin had still been going out with Jonnie when he'd had his accident, would he have felt like this? As if he'd die if he lost him?

What he and Kell had wasn't love. It couldn't be. Could it? Not yet. But maybe getting there. *Christ, who am I trying to fool?* He was torn by a mixture of shock and fear. He could deny it all he liked but he *did* love Kell. It had crept up on him, drawn him in. Except just as Gethin had risked opening his heart, it seemed fate had other ideas. *I can't lose him.* Gethin's life had been on hold since the day he'd found Jonnie cheating on him, and Kell had made him see he had to let go, move on, that they only had one life and time was too short to waste a minute of it. *Take a chance.* Gethin had taken it and now he needed Kell to live so he could tell him how he felt.

Don't die, don't die, don't die.

The police were waiting when Gethin came out of the ICU. They asked him to go to the station to make a statement. Gethin followed them on his bike.

He wasn't surprised when DCI Beckwith came into the interview room. The man with him introduced himself as Nigel Lane.

Gethin's anger surged back. "How the hell did you not realise you had Pavel and not Marek?"

"We hadn't realised there was a brother until it was too late," Lane said. "They'd exchanged their ID."

"We thought we were safe."

"How is he?" Beckwith asked.

"Holding his own."

"I'm going to see him this afternoon." Lane swallowed hard. "I know you're angry. We fucked up."

"How the hell did Marek know where he was?" Gethin asked. "What happened?"

Beckwith pursed his lips.

"For fuck's sake. You can tell me. What difference is it going to make?"

"We're only surmising until Kell can give us his version," Lane said. "But your escape from the van was captured by some enterprising guy on his mobile phone. Sold to a reporter who turned it into a scoop for the Metro. You were on the front page this morning."

"Shit."

Lane put his hand flat on the table. "Marek must have guessed where you might be. He kicked the door in. He probably hoped to find you both. We think he and Kell struggled. Somehow Kell managed to get to the door. A neighbour had already heard it being broken and called the police. The operator had caught a muffled sound when she spoke to the neighbour, thought it might have been a gunshot and we sent in an armed unit."

"Doreen Martineau?" The seventy year old who kept asking Gethin to change her lightbulbs and put her rubbish out.

"That's the one."

Gethin would buy her enough lightbulbs to last her the rest of her life. "You certain you have everyone in custody? Including Marek and Pavel's sister? And Charlton?"

"Yes."

"Can you hold them?"

"Warner's lawyer is fighting to get him out on bail. He might manage it. Marek won't. A tangled mess to sort out."

"Yep."

"Right. After we've done, we'll take your fingerprints for elimination purposes. Now let's have your version of events." Lane clicked on the recorder. "This is Detective Superintendent Nigel Lane interviewing Gethin Jones. The date is…"

From there, after calling to check if there had been any change in Kell's condition — the answer was no — Gethin went to see Jonnie. The look on Jonnie's face when he walked in was so full of hope that Gethin made himself smile when it was the last thing he felt like doing.

"How soon?" Jonnie asked.

"Just before or after Christmas."

Jonnie closed his eyes and pressed his lips together. "Before."

"I'll try," Gethin said.

Jonnie opened his eyes again. "You'll help me?"

"Yes, but you need to know that every step of the way I'll be trying to change your mind."

"Not going to happen. Tell me what we have to do."

We? Gethin knew he'd have to do almost everything. "You need a carer traveling with us, someone who knows how to handle your day to day needs. I suspect there's no point asking anyone here. They might lose their jobs. I'll try agencies. I need to find an airline that will take you and your chair, one that will give us seats close to the front. We need a place to stay in Geneva that's wheelchair accessible. A vehicle that can take your chair."

"I'll look online."

"Have you told your parents?"

"Emailed. They haven't responded."

"Fucking bastards." *But emailing? Really?*

Jonnie smiled. "Yeah. Gethin? Will you take your guitar? Play to me when...when it's time?"

Oh God. "If you want."

"I do want. No funeral. Cremation. Scatter my ashes..." He choked up.

Gethin struggled to hold himself in check. "You don't have to—"

"Yes I do. Tell you now and don't have to say it again. Scatter my ashes at the top of Mount Everest."

"What?"

311

"Joke."

Gethin sagged and managed to laugh. "Thank fuck for that."

"Out at sea. Don't care where. Sunny day. No wind or I'll blow back in your face. You might swallow me. Though you used to like that."

It was as though Jonnie had reverted back to the guy Gethin had once fallen for.

"I'll wear a mask, just in case," Gethin said.

Jonnie gave him a lovely lopsided smile.

When Angel opened the door and saw Gethin on his own, he frowned. "Where is he? I expected you both for supper."

"Kell's in hospital."

"What's happened?" Angel pulled Gethin into the house.

"He was shot."

Angel clutched his chest. "Oh my God. Is he going to be okay?"

"I don't know." If it hadn't been going to look corny, Gethin would have clutched his chest too. His heart had ached from the moment he heard what had happened.

Angel sagged. "Oh no. Poor Kell. Poor you."

"Can I stay the night? My place is a crime scene."

"Of course you can. Henry!" Angel picked up Winston and put him in Gethin's arms. "Stroke Winston. That makes everyone feel better. Kennedy will wriggle."

Henry came into the hallway. "Hi, Gethin. Where's Kell?"

"In hospital." Angel clutched Henry's arm. "Open the good wine. Gethin'll tell us everything."

Maybe not everything, but enough by the time he'd finished, to leave the men open-mouthed with shock.

"You can stay as long as you like," Henry said. "We'll give you a key."

"And while I remember." Angel handed him a cheque. "Here's the money."

"Thank you. I don't know when I'm going to be able to pay you back. I don't want to take on more work for the time being." Maybe never again as a PI.

"Don't worry about it," Henry said. "We can afford to lend it you. We can afford to give it you but—"

"I have to pay for this. But thank you."

Gethin sat with Winston curled upon his knee. He only drank half a glass of wine. If he had a call about Kell, he needed to be able to ride his bike.

When there had been no call by ten, he phoned the hospital. 'Comfortable' was all he could get out of them. So Gethin had an uncomfortable, largely sleepless night.

The next day he spent at the hospital at Kell's bedside. Kell still hadn't regained full consciousness and Gethin sensed the staff worrying about that, though no one voiced their concerns. At least the breathing tube was out. That had to be a good thing. He willed Kell to get better. Willed him to open his eyes.

Kell's friend Quin came to see him and he remembered Gethin from the party. Gethin went to get a drink while Quin sat with Kell. Gethin wanted to be there when Kell woke—because he *would* wake—but he knew others had claims on Kell too. Quin emerged red-eyed into the corridor where Gethin waited.

"Do they know when he might wake?" Quin asked.

Gethin shook his head.

"I forgot his birthday." Quin swallowed hard. "I never forget it because I know what a jerk his brother is but I forgot. Christ."

Kell's father came down the corridor toward them and Quin stepped into his arms, his shoulders heaving. Tobias patted his back.

"Sorry." Quin rubbed his eyes. "I told him to hold on. He was always saying that to me. Hold on or I'd fall in the water. Hold on or I'd fall off the cliff. Kell's the kindest... He doesn't deserve this."

Quin left and Gethin and Kell's father went into the ICU. Kell looked no different, still deathly pale. Tobias sat one side of the bed and Gethin the other.

Kell's father talked about Kell's childhood. "You remember how determined you were to ride your bike without stabilizers? You kept trying and trying until you could do it. Then there was the day your fingers were caught in the bike chain. I'm wondering now if Oliver deliberately pushed the pedal the wrong way to make matters worse. Then I bought you a new bike, a BMX. You loved that bike. I've never seen you take such good care of anything."

Gethin had never had a new bike. He'd made do with bikes that had belonged to other kids before him. The more Tobias spoke, the more Gethin realised what a privileged upbringing Kell had had—skiing holidays, vacations in the Caribbean, private schools.

"I didn't want him to be a policeman," his father said. "But he insisted. He wanted to make things fair, he said. Right wrongs. Put bad guys somewhere they couldn't hurt the good guys. I don't know what I was thinking letting him do it. It was too dangerous. I…" He took a shuddering breath and looked at Gethin. "Now I see it was because of Oliver that Kell went into the police. He couldn't do anything about his brother but he wanted to protect others from brothers like him. I knew Oliver was bad, but I tried to convince myself he wasn't *that* bad.

"I was away a lot. My wife came to me with these stories of what the boys had been doing and she laughed and I thought it was nothing. Just high jinks. I didn't want to see more than that." He pulled at his hair and for a moment looked like Kell. "What about you? Do you have siblings? Parents?"

"No siblings. My parents… They died when I was seven. A faulty heater gave off fumes. I was in a bed near an open window. They were in another room. I woke and they were already dead."

"That's terrible. I'm so sorry. Who brought you up?"

"A lot of people. Mostly me."

Kell's father sighed. "I'm sorry to hear that. I always thought Kell would make a good father."

Gethin wasn't sure how to respond.

"Being gay doesn't preclude the possibility," Kell's father said. "Kell's heart has always been so... Oh God."

"Where are my croissants?"

They started at the sound of Kell's hoarse voice. Gethin leapt to his feet. Kell blinked up at him.

"Hi," Kell whispered. "Hi, Dad. Did I nearly die?"

"Nearly." His father clasped his hand.

"Glad I didn't," Kell said.

Gethin opened his mouth and nothing came out.

"Bloody Dushkus," Kell whispered.

Gethin nodded.

"I know of Oliver's role in this." Tobias glanced at Gethin. "Your young man thumped him. Not hard enough. I shall be dealing with him. If he doesn't seek help, I'll..."

"What?" Kell asked. "Stop his pocket money?"

"Actually I will. He lives beyond his means. Perhaps it's time he lived inside them. I'll leave you two for a while and get a coffee while you chat. I'm delighted you've woken. When you're fit to be discharged, come home. I'll employ a nurse to look after you. Gethin can come too."

He bent and kissed Kell on the forehead, nodded to Gethin and left.

"Going to speak?" Kell asked.

"What would I have done if you'd died?" Gethin whispered.

"Picked yourself up and carried on. After a long period of mourning... Seven years wearing black sounds about right." He winced. "No, not black. You look too hot in black... Pink. Yep, that would work... No one would want you then."

Gethin rested his head on Kell's arm and let the tears fall.

The next weeks passed in a mixture of visits to the hospital to see Kell and visits to Jonnie and in between, Gethin managed to do some work. Apart from needing the money, it stopped him brooding. But seeing Kell's health improve lightened the load on Gethin's shoulders. When Kell went to stay with his father, it meant Gethin couldn't see him as often but he knew he was being well cared for.

Weekends were Kell's. Jonnie seemed less anxious about Gethin visiting. It was as though he'd gone to a different place in his head. Gethin sensed no change of heart, rather contentment borne of Jonnie finally getting what he wanted. Although Jonnie might have been content, Gethin wasn't. He still agonised about what he was doing. Without Kell, he thought he'd have fallen apart.

Kell's father opened the door when Gethin knocked.

"How is he?" Gethin asked.

"Still a terrible patient. Very hard to get him to take it easy."

Which was part of the reason Gethin had not given in to requests that he move into Kell's father's house. Gethin pushed open the door of the drawing room where Kell sat on the couch.

He looked up from the book he was reading and scowled. "I've just got to the exciting bit. You'll have to sit quietly while I finish it. Someone's about to get shot."

Gethin put his helmet on a chair and took off his leather jacket.

"I don't see why you have to stay with Angel and Henry," Kell said. "You could live here."

Gethin had given up his flat and moved in temporarily with his friends. Kell patted the cushion beside him and when Gethin dropped down next to him, Kell flinched.

"That's one reason." Gethin kissed him and moved back when Kell tried to deepen the kiss. "You need to fully recover."

"And the other reason?"

"My head's not where I'd like it to be." He tried not to talk to Kell about Jonnie, about all the hassle he was having sorting this thing out, how at every step it felt like there was a mountain to climb and that guilt still surged like bubbling lava in his veins.

316

He took hold of Kell's hand and stroked his fingers. Kell let out a low groan and tossed the book over the back of the couch.

"I thought you wanted to read the exciting bit."

"Until an even more exciting bit popped up. See what you've done?" Kell pulled his hand onto his crotch. Gethin felt the hard outline of his cock.

There was a knock at the door and their hands sprang apart. Kell pulled a blanket over his lap as his father walked in.

"Something to eat? Drink?" he asked.

Kell shook his head. "We're fine, thanks."

"I'd love a coffee, please," Gethin said.

That earned him a glare from Kell and a laugh from Kell's father as he left the room.

"Dad told me he'd cut Oliver out of his will."

Gethin raised his eyebrows. "Does Oliver know?"

"Yeah. He's not happy. I think Dad wanted to make a point."

Gethin wanted to make more than a point. He was quietly looking into Oliver's life. He didn't want to cause trouble for his wife and kids but there was no way he was letting him get away with what he'd done to Kell. He'd get what was coming to him.

Gethin changed the subject. "I had a cheque from Dieter's mother today."

"How much?"

"Four hundred pounds. I don't have the heart to ask for more."

Kell rolled his eyes. "It's a wonder you're still in business. Any more news on the investigation? Have the police found out why you were selected to get the information off Charlton's computer?"

"Unflatteringly, it was part by chance because Marek wanted an inexperienced sole operator. He didn't expect me to be able to decrypt the data, just obtain it. Marek and his sister intended to syphon off Warner's money."

Kell pulled Gethin's hand under the blanket. "Going to tell me why you were so worried about their reason for choosing you?"

Gethin hesitated as he usually did. He'd lost count of the number of times Kell had asked him the same question. He pulled free of Kell's hold and Kell grabbed his hand and held tight.

"I'm not going to let go until you tell me." Kell rubbed Gethin's knuckles with his thumb. "You have to open up about stuff or it's only ever going to be me who does the talking and you'll get fed up of me, duct tape my mouth, and that will be it."

You talk about everything but the one thing I want to hear. Gethin almost asked the question he'd bottled up since Kell had been shot, but swallowed it instead. He wasn't sure Kell would ever tell him the truth about what had happened when Marek turned up at his flat. He knew the version Kell had told the police was shaky. Maybe telling Kell what he wanted to know about his past would open the gates.

"You're a cop and I haven't always been on the right side of the law. I'd lose my PI license if anyone found out what I'd done."

"As if I'd tell anyone. What did you do? Move your name off Santa's naughty list onto the nice list? Send a van load of pizzas to 10 Downing Street?"

"Let myself be persuaded to build a program and insert it into a company's accounting system. It was supposed to be a—look what can happen to you—type of thing, but the guy who'd *persuaded* me stole the money I thought we'd give back, then ran. I closed it down but he got a few million before I did. He was arrested, went to prison. He didn't give me up."

"But you worry he still could?"

"It's a niggle at the back of my mind that I might be linked to the crime."

"But that's not happened."

Gethin shook his head.

"You know that worrying about what *might* happen is a waste of time."

"Yeah."

"How old were you when you did it?"

"Sixteen."

"Fuck. A master hacker at sixteen?"

"It was all I did. Messed around on the computer or played my guitar."

"You didn't spend all your time wanking?" Kell gaped at him and Gethin laughed.

The door opened, Kell's father came in with a tray of drinks and a plate of biscuits, and Gethin pulled his hand from under the blanket. When they were alone again, Kell yanked it back underneath and moaned when Gethin stroked his cock.

"Will you stay tonight?" Kell asked.

Gethin hesitated.

"You're depriving me of my medicine. Your irresistible arse. Except it is resisting me." He scowled.

"You have to take it easy. You know what the doctors said."

"Not just the doctors, is it?" Kell turned sharp eyes on him.

Gethin met his gaze. "It will be over with Jonnie soon. I booked the flights today. Four more weeks."

He felt Kell bristle, but Gethin kept hold of his hand and stroked his fingers.

"I can't wait that long," Kell said. "I want us to move in together *now*. My father's driving me mad. I've been researching flats online. I want you to look at them. I'm going to continue to rent my old one out and we can choose something we both like."

"I'm hardly working. And you're not. How are we going to afford anything?"

"The police are still paying me. And I have savings. Plus I have stuff in storage including a double bed. Please."

"Okay."

Kell's eyes widened in shock. "Did you just say okay?"

Gethin nodded. He figured it would take a month to get a flat sorted out and by then, Jonnie…

Kell lifted his tablet from the floor and clicked it on. "Look at this one in Greenwich. I really like it. We can move in next week."

Kell looked so excited, Gethin didn't have the heart to say no.

"Okay."

319

"Shit. Is it that simple? There's a catch. What is it?"

"You still have to take it easy."

Kell's smile told Gethin he'd lost that argument before he'd started.

There was a knock on the door and Kell's father popped his head round. "The Crown Prosecution Service lawyer called. She wants to go through your statement."

"Gethin and I are moving in together," Kell said.

"About time," said his father. "You're driving me mad."

Chapter Twenty-Nine

19th December

"You okay?" Kell asked. "Stupid question. You're not. Sorry."

Gethin put his bag and guitar down by the door of their flat and pulled Kell into his arms. He didn't want to let him go and when Kell clung to him as if he couldn't bear to let Gethin go either, Gethin almost broke down.

"I'll try harder when I get back," Gethin said. "Be a different man."

Kell put his finger over Gethin's lips. "Don't be too different. I like you awkward. I'll be thinking of you. You won't be alone."

Gethin nodded, picked up his things and left.

These past few weeks had taken their toll on his relationship with Kell. They'd moved into the flat two weeks ago, but Gethin's heart hadn't been in decisions about furniture, rugs, and crockery. What should have been fun, felt like a chore, unimportant in the grand scale of things and he knew he'd disappointed Kell. Part of him wished they could have waited until this thing with Jonnie was over, but Kell needed him and he needed Kell, so Gethin had agreed to move in. It had been the right thing to do. Visits to see Jonnie were still difficult when Gethin was counting down the days. But when Gethin got back to Greenwich, Kell made his world turn again.

Now there were no more days. At least only one more. Gethin caught the DLR into London and the Heathrow Express from there. It hadn't been easy to find a nurse who was prepared to make the trip to Switzerland, particularly this close to Christmas, but Lawrence had turned out to be an okay guy and Jonnie liked him. Gethin was meeting them at the airport for Jonnie's final journey.

The three of them made it to Geneva with everyone still speaking and Jonnie's wheelchair in working order which was a huge relief. Jonnie was high as a fucking kite and Gethin had never felt so wretched in his life, apart from when Jonnie had been injured and Kell had been shot. They'd had to carry Jonnie on and off the plane and Gethin had spent the entire day thinking people were looking at them wondering if they were taking Jonnie to die in the Geneva clinic — not a clinic, a house. He'd been told off for saying clinic.

They kept the appointment to see the physician who'd prescribe the drugs needed to end Jonnie's life and from there they went to the hotel. Jonnie fell asleep the moment they got him into bed. He'd begged Gethin to sleep beside him and Gethin had. Well, he wasn't asleep, but he *was* beside him. Lawrence snored in the other bed and Gethin lay thinking. He was emotionally drained, physically exhausted.

For the last couple of months, his life had been consumed by worry, not just about what he was doing for Jonnie, but anxiety about Kell. The bullet had nearly killed him. If it had struck a millimetre either side, he'd have bled out. The thought of losing Kell choked him, and he still couldn't bring himself to feel right about helping Jonnie to die. Life was so precious, you had to hang onto it with everything you had. But Jonnie's life wasn't *his* to control and he *did* understand why Jonnie felt as he did. Gethin just didn't have to like it.

When Kell had kissed him goodbye this morning, Gethin had promised to be a different man when he came back, but he wasn't sure it would be that easy. He was appalled at the thought of being haunted by what they were going to do tomorrow. Yet if he didn't close the door on it, there would be no happy ending for him and Kell.

After Lawrence had gotten Jonnie up and dressed the following morning, Gethin sent the guy to the airport to see if he could catch an earlier plane home. What had to be done now, Gethin could do himself.

Jonnie didn't want breakfast and Gethin couldn't face it. The specially adapted cab they'd used yesterday that enabled Jonnie to stay in his wheelchair, was waiting for them when they emerged from the hotel. Once the chair was locked into place in the vehicle, Gethin strapped himself in at Jonnie's side. He kept hold of his guitar.

"Want me to tell the guy to take a drive around?" Gethin asked. "Look at the mountains? The snow?"

"I've seen enough. Wish it was snowing though. Like to feel snowflake on my tongue."

Gethin swallowed. "You can still change your mind."

"I know."

This was surreal. By the end of the day Jonnie would be dead. The lump in Gethin's throat felt like a boulder.

As this day had grown ever nearer, Jonnie had become easier and easier to be with. It was after leaving Wellbrook that Gethin struggled. But sitting in Jonnie's room and watching TV, DVDs, they'd laughed together. He never mentioned Kell to Jonnie, but he wondered if Jonnie guessed he had someone in his life.

The other band members had come to see him. Said goodbye. Which was more than Jonnie's parents had managed. *The arseholes.* Gethin had contacted them. His mother had said it was too painful, that they'd lost Jonnie the night of his accident. Gethin found it impossible to believe parents could be so heartless.

When they arrived at the house, the driver lowered the ramp so Jonnie could roll out of the vehicle. Gethin paid him, and he drove away. An ordinary cab could take Gethin back to the airport.

Jonnie stared at the unprepossessing building in front of them and a muscle twitched in his cheek. "Not the Ritz."

"You don't have to do this."

"Throw snowball at me."

"Seriously?" Gethin asked.

"Yes. Be able to hit me for once."

Gethin balled up some clean snow, moved back, and threw it at the arm of the chair. Jonnie laughed. Gethin threw ball after ball and none of them hit Jonnie straight on. Out of the corner of his eye he saw someone at the door of the house but he kept throwing and finally made sure one ball of snow landed on Jonnie's head.

"Bastard," Jonnie said but he was laughing.

Gethin brushed off the worst of the snow. "You don't have to—"

"Stop it. You're allowed to ask me one more time…and that's it. Okay?"

Gethin nodded and they went into the house, his heart feeling like a lump of lead in his chest.

There was all sorts of stuff to go through. Questions to answer. Forms to fill in. Declarations to make. Gethin wished Kell was there. Wished he'd been able to tell him what this was like, but Gethin had felt it was his pain to bear. While he sat waiting for them to do whatever they were doing with Jonnie, he strummed his guitar. He wasn't sure he could keep the emotion from his voice in order to sing, but he'd try.

When someone came to get him, Gethin could hardly push to his feet. They talked to him in English, but it could have been some alien language. He was shown into Jonnie's room where he sat in his wheelchair next to a bed.

"You okay?" Jonnie asked.

Gethin nodded. *No, I'm not fucking okay.*

A guy in his forties explained to Gethin what he already knew, that Jonnie would take an anti-emetic followed by a fast-acting lethal barbiturate, prescribed by the physician they'd seen yesterday. It would be dissolved in drinking water and Jonnie might want to have something sweet afterwards to take the taste away. He'd fall asleep within two to five minutes and death would follow. He had to take the lethal dose himself. It couldn't be given to him. The plan was he'd manoeuver the glass into position, then suck the liquid up through a straw. A nurse, as well as the other guy, would stay with them until the end.

"Can come in now to say goodbye," Jonnie said. "Then I want them to go."

The door opened and much to Gethin's shock, Jonnie's parents walked in. They were both sobbing. Gethin had to leave the room. Their grief would pull his to the surface. He leaned on the wall next to the door and took deep breaths. He'd asked them to at least contact Jonnie, say *something* to him, but he hadn't expected them to come to Switzerland.

When they emerged, his mother glared at him but Jonnie's dad pulled her away before she could say anything. Gethin wanted to tell them he'd tried his best to talk Jonnie out of this, but maybe they wouldn't believe him. A moment later, his dad came back and Gethin braced himself.

Jonnie's father held out his hand and Gethin shook it. "Thank you. He told us he wouldn't ever see us unless we agreed to do this for him, bring him here. All this time, we waited. His mother couldn't... Thank you for doing what we couldn't."

Gethin watched him walk away down the corridor. *Oh God, Jonnie. Manipulative to the fucking end.*

Jonnie smiled when he went back in. "Whisper," he said.

Gethin leaned in and put his ear to Jonnie's mouth.

"You are the best thing that ever happened to me... Wish I'd seen it sooner. I'm an idiot. Loved fucking you... Miss that so much... Can't do this knowing I've lied to you... I remember what I did to you. Remember I hurt you."

Gethin sighed.

"Didn't at first, but when memory came back, I was frightened you'd leave me... Sorry. Wish I'd not done it... Wish I could go back in time and make everything turn out differently."

Gethin straightened. After Kell had suggested it, Gethin had wondered whether Jonnie *had* remembered. "Doesn't matter now."

"Don't deserve you."

"Would you have jumped even if I'd told you not to?"

Jonnie gave him a crooked smile. "Yeah. Because I'm stupid. Thought I didn't need you and I've always needed you... But you didn't need me and I couldn't bear that. You've been the best

friend anyone could ever have… I love you for doing this for me."
Tears trickled down Jonnie's cheeks and Gethin wiped them away.

"Play guitar now please."

Gethin sat on the chair and started with one of the tunes
Jonnie had written, one that gotten them an agent well before
Gethin joined the band. He went through several of Strip Jack's
best songs, his voice just holding together, then played a new one
he'd written called 'Walking into the sun.' It was about a vampire
who decided to kill himself because he missed being human so
much. He watched as Jonnie drank the anti-emetic, then used his
finger control to move the glass with the barbiturates into position
so he could use the straw to suck it up. But he didn't drink.

"I'm going to ask you one last time," Gethin said. He stood,
pulled a piece of paper from his pocket and held it out with
trembling fingers so Jonnie could see what it was. "I bought you a
return ticket. We can leave here now."

"Love you for trying, but not leaving. Sing that one again. It's
not bad. Needs a few tweaks."

Gethin stuffed the ticket back in his pocket, picked up his
guitar and began to sing.

"Want rain on my face
Snow in my hair
You by my side
A life in the sun.

Watch clouds in the sky
The sea rolling in
Want to feel warm
A life in the sun.

Want light on my face
Colour in my life
You by my side
A life in the sun.

But you have to stay
So I'll smile and be glad
One minute is mine
Of life in the sun.

I'll never grow old
I'll never be sad
One moment of time
Of life in the sun."

Jonnie used his finger to move the glass until the straw was in his mouth, then sucked at the lethal cocktail until it was all gone.

Gethin set his guitar aside and leaned over. "Something sweet. My kiss." He pressed his lips against Jonnie's, then pulled back. "You were loved. I want you to know that."

"Thank you," Jonnie whispered.

Gethin stood still, his heart galloping.

Jonnie blinked. "Is it snowing?"

Gethin glanced at the window. "Yeah."

"Take me out, Dart. Please. Please."

"Not advisable," said the man.

The nurse shook her head. "He must stay in room."

"For what?" Gethin lifted Jonnie into his arms and ignoring the protests carried him down the stairs and out the door.

"Snow in your hair. Light on your face." Gethin turned in the snow with Jonnie's face tilted to the sky.

Jonnie put out his tongue and laughed as a flake landed there. He looked straight at Gethin. "Be happy for me." His speech was more slurred. "Be happy for...yourself. This is...what...I...want. Thank...you."

He closed his eyes.

Not dead, but sleeping now. Gethin sank down in the snow with Jonnie cradled in his arms, glad Jonnie didn't have to spend another day unable to move. It wasn't up to Gethin to decide whether this had been the right or wrong thing to do. Jonnie had wanted it and Gethin had made it possible. If that made him a bad person, so be it. He gave Jonnie one last kiss, felt Jonnie's exhalation pour into his mouth and he breathed in Jonnie's final sigh. *Your life in me. You live on in that.*

When he could no longer feel Jonnie's heart beating, Gethin carried him back inside.

Kell sat in the car he'd hired wondering if he'd done the right thing in coming to Geneva, aside from the fact that he hadn't been supposed to fly yet. Gethin had unwittingly supplied him with enough information that he'd been able to work out the timing and it had seemed like a good idea to be there for him after...*after*. Now he wasn't so sure. Through the side window of his car, he'd watched Gethin carry Jonnie out into the falling snow and understood Jonnie had just died in Gethin's arms.

He waited for several minutes, then made his way to the house and pressed the buzzer. "*Taxi pour Monsieur Gethin Jones. J'attends dans la rue.*" Then he slipped back to the car.

Just when he was beginning to think he might have to go to the door again, Gethin emerged carrying his guitar case and backpack. Kell pulled his hat down low and turned his head away as Gethin climbed in the back.

"You sure you're for me?" Gethin asked. "I didn't call."

Yes, I'm sure. "*Oui.*"

"Airport, please."

"*D'accord.*"

Kell was certain Gethin would register it was him but every time he glanced in the mirror, Gethin was looking out of the side window. No tears but his face was pale. Kell had pulled up at the car hire return in the airport before Gethin spoke.

"Can't you drop me off at departures? Crap. *Departs, s'il vous plait.*"

Kell jumped from the car and pulled open the rear passenger door.

Gethin climbed out with his backpack and guitar. He reached for his wallet and his eyes widened. "Kell?"

"Seven thousand three hundred and ninety-seven francs." He held out his hand. "Plus tip. Make it generous."

When Gethin laughed, Kell breathed a sigh of relief. He handed the keys to the rental car guy and waited for his receipt.

"What the fuck are you doing here?" Gethin asked.

"I've come to take you home."

Gethin gave a choked groan, put down what he was holding and stepped into Kell's arms. He pressed his face into Kell's shoulder and Kell could feel him shuddering. Kell held him tight for a long time until Gethin finally straightened.

"You're on the same plane?" Gethin asked.

Kell nodded.

"We're too early."

"Doesn't matter. We can sit and wait. Want something to eat?"

Gethin nodded. "Yeah, that would be good."

He took Kell's hand in his, squeezed his fingers and didn't let go.

Kell took him to Altitude, one of the airport restaurants that overlooked arriving and departing planes. Snow covered mountains towered in the distance and Kell stared at them trying to figure out what to say. Once the food had arrived, he took a deep breath and spoke. "Was it awful?"

"Yes and no, but it's done. I just have to live with it now."

"You'll be able to, right? Only I've signed a twelve month lease on the flat."

Gethin looked straight at him and managed a small smile. Kell was grateful for that. Kell was joking, but knew Gethin had understood what he was saying.

"I thought…" Kell swallowed hard. "Now might be a good time to tell you what happened when Marek came to your place."

On the other side of the table, Gethin froze with a sandwich halfway to his mouth.

"Not quite what I told the police, but I think you'd guessed that. Marek wanted to shoot you first, not kill you outright, but make you watch while he…did stuff to me before he finished me off."

Gethin reached across the table and took Kell's hand. "What did he want to do?"

"He'd talked about fisting. I knew he wanted to. I didn't. I wasn't going to let that happen, but that morning he said he was going to shove his whole arm inside me, rip my guts out through my arse, drag my…yeah, well, he was inventive. It's amazing how strong you can be when you're fighting for your life. We struggled, the gun went off and he sort of shot himself in the side. I backpedalled away and he fired straight at me. I fell off the side of the bed. I think he thought I was dead. I *thought* I was dead. Well, not quite but I was pissed off.

"He sat on the floor trying to staunch the flow of blood from his side and he didn't spot me crawling toward him. I grabbed the gun, pointed it and pulled the trigger."

Gethin held his hand tighter.

"I didn't have to. I could have kept the gun on him, called the police, though I was struggling to stay conscious. But I could have… I didn't have to kill him but I did."

"I'm glad he's dead."

"I am too but… I know I shouldn't have done it."

"Yeah you should. He'd have fired at you again if he'd realised you weren't dead."

"I didn't kill him in self-defence though. I killed him because I wanted him dead. I didn't want him to kill you, but I didn't want him to have his day in court either. The fucker would have made a meal out of the fact that he and I had…"

"You did exactly the right thing. And it *was* self-defence."

"I don't think I want to be a cop anymore."

"I *know* I don't want to be a PI."

Kell smiled. "What *do* you want to do?"

"Do something that gives me time to write music. Maybe I can do some freelance IT work. What do *you* want to do?"

"I'm thinking I might like to be a sex slave."

Gethin laughed.

When they finally got back to their place in Greenwich, Kell felt as though Gethin had hardly let go of his hand since they got on the plane. Kell wasn't used to such a public display of affection and suspected Gethin wasn't either, but when a friend had just died in your arms, how could holding hands not be right? Kell unlocked the entrance on the ground floor and they headed for the lift.

"I have a confession to make," Kell said.

"What have you done?"

"You know we've not been in the mood for Christmas? Well, I gave Angel a key and asked him to come this morning with a tree and decorations. I told him he couldn't decorate it himself, despite him pleading. I want us to do it, though I have no idea what we'll have ended up with. He and Henry have invited us for drinks on Christmas Eve. I said yes. My dad invited himself here for lunch on Boxing Day. I said yes. My dad also offered us a holiday as a Christmas present. I said yes to that too. I'm in a yes mood."

Gethin smiled. Kell opened the door and gestured for Gethin to go in. Their top floor apartment was only a few years old. It was warm and clean with two large airy bedrooms and big high-ceilinged living space that incorporated a kitchen with an American style fridge-freezer, much to Gethin's delight. Kell had complained he'd been more enthusiastic about that than the stylish bathroom with twin sinks and open shower.

They hung up their jackets and Gethin put his guitar and bag on the floor in the hall. When they walked into the living room, Kell gasped. A huge artificial tree stood in front of the window, thousands of white lights twinkling, but as Angel had promised, not a decoration in place.

"It looks real." Gethin walked toward it, and laughed. "Come here."

Kell joined him and saw the plush squirrel Angel had hidden in the branches. As Kell reached for it, the squirrel squeaked, wriggled, and made him jump.

"Shit, I thought it was alive for a minute," Kell said.

"Motion activated."

There were boxes of decorations stacked at the side of the couch, and the loose cushions Kell had picked out from John Lewis had been replaced by ones featuring reindeer, huskies, stars and penguins.

Kell wanted to drag Gethin to bed but he wasn't going to. For a start, he'd prefer Gethin to do that to him, but first he wanted to decorate the tree, and create a happy memory to end a difficult day.

Gethin headed to the kitchen, opened the fridge and gaped. "Did you buy all this?"

Kell joined him. The fridge was packed with food: several varieties of cheese, two boxes of mince pies, brandy butter, a side of smoked salmon, a packet of Parma ham, parmesan, pasta and pizzas. "No. Angel must have."

A saucepan sat on the hob and when Kell lifted the lid the scented aroma of mulled wine poured out—oranges, nutmeg, cinnamon.

"Heat it up," Gethin said.

"Are you hungry? Want a mince pie?"

"Not yet." Gethin grabbed the iPad and a few moments later, they had Christmas music playing.

By the time Kell carried two mugs of mulled wine to the coffee table, Gethin had opened one of the boxes of decorations. It was full of silver snowflakes. He sat staring at it and Kell wondered if he was thinking of Jonnie's face tilted to the sky, if snow was always going to make Gethin sad.

"They're all different," Gethin said.

"What?"

"Snowflakes are all different and these decorations are too. They're fantastic. Angel has such good taste, but only for everyone else, not himself."

Kell smiled and opened the other boxes so they could choose what to put on the tree.

Two mugs of mulled wine later, they stood back and looked at what they'd done.

"I have the feeling we were supposed to choose a colour and we've put everything on," Kell said.

The tree was a mixture of delicate ornaments, hand crafted wooden Santas and angels, metal reindeer, sprigs of red and burgundy berries and dozens of stars. They'd moved the coffee table for Kell to climb on to put a star on the top. Kell switched off the main room light and they stood and stared at the tree.

"I like it," Gethin said.

"So do I."

"You know why I like it?"

Kell glanced at him.

"We've no curtains or blinds at that window so the people in the block opposite can see in — usually. Now they can't."

Gethin reached to unbutton Kell's shirt and Kell sucked in a breath.

"Too slow." Kell grabbed him, then they were mauling each other, kissing and grabbing and humping, and they still weren't close enough.

Gethin slid his hands under Kell's shirt, one hand worming into the back of his chinos, onto his arse and Kell rocked into him, pushed his cock against Gethin's. Clothes began to fly. They worked together to rid themselves of everything they wore until they stood plastered together, joined head to toe, lips locked. Kell was drunk on the taste of him, desperate to make him happy again.

When Kell pulled back to breathe, he took in the beauty of Gethin's body in the shimmering light from the tree. He'd been beautiful before, but he was more toned now with ripped stomach muscles, his cock framed by his hip bones, plus that sexy tattoo. He looked like a Christmas angel come to life. Kell's fingers moved instinctively to the healed scar on his chest and Gethin caught his wrist.

"It's such a pity you're never going to be able to tell a new guy how you got that," Gethin said.

Kell's heart lurched when he took in what Gethin was saying, though he hadn't actually said it. "And it's such a great line," Kell whined. "*I was shot.* Bound to get me a fuck."

"Oh it's going to get you a fuck."

Kell laughed. Gethin kissed him again, his arms wrapped around Kell, cupping his buttocks, grinding their cocks together.

"Flaw in my plan for not moving from this spot," Gethin said with a groan. "See if Angel left us condoms and lube."

"Nope. We have to go the bedroom."

"Fine, then the foot of the Christmas tree, the couch, the coffee table, the counter, the rug and the walls in here – will all have to wait." Gethin lifted Kell up and carried him, and Kell wound his legs around Gethin's hips.

He laid Kell down on the bed and crawled on top, kissing him again as they writhed together.

"Oh fuck, you drive me crazy," Gethin whispered.

"In a good way?"

"Apart from squeezing the toothpaste from the top, yeah."

Kell stopped moving.

"What?" Gethin looked down at him.

"Is that it? All I do that annoys you is squeeze the toothpaste from the top?"

Gethin quirked his mouth. "I think that's it." He forced his hand between their bodies, caught hold of Kell's dick and squeezed at the bottom. "See how good that feels?"

He gave Kell the hand job that Kell had first given him, little by little working his way up his cock and all the time staring into Kell's eyes.

"I love you," Gethin whispered.

Kell stopped breathing, forgot how to breathe, thought breathing was overrated until he had to gasp.

"Aren't you going to say anything?" Gethin asked.

Kell opened and closed his mouth like a stranded fish.

"I've said the word before but I've never meant in the way I mean it with you." Gethin gave him a shy smile. "I wish I'd never said it before. I wish you were the first person who ever heard those words come from me, because I know now that you're the first person I've ever truly loved. I feel as if I've been waiting for you so I could begin to live."

Kell smiled. "This is turning out *much* better than I expected. I thought I was going to have to say it first. Now I'll make you wait."

Gethin growled and let Kell's cock slide faster in his hand. "Going to say it soon?"

"Remember I've been injured," Kell said.

"How long are you going to use that excuse?"

"For the rest of our lives."

The look that passed between them then stopped Kell breathing and stopped Gethin's hand moving on Kell's cock.

"I love you," Kell whispered.

"Is that just to get me to move my hand? Anyway, how long was that before you said it? Ten seconds?" Gethin laughed.

"I love you. Now I've said it more than you. I win."

"Whatever you like." Gethin dropped his head and Kell slid into bliss.

The End

About the Author

Barbara Elsborg lives in Kent in the south of England. She always wanted to be a spy, but having confessed to everyone without them even resorting to torture, she decided it was not for her. Vulcanology scorched her feet. A morbid fear of sharks put paid to marine biology. So instead, she spent several years successfully selling cyanide.

After dragging up two rotten, ungrateful children and frustrating her sexy, devoted, wonderful husband (who can now stop twisting her arm) she finally has time to conduct an affair with an electrifying plugged-in male, her laptop.

Her books feature quirky heroines and bad boys, and she hopes they are as much fun to read as they are to write.

She loves hearing from readers and can be contacted at barbaraelsborg@gmail.com If you'd like to hear about future releases please ask to be put on her mailing list.

Books
There are a few linked books in this list but all can be read as stand-alones.

Contemporary MMs
Cowboys Down
With or Without Him
Give Yourself Away
With or Without Him
Falling (Fall and Break book 1)
Breaking (Fall and Break book 2)
Drawn In

Paranormal MMs
Dirty Angel
Bloodline (Norwood book 2)
The Demon You Know (Norwood book 3)

Contemporary MMFs
Anna in the Middle

Susie's Choice
Girl Most Likely to
Talking Trouble
Just What She Wants (novella)

Paranormal MFs and MMFs

Perfect Trouble MF
Power of Love MF
Kiss Interrupted MF
Jumping in Puddles MF (Norwood book 1)
Rocked MMF
The Small Print MMF
Worlds Apart MMF
The Consolation Prize MF (Trueblood book 1)
Falling for You MF (Trueblood book 2)
Lightning in a Bottle MF ((Trueblood book 3)
The Misfits MMF(Trueblood book 4)
Fight to Remember MMF(Trueblood book 5)
Lucy in the Sky MF (sci fi)
Taking Stock MMF (sci fi)
Just One Bite MF novella

Contemporary MFs

Strangers
Summer Girl Winter Boy
Kiss a Falling Star
An Ordinary Girl
Perfect Timing (Bedlingham brothers book 1)
Something About Polly (Bedlingham brothers book 2)
Doing the Right Thing (Mansell brothers book 1)
Finding the Right One (Mansell brothers book 2)
Digging Deeper
The Princess and the Prepper (novella)
Snow Play (novella)
On the Right Track (novella)

Short Stories (MF)

Saying Yes
The Bad Widow
The Gift
Dragon Race
Two Birds, One Stone

Romantic Suspense (MF)
Chosen
Crossing the Line

Printed in Great Britain
by Amazon